BOOK I

THE MERCHANT AND THE MENACE

BY DANIEL FRANCIS MCHUGH

Copyright 2012

Daniel Francis McHugh

http://www.seraphinium.net

All rights are reserved. No part of this book may be used or reproduced in any manner whatsoever without written permission from the author.

McHugh, Daniel F. (2012).

The Merchant and the Menace

(The Seraphinium Series, Book 1)

THE SERAPHINIUM

BOOK I

THE MERCHANT
AND
THE MENACE

DANIEL F. McHUGH

DEDICATION

This book is dedicated to the person who collaborates in the fulfillment of my dreams,
Jennifer Jo.
AND
To the three Fates who have filled my life with unbridled joy,
resonant laughter
and
uncontrollable glee.
Lilywynn
Liza Bean
And
Pryor Maeve

Many thanks to those who spent days editing this jumble of thoughts: Jennifer McHugh, Judy Pryor, Daniel Woolsey, Sue Elworth, Michael McNamara and the beautiful Lillian McHugh.

Additional thanks to those early readers for their gracious support and insight: Timothy Feeney, Daniel Quinn, Bill Mazurowski, Emily Douville, Kurt Steib, Ron Forresta, Timothy O'Reilly and Joseph Felicicchia.

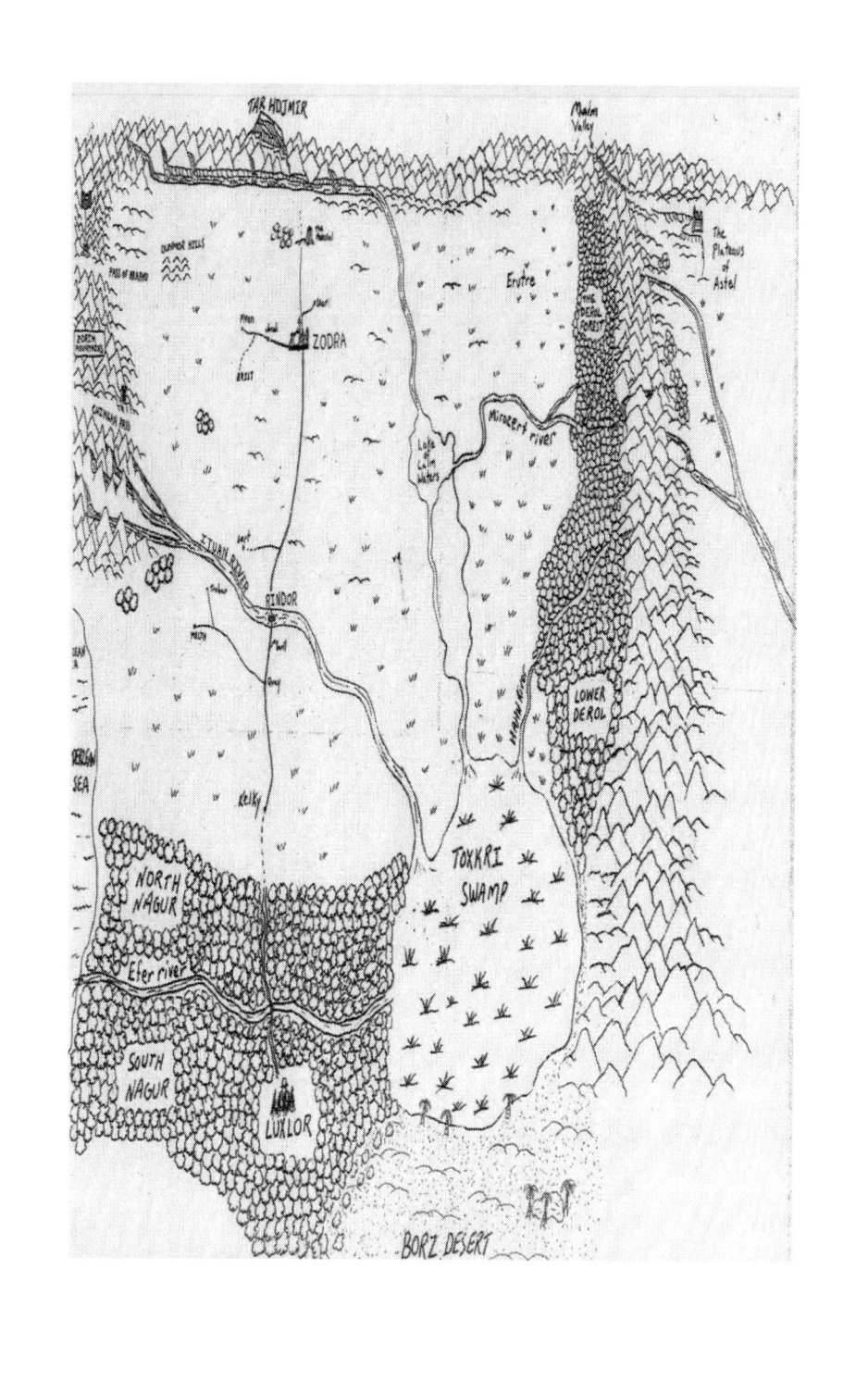

TABLE OF CONTENTS

PROLOGUE
CHAPTER 1: THE TOUCH
CHAPTER 2: PARTING
CHAPTER 3: THE RACE
CHAPTER 4: THE ALMAR THRONE
CHAPTER 5: UP THE WINDING STAIRCASE
CHAPTER 6: FLAME OF THE MALVEEL
CHAPTER 7: MYTHS AND LEGENDS
CHAPTER 8: THE STONE CHAMBER
CHAPTER 9: STEPPING FROM THE SHADOWS
CHAPTER 10: BIRTH OF THE SERAPHIM
CHAPTER 11: DOWN THE WINDING STAIRCASE
CHAPTER 12: THE COMFORT OF SLEEP
CHAPTER 13: THE KING'S SERVICE
CHAPTER 14: THE ORPHAN'S WIDOW
CHAPTER 15: RECRUIT
CHAPTER 16: WAVES IN THE POOL
CHAPTER 17: THE BLACKSMITH'S APPRENTICE
CHAPTER 18: THE MERCHANT AND THE MENACE
CHAPTER 19: LED THROUGH DARKNESS
CHAPTER 20: THE LESSONS OF PREJUDICE
CHAPTER 21: TO EACH HIS OWN
CHAPTER 22: BRIDGE TENDER, GATEKEEPER
CHAPTER 23: THE SINGING MERMAID
CHAPTER 24: SUMMONS
CHAPTER 25: REVELATIONS ONE
CHAPTER 26: THE BLACK OBELISK
CHAPTER 27: TAPESTRY
CHAPTER 28: KNOWLEDGE IS POWER
CHAPTER 29: THE FOX AND THE HAMMER
CHAPTER 30: THE GATES OF ZODRA
GLOSSARY OF CHARACTERS AND LOCATIONS
GLOSSARY BY LAND OR RACE
GLOSSARY OF MAPS

PROLOGUE

Steff froze and his eyes widened. He stared at Lord Giar as a breeze dodged past the thick trunks of the deep wood and rustled the leaves above. Giar crouched beside a dying fire and stoked the blaze with a stick. Flames grew but darkness swallowed their light only a few feet from the pair. Giar's conversation remained casual, but the elder Elf's free hand caused Steff's alarm and fixed his attention.

Giar held the hand close to his body, just visible inside the folds of his cloak. He manipulated it rapidly, creating complex signals. Signals used by the spies of his country to communicate silently.

"We made excellent time today, son," spoke Giar calmly as his fingers danced. He leveled a penetrating gaze at Steff. "The real test will come on the plains to the north. We have many leagues ahead of us."

Steff ignored his father's words. He squinted through the darkness at the hand as it twitched within the cloak. Steff struggled to decipher the code. Giar only recently passed its secrets to the young man.

"...something ... in wood. Remain calm ... "

"The horses could use a rub down and some water. Do you have any oats in your pack?" continued Lord Giar as he dropped the stick into the flames and motioned to the tethered horses.

The fire greedily consumed the fresh fuel, flaring for a moment more. Steff glanced to a few small bundles stacked beside the horses at the edge of the forest clearing. The young Elf's longbow and quiver lay beside the packs. Steff turned back as his father continued.

"Our mounts earned a few sweet oats and some water before we turn in," stated Giar.

His hand continued to flicker.

".... retrieve your bow ..."

"Yes, father," replied Steff nervously. The boy grimaced and fought to remain composed. "I'll see what we have."

He rose from the fireside and calmly walked to the bundles. Steff rummaged through the first pack, well aware it contained no oats. He discarded the bundle directly atop his bow and quiver then checked the second.

"I can't find them. The light is too low," said Steff. "I'll bring them closer to the fire."

Steff dropped the second atop the first then scooped the bundles, bow and quiver from the ground. He slowly walked back toward the fire. The horses whinnied and grew restless.

"I may have forgotten to include the oats in our provisions," stated Lord Giar. "The horses can feast on grasses once we reach the plains in the morning. What do we have for a meal?"

Steff knelt and laid the bundles beside the fire. One hand locked on the bow beneath the burlap, the other wrapped around the shaft of an arrow within the quiver. One of the horses stamped and threw its head. The other strained on its tether. Steff stared at his father's gesticulating hand.

"... in the wood ... behind me. Malveel ..."

Steff sucked in a deep breath. His eyes darted upward. His father smiled pleasantly at the young man, but Steff noted tension in Giar's stance. The Elf lord's hand inched toward the dagger sheathed at his side.

"The horses," blurted Steff. Panic edged into his voice. "We could ... I could try again. Perhaps we could find something ...."

"No," frowned Giar as he spoke in a firm voice. "There is no going back. The horses are exhausted. I must deal with our problem. Remember this lesson when you return to Luxlor. We must properly prepare for all contingencies. Our people must learn from our mistake. The Grey Elves need to prepare the next time they journey from Luxlor."

Steff struggled to keep his concealed hands steady. The burlap trembled as he slowly drew an arrow from the hidden quiver and notched it upon his bowstring. The horses grew more agitated. Steff gazed wide-eyed at his father. Giar leaned toward his son.

"I love you, lad," whispered Giar. "Will you do as I say?"

Steff nodded in agreement. A loving smile crossed Lord Giar's face. His hand wrapped about the hilt of his dagger. The Elf lord drew in a deep breath. His eyes pierced Steff with their intensity.

"RUN!" cried Giar.

The Elf lord spun toward the tree line. A long, pointed dagger whipped from beneath his cloak and hurtled into the night. Something monstrous and black burst from the darkness. Tree limbs snapped. Red eyes, filled with molten flame, bore down on them.

Steff leapt to his feet, drew the arrow back and hastily took aim. A terrifying roar drowned out the high pitched twang of his bowstring. The shaft whistled past his father. It ricocheted off the beast with a loud CRACK! The creature's eyes flared and crimson fire poured forth.

Giar danced to his left, avoiding the deluge of liquid flame. The Elf lord's head snapped back toward his son. His wild eyes locked on those of Steff as he ripped a short sword from its scabbard.

"RUN!" he bellowed again.

Steff obeyed. He wheeled and dashed into the darkness of the Nagur Wood. He vaulted fallen timber and plunged through thickets. Branches slapped his face and thorns tore his flesh. The Elf lad was uncertain of his direction or the location of the path. His lungs burned as he ran on and on. The screams of Lord Giar carried through the wood. Tears welled in Steff's eyes. How could he abandon his father?

He slowed.

His duty was to the kingdom. Giar's orders were clear. Steff must return and warn his people of the Malveel threat. Luxlor was in danger.

A faint cry pierced the stillness of the wood then abruptly silenced. Surely there was no hope for one man against a Malveel lord.

Steff stopped, dropped to his knees and sobbed.

"Not much of a chase," growled the darkness around him.

Steff's head snapped up and he frantically searched the wood. He flung the bow to the ground and snatched his own dagger from its sheath, holding it awkwardly before him.

"Sh- show yourself," stammered the Elf.

A pair of red orbs flared to life a dozen yards in front of him. They hovered before Steff then slowly circled through the wood.

"My brother, Methra, leaves me the tiny one," croaked the voice. "I hoped for a bit of sport from our chase, but you disappoint me, Elf."

The orbs vanished into the darkness and silence enveloped the wood. Steff's eyes darted about, snapping toward any movement, perceived or imagined. He lifted his blade higher.

"What ... what do you want?" stuttered Steff.

"We seek the Seraphim!" snarled the voice from directly behind the Elf boy.

Steff whirled on the sound. The orbs were closer. The boy staggered backward, trying to put distance between himself and the hate filled eyes. He could hear the Malveel's hoarse breath rasping between jagged fangs.

"The power of the new Seraph draws us. It is close," continued the Malveel. Contempt filled its voice. "You are not the Seraph."

The orbs disappeared once more. Steff spun this way and that, slashing the darkness with his dagger. Panic overwhelmed him.

"Do not .... do not test me, Malveel!" cried the Elf in desperation. "My powers are .... you cannot stand against the New Seraph!"

Silence hung in the wood. Steff slowly turned, trying in vain to penetrate the gloom. Seconds dragged on. He saw nothing and heard only the light breeze as it buffeted the leaves in the canopy above. His heart slowed and his despair grew. Steff's shoulders drooped and gradually his blade dipped toward the forest floor.

"You ... you dare not taste my power," called the boy feebly into the void. Perhaps the Malveel feared this being they hunted. "The new Seraph ... I ... I hold your doom."

"Hardly," sneered the creature in Steff's right ear.

The boy spun. Blazing eyes and glistening fangs hovered inches from his face.

CHAPTER 1: THE TOUCH

Kael scowled at the ceiling inches above his bunk. He was so close to finally convincing his father to let him journey to Luxlor when rumors of trouble in the Nagur Wood reached the village. Would Brelg call the trip off and spoil Kael's first chance for a bit of adventure?

The boy rolled onto his stomach with a dejected sigh and glanced below at his sleeping brother, Aemmon. The absurdity of the sight that greeted him, made it difficult to continue his brooding.

Aemmon, nearly a man now, lay in the lower bunk. Half of Aemmon's lower legs dangled over the end of the small bed their father, Brelg, had fashioned for the boys when they were young. Aemmon's right arm stuck out from beneath a woolen blanket, knuckles lying on the wooden floorboards.

In the early morning light, Kael could just make out Aemmon's dirty blond hair jutting out from under a goose down pillow. The snore that rumbled from under the pillow kept rhythm with the bulk heaving beneath the dark blanket.

Aemmon looked so content, Kael found it difficult to disturb his brother's slumber. Instead, he grinned and dug beneath the blankets of his own bed. He and Aemmon had a bit more time before they needed to start the day's chores and Kael's bunk still fit him so comfortably.

Contentment filled the boy. Many a night he crawled into this bunk for sleep and many a morn he reveled in its warmth. Memories flooded him now, memories of wondrous stories told to him and Aemmon by their father as the pair of small boys yawned and drifted to sleep, memories of their mother always standing at a bedside when one of them woke from a nightmare.

Other memories crowded his reverie, memories of worry and sleepless nights, memories of the sound of his father's boots as Brelg paced the hallway outside his mother's room, memories of a healer shaking his head in confusion and finally, memories of tears soaking the blankets on this very bed.

Kael's smile disappeared and he quickly sat up and threw his legs over the edge of his bunk. He noiselessly dropped to the ground, landing in a crouch beside Aemmon. A twinkle danced in his eye.

"Aemmon, get up," he whispered just inches from the lumpy pillow.

The deep snoring sputtered then stopped.

"Huh?" came a confused reply from beneath the pillow.

"Get up," said Kael softly. "Father hasn't cancelled our trip yet. Maybe if we ignore the news, he will too?"

Aemmon moaned and the big hand lying on the floorboards slowly rose and dragged the pillow from atop his face. His chiseled features remained placid and his eyes closed.

"When I open my eyes I'm going to see sunshine, right?" mumbled Aemmon.

"Not exactly," chuckled Kael as he glanced out the tiny window of the room atop their father's inn. The sky was awash in the rosy hue of dawn. "You may see a bit of 'shine', but you certainly won't see any 'sun' yet."

Aemmon grumbled once more and plopped the pillow back over his face.

"C'mon Aemmon," pleaded Kael. "I won't be able to go without you."

The pillow didn't move. Kael frowned and softened his tone.

"I can understand if you don't want to go to Luxlor," he murmured sheepishly. "I wouldn't want to force you into anything. I suppose I could always try again next year."

Aemmon dragged the pillow from his face once more, but this time his eyes were wide open and his smile etched with accusation.

"You're not fooling anyone with that sad tale," announced the big lad. He broke into an imitation of a simpering Kael. "I could always try again next year."

Kael grinned and the pair chuckled. Aemmon sat up and rubbed the sleep from his eyes while Kael dressed. In a moment,

Aemmon stood, producing a loud groan from the floorboards in their room. He dressed and the boys made their way to the main stairway of the inn.

They moved quietly in order not to wake any of the lodgers. Kael dashed down the old wooden staircase without making a sound. He turned and suppressed a laugh. Aemmon took each step slowly, wincing as the knotted wood creaked and popped under his impressive weight. After quite some time, and considerable frustration, Aemmon reached the bottom of the staircase.

"How do you do that?" he whispered.

"You looked as if the whole staircase was about to collapse," chuckled Kael as he clapped his younger brother on the back.

Aemmon smiled, gave his brother a poke to the ribs, and the pair walked out the rear door of the inn toward the stables. In the early morning sun, the differences between the brothers were quite evident. Aemmon was a classic example of a young man from the Southlands of Zodra. He was tall, with his bulk comprised mostly of muscle. His blond hair and blue eyes mirrored many Southlanders' traits.

Kael, on the other hand, stood out. He was smaller than most and his wiry body held a darker complexion. The single most striking characteristic of Kael was his hair. It was jet black. Dark hair was unusual for a Southlander, and Kael's hair was darker than a raven's wings.

The pair strolled along and Kael noted heaviness in his brother's step.

"What's wrong?" asked Kael.

Aemmon stopped and the sadness in his eyes disturbed Kael. They stared at one another for a long moment.

"Everything will be fine," Kael blurted cheerily. "These recent stories about the Nagur are nothing. The ale starts talking when the loggers stay in the common room too long. There's nothing to any of it. You know that, right?"

Aemmon frowned deeply.

"Do you think Old Sarge would allow us to go on this trip if he didn't think we'd be fine?" sighed Kael.

"No, course not," his brother replied.

"The only way to get to Luxlor is through the Nagur Wood. You're not afraid of the Elves are you?"

"No," returned Aemmon with a shake of his head. "Father's been trading with them for years."

"Well, as for the Nagur, the stories we heard are just that, stories, made up by lonely men who spend far too much time out on the open road," Kael shook his head and smiled broadly. "Besides, where's your sense of adventure?"

"My sense of adventure is still sleeping in our room, as I should be," yawned Aemmon with a smile. "And neither the Elves nor the Nagur concern me."

"Then what?" prodded Kael.

Aemmon frowned once more and his eyes focused on the ground at his feet.

"Oh ... nothing," murmured the lad. "I ... I just wish things didn't need to change. I like them the way they are."

Kael looked quizzically at his brother and chuckled.

"You and I going on our first trading journey isn't going to turn the world upside down, Aemmon!"

Aemmon paused and searched Kael's face. He flashed his brother a light grin and arched an eyebrow.

"Maybe ... maybe not."

The larger boy grabbed an ax from the stable wall and went to split logs for the woodpile. Kael watched him go and doubt entered his mind. Why was Aemmon so reluctant to go on this trip? In the past, his brother always brimmed with confidence. Nothing bothered him. No challenge was too great.

The loud thunk of the ax lodging deeply into a log drew Kael from these thoughts. He hustled to the shed, retrieved a bucket and entered the inn. He filled the oaken bucket from the kitchen pump and stepped into the dining area. His father, Brelg, was eating breakfast. Kael hefted the heavy bucket toward a dark corner of the common room, hoping to avoid any notice.

"Good morning, boy," said Brelg without raising his eyes from his food.

"Morning." answered Kael as he froze in his tracks.

Brelg frowned, glanced up and waved the boy over. He pushed a chair back from the table and motioned Kael to sit.

"I've a bit of a problem. Perhaps you can give me some advice," began Brelg.

Kael smiled and took his seat at the table.

"An extremely persistent young man I know has been pushing to help me expand my business. He's rather young, so I'm not sure I'll approve, but his resolve is slowly wearing me down," grumbled Brelg. "I was ready to concede when recent news caused me to become a bit apprehensive."

Kael smiled broadly.

"I'm sure he's quite competent, sir," replied the boy. "Besides, what could go wrong?"

Brelg frowned and placed his fork upon his plate.

"Seriously Kael. This business in the Nagur Wood causes me concern," said Brelg. "I know how much you want to experience a bit of the wider world, but maybe this isn't the proper time."

"You know how the loggers talk when they've been in the common room all night," frowned Kael. "One acre of cleared forest becomes ten. A six point buck becomes twelve. What does their story amount to? Some unfamiliar tracks. A feeling of being watched or tracked. Both are easily explained by a large bear and the fertile imaginations of men alone on the open road."

"Mr. Drovor is a very sensible man," returned Brelg with a frown. "He does tend to exaggerate things a bit, but this time his story seems ... different. I'm a fair judge of men, my boy. I must be in this business. The usual twinkle that dances in Drovor's eye when he spins a tale was missing."

"Well, you've often said that I've learned the business pretty well myself," said Kael proudly. "My advice to you is to forget Drovor's tale. How many times has he stood in the common room describing how he out maneuvered a band of highway bandits or outran a pack of starving wolves?"

Brelg furrowed his brow. Kael tried to change the subject.

"Don't forget," said the boy. "A candidate for the Zodrian Guard rides with me."

Brelg smiled and his eyes took on the faraway look Kael often noticed when they spoke of the Zodrian Guard and the capital city.

"That would be a fine day, wouldn't it?" whispered Brelg lightly nodding his head. "If Aemmon were chosen for the Guard …"

Brelg's voice trailed off. Kael smiled and put a hand on his father's shoulder.

"That would be a fine day for all of us, even mother."

"Yes, if she were here she would be proud of you both," sighed Brelg. "She loved you dearly. However, I think she watches me from somewhere shaking her head in disapproval over this trip you've concocted."

"Mother never objected to your trips," said Kael with a sly grin. "As I recall you went on plenty, leaving the three of us to manage the inn."

"Business is business," huffed Brelg. "Besides, I was younger then and settling down proved difficult."

"Exactly," winked Kael.

Brelg frowned deeply at the smiling boy. Kael continued to grin until Brelg chuckled and tousled the boy's mop of black hair.

"Get to work," laughed Brelg. "Or you'll never get out of here."

Kael spun and dashed toward the kitchen to retrieve a mop.

"You better hurry with your chores," called Brelg after the boy, "and tell Cefiz to get the stove fired up. I don't want my customers slipping on a wet floor, on their way to a breakfast that has yet to be cooked."

Cefiz, the inn's handyman and cook, stood yawning in the kitchen.

"You best get your fires started or he'll have your head," smiled Kael.

"Who? Good old Sarge? Angry with me? You must be joking?" Cefiz laughed.

Kael always grinned when Cefiz called the demanding innkeeper "Sarge". Aemmon and Kael picked up on the moniker and often used it to refer to their father, but never in his company. Brelg, on the other hand, took to calling Cefiz "chubby", and constantly teased the cook concerning his expanding waist.

In Kael's early memories, Cefiz was a powerfully built young man employed by the inn to carry out odd jobs and general maintenance. Since the death of Kael's mother, Cefiz became the cook of the inn as well. His hair had begun to frost and a noticeable paunch hung over his belt line.

Cefiz pulled wood chips out of a box and stuffed them into the stove.

"So today is the big day?" yawned Cefiz.

"Today is the day," repeated Kael with a smile.

"I suppose you still don't care for my suggestion?" said Cefiz.

"Just as I told Sarge," said Kael eyeing the door. "I'm not a boy anymore. I don't need you to come along and watch over me. Besides, I think your 'suggestion' came from Sarge more than yourself."

"Are you accusing me of being a deceitful scoundrel?" smiled Cefiz.

"Not a deceitful scoundrel," said Kael. "Just a loyal one."

Kael retrieved his mop and returned to his bucket in the common room. While he scrubbed the stone floor, he contemplated his journey through the Nagur. Were any of the dangers real or the stories true?

An inn is a wonderful place to pick up bits and pieces of information. Kael excelled in this ability. He badgered customers for stories from their travels. He lingered over tables where woodsmen or hunters were discussing events in the faraway corners of the kingdom. He ferreted out all he could about places he would never visit and people he would never meet.

However, the recent rumor of trouble didn't come to Kael by the usual ways of a small village. No local washerwoman or merchant passed the information onto him in casual conversation. Instead, Kael found out in the manner he gathered most of the truly important information in the town of Kelky. He used the Touch.

For as long as Kael could remember he was able to employ the Touch. It was as natural to him as breathing. However, something warned him it wouldn't be considered normal by others, so he spoke to no one about it, not even Aemmon.

Usually, he performed the Touch when he was engaged in one of his boring chores in and around the inn. He might be washing dishes in the kitchen, mopping the common room floor or hanging laundry in the yard when the desire struck him. He concentrated, forcing his mind to block out all distractions. The banter in the common room faded, the chickens in the yard went still and the rushing of the wind quieted.

Kael focused on what he needed to "touch". Not in a physical way. Instead, he reached out to an event with something other than his hands. He forced his senses to "brush" against the scene he wished to view. Even if a conversation were whispered in a room full of rowdy patrons, Kael heard it as if he sat hunched over a table with its participants.

The Touch is how he came to hear the rumors concerning the Nagur. A few evenings earlier, two loggers ate dinner in the common room. They were fresh from an excursion to the forests of the lower Zorim Mountains where they cut for weeks then bundled their timber and circulated through the small villages of the Southlands selling their haul.

Often, the loggers held back a portion of the wood and traveled to Luxlor. Although the Grey Elves lived within a massive forest, they never put ax to living wood. They often referred to themselves as "guests" within the Nagur and refused to harm it. The Grey Elves paid a premium for the fresh lumber and the loggers claimed a tidy profit in the Elf city.

This pair of loggers sat within the common room of "The King's Service" as their foreman returned from Luxlor. He joined the men at their table as Kael passed with an armload of dirty dishes.

"Drovor," said one of the loggers. "How did you fare? Profitably I hope."

"Aye," replied Drovor. "The Elves always pay a fair price for timber. I unloaded a full ..."

Kael stepped past the kitchen door and dumped the stoneware dishes into a tub of hot water. His hands plunged in, retrieved a horsehair brush and he slowly began to scrub the hardened mess from the plates. A moment or two into his chore, the boy let his mind wander. Boredom quickly overcame him as he stacked the third of the cleaned plates. He closed his eyes and let himself calm. The bustle of the nearby common room faded. The chatter at the bar grew faint. The Touch drifted from his body.

Kael stood over the tub of soapy water, but another part of him passed through the kitchen door and back into the common room. He couldn't "see" the room or its occupants, but was well aware of everything and everybody in the dining hall. In fact, the Touch gave Kael more clarity. Rushing through life distracted him, but the Touch let him sit back and truly observe.

He sensed the loggers and moved the Touch toward their table.

"... are always quite free with their coin as long as you treat them fairly," Drovor was saying.

"Thank heaven. We'll be out of a job if the Grey Elves ever decide to cut the Nagur," said one of the loggers.

"True," muttered Drovor.

"What's bothering you?" The other man asked. "A fine haul, no accidents and a tidy profit. What more could you want?"

"The Nagur," stated Drovor. "Something felt wrong. Something was wrong."

"The only thing wrong with the Nagur is the fact that we don't cut there and sell the wood back to the Grey Elves," said the first logger.

"That's what you think, eh?" An edge entered Drovor's voice. "Sell 'em their own wood, that's your plan?"

"Sure, why not?" continued the man. "The Elves don't even travel north of the Efer River much. The whole of the North Nagur is there to be cut. We travel all the way to the Zorim for wood that can be had on the Elf's very doorstep."

"Let me tell you something," growled Drovor. "Cutting the Nagur is one of the dumbest things you could do."

"That's hogwash. We could be rich if ..."

"Dead!" cut in Drovor. "You could be dead. Men have tried it before. Men like yourself who see nothing but coin in front of their faces. Men who haven't been on the crews long. Off they go to cut the Nagur and after four or five weeks with no news, everyone realizes you can't, or shouldn't lay an ax to that wood. They end up as just another group of fools who tried to log the Nagur and were never seen again."

"How?" asked the first logger. "The Grey Elves?"

"No," scoffed Drovor. "The Grey Elves are good people. I should know. I've dealt with 'em for years. Actually, I've never had a clue as to why those men disappear. That is until now."

Kael heard the creak of a chair as Drovor leaned in close and lowered his voice.

"I saw some strange tracks this last visit. Tracks of something big. Never seen the like. Maybe .... eighteen feet long."

"What d'ya think made 'em?" asked the first logger.

"Don't know," replied Drovor. "But I decided not to press my luck and got out of there as fast as I could. I picked up my pace and had a strange feeling someone ...."

"Don't fall in and drown," laughed Cefiz, breaking Kael's concentration.

The Touch lost its hold on the common room and Kael lurched as his senses sprang back into his consciousness. A loud crash snapped Kael's eyes open and his breath came in short bursts. The small earthenware bowl he had been washing lay in broken shards at his feet.

"Sorry to startle you, lad," chuckled Cefiz. "You looked as if you were about to pass out into the wash tub. I would hate to inform Sarge that you drowned in the dishwater while I was outside collecting fuel for the fires."

Kael turned to find the cook standing upon the threshold to the yard, hefting a stack of split wood. The boy blinked and ran a hand through his dark hair.

"Uh, thanks," smiled Kael weakly. "Didn't sleep well last night."

That was two nights ago. Now Kael rushed through a day of chores in the hopes that he and his brother could head off into the very wood from which Drovor raced. The boy thought over the foreman's story for the past two days. Slowly he convinced himself that Drovor imagined much of what he saw. Certainly, a bear or other large animal was responsible for the tracks. What other explanation was there? An animal certainly wouldn't attack only those cutting trees. The whole idea was absurd.

Kael left the kitchen and went to help Aemmon bring firewood into the main hall. They proceeded to work on the remainder of their chores for nearly two hours.

As Kael fed the chickens, a rickety old cart slowly headed up the southern trail. The boy smiled at the old man driving the cart.

"Jasper. Good morning," called Kael.

"Kael. Already feeding the chickens eh? You woke early today," called the old man on the buckboard.

Jasper stopped and stepped down in front of Kael. The tinker was old. How old, Kael couldn't be sure. Jasper's stark, white hair lay cropped close to his scalp. He wore silvery stubble on his deeply tanned and lined face.

In contrast, the old tinker's eyes defied age. Neither young nor old. Every time Kael talked to Jasper, the intensity in the old man's eyes startled the boy. Those eyes were a piercing, silver blue. They captured your attention.

Jasper wore a heavy leather jerkin which shared the shade and texture of his complexion. He sported sturdy wool pants beneath it. Normally, a pipe hung lazily out of his mouth, but today it wasn't present.

"Come around, boy. Come around," coaxed Jasper, motioning Kael to the back of the cart.

A stern faced, broad shouldered Zodrian sat on the open gate.

"Good morning, Rin," Kael remarked.

The man hopped from the back of the cart and stepped from Kael's path.

"My son is quiet as usual," Jasper stated. "So I will conduct our business. Take a good look over the merchandise, Kael, while you tell me how your family is getting on. You know I haven't visited Kelky in months."

Rin untied a bundle and spread the contents out for Kael to see.

"You've been gone for quite some time this season. My brother misses your stories by the fire. You captivate him with news of the greater world," Kael paused. "How much for the Elven blade?"

"Ah!" said Jasper "Now there is a man with a keen eye. That is a quality piece of weaponry. What do you offer in trade?"

"How does a free meal and a night's lodging sound?" Kael offered.

"Kael," frowned the tinker. "One should never take an opponent for a fool. You know I'll receive a meal from your father for simply trading some news of the world before the fire tonight. Now come, come. Try me again."

After some consideration, Kael sighed, "I own a Westland bow. It isn't much, but I take good care of it."

"Done!" cried the old man with a laugh. "The dagger is yours. You outfox me again, my friend."

Kael knew he didn't outwit Jasper. In fact, he grew accustomed to their bargaining sessions ending in a "victory" for Kael. He was sure the tinker allowed him to win. Possibly as payback for the kindness shown by Brelg.

Kael ran his fingers over the intricate detail in the ancient dagger, marveling at the beautiful design trapped under years of tarnish. Jasper questioned the boy on the health of his family and the happenings of the town. Kael didn't intend to pass along Drovor's rumors, but as always with Jasper, the boy started to talk and found himself desperate to tell all he knew.

"Kael, elaborate on this trip you plan," suggested Jasper unexpectedly.

"Jasper, how did you know we ...?"

"Remember, Kael. One of my talents is information. I know everything because I must. That is how a traveler survives in this world. Now tell me of your journey," said Jasper.

"Well," Kael began. "My father is interested in obtaining more Elven rope and medicines. So we decided I should go to Luxlor to buy them."

"You mean 'you decided' don't you?" frowned Jasper.

"Father is reluctant to let me go," replied Kael grinning, "but I pestered him enough."

Jasper turned to Rin.

"Old Sarge grows soft as the years go by, eh Rin?"

The straight-faced Zodrian nodded then allowed a slight smile to creep across his face. Jasper turned and walked toward the inn with Rin following.

"I must transact some business with your father. I suggest you stop dawdling if you want to leave before high sun," called the old trader and he disappeared behind the inn's front doors.

Kael inspected the dagger he purchased. Surprisingly, the seven-inch blade held a sharp edge even after its apparent neglect. The handle was made of a blue stone, but was so dirty Kael couldn't determine what type. With a bit of cleaning and sharpening, he he was sure the blade could be restored to its former beauty. Kael rubbed some of the grime from the stone and the light played off its surface. The boy determined that he probably did get the better half of the bargain. He tucked the blade in his tunic and ran to retrieve the Westland bow.

Kael descended from his room into the main hall. He noticed his father sitting at a corner table with Jasper and Rin. Kael approached the table with his bow.

"Excuse me, gentlemen," said Kael

"What is it you wish, Kael?" asked his father as all three men turned to look at him.

"I came to give this to old Jasper," said Kael holding out the bow.

"Kael!" said Brelg sharply. "Plain 'Jasper' is the man's name. Don't be rude."

Brelg turned to Jasper and shook his head.

"The boys' mother was in charge of teaching them proper manners," said Brelg frowning. "I'm afraid I've been a bit lax in that department."

Jasper grinned and waved off any insult he may have received. The innkeeper turned back to his son.

"And what does Master Jasper want with your bow, Kael?"

"I traded for something," said Kael.

"You traded for something? What are you thinking? That bow puts good game on our table in some of the leaner months. How could you trade away something that important? And what frivolity did you trade for?" said Brelg in a growing voice.

Kael pulled the dagger out of his tunic, and awkwardly held it forward. Brelg shot a glance at Jasper and back to Kael.

"So you trade a fine hunting bow for a toy to play soldier, is that it? I'm astonished at you, boy. If you think this deal through, you'll see your folly. I'm sure Jasper would reconsider his deal ..."

"Now hold on, Brelg. The boy made a sensible trade you know," cut in Jasper.

"How so?" Brelg asked respectfully.

"Well, if he means to travel the Nagur, he may need a weapon. A dagger draws more quickly than a bow."

"Your words are true, but do you really think he'll need it? If so, I would just as soon neither of my boys journeyed today," said Brelg.

Kael looked over his father's shoulder with a pained expression. Jasper's eyes met the boy's and a smile flashed across the old trader's face.

"Oh, of course not, Brelg. There is really no need for it, but better to err on the side of caution, eh? Let us call the dagger a loan to carry with him through the Nagur. Next time I'm in town, I will pick it up. Mind you, Kael, don't act foolishly and trade away my property," laughed Jasper.

"No sir, of course not," stammered Kael.

"Well, it is settled then," said Brelg. "Now Kael, get to your chores. I've some more business to discuss with Jasper and you're running late."

"Yes, sir," said Kael. He spun from the men and dashed out to the stables.

Kael entered the low building and tied on a long leather smock. His father puzzled him. When most men visited the inn, old Brelg made it perfectly clear who was in charge. However, when Jasper and his quiet son appeared at "The King's Service", Brelg demanded perfect manners. Brelg too became reserved and polite. Kael assumed this was out of respect for the old trader's age and knowledge. An innkeeper needed information about the wheat crop in the fields outside Ymril and the fishing hauls on the Derzean sea to help set his prices. However, this politeness was uncommon for Brelg.

Aemmon stood in the stables holding a shovel and a bucket. A sour expression crossed his face.

"I hate cleaning the stables."

Kael burst into laughter. "That's one thing we certainly agree upon!"

Kael picked up another shovel and went into the nearest stall. The pair worked for nearly an hour. In addition to cleaning the heavily laden floor, they filled feedbags, carried water into the troughs, and finished by giving each horse a brush and rub down. Finally, a broad smile crossed Kael's face.

"Aemmon, get the harness for Battle-ax. We're almost ready to go."

Aemmon frowned and walked to the end of the stables. He took a small harness from the wall and entered the last stall. Kael heard a few muffled groans and finally Aemmon emerged holding the end of a leather strap. As he backed out of the stall, the strap went taut. Aemmon gave a pull.

"C'mon," pleaded Aemmon. "Be a good girl."

"You need to be polite to her or she won't be polite to you," laughed Kael.

"You know it doesn't matter how I act toward her. She refuses to do anything I say. Come over here and help me," pleaded Aemmon. "She listens to you."

Kael approached the stall smiling. Inside, a small donkey stared defiantly at Aemmon, her legs stiffly braced against the compacted earth. As Kael entered, the donkey's stance relaxed. Kael cupped his hand around her ear and whispered soothingly. The donkey stepped slowly from the stall and pulled Aemmon out of the stables.

Aemmon glanced over his shoulder, rolling his eyes at Kael in exasperation. Kael shrugged his shoulders and followed into the yard. In the courtyard the boys tied empty saddlebags to the donkey, and then the bag of provisions for their trip. Next, they entered the kitchens for some breakfast. Cefiz stood at the cutting board slicing a large ham.

"All of your work is done?" he questioned.

"Absolutely," said Aemmon, staring at the ham.

"Stables, hens, pigs, horses, floors, dishes, everything?" said Cefiz solemnly.

"Please, Cefiz. Don't tease us. We're hungry!" pleaded Kael.

"Did you get Battle-ax ready?" asked Cefiz raising a questioning eyebrow as he sliced.

"Yes, sir," groaned Aemmon.

"Let's see, am I forgetting anything?" smiled Cefiz.

Aemmon's stomach growled loudly. The trio laughed and Cefiz forked ham onto two small loaves of bread.

"I also cut some ham and put it into this sack for you. It'll be nice to stop for a quick bite when you're into the Nagur a ways. You should start getting hungry about then," he paused. "Well Kael will, but Aemmon will be hungry twenty feet from the front gate!"

Aemmon blushed. He finished stuffing half of his loaf into his mouth and was munching furiously. He chewed some more and gulped hard.

"I could do without food for a couple of hours if it means getting this over with," grumbled Aemmon.

"Oh, you won't run into any trouble in the Nagur, Aemmon," said Cefiz. "On a sunny day like this it's an easy journey. The trail is well marked. Nightfall is when it's easy to get lost in the Nagur. You can't see a yard in front of your face."

"How do you know that, Cefiz?" asked Kael. "Did you ever travel the Nagur?"

"Oh, when the Sarge could spare me," smiled Cefiz. "I used to go on trading trips for the inn. I haven't been able to go to Luxlor since ..."

The cook trailed off and resumed slicing ham.

"Ever since mother died." finished Aemmon.

The three men grew silent for a while. The cook finally coughed and cleared his throat.

"An inn can't survive without a cook. I don't think I've left this town in nearly ten seasons," frowned Cefiz. "You boys better get going. You want to be through the forest before sundown."

Kael picked up the sack and headed for the door. Aemmon finished picking at the scraps left on the cutting board and followed. As the boys walked toward Battle-ax, their father and Jasper approached.

"Well, it's close to the time you two should be on your way," said Brelg. "Did you pack everything you need?"

"Yes, father," answered Kael.

"Remember, Kael," said Jasper. "I'm a man who's traveled the Nagur many times. There are a few simple rules to follow to ensure your safety.

"First, do not stray from the path. The forest is thick and overgrown. It's easy to lose one's way once you step from the path.

"Second, respect the Wood. I'm not a superstitious man, but mystery befalls those who harm the trees. If you need firewood, collect kindling from the ground. Never lay an ax to the trees.

"Finally, if you do get lost, listen for the sound of rushing water and move to it. This will most assuredly be the sound of the Efer River or a creek flowing to it. Once you reach the river, follow its banks and you should find a bridge and the path to Luxlor."

"Thank you, sir," nodded Kael as he glanced to his father.

With that, the two boys moved toward the donkey. Kael grabbed the reins and led her to the south road.

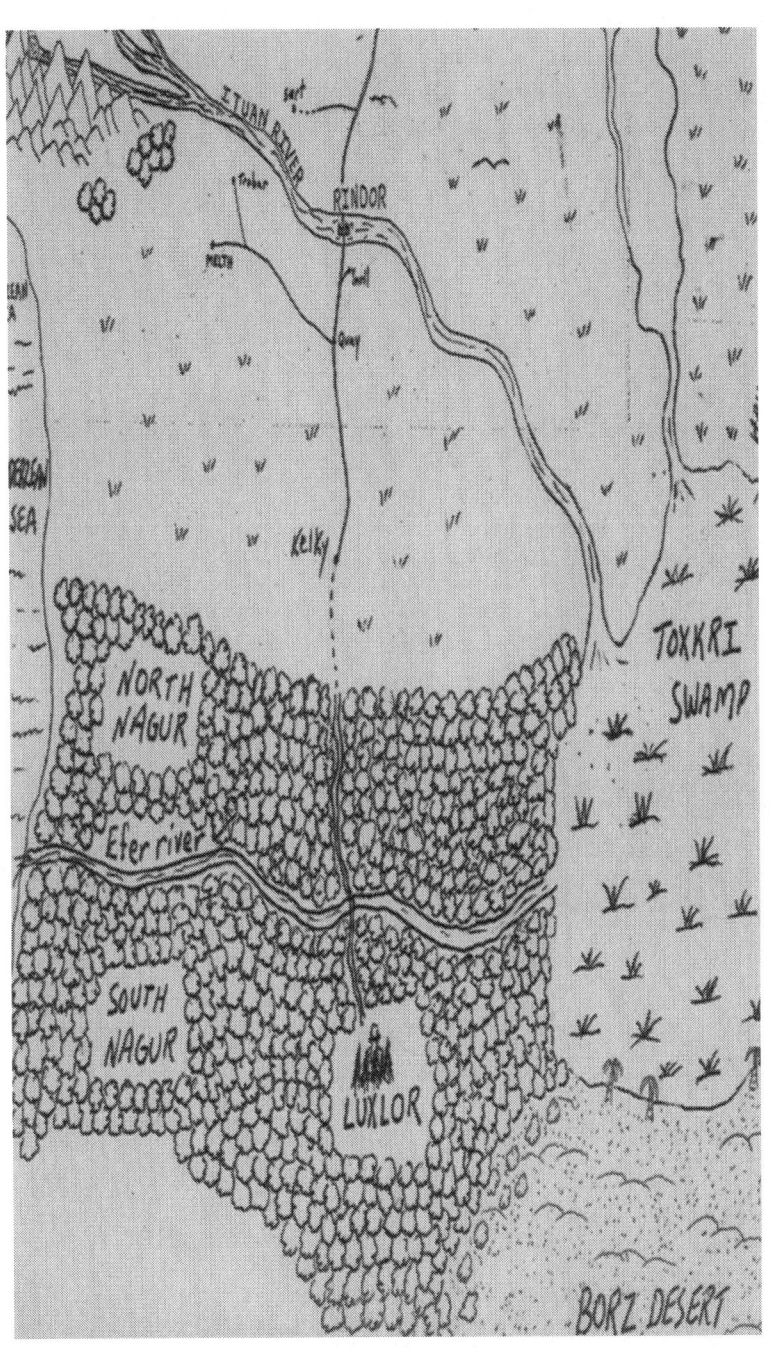

CHAPTER 2: PARTING

The road out of Kelky ran due south, crested a low hill and meandered in a southeasterly direction. Once the boys passed the hill they were alone. Not many travelers left Kelky to head south. After ten minutes leading the donkey down the dirt road Aemmon broke the silence.

"I'm glad we finally left. I expected father to make us do chores all day," muttered Aemmon.

"If he had his way, he would," said Kael. "We just needed to keep working on him."

He glanced at his brother.

"You seem to be getting more comfortable with the idea of this trip. Am I correct?" asked Kael.

"Comfortable? No," replied Aemmon. "Resigned to it? Yes."

They continued on in silence for several hours until Kael held up his hand.

"Did you hear that?" asked Kael.

"No, what?" replied Aemmon.

"I heard some thunder in the distance. Might be my imagination, but we really don't need to get caught in a thunderstorm this afternoon. We should try to quicken our pace."

The boys walked quickly and the donkey followed. The sky remained clear and sunny for another half hour, but then a dark, brooding cloud appeared on the Northeastern horizon. Soon the wind picked up, and Kael knew the storm moved their way. The Nagur appeared several leagues ahead when the first, fat raindrops splattered on the dry and dusty path. The pair hurried south. Within minutes a true downpour began and the young men were soaked.

At first, the storm was a nuisance. Kael found it difficult to keep his eyes on the path as the swirling wind slapped sheets of rain into his face. His cloak blew open and with his free hand he fought to keep it tightly wrapped about his body.

Aemmon fared no better. The large lad struggled to keep rainwater from pouring down his neck and smoothed his matted blond curls from his eyes.

Battle-ax occasionally fought their progress and the donkey froze when a particularly loud thunderclap ripped the air.

The path flowed like a small tributary of the gullies in the surrounding landscape. Each footstep sank deeper and deeper into the muddy trail and their footing became unsteady. The pair made poor progress. A flash and a roar filled their senses and a lone oak to their east stood split and smoldering from the force of a lightning bolt.

"We've got to find someplace to get out of this storm for a while!" yelled Kael over the howl of the wind.

The boy was worried about how much time they wasted, but fighting through the storm became useless.

"How about there?" pointed Aemmon.

About a hundred yards ahead and nearly two-dozen to the west stood a small grove of trees. Kael nodded agreement and led Battle-ax down the road. When they came close to the grove, they left the road and scrambled through the rain-swollen gullies toward the temporary shelter. Slipping and straining, they made their way. Finally, Kael clawed his way up the remaining mud wall and coaxed the donkey behind him.

Aemmon grasped the branches of a thistle, pulled himself up and tumbled backward as the bush uprooted. His right foot became lodged in the gnarled roots of a stunted oak he had used for footing.

Kael was tying the donkey to a tree when he heard Aemmon shout. He hurried back to the edge of the gully to find his brother dangling down the eight-foot wall. Aemmon's boot was locked in the oak's roots.

Kael winced at the sight of Aemmon's leg twisted in the wrong direction. He slid down the muddy wall and grabbed his brother by the shoulders. They struggled with Aemmon's weight for a few moments before Kael managed to lift his brother high enough to release the boot from the tree roots. The pair tumbled into the gully with Aemmon howling in pain.

"Are you all right!" shouted Kael over the wind and rain.

"Of course I'm not all right," growled Aemmon through clenched teeth. "My leg …… it hurts."

Kael moved over and pulled his brother's hands from the injured knee. He rolled up the pant leg and inspected the injury. Aemmon's knee was swollen and discolored.

"Well, this isn't the best place to wait out the storm front," shouted Kael. "We've got to get you up this hill and under cover."

Kael stood and grabbed his brother's hand, helping Aemmon to his feet. Twenty yards south, the gully's walls stood less steep. Kael scrambled up and over the edge and held his hand down to assist his brother. After considerable effort and grumbling, Aemmon reached the top. Kael supported his brother as they made their way back to the grove. Aemmon was quickly propped against a tree trunk.

"How does it feel?" asked Kael pointing to the injured knee.

"Awful," replied Aemmon. "What are we going to do now?"

"Well, you can't go on. I see no point in trying to continue. That knee cancelled our journey, and this storm put an end to our return home."

Kael stood and approached the donkey. He retrieved a thick woolen blanket from a pack. Kael spread one end of the blanket over Aemmon then ducked underneath and huddled next to his brother. Aemmon flashed a weak smile then pulled the blanket further over his head to keep the rain at bay.

They sat in the limited shelter of the grove for nearly half an hour. The wind blew fiercely and the rain poured. Water drowned the ground about them and soaked their clothes.

"You know," said Aemmon, "a little distance into the woods we may find shelter and firewood. We might be able to dry off. I could easily get that far if it guaranteed a warm shirt and a dry spot to sleep."

Lightning flashed through the sky and thunder rumbled the earth. The downpour doubled its intensity.

"Well, this coming from the man who didn't want to set foot in the Nagur," shouted Kael over the roar.

"Some things are more pressing than others," grimaced Aemmon in return.

Kael rose and walked over to Battle-ax. He strapped some of the donkey's load on his own back and cleared a spot for Aemmon. The injured man struggled over and onto the donkey. In minutes the little group traversed back to the road. The swirling wind whipped rain into their faces and stung their cheeks. After thirty minutes of slow travel, they reached the edge of the Nagur. Kael stole a glance back at his brother who winced with every step Battle-ax made.

Kael led the donkey past the trees and into the woods. The rain immediately diminished as the surrounding forest and its thick canopy encased the travelers. The wood held the musty odor of decaying vegetation. All around them huge moss covered oaks and elms towered under a sky of dark greens and blacks. Kael couldn't find a single hole in the darkness to see the sky above. The Nagur was a world unto itself, its own sky, boundaries and life.

The brothers found a large elm, recently fallen, just off the edge of the path. Kael helped Aemmon from the donkey's back to a spot against the trunk of the fallen tree. The boy cleared an area for them to sleep, dug a fire pit, unloaded Battle-ax and tied Aemmon's leg in a splint. Kael then collected enough dead wood to feed a fire for the remainder of the day and night. Aemmon scanned the dark forest as Kael prepared to strike his flint at the kindling.

"Jasper said fire was acceptable as long as you didn't lay an ax to the trees," said Kael.

He lit the wood and soon a hot blaze roared in the fire pit. Aemmon settled in against the elm and wrapped the blanket tightly around his big frame. Kael hung some of their wetter things on a line near the fire then retrieved a blanket of his own and settled in next to Aemmon.

They sat in silence watching the steam rise from their soggy clothes. Kael looked to Aemmon and the bigger brother offered a weak smile. Kael returned it with a wide grin then rummaged through his pack for the food Cefiz provided.

"Kael," said Aemmon, "I'm truly sorry I ruined the trip for you."

"Aemmon, you didn't ruin the trip. It was this storm coming out of nowhere. Don't fret over it," said Kael as he handed his brother a loaf.

"Ironic, eh? I kept hoping you would change your mind about going to Luxlor. I didn't want to travel to these woods. I was ... I didn't want to face this trip. Now we're here and it doesn't really bother me. I guess you need to go ahead and do something to overcome the fear of it," replied Aemmon as he took a bite of bread.

"Well, you certainly have gone and 'done it'," laughed Kael, nodding towards Aemmon's leg.

"I did at that," laughed Aemmon through a mouthful of food. "What a fool I am."

Kael gave his brother a playful punch to the shoulder then turned and surveyed the campsite.

"We set up a good camp. Plenty of firewood. Plenty of food. We might as well stay here for the remainder of the day, and leave for home first thing in the morning. That storm sounds like it hasn't died down," Kael said gazing up into the trees.

"Uh, Kael," said Aemmon hesitantly, "There's still plenty of time to reach Luxlor with speed and luck on your side."

Kael turned back to his brother.

"Don't be ridiculous, Aemmon," he said, "You can't possibly travel to Luxlor. The journey home will be tough enough."

"I don't intend on going to Luxlor, although it would be a nice place to see. I meant, you could make it there."

"And leave you here all alone. I wouldn't think of it. Besides, that donkey is too slow. It would be nightfall by the time I got there and the markets would be closed. It's pointless."

"Why take Battle-ax?" asked Aemmon, "What is the most important thing we are after on this trip?"

"The medicines father needs for the town," said Kael, "Also he really wanted the Elven rope."

"Do you need Battle-ax to carry a couple of lines of rope and a few pouches of medicine?"

"No," said Kael. "I brought her in order to bring back some carvings, food and any other items that drew our eye."

"So, you don't need her. We are stuck here until tomorrow anyway. Father will be disappointed and a touch wary about sending us a second time. Finally, I am not a child who needs you to stay here and watch me. To tell you the truth, even with an injured leg I can protect myself a good deal better than you. So do me a favor. Give me peace and quiet and go to Luxlor. I'll wait here until you return and we'll say nothing to Sarge about any of this. That way, he has his rope and medicines and everybody is happy," explained Aemmon.

"You're actually making some sense," smiled Kael.

"I don't hear you saying 'no'," grinned Aemmon in return. "I know how much you wanted this, Kael. I don't want to be the reason you miss it. Please go."

Kael stared at Aemmon for a long time. Finally, he shook his head and smiled.

"I will," said Kael, "but take my bow. Keep it close by with your broadsword. You should be able to keep any wolves away with the arrows and the fire. Don't let it die down."

"Wolves won't be a problem. We're not in the lean months yet. Don't worry about me, Kael," said Aemmon.

"Let me get some more wood for you, and then I'll be off," said Kael.

Kael piled extra wood on the fire, replenished the stack at his brother's feet and shook Aemmon's hand.

"It'll seem like only moments have passed by the time I return," said Kael as he gathered his belongings and headed down the path.

"Take care of yourself!" Aemmon called into the darkness of the forest.

CHAPTER 3 THE RACE

The forest swallowed him up as Kael moved deeper into its interior. A few bends and curves of the path and the exit from the woods onto the Southlands of Zodra disappeared. As he moved inward it grew darker. Kael wondered if this were due to the day growing longer or the woods becoming thicker. He walked on.

The boy lost track of time as he hiked down the path. The monotony of the forest lulled him. His mind drifted over happier times in Kelky, when his mother ran the day to day business of the inn and he and Aemmon spent afternoons playing in the fields around the village. Their father was often away on business in those days, but had since stayed close to home in order to raise his boys and keep the inn operational.

Suddenly, Kael sensed strangeness in the wood. At first he shrugged it off as irrational fears playing in his mind. Then, he convinced himself something was watching him. However, he neither heard nor saw anything to add credence to his fears. Kael increased his pace and jogged down the path. He desperately needed to make up lost time anyway.

After fifteen minutes at this tiring pace, Kael slowed and shook his head. The feeling was gone, and as he caught his breath he laughed. How foolish he felt. The fears and imaginings of a child got the better of him. Thank goodness no one was a witness to that stupidity.

After another hour, Kael stopped by the western side of the path. He was unable to determine if the storm raged outside the forest. The trunks of the trees were coated in water and drops constantly fell from the canopy of the forest. Kael was certain the hottest, driest days outside the forest appeared this way. The Nagur was a cool, wet, dank place, all to itself. Quiet permeated everything.

From his calculations, Kael felt he should be nearing the Efer River. As he sat propped against a tree, he listened for the sound of rushing water. He closed his eyes and let his mind stretch out and reach for that sound. Did he hear it? Maybe, just faintly, he heard the sound of water spilling over rock. It grew louder the more he concentrated and focused his mind. Yes, now he definitely heard the steady rush of water.

A loud snap interrupted the rhythm of the river. Then another. Kael's eyes sprung open, but his mind and ears stayed alert. The noise came from the eastern side of the Nagur trail. He rolled around the trunk of the tree and gazed into the woods on the opposite side of the path. Nothing. After a minute, Kael heard another faint crunching noise. His eyes shot in the sound's direction. Was that movement he saw? He couldn't be sure. A few more soft rustling noises and Kael was up and moving Southward down the path.

The boy fumbled inside his cloak for the blade Jasper gave him. He ran lithely, springing over rocks and fallen tree limbs, his ears on the alert. The rustling turned into a soft thumping noise that quickened as Kael increased his own pace. This was no longer his imagination. Something followed behind him and sounded as if it were gaining. When he reached an open stretch of pathway, Kael stole a glance over his shoulder. The boy was sure he saw movement inside the tree line. He increased his speed, pushing his body's endurance.

The sound of the river grew. Ahead of him the path widened and cleared. A narrow, wooden bridge arched over a small gorge. The Efer River rushed beneath the bridge. If Kael made it over the river, whatever followed would be required to do the same. Tactically, that gave him an advantage. If he had only kept his bow. Courage replaced fear. His goal became the bridge.

The path flew under his feet as he increased his speed. Behind him he heard a crash and glanced back to see a figure break free from the trees and onto the path. Kael leapt onto the bridge. His heart leapt as well. Jasper's blade flashed from beneath his cloak. The boy prepared to turn at mid bridge and face his assailant.

His hopes crashed. Ahead of him, three shadowy figures rushed from the woods. They took positions at the end of the bridge and notched arrows into short bows. Kael's heart sank. The bridge was to be his salvation. Instead, it was the perfect trap sprung by this group of thieves. Thirty feet ahead lay an arrow to the heart. Thirty feet below a nasty fall to the turbulent Efer. Thirty feet behind …….

Kael turned to see a hooded figure in green slowly advancing across the bridge. The figure gripped a sword and moved to within three yards of the boy. Kael clenched his teeth, spun the dagger's balanced weight in his hand and glared. His assailant froze. Kael was shocked to hear the snarl emit from his own lips.

"Yours is a bit bigger than mine, but both cut deeply enough! Stay back!"

The man on the bridge relaxed and stood straight, throwing back his hood.

"You possess backbone," said a handsome, young elf with dusky gray skin and dark black hair, "but you are hardly in a position to make demands. I am Eidyn, Captain of the Imperial Guard. Drop your weapon and state your business."

Kael's shoulders drooped and he glanced nervously between the trio on the bank and the lone elf advancing on him.

"How can I be certain who you are?" muttered Kael over the rush of the river. "The four of you might be thieves."

"Grey Elves do not become thieves! You were about to enter our lands. Who else would be guarding the entryway? Now comply with my demands or be taken by force. Those archers could have killed you long ago if they so desired."

Kael weighed the stranger's words and knew they held merit. He couldn't help but weakly smile at how poorly this trip was progressing. Now he stood captured by the very people he came to visit. He plunged the dagger into a post of the bridge and stepped toward the archers with his hands held high.

"I mean no one harm," said Kael. "I'm here to do some trading."

"Trading eh," replied Captain Eidyn. "It's extremely late in the day to be thinking of trading. The markets will be closed soon."

"Unfortunately, my companion was injured and needed attention. This took some time and forced me behind schedule. If you need someone to vouch for me, I'm to meet an Elf named Teeg when I arrive. He's a friend of my father. He should clear things up."

"If you use prominent names to impress me, you'll soon learn they do not," said Eidyn. "Lord Teeg will be notified of your arrival and we shall see if he supports your story."

The Elf moved forward and checked Kael for any other weapons. When he was satisfied, he turned and worked the dagger free from the bridge post. His eyes widened and he took a step back from Kael.

"Where did you get this dagger?" he demanded.

"From a friend," returned Kael.

"The owner of this dagger would not part with it easily. Turn around!" ordered Eidyn.

Kael complied. Eidyn bound Kael's hands behind his back and placed a gag in his mouth. The captain marched Kael to the opposite side of the bridge.

"Lieutenant Diom, make sure your men are as vigilant as ever," Captain Eidyn said to one of the bowmen. "The stories of trouble in the North Nagur are true. I bear much to report to his majesty. I don't know what role, if any, this prisoner plays in the trouble, but he wears the dress of a Southland villager without the features of one. You three will come with me. You others maintain your positions and guard the bridge. Support will arrive shortly."

Kael scanned the woods on the south side of the bridge and picked out the figures of Elves crouched behind trees and boulders. Eidyn moved ahead down the path and led the five men on their march toward Luxlor.

After a short while on the path, one of the bowmen left Kael's side to walk with Eidyn several yards ahead.

"Sir?" he whispered, attempting to keep his conversation low.

"Yes, Diom," answered Captain Eidyn.

"I was wondering sir. This prisoner, he hardly seems like much of a threat. I mean, he's just a boy. What worries you about him?"

"He may appear a boy, Diom, but after the things I've seen this week I'm taking no chances," replied Eidyn.

"Sir?" prompted Diom.

"Several nights ago, I came across tracks I'd seen only once, long ago," continued Eidyn. "Immediately, I assumed there was an unnatural to the north. I tracked it for the remainder of the evening and lost it."

"Impossible!" gasped Diom.

"I tell you it eluded me by some black magic," said Eidyn, "and that is not all that seems impossible. As I was returning home, I came across this boy. Taking the usual precautions, I trailed him."

Eidyn paused and furrowed his brow.

"He heard me," said the captain.

"No! This cannot be. No mere Southland lad could detect you. I myself find it difficult. You're like a shadow amongst the trees."

"Not only did he hear me, but he saw me. I took every precaution and still he saw me," exclaimed Eidyn.

Diom furrowed his brow in a troubled expression.

"Sir, I'm glad we spoke. I supposed it to be a trick of my imagining, but when you ordered our troops in the wood to maintain their positions," said Diom, "I swear the boy looked directly at Firn and Erlin's stations. For an instant, I was convinced he saw them as well."

Eidyn considered the news.

"Diom, this boy concerns me. Once I knew of my discovery, I moved to capture him. As heaven is my witness, he outran me. If he ran in any other direction than that of the bridge, he might have evaded me."

"Ridiculous! You are a champion of the Grey Elves. This boy could not outrun a champion of Luxlor."

"You saw it yourself. By the time he reached the bridge I was nearly spent. In another locale he would have outstripped me,"

Eidyn clenched his teeth. "When that boy heard me, saw me, then outran me, I knew I was dealing with something unusual."

Diom turned and looked over his shoulder as the group marched on. Kael diverted his eyes as his mind and heart raced. What were these men talking about? The boy was frightened and confused. His blood rushed and his senses were alert. He prayed that once they reached Luxlor his father's old friend, Teeg, would set things straight. Diom turned back to his superior as Captain Eidyn slid Kael's dagger from beneath his cloak.

"Not only did he accomplish these improbable tasks, but he carried this," whispered Eidyn.

"The Needle of Ader!" hissed Diom and he shot a glance back to the boy.

Kael was shocked and his eyes went wide as he gazed ahead at the dagger. The revelation that he carried a weapon of significance to the Elves was too much for him to grasp. His reaction did not evade the keen eyes of Diom.

"Captain," hissed Diom "He hears us and he understands!"

Again Kael was shocked. Something strange was going on. Eidyn wheeled around and marched back to Kael. The captain tore the gag from the boy's mouth and held the dagger to Kael's throat.

"Is this true?" demanded Eidyn in his Elvish tongue.

Kael's eyes were wide with fear.

"IS THIS TRUE?" demanded Eidyn once more.

"Yes," stammered Kael. "I.... I don't know what's going on here. Please, sir. I'm just an innkeeper's son on his way to Luxlor to trade some goods. I don't know about any trouble in the Nagur."

Eidyn's eyes narrowed.

"An innkeepers son. From what town?"

"Kelky," answered Kael.

Eidyn's face grew stern. He threw the gag to the ground and spun to face his troops.

"I want the three of you in a tight formation guarding the prisoner. It's time to move. Quickly!"

Eidyn thrust the dagger into his cloak, turned to the trail and ran toward Luxlor. Two of the Elves grabbed Kael under the arms and forced him forward at a similar pace.

Once again Kael's mind raced. What was going on? Did he step into the middle of a battle? Was he being mistaken for someone else? Certainly, he reasoned, this was not normal behavior for the Elves. Possibly there was a murder or theft in the Nagur, and he was in the wrong place at the wrong time. If they believed him to be at fault, would they arrest him or execute him? He desperately wished his father were with him.

After forty minutes at a steady run, the five men passed a guard outpost. Two Elves manning the post stepped into the road, but recognition of Captain Eidyn flashed across their faces and they quickly stepped aside. Within another five minutes, the group arrived at the outskirts of the city of Luxlor. Simple cottages of earth and wood appeared here and there in the surrounding forest. As they traveled onward, the number of cottages grew.

The trees in the city fascinated Kael. Their number didn't diminish as the group traveled deeper and deeper into the heart of Luxlor. More and more houses and cottages appeared, but the Elves constructed them in order to give the trees room. The citizens of Luxlor built their cottages, stores and other buildings around the trees. In some cases, the trees were an important part of the structure. They passed a cottage with a huge oak trunk sticking out of the middle of the roof and soaring high into the forest ceiling.

Dusk was approaching and Elves crowded the streets traveling to their homes.

"We don't need to alarm the populace by rushing through the streets," said Eidyn to his men. "Watch the boy closely."

The group slowed to a walk. Kael was allowed an opportunity to observe the people of Luxlor. Most of the men were about his height, somewhat short by Zodrian standards. All displayed the distinctive smoky gray skin and black hair common to the elves. Also, Kael noticed the Elves were predominantly slight of build, almost delicate. This feature coupled with their graceful, fluid motions made even the most mundane tasks appear a beautiful dance.

    As Kael was watching an attractive young woman glide by him carrying a basket of apples, he was pulled to a stop by the hand of one of his guards. He turned and stared forward. Stretching across the road in front of him towered a row of gigantic trees. Each spanned a width of ten paces with an unusual cloudy white bark that appeared smooth to the touch. The trees grew so closely together that Kael guessed his fist might just be able to pass between the nearest two. The giants created a formidable wall. Their towering mass securely protected whatever lie on the opposite side.

    Ahead, two of these titans grew together over a steel archway and a set of massive steel doors. Eidyn approached a guard stationed by the doors. After a few moments of conversation, the guard stepped away and the doors slowly swung a few feet open. Kael and his escort hurried through the opening before it was slammed shut.

THE ALMAR RING

The group stood in a passageway beneath the trees. A thirty foot, steel tunnel had been constructed and anchored to the forest floor ages ago. The trees were coaxed to grow against and around this tunnel. The passageway was so large, two carts could pass one another in the tunnel with room to spare. The high ceiling was lit by glass jars containing a greenish, glowing gel. As Kael gazed about in awe, he noticed Eidyn staring at him.

"For your sake, I hope you told us the truth about yourself," said the Elven captain. "You are about to enter the palace of Luxlor and the Almighty help you if you lie."

The Elf turned and strode ten paces to another set of steel gates. He whispered through a hole and the door swung open.

The group stepped into a wide, circular opening in the forest. The only trees visible were those they passed beneath. The wall stretched behind Kael to both his right and left. The line of living columns arced around the clearing, enclosing this portion of the Nagur Wood within their formidable defenses.

Sitting within the center of this circle and towering above even the giant white trees stood the palace of Luxlor. Shredded clouds skirted across the sky above as the remnants of the storm sprinkled the buildings with a fine mist. The last rays of the setting sun pierced the fleeting clouds and struck the palace. Its surface glistened in brilliant white.

"Its beautiful," mumbled the boy.

Eidyn smiled as he stared at his home.

"Yes, it is," he replied.

The Captain turned to one of several gatekeepers in attendance and issued a series of quick commands. The soldier spun and ran toward the palace. Captain Eidyn addressed the group.

"Diom, you are to take command of the prisoner. He is to be presented to the royal guard immediately. Hopefully, I will be afforded time enough to attend to business before the court is assembled," said Eidyn.

"Yes, captain," answered Diom with a salute.

The Elf captain spun and ran toward the palace. Diom nodded toward the remaining guards and prodded Kael forward toward the shimmering white structure. As they walked, Diom turned to the prisoner.

"How in heaven's name did you outrun the captain? No Elf is as swift," said Diom.

Kael furrowed his brow and questioned whether he should say anything. Was this a trick to get him to speak? Then again, what could he possibly say that might get him in greater trouble than he found himself? Diom waited a moment then scowled. Kael determined silence was not the best course of action.

"To tell you the truth, sir," replied Kael, "I was so frightened, I couldn't tell what was happening. I reasoned you were thieves."

Diom pondered Kael's answer then grinned.

"Swift or not, I know one thing you cannot outrun," Diom winked and tapped an arrow in the quiver strapped to his back. "Nothing outruns one of these. So don't give me any trouble while you're in my care."

"Absolutely not," replied a wide-eyed Kael.

CHAPTER 4: THE ALMAR THRONE

After several minutes walk, the group arrived at the palace. A small flight of steps led to a long corridor. The floor of the hallway was made of the same white-grained wood as the rest of the castle. Greenish light from jars similar to those Kael glimpsed in the tunnel radiated the hallway.

After passing several connecting corridors, the group reached a large set of doors guarded by a pair of Elven soldiers. Diom motioned Kael to a smaller doorway inset to the right. The group entered a cozy room filled with exquisite furniture. Rich tapestries of beautifully woven scenes from the palace grounds of Luxlor covered the walls. Busts of Elven royalty stood on pedestals throughout the room.

"Sit," said Diom pointing to an embroidered armchair.

Kael did as he was told. Diom took a chair opposite Kael and sat as well, staring at the boy intently. The other guards stood by the door to the room. It felt to Kael like hours went by before the door swung open. Diom jumped to his feet and stood rigidly at attention. An elderly Elf swept into the room and surveyed the scene. The Elf stood slightly under Kael's height and had a kindly, wrinkled face. He wore a blue robe with gold embroidery and carried a jumbled bundle of scrolls.

"Well Diom, it is good to see you in the city walls. How do you fare?" smiled the Elf.

Diom lowered his head and bowed.

"I am excellent, sir. I'm happy to see you are in good health," answered Diom.

"Couldn't be better. Well now, to the business at hand. I see you are in charge of a.... prisoner," the Elf turned toward Kael. "Kael Brelgson, how fare you?"

Kael stood somewhat aghast and froze as the Elf extended a hand in friendship while trying not to spill the scrolls.

"Come now, Kael. Don't be so taken aback. I am Teeg, you may remember me from seasons ago when I visited your father's inn. You were but a small boy then."

"Ah ... I do vaguely remember you," replied Kael extending his bound hands. "It's true, I was quite young then."

"Diom, I am sure that is unnecessary," said Teeg pointing at the leather constraint.

Diom glanced from the old Elf to Kael's wrists then quickly drew a dagger from beneath his cloak and cut the strap. Kael thanked Teeg and rubbed the blood back into his hands.

"I beg your pardon Master Teeg..."

"Oh, just Teeg is fine, Kael," cut in the Elf. "I know you have many questions about your experience, however, you need only wait a few short minutes before they are answered. Diom, your service was superlative as always. I will take our guest from your hands."

"As your honor wishes," said Diom and he bowed.

"Kael, please follow me," said Teeg.

The old Elf led Kael back into the hallway and past the guards stationed at the large double doors. The doors opened and Kael entered a long chamber with a highly vaulted ceiling. This room, although of great size, was furnished as ornately as the anteroom. Tapestries hung on the walls and pillars lined both sides. A sky blue carpet ran to a dais at the far end of the room. Upon the dais were four intricately carved chairs.

In the right center chair sat a tall, distinguished looking Elf. The Elf's black locks were beginning to frost. He wore sky blue vestments and a cloak with gold embroidered borders. To his right sat a beautiful woman in a light blue gown. Her black hair was braided with spun silver and hung over her shoulder, down her chest.

"Trust me, Kael," whispered Teeg as they walked the carpet, "be honest, polite and to the point and you shall be home in Kelky tomorrow."

Teeg nudged Kael as they stopped before the throne and the old Elf bowed. Kael hesitated and bowed as well. As he did so, he glanced around the throne room. A small gathering was present. The Elves in attendance were all richly dressed with colorful vestments and robes. Kael noticed Eidyn among those in the crowd. The Elven captain wore his cloak, a green tunic and pants. Several medals were pinned upon his chest. Other Elves sprinkled throughout the court were dressed similarly. The king raised his hand as Teeg and Kael approached. The court quieted.

"Lord Teeg, why do you summon a council of the king at this late hour?" questioned the stately Elf.

"Leinor, King of the Grey Elves. Before I address your question, I prefer that your son, Prince Eidyn, make his report to the court."

All eyes turned to Eidyn. Kael narrowed his eyes in confusion. Captain Eidyn was a prince?

"Eidyn," replied King Leinor. "What news have you?"

Eidyn stepped to the center of the room beside Teeg and Kael. He bowed deeply to first the king and then the queen. The queen smiled and nodded her head to him.

"Your highness, your majesty," said Eidyn, "my news is not good. I suspect your fears of an 'unnatural' in our homeland are well founded. These past twenty days I searched the forest from boundary to boundary for evidence of such a creature. Where the northern tip of the Nagur meets the Derzean Sea, in the place called Bothom's Hollow, I found tracks. They were faint and hard to pick out but I am certain. A Malveel prowls the Nagur."

A gasp emitted from several in attendance.

"I followed its tracks for days," continued Eidyn. "When I appeared to be close, the tracks disappeared."

"Impossible!" scoffed an old Elf in military garb, "A beast of such size cannot simply disappear. No such beast could elude you."

"Thank you for your confidence, General Chani. Nonetheless it is true, the track went cold. After several days of searching an ever increasing circle, I admitted defeat and moved on. My task then led me to the Eastern edges of our homeland. There by the Toxkri Swamp ...," Eidyn paused and studied the court members in attendance.

"Eidyn, I spoke to your cousin Gwinnen. She is not amongst those assembled here and retired to her chambers to rest. Please continue," prompted Teeg.

"There I found the bodies of Lord Giar and his son Steff," stated Eidyn solemnly.

A murmur broke out in the Elven court. Kael registered the dismay on the faces of the noble men and women. The soldiers, however, stood steady and stone faced.

"Eidyn, this news is grave and makes my heart heavy," said King Leinor. "Please my lords and ladies. We must contain our grief and determine the cause of such a catastrophe."

The murmur quieted and order was restored.

"Eidyn, how did they perish?" asked Leinor.

"My lord, their bodies appeared to be torn to shreds by a beast of some kind. I discovered the same tracks as those at Bothom's Hollow. I determined they were set upon by the Malveel I failed to shadow."

Eidyn bowed his head.

"Unfortunately, their condition did not allow me to bring them home to Gwinnen for proper burial. I interred them where they fell and said the rites over their graves.

"I decided to return to Luxlor as quickly as possible with this news. I headed toward the Nagur path. After several days travel I nearly reached my objective when I almost stumbled into the path of this boy," Eidyn said pointing at Kael.

The court assembly turned to study Kael. Many of the members of the court were still reeling from Eidyn's news. Their shock already turned to anger and he felt its focus.

"As you well know, my lord. I am a trained officer of your elite corp. Two days previously I discovered the mutilated bodies of my kin and knew of the presence of an 'unnatural' in the Nagur. Believe me when I say I was using all of my skill and training to detect anything unusual. However, with the Almighty as my witness, I nearly walked into the path of this... this boy.

"I neither heard nor saw him until the last moment. Luckily I was able to conceal my movements and avoid detection. Also, as we know, many of our enemy's emissaries are not what they seem. His appearance was not threatening but I took no chances. I allowed him to continue for an hour and trailed him distantly.

"Unexpectedly, he stopped and sat near the edge of the path. I determined to get a closer look at the boy, so I moved in slowly. Again I took all the necessary precautions. However, I was overheard."

General Chani's face screwed into a look of distress and he cleared his throat.

"I don't know how, but he was aware of me," continued Eidyn. "He broke and ran. I experienced trouble keeping up because I wanted to remain concealed and followed in the wood. He remained on the path and eventually made the Efer... his only error in judgment."

"What are you saying Eidyn? He was in the Nagur. There is no escape from us in the Nagur!" exclaimed General Chani.

"I mean what I say, General. This boy outran me. I am not ashamed to say it. With his silent ways and speed, I dare say had he avoided the river and entered our wood, he would have eluded me. As providence would have it, he ran directly to my men stationed at the Efer crossing. Once he was outnumbered and in their sights, he surrendered."

"Might this mere boy be capable of the deed perpetrated on Lord Giar and Steff?" asked the general staring at Kael. "Giar was a trained veteran of the military. He served on my personal staff. Should this boy be allowed in the court unbound? Captain Eidyn, is he a captured prisoner or a guest?"

Chani glanced to the other officers in the room with concern.

"I'm unsure of the capabilities of this boy, if that is what he is," stated Eidyn. "However, he was armed."

Eidyn removed a canvass wrapped object from beneath his cloak.

"My lord, the boy carried the ...."

"Silence! Stay your words Captain Eidyn," boomed a voice from the doors of the king's court.

Kael wheeled and stared at the opening. There on the threshold stood Jasper the trader and his son Rin. The duo stepped into the middle of the court and stopped near Teeg and Kael. The entire court, including the king and queen, crossed their hands over their hearts then held them out, palms upward. Jasper quickly returned the gesture and turned to face the throne.

"Hail, Lord of the Elves and protector of the Holy Wood. Hail Eirtwin, Mother of the Elven people," said Jasper.

"Hail and well met Ader, Chosen of Avra. You are not long from our lands, yet return at an opportune hour. The Holy Nagur is troubled," returned Leinor.

Jasper turned and approached Eidyn. He took the wrapped object from the Elf's hands. Kael stared in shock and disbelief. His old friend radiated power and control throughout the room. Eidyn readily released his burden, bowed lightly to the man he called "Ader" and backed away. The throne room's full attention focused on the old man. Kael was filled with courage and edged closer to the tinker.

The boy took a deep breath and started to speak, but a sharp look from Jasper erased any notion of continuing. The trader's eyes left no doubt how serious the situation was and that Kael was expected to remain silent. Kael's courage departed as easily as it came and he too stepped back to allow Jasper center stage.

"My lords and ladies, you received quite a shock today. I suggest you all return to your homes. Nothing can be done now. I must take counsel with your king," stated Jasper.

Leinor stood and bowed, acknowledging his agreement. The king motioned to his guards and the doors to the chamber were opened. The nobles and military personnel filed out. Kael stood in the emptying court stunned. Jasper ordered the nobles of Luxlor to their homes, and they obeyed!

"I require General Chani, Prince Eidyn and Lord Teeg remain," announced Jasper.

Once the room cleared, Jasper directed the group closer to the king's throne.

"Ader, you heard of the deaths of Lord Giar and his son Steff?" asked Prince Eidyn.

"Most unfortunate," stated Jasper with a heavy frown.

"I sent them toward Erutre to warn Chieftain Temujen of the increased boldness of the 'unnaturals'," stated Leinor.

"Of course," said Jasper. "This is a time for all of the lands to share information and show aid to one another."

Kael was anxious for answers, but so far complied with Jasper's obvious demand for silence. The boy's mind reeled and the uncertainty of his situation sent his heart racing and the blood rushing through his veins. How was this situation spinning so far out of his control? Better still, how did his old friend confidently storm into the Elven court and take control? Even the king deferred to the tinker's wishes. And why was everyone calling him "Ader"?

Kael shook his head to clear the confusion. When he glanced upward he noted Queen Eirtwin's intense scrutiny. She had been silent throughout the proceedings. However, her penetrating stare processed all. She smiled.

"Ader," said the queen. "You should introduce us to this young man. You called him 'Kael', did you not?"

"What?" said the king. "Kael, you say?"

"King Leinor and Queen Eirtwin, this is Kael Brelgson from the tiny village of Kelky, not more than a day's journey from your borders," said Jasper pulling Kael closer to the king and queen.

Kael stretched out his hand toward Leinor. The king smirked and awkwardly accepted the handshake. Kael then turned to the queen and stopped in confusion and uncertainty. She laughed and offered him her hand to kiss, which he did readily.

"I .... I'm pleased to meet you both," stammered Kael.

"The pleasure is all ours," replied the queen bowing her head.

"Very well," commented Jasper. "That should do for the courtly pleasantries. Now that I am here, we know who the boy is and he may go about his business."

"Ader, I don't mean to question your judgment, but are you certain? This boy has skills he should not possess!" stated Eidyn with concern.

"I don't understand," said Kael. "Why do they call you 'Ader'?"

The boy turned to King Leinor.

"His name is Jasper and that man by the door is his son, Rin."

The king and queen smiled and glanced at one another. Eidyn and Chani looked perplexed. Teeg stared at the ground and frowned.

"Do you see what you caused?" growled Ader as he spun toward Teeg.

"I felt it was time," shrugged Teeg.

"Well I didn't," grumbled Ader.

Rin approached from his position by the door.

"Ader," he said calmly.

"What is it Manfir?" asked Ader still scowling at Teeg.

"Where is the boy's companion? Where is Aemmon?"

Ader turned toward the boy.

"Kael, your brother, where is he?" asked Ader abruptly.

"He injured his leg. He's waiting for me on the other side of the woods," replied Kael.

Ader glanced at Manfir.

"What say you?"

"He is capable," said Manfir dryly. "We detected nothing on our ride. The danger seems to have passed."

"Yes, but we obviously missed the danger on our first pass through the wood," frowned Ader. "If we had been more diligent, Lord Giar and Steff might never have fallen and Kael would never have been allowed on this folly of a trip.

"Nevertheless, it is Aemmon Brelgson who concerns me now. The danger may be past, but precautions should be taken. Decisions must be made. Eidyn, you endured a strenuous and emotional fortnight. You will go to your chamber and rest. Also you will keep everything you saw and heard in the Nagur and here tonight completely confidential. Is that understood?"

"Yes, Ader," said Eidyn, bowing and departing.

"General Chani, you will dispatch a squad of your corps to find and guard Aemmon Brelgson on the north edge of the Nagur. I do not anticipate any further trouble. The attack on Giar and Steff must have been the creatures assignment and they do not like to tarry once their work is done."

"As you command," declared Chani, and he also bowed and departed.

"Lord Teeg, you will occupy the time of our young friend until his departure tomorrow. See to it that he obtains the goods he came for. I'm sure my wishes concerning Kael are understood," said Ader sternly.

"Perfectly, my lord," replied Teeg arching an eyebrow.

"Wishes about what, Jasper?" asked Kael in confusion.

"Kael," said Ader calmly turning to the boy. "By now you must realize that I am called 'Ader' in these lands. To avoid confusion with our hosts, please do the same. You are mixed into something you should not be. None of this concerns you. You were dragged into it by happenstance. As a favor to your father, I extricated you. Please get your things tomorrow and go home. I must discuss certain matters with the rulers of this land. Teeg, show him the remainder of the castle."

Before Kael could object, Teeg took him by the arm.

"Come, Kael," said Teeg with a grin, "it is a fascinating place."

The old Elf led him toward the door.

"Kael Brelgson," called the queen from behind him. "It was a rare treat to meet you."

The last thing Kael heard was the voice of King Leinor as the doors to the chamber were pushed shut behind him.

"Please Eirtwin, the boy is confused enough. Do not further it."

Teeg led Kael down the passageways of the palace. They passed door after door. Kael wondered what all the rooms held. Finally, Teeg stopped and pushed one open.

"This will be your chamber for the evening, Kael," said Teeg.

They entered a huge room that could easily hold the stables of "The King's Service". It contained a desk and a large table to the left. On the wall opposite the door, maps were mounted. To the right of the door stood a large bed carved of the same beautiful white wood. Large windows looked out over the palace grounds.

"That is the biggest bed I've ever seen," said the wide-eyed boy. "It's bigger than the room I share with my brother back home."

The idea of Aemmon in the woods with a creature roaming around leapt into the boy's mind. His excitement dissipated and he moved toward the windows, staring out as darkness settled on the Nagur Wood. Teeg noticed the change in temperament.

"Kael, your brother will be fine. The attack on Giar and Steff was two days travel from the Nagur path."

Kael chewed on his lower lip and turned back to the Elf.

"Master Teeg," said the boy. "What's going on?"

"Nothing, Kael. Just as Lord Ader said. Don't worry. We will acquire your goods in the morning. You may pack up and get back to Kelky by the end of the day tomorrow."

Kael's eyes narrowed at the old Elf and he scowled.

"Well, at least tell me why you keep calling Jasper, 'Lord Ader.'"

Teeg paused and stroked his chin in thought. Finally, he smiled and looked into Kael's eyes.

"Kael, do you know the name 'Ader'?" asked Teeg.

"It is a common name in some of the lands," replied Kael. "Some people give the name to a child for good luck or in reverence to the Seraph Ader."

"And who or what is the Seraph Ader?" questioned Teeg.

"Well the myth is that the Almighty Avra created the Seraphim or Guides to watch over his people in times of trouble. They support Avra and perform his bidding."

"Good," responded Teeg. "Brelg and Yanwin taught their sons well. However, what puzzles me is the use of the word 'myth'."

"My mother and father trained us in all the stories of lore that they knew," said Kael. "We were even taught to read using bits of the Delvin scriptures. But those were just stories, Master Teeg. Fables from the past."

Teeg turned and walked to the door. The old Elf smiled over his shoulder.

"Kael," said Teeg. "Every fable is based upon some amount of truth. The trouble is discerning where the truth ends and the fiction begins. You may discover more truth in those old fables then you ever thought existed.

"Make yourself comfortable. Food and drink will be provided to you. Then I suggest that you get a good night's rest."

Teeg left Kael in the royal guest chamber of the castle of Luxlor. The boy returned to the window and watched as light after green light appeared in windows and doorways throughout the palace grounds. The Elves' lights burned strong and bright, banishing the darkness and calming Kael's fears.

Flaming red eyes glared in the darkness.

"You failed me", hissed the hooded figure on the dais.

"No ... absolutely not my lord,...I ... it will take more time," stammered the colonel. His vision swept to the corner of the cold, stone chamber where the body of his superior smoldered.

"My servants do not fail me," snapped the dark figure as he raised a hand toward the body in the corner. "Your general failed..... Do not join his fate."

Izgra the warlock slowly turned and motioned to a dark area behind the platform. A curtain rustled aside. Something even darker slid from beyond. The colonel gasped as the inky blackness coalesced into a nightmare and slowly bore down on him through the shifting shadows created by torchlight. His back met the rough wall of the chamber.

"Please! Do not let it harm me, Lord Izgra!" cried the colonel. "I am useful and will continue to be so!"

Izgra silently turned away and slipped from sight behind the heavy, black curtain.

The creature prowled closer. Six yards long with a jet black, scaly hide. Its bulk was tremendous. Chest and shoulders larger than any warhorse the colonel ever laid eyes upon. Closer. The colonel slid down the wall, raising his arms to shield himself. The beast's huge forepaws were tipped in razor sharp claws, longer than the dagger sheathed at the colonel's side. Upon its back two gigantic, leathery wings lay folded across the ridged hide. The wings created an eerie, rasping noise that sounded strangely melodic. The nightmare crept forward, swaying to the rasping.

The maw of the beast came into focus. A heavy, wide jaw held a row of long, pointed teeth. Deep set, angular eyes boiled red with an evil rage. Thick brows, encrusted with stone, supported a crown of blunt horns.

It halted within a yard of the colonel. A guttering torch bled light onto its snarling muzzle and those crimson eyes held the army officer fixed to the wall. They inched closer and acidy drool spattered on the floor at the colonel's feet, blackening the stone.

"P-Please Lord Izgra .... spare me from this hideous creature .... I beg you," the colonel cried as he fought to avert his eyes from the hypnotic gaze.

The beast shifted its weight forward and hovered over the man. A guttural rumble issued from the depths of its cavernous chest. It threw its head back and a cold laugh boomed from beneath quivering lips.

"Hideous creature. One day I will snap your bones and suck the marrow for those remarks," growled the beast, "but today you are still valuable to my master."

Its weight shifted backward.

"Know that you speak to Sulgor, Lord of the Malveel. As old as the mountains. Immortal. Guides and Guardians tremble at our sight. Obey me and you shall live."

As the creature spoke its mouth curved into a wicked smile, exposing the massive black fangs that dripped with spittle.

"The General failed to secure our quarry," Sulgor glared at the charred body in the chamber's corner. "You will start where he left off. You will return to the city of Zodra and spread the story of a cowardly ambush by the Keltaran giants of the West. The giants waylaid you and the General while you rode on a scouting mission. The General fought the giants bravely, but his decision to ride with only his aide-de-camp and no troop escort was a foolish one. It cost him his life."

The creature paused.

"You suffered grave injury but were able to escape death."

The colonel remained trembling near the floor of the chamber during this exchange, his eyes caught in the charmed gaze of the Malveel King. However, the news of his impending release emboldened him. His mind raced through different ways to achieve the deception suggested. It would be difficult to convince the king's military staff that the General was killed and that he, Colonel Udas, somehow escaped a dozen Keltaran giants. A grave injury? How might he feign a grave injury?

The Malveel hovering above him smiled as it saw recognition enter the colonel's mind.

"How am I to ...?" muttered the man slowly.

With lightning speed the creature's claws slashed down upon the colonel's forearm, severing it from the elbow. The armored limb spun through the air and clattered off the stonewall ten yards away.

Three hulking Ulrog stone men rushed into the room. One sprang forward and threw a powerful chokehold about the colonel's neck stifling his screams of agony and terror. The second clumsily looped a noose around the stump of the man's right arm, pulled the noose taught and stabbed a searing hot torch onto the gushing wound. The third lumbered forward with a pair of bulky, military saddlebags, dumping them at the restrained man's feet and spilling the contents across the chamber floor.

Even through madness and terror the Zodrian colonel recognized a small fortune in gold and precious stones. The Lord of the Malveel sneered at the struggling human.

"When you recover, collect your treasonous bounty and attend to my master's business!"

CHAPTER 5: UP THE WINDING STAIRCASE

Kael tossed and turned the entire evening and did not feel rested when he woke before sunup. He was worried how Aemmon fared during the night in the Nagur. He dressed quickly and moved to the doorway. What was he to do? Was he allowed to roam the castle without an escort? His hand shook as he grasped the handle and pushed the door ajar. Kael inched forward and pressed his eye to the opening.

The green glowing jars radiated light throughout the castle. The corridor was empty and Kael's sharp ears picked up no sound of activity. The boy slipped from his room and silently moved down the hallway. The blood raced through his veins and his senses were on full alert.

He let those senses direct him. He crept past portraits of dignified Elves and displays of ornate weaponry, pausing only briefly to ponder their beauty. Each step provided a new wonder hidden in an alcove or resting on a pedestal of intricately carved white wood.

A sudden turn in the corridor and Kael stood before the opening to a winding staircase. He stepped in and looked up the center of the stairwell. It appeared to rise forever. His curiosity was piqued again. He nervously glanced around and then ascended the staircase.

At first he proceeded slowly, expecting to find a guard or opening around each turn. With every step his courage grew and he raced up the staircase. Glass jars rested in iron mountings on the walls, radiating greenish light up and down the stairwell. Finally, Kael spied an opening above him and slowed to investigate. He stepped into the center of a small, square room. Shutters were set in each of the four walls of the room. A mosaic set into the floor displayed a large compass.

Kael walked to the shutters above the "E". He threw their latch back and they noiselessly opened. He gasped. Below him the palace and its outbuildings lay spread across the circular clearing. The tops of the gigantic white trees swayed below him. Beyond and still further below the ring of white sentinels lay the green canopy of the Nagur, stretching out in waves of lush forest to the eastern horizon. Mist rose out of the forest rooftop, as the sun burned the early dew from its foliage. The sky to the east was aflame and a sliver of sun peeked above the horizon. As Kael gazed to the East, he saw the outlines of snowcapped mountains.

"Tis a beautiful sight is it not?" said a soft voice behind him.

Startled, Kael turned to find Queen Eirtwin standing in the center of the room.

"Your keen sense of hearing must come and go," she laughed.

"Pardon me, your highness," said Kael. "I didn't mean to trespass."

"You haven't. The observatory is for all to use. I must admit however, at this early hour I'm customarily the only one up here," said Eirtwin. "You see, most Elves love their forest home. I do as well, but there are times I long to see the blue skies and feel the rays of the sun."

"Do you come up here often ... my lady?" asked Kael.

"Yes, it's a habit from the days of my youth. When I was young, my sister and I stole up here and whispered dreams of our future. Now I sit here alone, burdened by the thoughts a ruler must ponder. The concerns of my people. Their wellbeing. Food. Shelter. Protection."

"Your sister no longer joins you?" questioned Kael.

"Unfortunately no," answered the queen. "She passed into the hands of Avra."

"I am ... uh ... terribly sorry," said Kael, his vision dropping to the floor.

The pair stood in silence for a few moments. The queen's gaze penetrated the boy as he ran his hands through his hair and shifted on his feet. Finally, she turned and focused on the sun as it crept up over the horizon. Its light was dazzling and the Nagur blazed in green. Flocks of birds swirled from treetop to treetop.

Snow white clouds drifted lazily overhead and occasionally a circling hawk cried out.

The queen smiled and turned north. She unlatched those shutters and swung them open. Kael caught his breath again. The massive forest fanned out beneath them. He walked to the opening and looked to the palace grounds below. The dizzying height gave him an appreciation of his earlier climb. He guessed they were perched over forty yards above the forest floor. The castle and its surrounding buildings filled the hollow in the forest.

"Your home lies almost due north of Luxlor, approximately there," pointed the queen.

"You know my village?" asked Kael.

"The happenings in Kelky are always of an interest to us," replied the queen.

"Why do you care about our little trading town?" asked the boy.

"Kael, you will learn that all towns down to the smallest hamlet, including every person in that hamlet, affect the overall. Everything contributes to the whole, and without that tiny addition the whole changes dramatically."

"Even someone like me?" said Kael.

"Especially someone like you," laughed the queen.

"Your majesty?" came a distant call from below in the stairwell.

"Lord Teeg searches for me ... or perhaps you," said the queen. "We must go."

She leaned over and kissed Kael's cheek. He blushed furiously as Eirtwin led him down the stairwell. Teeg and Ader stood at the bottom of the observatory tower.

"I was looking for Kael and came across Lord Ader here," stated Teeg. "He informed me that both of you were up above."

"Eavesdropping is not one of your duties is it, Lord Ader?" said the queen arching a brow at the old trader. "Fear not, your wishes are being followed."

"My lady does me an injustice," replied Ader. "I merely searched for the boy. He leaves with Manfir and I in one hour. We will escort him to his brother and then home to his father in Kelky."

"I packed a horse with the goods he sought and other things which may interest his father," said Teeg.

Kael hastily pulled a pouch from around his neck and untied its drawstring.

"I carry only enough money for a few vials of almar chinchur and some lengths of rope," said Kael.

"The goods are a gift from the queen," said Teeg putting a hand on Kael to stop him.

"You were a guest traveling to our lands and were treated poorly at my son's hands. Please accept my gifts, Kael," added Eirtwin.

"My mother always said 'Never take something for nothing, you will lose more than you get.'" said Kael and he handed the pouch to Teeg.

"Your mother taught you well. I approve," said Eirtwin. "Farewell, Kael Brelgson."

Queen Eirtwin turned and gracefully moved down the passageway out of sight. Kael's spirits dropped upon her departure.

"She is a woman of great presence," said Ader sensing Kael's mood. "When she enters a room it becomes filled with light. Her spirit is strong."

"Indeed," concurred Teeg and he waved to the boy. "Kael, follow me."

Teeg led Kael and Ader through the corridors of the palace to a large wooden door. The doorway led to a courtyard. On the other side of this courtyard stood the stables. Manfir walked out leading three horses.

The first of these horses was a large black stallion. The powerfully built horse wore battle armor across its head, chest and flanks. The silver armor was polished to a brilliant shine. Kael was struck by the animal's ability to inspire both beauty and fear. Ader left Kael with Teeg and went to speak to Manfir. Kael noticed one of the horses carrying burdens.

"Are we going to ride to Kelky?" asked Kael.

"Of course," answered Teeg.

"I ... I don't carry enough money to pay for a horse," broke in Kael nervously.

"No sense in arguing. The pouch you gave me was to pay for the gifts from the queen, and the mare is one of them," said Teeg.

"I didn't think her gifts included a horse. I can't accept such a gift. My father would be furious," said Kael.

"Tell him a bit of gold goes a long way in Luxlor," laughed Teeg. "I'm sure he'll understand Elven generosity."

Kael frowned and realized his arguments were useless. He shook his head and changed the subject.

"Is that beautiful stallion Ader's mount?" asked Kael.

"No," replied Teeg. "That is Manfir's warhorse."

"Oh. Makes sense I suppose. It takes a young man to handle a horse like that," said Kael.

"Ha," laughed Teeg. "I say again. Fables are built on fabulous truth and life is full of surprises!"

Ader finished talking to Manfir and walked toward them.

"Kael, you will ride the chestnut with the packages on it. The other is for Aemmon when we reach him."

Ader turned toward the stables and a look of concentration crossed his brow. Kael heard a deep whinny and the stamp of a hoof. Another stallion pranced from the stables. Kael stood mouth agape. Manfir's black stallion was huge, but Ader's steed stood a full two hands taller with considerably more bulk. The horse pranced over to Ader and nuzzled his chest. The stallion was dark gray in color and bore a strange, five-point marking upon its forehead.

As Kael stood marveling at the beauty of the creature, it turned and eyed him. Its huge nostrils flared and it took in the boy's scent. The horse let out a low rumbling whinny, approached Kael slowly with its head lowered and nuzzled his chest. Kael's body was rigid and his arms lay locked to his sides. The boy's wide eyes danced between the giant stallion standing before him and the amused grins of his companions. Slowly he raised his hands, took the huge head into his arms and gently stroked it.

"I've never seen Tarader allow any other to handle him but you, my lord," said Manfir approaching the group.

"It seems he is intrigued by the lad," said Ader smiling.

"Truly remarkable," stated Teeg.

Kael released the horse and mounted the chestnut mare, a fine Erutre horse in its own right. Manfir mounted the black stallion and moved toward Ader. Ader spoke briefly to Teeg then turned to Tarader. The horse dropped on its front knees and the old tinker mounted. With no effort at all the horse rose and moved toward the opening to the street beneath the castle walls. Kael and Manfir followed.

"Thank you for everything," called Kael over his shoulder to Teeg.

The old Elf smiled and bowed.

The trio created quite a stir as they traveled through the city streets. Elves, young and old alike, bowed heads and placed their hands on their hearts. They finished their greeting by extending their palms upward. Ader's face remained stern and occasionally the trader bowed his head, extended his right hand and mumbled something. The Elves smiled and bowed in gratitude, but Kael swore he heard the words "ridiculous" and "nonsense" in Ader's ramblings.

They passed through the gate in the wall of giant white trees and through the outer city streets. Soon they were out of Luxlor and on the Nagur path. They made excellent time to the bridge and dismounted to lead their horses across its narrow expanse. Kael glanced about the woods and after concentrating was able to discern at least a dozen figures hidden within its shadows. He noticed Diom covered in his Elven cloak, motionless amongst several brambles to his right. The Elf's face was colored to match the patterns of the brush.

Kael smiled broadly at the Elven soldier and waved heartily.

Diom remained like a statue save for the tightening of the muscles in his face. The trio reached the northern side of the Efer and mounted to ride on.

"Kael, never embarrass an Elf," frowned Ader.

"I wasn't trying to embarrass anyone," replied Kael returning the frown. " I wanted Diom to know I hold no ill will from our encounter."

"The Elves take pride in their stealth," returned Ader with a slight scowl. "By pointing out Diom, you shame him before his men."

Kael furrowed his brow.

"That is ridiculous. They were all clearly visible."

"How many did you see?" asked Ader arching a brow.

"All of them, I assume," returned Kael. "About two dozen."

"I counted fifty Elves at the crossing," replied Ader with a grin. "They doubled the garrison after Eidyn's report to the council.

The old man turned from the boy and let his mount canter ahead. Manfir pulled up alongside Kael.

"Ader tries to teach you respect," said Manfir in his deep, stolid voice. "The world is a dangerous place. Confidence is an ally, but it can also become an enemy. What you know is important and certainly assists you in times of trouble. However, it is what you do not know that will get you killed. That and pride. Pride is the foolish man's executioner."

"I'm sorry. I didn't intend to be disrespectful to Diom," said Kael drooping his head. "It's just that the last day has been so ... serious. I'm happy to be going home."

The boy flushed as he considered the Elven soldier.

"I'm the one who should be embarrassed, thinking myself as capable as experienced men. I must sound like a fool trying to prove how many of the Elves I spotted while men like yourself find such tasks commonplace."

The big man's face remained placid as he glanced at Kael then spurred his giant black stallion forward to keep pace with Ader. He turned over his shoulder and called back.

"Me? I saw no Elves, Kael. That is why I am ever vigilant."

The trio trotted on in silence. After some time, Kael pulled the chestnut alongside Ader. He was curious about many things and was put off for too long. He needed answers. Kael started out cautiously.

"Ader, where did you come upon such a beautiful horse?"

"He was a gift to a friend," answered Ader. "I am sometimes allowed the use of his strong back."

Kael assumed the queen of the Elves gave the old trader the mighty stallion.

"Where did he get such a curious name?" asked Kael.

"Kael, do you know the old tongue?" Ader inquired.

"Some," said Kael.

"'Tar' means?" questioned Ader.

"'Tar' is the word for 'mountain'," answered Kael brightly. The boy took a moment then grinned. "Ah, I see. He is 'Mountain of Ader'. That is clever."

"I never approved of it," said Ader frowning. "He isn't mine anymore than he wants to be. We are friends. When I need him, he helps me. When he needs me, I help him. Others contrived that name a long time ago, but I don't use it."

"Why do you call yourself 'Ader' among these people?" prodded Kael abruptly.

"It's my name here," replied Ader.

"What do you mean 'here'?" countered Kael.

"Just what I say. I'm known in different lands by different names. People sometimes speak a different tongue in faraway lands. They change your name to suit their taste. I'm a traveler and a tradesman. I must change my name to fit in comfortably with those I transact business."

"But you don't simply 'fit in' at Luxlor. You're a guest of the king and queen," exclaimed Kael.

"So were you," returned Ader. "The Elves are a hospitable people."

"That's true," frowned Kael, "but I didn't burst into the royal court and begin to order princes and kings to do my bidding."

"The Elves are an isolated people, Kael," replied Ader. "Their news of the world is limited. They treat me well because they seek to learn about the world outside their forest. They seek my counsel because I'm old and world wise. They pay me with their hospitality and a certain tolerance of my rough behavior."

"I'll accept that, but you must admit that you're not the poor trader you portray in Kelky. This horse alone must be worth hundreds of gold coins," stated Kael.

"I said, he isn't mine to trade or barter. Besides, if I arrived in Kelky as a wealthy man, the people would buy none of my goods for fear they were overpriced by a money gouger. Then they would try to sell me theirs at an inflated price, surmising that I held enough coin to be gouged. If I look poor, the locals, including your kindly father, keep their prices fair. That is how the world works, Kael." said Ader.

CHAPTER 6: FLAME OF THE MALVEEL

Again they rode on not speaking, but the forest was alive with sound. They traveled some time and Kael felt an uneasiness creep over him. A chill shot through his body and his heart raced. Ader abruptly stopped. The old man raised a hand as a signal for the others to follow suit. There was an ominous silence.

"What is it?" whispered Kael.

"We are close to where you parted with your brother," said Ader without turning.

The old man's eyes scanned his surroundings

"I see nothing," stated Manfir flatly.

"You need not see something to be alerted to its presence," said Ader. "Proceed cautiously."

They trotted forward, cresting a small hill in the path. Kael noted a thinning of the trees ahead. He knew they were close to the northern end of the Nagur. Ader cautiously led them forward.

"Ader, what is it you fear?" asked Manfir.

"A great evil is present here."

Manfir drew his broadsword from the scabbard strapped to his back. He clutched his horse's reins with one hand and held the blade out with the other. As the group moved along the path, all the horses grew skittish. Kael leaned forward and spoke soothingly to the chestnut and the little horse calmed.

A breeze rustled through the trees from the path ahead and the smell of death filled Kael's nostrils. The boy's breath quickened and his cheeks flushed. They rounded a bend in the path and were able to see the opening of the forest to the fields beyond. The light from the opening illuminated the path ahead and Kael saw lumps strewn about the road. Immediately he knew they were the bodies of the Elven squad sent by General Chani. His stomach twisted into knots and he covered his mouth and nose to prevent from getting sick.

The trio reached the battle scene and Ader motioned them to halt and dismount. Manfir dropped from his horse and removed a long shield strapped to the side of the stallion. His eyes never stopped scanning the forest around them. Kael slowly slid from his horse and staggered toward Manfir.

The ground was covered in Elven blood and bodies. Many were so savagely mutilated that they were unrecognizable. The bodies were scattered across the road and into the woods on both sides of the path. Ader bent close and examined the remains of one of the Elves propped against a tree. The body was burnt beyond recognition and the tree trunk was charred black. Manfir approached.

"A surprise attack," stated Manfir. "It's evident by the way the bodies are spread throughout the area, defending no single position."

"What are you talking about?" asked Kael fighting nausea and panic. He averted his eyes from the horrifying corpse.

"When you are aware an attack is imminent, you choose a location and defend it," replied Manfir. "These men are strewn about the locale haphazardly. Some men are on the north side of trees, some on the south. Some are on the east of the road, some on the west. These men were surprised and forced to defend themselves with the enemy in their midst."

"I don't care how this happened!" exclaimed Kael, squeezing his eyes shut. "What of Aemmon?"

"I don't see your brother among the bodies," replied Ader solemnly. "A closer inspection is in order."

Kael's chestnut reared on its hind legs, tearing its reins from the boy's hands. Its hooves flailed the air. Kael's eyes snapped open and he struggled to retrieve the reins. The horse spun and bolted out of the woods into the fields beyond. Tarader and the black stallion whinnied and backed toward the forest opening. The trio of men followed the animals' gaze back down the path into the forest's interior. Thirty yards away, a large creature emerged from the woods on the east side of the path.

It was huge. Kael guessed the beast was at least fifteen feet long. Although it stalked forward head held low, its shoulders were almost as high as the head of Manfir's stallion. Patches of scraggly hair covered its scaly black body. Its head was like that of some giant hound, a short, wide muzzle and a large, black maw. Its dark coloring made it nearly invisible as it emerged from the dark wood. Deep, blood red eyes bore down on the men.

Those eyes approached slowly and confidently. Manfir readied his broadsword and held his shield up.

The boy noted something hanging from the great jaws of the beast. The monster dragged it along the ground, a scaly bell partially obscuring its burden. When the beast crept to within fifteen yards of the men it dropped its load and rose to its full height. Aemmon's body lay on the forest floor.

Kael froze in fear and shock, unable to scream. The creature crouched and licked the blood seeping from puncture wounds on Aemmon's broken neck. Its malevolent eyes drifted to the travelers and the right side of its mouth curled into a snarl. A harsh guttural voice called out.

"This is not the one we seek. I judged it might be, for it possessed power," the beast nodded into the woods where Kael's keen eyes saw the lifeless body of another of the creatures with its head neatly severed. "My brother Quirg fell, but its power was no match for Methra."

The creature's chest puffed outward.

"What is it you seek?" asked Ader calmly.

"I seek the new Seraph. Perhaps he is here among you?" hissed the beast. "We feel his presence. He creates a heavy pulse in the spirit pool. I must seize him for my master."

The creature stepped over Aemmon's body and moved toward the group. A forked, black tongue tested the air.

"Hold your ground, Malveel!" commanded Ader as he held up his hands.

"Your spirit is strong old one. Its pattern is familiar," pondered the creature as it slowed.

"Perhaps you remember our encounter on the peaks of the Great Mountain, Methra."

The red eyes of the beast went wide. A low rumbling formed in the depth of its belly and seeped out as a hiss.

"Ader....", came the voice of recognition.

"I'm not as young as I was then, but a man changes after a thousand years," growled Ader. " Amird the Deceiver saved you from me then. He can't save you now!"

"SAVED! I was not saved." snapped Methra. His eyes narrowed and sparked with crimson fire. "You disappeared from me. Else your bones would be bleaching as we speak!"

A bright green glow formed around the outstretched hands of Ader. The glow came alive and leapt about on his hands like a flame.

"Amird allows his bastard children to stray too far from home this time," shouted Ader. "It is unfortunate you can't use those wings to flee from here. I'll not allow you to escape a second time."

The creature rose to its full height and enveloped its body in the protection of its heavy, armor-plated wings.

"Their purpose has never been that of escape, old man," smiled the beast wickedly. "I will bring your charred body back to Amird as an offering!"

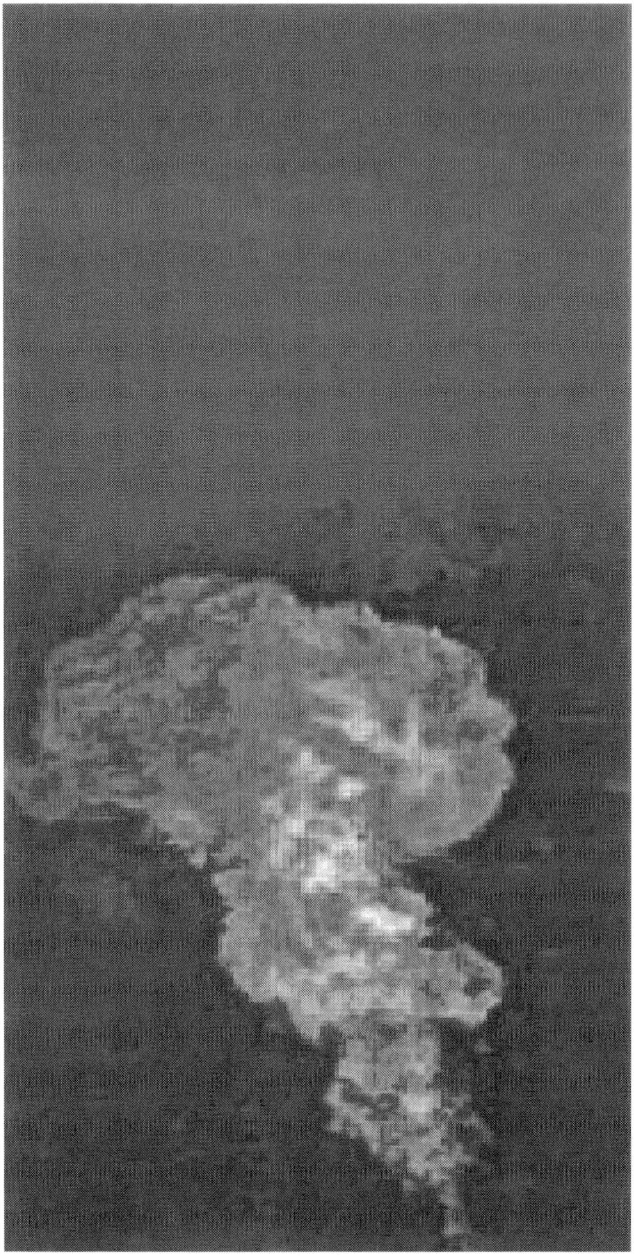

Waves of crimson fire burst from Methra's eyes and shot across the road toward Ader. In the same instant, the green glow around Ader's hands pulsed and encircled his body. The crimson wave of flame was so bright it blinded Kael as it engulfed the trader. The boy shouted in alarm. However, the wave of red flame diminished and Kael clearly saw the form of Ader standing unscathed within the green globe.

Methra roared in frustration and moved forward, hurling flame as he advanced. His efforts were rewarded as the deluge of fire penetrated the pulsing green globe, forcing it to contract. Ader's clothes smoldered and he cried out in pain, closing his eyes.

The veins in the old trader's forehead pulsed as he struggled to maintain the protective sphere. In a few moments the green light grew in strength and expanded. The flames from Methra's eyes once again were left inual by Ader's shield. They struck the globe and were harmlessly turned aside.

Manfir backed away from the combatants, putting distance between himself and the dance of fire. His blade was drawn and his shield held high. Kael stood behind the silent warrior trembling. The beast slowly circled Ader, unleashing bursts of red flame at the old man.

The red flame remained ineffective against the green shield. Inside the pool of pulsating light, the old trader stood with arms raised and hands held high. His eyes remained tightly shut and his brow furrowed in concentration.

Kael's heart pounded as he tried to shrink down behind the broad shoulders of Manfir. He closed his eyes, trying to banish the terror that washed over him. A roar snapped them back open as a fresh wave of red flame slammed on top of Ader.

The boy's breath came in short bursts, each pant filling his lungs with the acrid scent of brimstone and smoldering tinder. Kael fought hard to control himself. His eyes darted down the Nagur path. He wanted to run, but his legs felt like columns of stone. He wanted to scream, but his desire to disappear was even greater.

His mind reached out for an anchor to rescue him from this madness. He longed to see his father marching down the path toward him. An image of his mother filled his mind. Aemmon!

Kael turned and stared at the lifeless form of his brother laying on the dirt path. The boy edged from behind Manfir, drawn to the body. The battle raged before him but it no longer mattered. He stood tall and a tear streaked down his cheek.

Questions flooded Kael's mind, but ultimately he was left with just one. Why?

A roar from Methra ripped Kael's attention back to the fight. The creature circled right and attacked the old trader once more. Kael felt the hair on the back of his neck tingle and stiffen. Ader's hands adjusted to the flow of the crimson flame. The green sphere thickened near the points of attack as the old man manipulated his own powers. A new wave of crimson fire splashed across Ader's shield. This time Kael sensed exactly how the trader responded. Kael's body came alive. He felt the flow and structure of Ader's power and found himself following along as the old trader influenced the composition of the sphere.

Methra struck again and Kael guessed the old trader's response before it occurred. The boy understood. Ader diverted power from other areas of the globe to suppress each attack.

Manfir backed into Kael and pushed him further from the battle as Methra's movements brought the beast closer.

"Old one, you were no match for me on the Great Mountain and you are no match for me now. Lord Izgra will be pleased when I return with your blackened bones," growled Methra.

"He is lord of nothing, and the king of emptiness! His servants are witless mongrels he uses to inflict his pain!" shouted Ader.

A wave of red flame lashed out at the trader. This time however, the trader reacted slowly to the attack. Methra's flame scoured the surface of the globe and Kael sensed Ader's power weakening.

The boy's panicked eyes darted to the old man. Ader's clothes smoldered again and his face was red and sweating. His eyes were tightly closed and his brow knit in furious concentration.

Methra circled and threw spattering bolts of flame at Ader. The creature's upturned sneer divulged its thoughts. Methra was winning. He wore down Ader's defenses.

"You grow weak old man. Maybe a thousand years HAS changed you," hissed Methra.

"A thousand years of watching you and your kind scurry and whine under the heel of a madman," replied Ader.

"DIE THEN!" shrieked the creature.

The bubbling cauldron of Methra's life force spewed forth a deluge of crimson flame. It shot across the forest and engulfed the entire form of Ader and his shield. Kael completely lost sight of his friend, as Methra poured forth his hatred.

The frightening onslaught subsided and Ader slowly came back into view through the smoke and haze which hung across the forest path. The grizzled old man stood motionless, centered in the tattered and weakened green sphere. Methra stood heaving with exhaustion. The monster was momentarily wasted as well, but his power was evident under the surface, building to erupt again.

Ader, arms still raised, gasped for breath and crumpled to his knees. His clothes were black and sooty. His beard and hair singed. His face and hands red and blistered. The green light surrounding him flickered and thinned.

Methra, his head and body slumped low, panted and slobbered like a dog in the summer sun. A wicked sneer played across his face.

"I have you now old one. I will become Izgra's favorite for destroying you. I will supplant Sulgor and lead the Malveel," wheezed the creature.

Kael sensed Methra's power returning. The Malveel's greedy dreams fed his confidence.

"Your death has been a long time coming," snapped Methra.

Kael desperately wished to act. Panic consumed him. He yearned to stop this insanity. He longed to make this creature vanish.

"However," hissed Methra, "my errand is to discover the new Seraph and capture or destroy it. Perhaps I shouldn't kill you, but torture you to discover its whereabouts."

Kael watched the red wildfire surrounding Methra sputter and spark. The power grew. The green globe looked weaker than ever.

"I suspected this boy as the Seraph," snarled Methra as he nodded toward Aemmon's corpse. "His spirit was strong. Yet he was no match for the Malveel."

Kael recognized the ploy. The pause in the battle allowed Methra time to rebuild his strength. The boy sensed power returning to the beast. Kael's desperation grew. The mention of his brother's murder outraged him. He hungered to crush this evil thing. He wished to stamp out this raging fire of hatred. Snuff it out.

Kael's feelings of anger, loathing, sorrow, fear and panic transformed into a desperate need as he witnessed the Malveel preparing one final assault on Ader. Need charged to the front of his mind. The Need to help. The Need to punish. The Need to avenge. Need coalesced into a thin veil of crackling blue flame around the boy's hands.

"Kael! NO!" shouted Ader.

Something inside the boy lashed out. A small, blue bolt of flame sped through the forest air toward the Malveel. It struck Methra's forepaw, searing the hair and scales off a small area. The creature thrashed its body back and forth, howling in pain and anger. Flames meant for Ader sprayed the forest, igniting the trees. Methra wheeled to face Manfir. The creature's body coiled toward the forest floor.

Kael's eyes widened in horror. Fear once again reigned supreme. What did he do? How did he do it? He glanced at his hands. The blue flame slowly dissipated. The Malveel inched forward.

"So, my errand is near an end," hissed Methra.

Manfir tightened his body and braced himself in a fighting stance, his shield and blade held high. Kael stumbled backward, lost in fear and confusion. He felt the creature's hatred wash over him. He desperately wanted to be home at "The King's Service". He longed to see his father. His thoughts cried out to Aemmon. He felt utterly alone. The boy spun and fled down the Nagur path.

"Methra, you lap dog, come and finish me!" cried Ader.

"Later," snarled the beast, eyeing the running boy, "but first...."

The creature sprang, in one leap reaching Manfir. Razor sharp claws lashed out, knocked aside the shield and slashed deeply into the warrior's face and shoulder. Manfir's sword glanced ineffectually against the heavily armored scales of the Malveel. Without halting, the creature passed the warrior and scrambled toward Kael. The boy ran like he never had before, but heard the curses of the monster grow as it closed the gap.

"Methra will tear out your innards, boy," growled the Malveel.

Kael sprinted down the path, his heart gripped by terror. The voice sweetened.

"Do not run from me, boy. I must speak to you. Slow down."

The voice floated down the path in a strange singsong manner. Kael's racing heart slowed and he filled with the desire to comply and obey this voice. He was exhausted. His mind reeled. The death of his brother and all those Elves, as well as the emotional events of the last few days took their toll. He stopped and bent over to catch his breath. Methra was there instantly. The Malveel approached to within ten yards and crouched low.

"Look at me," commanded Methra.

Kael turned toward the creature and met its gaze.

"Much too impish and young for what I expected," assessed Methra. "The other one with all the cursed Elves appeared much more like the genuine article. Izgra wants the new Seraph brought to him alive or dead."

Kael stood motionless, caught in the creature's hypnotic gaze.

"Your display of power proves you to be the Seraph," said Methra, licking his oozing wound, "but why should I bring you to Izgra? He will turn your mind and make you his right hand. My wound shall serve as the perfect excuse for your demise. I shall claim you were too powerful and I fought you to the death, receiving injuries along the way. Does that sound good to you, boy?"

Kael stood mesmerized, nodding his head in agreement. Methra snorted.

"A savior! A mighty throne! What a story! Izgra has been fooled by the Scribes and their mindless prophesies," chortled the beast. "I shall snap your neck and drink your blood so you are less a burden to carry."

The Malveel rose from its crouch and approached Kael with an evil sneer. Its gaze remained fixed on the boy's eyes and held him in place.

Methra covered half the distance to Kael in one step, when unexpectedly the beast's eyes were averted to something behind the boy. Kael heard a rustling in the wood and felt the ground tremble. Methra glanced to the woods and his eyes went wide. A huge figure broke from the tree line. The boy felt a rush of wind as a giant, three yards tall and wearing a tunic of brown wool, swept past him.

Methra rose to his full height, nearly the same as the giant. The creature clawed at the air in front of him and sent searing flames at the approaching figure. The huge man never hesitated. He stepped through the crimson flames, knocked aside the flailing claws and clutched the Malveel about the neck with two enormous fists.

"I will not allow such an abomination in my holy wood!" boomed the giant. "Your business here is finished ..."

Methra's claws raked the giant's powerful forearms, but to Kael's amazement they left no mark. Flames leapt from the

Malveel's eyes and engulfed the giant's head. This too caused no damage.

"... And it is you whose neck needs snapping," bellowed the giant.

Methra's final hiss was cut off by the sickening crack of his neck breaking. The flames vanished and the red glow in its eyes faded to black. The giant casually tossed the dead Malveel to the side of the path and turned to Kael.

The boy was surprised to see the visage of an old man. His curly gray hair cascaded to his shoulders and intertwined with his long beard. Dark piercing eyes stared at Kael from beneath the giant's bushy brow. He knelt in front of Kael and inspected the boy.

"You are uninjured," stated the giant as a fact, not a question.

Kael nodded his head in agreement.

"That is good. Come," said the giant placing a hand around Kael's back and leading him down the path.

Kael numbly followed, too afraid and overwhelmed to even thank his savior properly. The boy glanced over his shoulder once to be sure the Malveel was motionless.

After a brief walk they encountered Manfir and Ader struggling toward them. The giant stopped and watched them approach. Manfir helped support a weakened Ader. The old trader's clothes were tattered and burnt. His face and hands were raw and blistered by his encounter with the Malveel.

Manfir's cloak and shirt were soaked dark red. He bore deep slash marks from the Malveel's claws, and the bone of his shoulder was exposed. Blood oozed from the wounds and his face was ashen and pale.

When Ader reached Kael and the giant, he released his grip on Manfir and dropped to his knees. Manfir staggered and put a hand to his sword. The giant scowled at Ader.

"Brother Ader, unholy creatures roam my world."

"Forgive us, dear Hilro," rasped Ader, "the times produce unfortunate events."

Manfir let the tip of his sword fall to the earth and he fell to his knees in exhaustion.

"Death is at work in my woods. Unnatural death. I will not allow it. Look at your comrade. I see his spirit fading as we speak," said Hilro pointing to Manfir.

Once again Kael could not explain the sensation, but something within him felt the life force of Manfir slowly slipping away. He turned to Ader in panic and realized the trader was nearly spent as well. Kael needed to do something. These men were fading away in front of him.

He spun to face Hilro. Kael was sure of one thing. This strange being could help. The giant exuded power. As if in reply to Kael's silent plea, the giant moved toward the two men.

"We shall tolerate no more death in my wood today," announced Hilro.

Hilro walked over to Manfir and bade the man rise. The giant's massive hands cupped Manfir's face, making the warrior look like a child. A rainbow of light flowed from those hands and surrounded Manfir.

Kael watched in awe as the fountain of Hilro's life force emitted streams of color. They flowed into Manfir's body. The warrior's eyes closed and he dropped his blade as he was bathed in rays of light. Kael felt the giant's energy filling the man and making him whole again.

Hilro pulled his hands from the warrior's face. The shredded and bloodied remains of Manfir's shirt lay dangling from his exposed shoulder. The wound was healed, leaving a large v-shaped scar. Hilro turned to Ader and held his hands above the trader.

Streams of green light emitted from Hilro's hands. They swirled around Ader and seeped into his body. The sphere that encased Ader returned, strong and bright. The light spun in a whirlwind around Kael's old friend, then jumped into Ader's body, reviving him.

"Thank you," said Ader as he emerged from the cascade of light.

The trader's hands and face were still slightly raw and blistered, but he showed a remarkable improvement over his previous condition.

"The children of the ancient race must not be left as such," said Hilro pointing to the sight of the massacre. "Use them to feed the trees."

"As you say, Hilro," said Ader bowing his head.

"Ader, I must interfere in your duties. These matters concern me. I do not care for the like of that in my wood," stated Hilro pointing toward the Malveel.

"I understand brother. We must ere be vigilant against such things," said Ader.

"Tis time," said Hilro nodding toward Kael.

"You are right," said Ader.

The giant briefly looked over Manfir and Kael, then spun on his heel and strode into the forest. Manfir and Ader approached Kael.

"Are you injured?" asked Ader.

"No," replied Kael.

"What were you thinking, attacking a Malveel like that? Have you no sense?" questioned Ader.

"I ... I thought you needed help," said Kael. "Besides, I wasn't aware I was attacking anything until it happened."

"Ader, I must agree with the boy. The creature held you at a disadvantage. You were in danger," said Manfir.

"My danger is my concern," said Ader. "We nearly lost Kael to one of Amird's lesser servants!"

"He didn't carry himself as a lesser servant." stated Manfir. "He maintained all the power of a Malveel of the first order."

"We shall face much worse than Methra the Worm in the days ahead," scowled Ader. "The Malveel was old and fell out of favor with his superiors over the years. The once proud Methra was reduced to a messenger for the enemy..."

Kael wandered away. His eyes drifted from one Elven body to the next. His breathing slowed, his shoulders slumped and he dragged his feet as if they were encased in lead. The Southlander turned and stumbled down the path toward the body of Aemmon. Ader noticed the movement.

"Kael, we must make haste to Luxlor and protection," said Ader. "We don't know what other creatures of Chaos scout the wood."

Kael slowed his trek toward the body of Aemmon. His hands covered his face and his body shook with sorrow.

"Kael ... " began Ader once more.

Manfir reached out and put a hand on Ader's shoulder, halting the old man's words.

"You have seen too much of death over these long years for it to hold much meaning," said the warrior soberly. "Stay your comments and give the boy a moment to grieve."

Ader looked into Manfir's eyes as the boy finally reached his brother. The old trader nodded as Kael dropped to his knees beside the lifeless body of Aemmon. Kael wrapped Aemmon in his arms and softly wept.

Chapter 7: MYTHS AND LEGENDS

Kael was uncertain how much time passed when a soft hand upon his shoulder startled him.

"He should be buried like a warrior," stated Manfir from above.

Kael raised his eyes and nodded his agreement. Manfir found a spot near the side of the road. Kael joined him and together they prepared a grave for the young man's body. When it was complete, the big man returned, picked up Aemmon and placed him in the shallow pit. The trio stood over the grave for a few moments and Manfir murmured a soft prayer. Kael stood by silently fighting the urge to cry out as Manfir covered the body of his brother with rocks and dirt. When Manfir completed the task he turned to Kael.

"Lord Ader and I must attend to the Elves," said Manfir. "Linger if you must, but we cannot tarry in these woods too long."

The two men left the boy to his sorrows and proceeded to bury the fallen Elves. There was no time to spare and so the dead were interred in the spots where they fell.

Kael shook as he stood over the grave of his brother. How could he be gone? How did this happen? Why? Questions flooded his mind?

An hour passed when Ader approached.

"Come Kael. It's time for us to leave this place. There is much work ahead for both you and I. Manfir will return to Kelky to seek out your father. He has retrieved your mount. You and I must return to Luxlor."

Kael turned and looked into the stern eyes of Ader. He wanted so many questions answered, but at the moment he didn't have the heart. He put his trust in the old man and let Ader lead him to the chestnut mare.

Manfir sat on the back of his black stallion and nodded to the boy as Kael approached.

"Kael Brelgson, fare you well," said the grim man. "Know that you are in my prayers."

The Black spun north and Manfir spurred him forward. The warhorse plunged up the forest path and disappeared from sight.

Kael mounted, turned and took one last look at the grave of his brother. The duo then prodded their horses and rode back toward Luxlor.

Their journey proceeded in silence for over an hour. Kael was lost in thoughts of Aemmon. Their life together at "The King's Service". Years of conversation while they finished their daily chores. Shared dreams and fears. How much their lives changed after their mother's death. Their father's withdrawal into sorrow. A sorrow that hung over the inn for many years after. What of his father? Brelg would be devastated. How could Kael adequately explain the horror that befell his brother? What was happening?

"What is happening is hard to explain," said Ader guiding his stallion next to the chestnut.

Kael was shocked that the old man read his thoughts. All of this was too much for him to comprehend, but one thing was for certain. Ader or Jasper, whatever he called himself, was much more than the people of Kelky believed, and Kael's sorrow turned to anger.

"I'm confused," said Kael staring at the trader through narrowed eyes, "and you're part of that confusion."

The trader sighed and took a moment to let Kael's anger pass.

"Kael, do you know anything of history?" asked Ader somberly.

"Yes, a bit," answered Kael hesitantly. "My mother tried to keep us well educated."

"Do you know of ancient history?" questioned Ader, "The time when the world began."

"I ..... I'm not sure what you mean by the term 'history'," said Kael. "I know the story of creation and other religious tales."

"You call them 'tales'. Don't you believe in them?"

"Who's to say what is truth and what is fancy. I'm sure they're just stories to explain how things are the way they are," returned Kael.

"What's the story of creation?" asked Ader abruptly.

"Avra decided to create man," said Kael. "So he fashioned the world and all things in it as a place for man to dwell. Then he set man on the world."

"Good, but what of the Elves?" coaxed Ader.

"I'm not sure about the Elves," said Kael. "I never really considered them."

"Well then, what about me?" asked the old man.

"What about you?"

"How do you explain my existence?" said Ader.

The boy looked puzzled.

"I am not an Elf," continued Ader.

"No, you're not."

"Am I a man?"

"I ... I'm not sure. Until yesterday I would have said yes, but no man is able to do what you did today," said Kael.

"No man can do what you did today either, Kael. Did you think of that?" asked Ader.

"Yes." whispered the boy dropping his head. "That only adds to my confusion."

Ader did not press the issue and they cantered forward in silence. Kael kept trying to make sense of all he had seen and done in the last day. However, images of his brother intruded his musings and filled him with sorrow.

"We'll take this slowly," said Ader. "You need to know many things now, and some things may wait. Therefore, I'll start at the beginning and I do mean the Beginning.

"Nothing. Darkness. An abyss. Disorder. It was and had been. Eternal. Limitless. This is how I can best describe it. Then, something stirred in this blackness. Something separated itself from the chaos and formed a pattern. Something that had been and will be. Something that was both part of the void, but distinct from it.

"From disorder came order. The something took shape and forced its will on its surroundings. Avra, my Lord and Father let himself become. Like a whirlpool in a raging river, he was a constant. As the rapids of Chaos rushed by in random surges, He spun and held his place.

"There is a duality in all things. Just as there is an up, there is a down. Hot and cold. Light and dark. Duality is the nature of the world. You have two eyes, two arms and two legs. Why not seven, four and three? The root of all the universe is two. Just as Avra was born from Chaos, so was Chaos born from Avra. When our Creator separated himself from Chaos, he not only gave himself an identity, He gave an identity to all that He left behind. That identity was Chaos. Have you ever paddled a boat through the water, Kael?"

"Yes," answered the boy furrowing his brow.

"Then you must notice the wake you create behind you. A uniform replica of the prow of your boat, etched in the water by your passage. Before the vessel arrives, the water slides about haphazardly. However, once the boat passes, the water in its wake is given shape, an identity all its own. When Avra allowed himself to form, the duality of all things created his opposite, Chaos. There are two forces at work on all things in this universe, the order of Avra and the disorder of Chaos."

"If Chaos is an equal force taking shape in the universe, why do people worship Avra? Why not worship Chaos as well?" asked Kael.

"The simple fact that you exist answers that question," answered Ader. "Chaos by its nature does not create. Chaos strives to break down order, to tear apart anything cohesive. Chaos corrupts and defiles. We show our gratitude and obedience to Avra simply because we wouldn't exist without him.

"Once Avra separated himself from Chaos he desired to commune with beings like himself. He wished to share the bounty of his power. Thus he set forth and created the universe and all the worlds contained within it. Every rock, tree and speck of sand is the product of Avra's love and imagination. He poured forth his blessings and created a realm of fantastic magnitude. Each of us is a small part of Avra's limitless force. You are part of Avra and He is part of you."

Kael paused and tried to reconcile such a weighty concept.

"It's a bit much when you first discover it," smiled Ader, "but as the idea lingers, it settles a man's soul. To know that you're part of the all powerful Creator and he is a part of you, fills you with an unparalleled confidence."

"But Avra doesn't decide to create people," said Kael. "People do. A man and a woman."

"True," replied Ader, "but remember, all men and women are products of those before them. Ultimately, all people are the products of the first humans put on this world. So they are all creations of Avra's first creations. Since all people are part of Avra, whatever they create from themselves is part of Avra."

Kael blinked hard.

"Avra set us on this world to emulate him, to create order from disorder, to grow, learn and produce," continued Ader. "Avra wanted man to rejoice in his world, to live every day striving to create and bring beauty into the world. Creating and nurturing life is part of that plan."

"Then why would someone ever choose to follow Chaos?" asked the boy.

"The answer to 'why' can only be found in the heart of each and every man," returned Ader, "but the answer to 'how' is quite simple. Free will."

Again the boy stared at the old trader with a puzzled expression.

"Avra's desires for us are just that, his desires. What of our own? When a man chooses to cheat his neighbor, he fulfills a desire all his own. Avra might easily create a race of men subject to his wishes. They would follow each and every command of their master, but that was not what our Creator wanted. He wished to share his existence with beings made in his own image, beings capable of making choices and striving toward unlimited potential. Creations enslaved to the will of another possess no such abilities.

Their potential is constrained by the boundaries set by their master."

"So Avra placed men and Elves upon this world and set them free to do as they wish?" asked Kael.

Ader frowned.

"Yes and no."

"That's not an answer." scowled Kael.

"It's a difficult question, my boy," said Ader. "The Elves upon this world are a somewhat ... unique situation."

Ader hoped that would suffice but Kael stared at the old trader.

"The Elves are a creation for a different place and a different time," resumed Ader. "As I said, Avra created many worlds, or more precisely planes, upon which he created many beings. The Elves are not originally from this world. They are from a higher plane."

"Then how did the Elves get from this .... higher plane to our world?" asked Kael.

"That is a lesson for another time." said the old man, "We must make speed and return to Luxlor."

Ader's refusal to answer bothered Kael. He wanted those answers. His brother was dead and Kael barely escaped death at the hands of a hideous creature bent on his destruction. He needed to know more to help him explain the madness of this day.

"Well, at least tell me what part you play. Why should I trust you or do any of the things you tell me?" stated Kael angrily.

The old man frowned and searched the boy's eyes.

"Oh, we both know how ridiculous that question is don't we? You already guessed correctly who I am," said Ader. "However, you're going through a trying time, so I'll humor you. I am Ader, third Seraph of our Lord Avra the Creator of this existence. You talk of myths and rumors, religions and stories. I am those myths and rumors. I've been on this world for what seems an eternity. I'm a guide, a helper and a confidante. I'm here to help man when he seems at his most helpless. It's my job to nudge, nay even to push them in the right direction. Does that tell you enough?"

"Umm, well, maybe," returned Kael.

The boy was embarrassed by his own uncertainty. His mind searched for questions. A moment ago he possessed so many, but now he felt even more confused. He desperately wanted to keep the conversation alive and think of anything other than Aemmon.

"Well, how old are you?" asked Kael, grimacing at what he deemed a ridiculous question.

"Age is irrelevant. I've been around quite a long time by your standards. Even by my own. However, Avra is ageless. To him I'm merely a baby."

Undaunted, Kael asked. "Well, how about in a time frame I understand?"

"Oh, several thousand years, at least. I lost count centuries ago. Years are meaningless to me. Events are what matter. How will they unfold and affect this world? Some of those events are centuries in the making, others just a few short years. However, both tend to affect this world with the same significance," said Ader.

"Do you.... talk to Avra. I mean, is He real?" asked Kael.

"Of course He's real," scoffed Ader. "Look around you. How do you think all of this was created?"

Kael paused then clenched his teeth.

"Why does He allow ...", Kael choked on the remainder of his question.

Ader paused once more to allow the boy to rein in his emotions.

"Kael, we all die," said Ader softly. "Every one of us is born with a certain amount of life force. Eventually, our life force runs out. Those are the people who die of old age. Other times, our life force is snatched from us. Disease, famine and war are some of the reasons. Why? Chaos strives eternally to break down this beautiful world and turn it back into the seething abyss that it once was. Like the waves of the sea breaking on the shoreline, so is Chaos. Wave after punishing wave eventually breaks the rock down. Chaos attacks the heart of man. Chaos rules the weak of spirit and tempts him to turn on his brother. Without order, the world is an ugly place indeed."

"Then Chaos is what killed my mother?" asked Kael.

"No, your Mother died of disease," answered Ader, "This world is not a paradise Kael, nor was it meant to be. Avra created a place for man to rejoice in his successes and a place to learn and strive to overcome his failures. Man struggles to survive everyday. Food, water and air are just the basics for survival. If man needed nothing and he was able summon all he wanted, he would be a god himself. One day someone will cure the disease your sweet mother died from, and mankind will move forward."

"Why hasn't it been cured already? Why her?"

"To Avra, a millennia is a heart beat. Time has no meaning. Do not misunderstand me. Every man woman or child is infinitely important to him. I do not diminish the life of your mother. However, she was born with a certain amount of life force, and the disease, another creation of Avra, overcame that life force. Her spirit is an altogether different matter," stated Ader.

"What do you mean?"

"When we are born, Avra's hand passes through the water of life and creates our swirl in it. In some cases, his hand thrusts the water aside and a powerful wave is born. I am thousands of years old. Avra's hand moved powerfully indeed. In other cases, his hand barely stirs the water. These people are short lived.

However, in both cases, the individual is free to build or spoil their spiritual force. Do you rejoice in the world, entering everyday with a feeling of thanks? Do you treat others as if they are the most important thing in the world? Do you show grace to those who wrong you? Pity to those who suffer? These are the qualities that enhance the spiritual force of an individual. Your mother's spiritual force was never taken from her. Her life force merely drained away. She continues to thrive in the presence of Avra."

The trader paused and Kael's face wrinkled in concentration. Ader told him things his mother and father taught him his whole life. Things he heard, but never really listened to or understood.

"What about that ... that thing that killed Aemmon? If Avra gave life to that, why would I want to believe in or follow him?" demanded Kael.

"That is an altogether different subject, and I must admit, one I'm not ready to discuss with you. Besides, you are so taken in by our conversation that you lose track of our surroundings. Diom must be pleased that you were unable to detect him this time."

Kael looked up from the path to see the Efer Bridge standing in front of him. He searched the woods around the bridge and again picked out the faces of Grey Elves among the shrubs and trees. Diom was not among them.

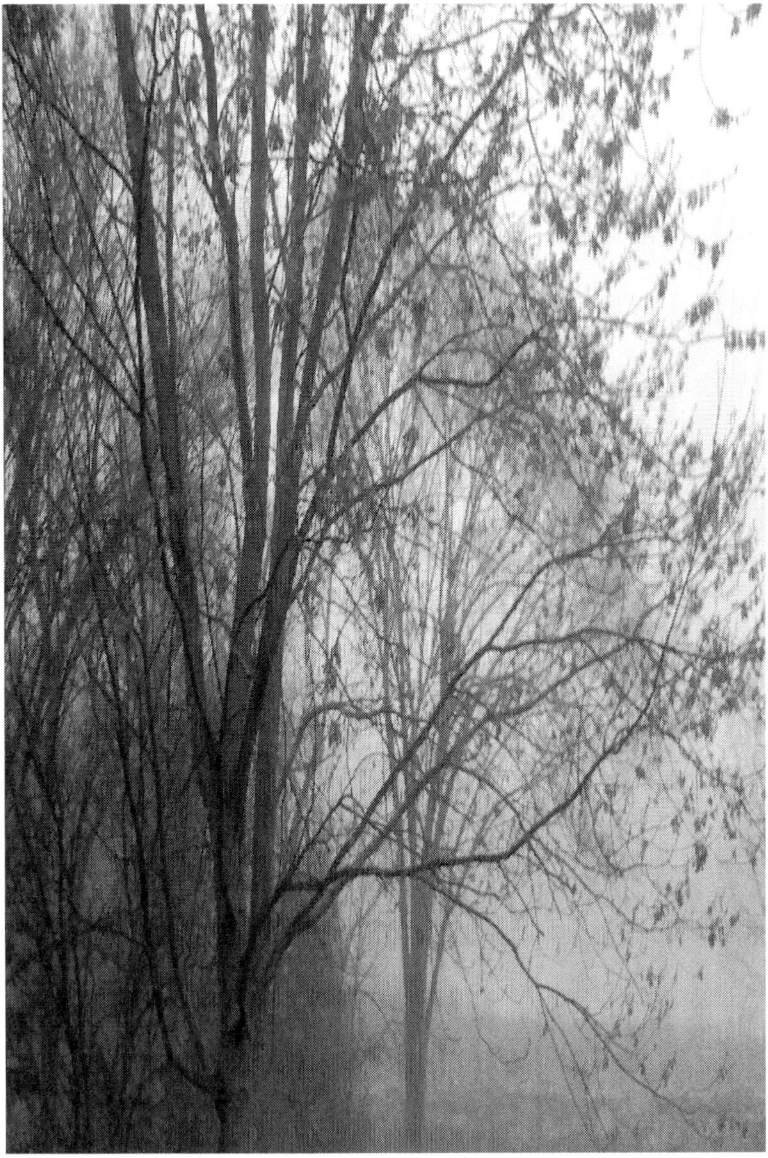

"Diom was about a league back in the North Nagur. Apparently, King Leinor and General Chani expanded their perimeter of defense."

The pair rode on in silence past the small cottages on the outskirts of the Elven kingdom and toward the white wall. They passed few Elves at first, but as they journeyed deeper into the Elven kingdom, the streets crowded. Many of the Elves greeted Ader with the traditional opened palms then placed them across their hearts. Some showed this sign of respect then quickly turned to others and whispered. Kael knew the ways of an isolated village. Rumors of their hasty return would spread quickly.

Kael noticed a boy keeping pace with the riders as they made their way past shops and street fairs. The boy stole glances at the pair as he dodged fruit stands and meat carts. As Kael turned to Ader to point out the boy, he noticed the old trader looking in the same direction. When Kael swung back, the boy was gone.

The journey proceeded rapidly and Ader led them to the stables of the palace. Runners were sent ahead to announce their return and Teeg awaited them in the stable yard.

"Greetings Lord Ader and Kael Brelgson, I didn't anticipated such an early return to the palace," announced Teeg somberly, "and you're without Manfir. I fear grave tidings come with you."

Stable boys took the chestnut by the reins and led her into a stall. Ader swung himself down from Tarader's broad back and the huge stallion trotted to the water trough and drank deeply.

"Grave indeed, Master Teeg. However, the news remains ours until we find a suitable venue. The king and queen must summon their counselors and generals."

"This has been done. They gather in the palace hall as we speak. Your early return prompts concern throughout the palace. Please, adjourn to your chambers and refresh yourselves. Might I suggest a new cloak, the burnt and tattered edges of that one caused enough fright in the city for one day."

"Ah, I'm a fool. I'm so caught up in my pondering, I announce to the world our troubles," frowned Ader. "We will depart and bathe."

"All will be ready when you return," said Teeg.

One of the stable boys led Kael to the guest chamber he occupied the previous evening. Fresh clothing was laid on the bed and a large bath was drawn. He undressed and slid into the hot water. Immediately, he relaxed. Kael realized his entire body was tense from the moment they encountered the battle scene.

It felt good to relax, but the emotions he fought to control came into stark focus. Kael let himself go to those emotions and lay in the tub sobbing. He slid deeper into the water and closed his eyes, squeezing tears upon his cheeks. The copper tub cradled his body and before he knew it, Kael was fast asleep.

CHAPTER 8: THE STONE CHAMBER

Sulgor crouched low in front of the dais with his eyes averted from Izgra's gaze. It rankled the Lord of the Malveel to bow down before this mortal being. The Malveel fought the urge to leap forward and tear out the throat of the human. What did Izgra know of their battle? This elf and human mongrel dwelt on earth for a fraction of Sulgor's existence.

However, Sulgor comforted himself in the knowledge that his master held plans for the Half Dead. Plans that would leave Izgra a shell of his former self. Plans that Izgra could not escape even if he dared try.

These thoughts emboldened the Malveel lord and he glanced upward at the hooded figure. Sulgor appraised the only being beside Amird whom he had ever bowed before. Izgra was in direct contact with Amird and Sulgor surmised the weak human was utterly in the Deceiver's control. Sulgor wondered how much of Izgra's thought was still his own, but the Malveel believed Amird probably controlled all.

Sulgor slowly rose and his chest grew. He was Amird's first creation. Molded from the rock and magma in the steaming pits of Tar Kreng centuries ago, the Lord of the Malveel had ruled over Amird's creations in the absence of the Deceiver. When the plan was complete, he would be restored to his rightful place. Izgra would be no more and he, Sulgor, would reign as master of the Malveel, Ulrog and all other beings in Amird's thrall.

"Your brethren fail me," snarled Izgra from behind the cowl of his jet black robes. "They possessed the opportunity to remove the threat and they were unable to complete the task."

"They may be slow in returning. Who is to say what the outcome of their journey to the Nagur is?" snapped Sulgor.

Boney, decaying hands shot from beneath Izgra's robes and flashed out toward the Malveel King. Crimson fire slammed the giant beast back to the ground as flames crackled and hissed about the scaly body. Sulgor writhed in agony and gnashed his long, razor sharp fangs. The beast desperately tried to retreat from the fire.

"I am the one to say!" shrieked Izgra. "Your Lord and Master!"

The flame halted and Sulgor shrank further from the dais. Izgra's hands remained poised in the direction of the Malveel. Spasms of pain racked the beast's body.

"The sooner you come to realize that I am Amird and Amird is me, the sooner you will halt this rebellion against my authority. You were our first, Sulgor, and our strongest. However, even the strongest servant must be put down if he does not obey," stated Izgra. "Do you understand?"

"Yes ..... my lord," snarled the Malveel King bowing his head. "I serve only you."

"Good," replied Izgra. "Your brethren did fail me. I feel all of the beings created by the power of Amird. Methra and Quirg are no more."

Sulgor's eyes widened with surprise. He dare not ask how the warlock discovered this news. The Malveel glanced at the figure on the platform. It was true that his master favored the warlock with great power. Izgra's eyes glowed red with the fury of Chaos. The Malveel barely distinguished the decaying face of the self-proclaimed "vessel of Amird".

"What is worse," rasped Izgra, "they encountered the Old Man in the woods. The battle was short-lived, but I felt his surge in the spirit pool. I hoped not to rouse him at this early stage. He was to be dealt with later."

"What are your wishes?" asked Sulgor, lowering his head further.

"Methra was close. I felt something. It was just a flicker, but the new Seraph makes his way into the world. We must hasten our plans," said Izgra. "Contact your assets and step up the pressure in both the West and the South."

"As you wish, my lord." consented the Malveel as he backed from the dais and exited the stone chamber.

CHAPTER 9: STEPPING FROM THE SHADOWS

"Kael, wake up," whispered Teeg.

The boy came to with a start. The old Elf was standing over him holding a robe.

"You slept quite some time. Do you feel refreshed?" said Teeg.

The bath had lost its heat and Kael shivered.

"Uh, yes. Sorry. Did I miss the meeting?" asked Kael.

"No. It took time to gather the king's court and there is much to discuss."

Kael rose and accepted the robe.

"Is Jas.... Ader there?"

"That is the other reason the meeting is delayed. Lord Ader tends to prioritize differently than most. He stopped in his chambers briefly, then left and cares for some other.... business. Nevertheless, he's due to return shortly and we'll be getting underway. I anticipate you desire to be a part of the proceedings?"

"Oh, yes!" exclaimed Kael.

He stepped from the bath, hurriedly dried and dressed. Teeg waited patiently, using the time to explain the history of the artifacts found in the room. When Kael was finished, they walked down the hallway to the palace court.

The court bustled. Runners and pages provided refreshment for the lords and ladies. Small groups of nobles huddled together conversing intently. Military personnel marched into the great hall carrying charts and maps to the large table where General Chani sat. Eidyn stood beside him and looked up as Kael and Teeg entered the hall. His gaze pierced the boy. In fact, many eyes in the room fixed on Kael. The assembly briefly hushed. Kael's face flushed then returned to normal as conversation built once more and eyes returned to their previous attractions.

Teeg led Kael toward the front of the room. They halted to the right of the platform holding the thrones of the king and queen.

The old Elf and the boy sat in a set of chairs placed against the wall and waited. General Chani poured over his maps.

Once again the room abruptly quieted. Kael looked up to see King Leinor, Queen Eirtwin and Ader stepping from behind a blue tapestry hanging behind the dais. Nearly every eye focused on the trio. However, Kael's keen senses focused his attention to the opposite end of the great hall. He noted movement as a large cloaked and hooded figure slipped into the room and disappeared into a shadowy corner behind the assembly of Elves.

"Thank you all for coming on such short notice and waiting for so many hours as the queen and I sought council from our dear friend Ader," announced King Leinor.

"As you all know," continued the king, "dire news surfaces. The deaths of loved ones at the hands of the unnaturals reaches us. The Deceiver's slaves venture much farther from his realm than ever they dared in the past. Our homeland is threatened. The lands of our allies are under siege.

"There is much to discuss. However, before we commence, all here must be informed of the facts. Rumors swirl and build, but we must only act on the facts. Often, the enemy uses rumor to send us charging in the wrong direction. First, General Chani, commander of the our defense forces, will recount recent events in and around the Nagur."

General Chani stood and cleared his throat.

"We are under attack," began Chani. "Scouts confirm Prince Eidyn's story and found additional evidence of unnaturals prowling our wood."

A gasp arose in the chamber.

"Units near the Toxkri confirm several sets of tracks leading in and out of that cesspool. The Malveel are hard pressed to remain hidden in the open grasslands to the north and use the Toxkri Swamp as a means of reaching the Nagur undetected. The creatures are extremely hardy and resourceful. How they navigate that maze without drowning in a bog or quicksand I'm unable to discern. However, if they map a path through the Toxkri and pass it back to their master, we lose our natural defenses to the east."

Kael noticed Teeg's mouth upturn in a slight smile. As the old Elf turned and saw the boy he quickly became somber again. Chani addressed the court.

"Of course, our northern borders are protected by both the might of the Zodrian Guard and the deadliness of the Erutre cavalry. However, this too becomes subject to second-guessing. If these forces are heavily engaged along the northern mountains, a force of some size might be able to cross cut the plains and make a move on our borders. The Efer is a good line of defense, but if the enemy is there, the situation is dire indeed. I took the liberty of extending our defensive forces much further into the North Nagur than we ever previously allowed."

"Why not move our forces to the Nagur's edge?" asked a distinguished looking Elf, "The scouts could pick up movement in the plains many miles away, and fighting from the forest against an opposing force is a desirable advantage."

"Queen Eirtwin's cousin Paerrow. A well respected lord," whispered Teeg to Kael.

"You are correct, my lord." replied Chani. "However, that theory is predicated by knowledge of where the enemy will strike with the main body of its force. The entire Nagur Wood is a massive area to cover with our forces. We would be spread thinly across this line. If the enemy surprised us in any way, the consequences might be grave. If they were able to sever our main body in two, we would be devastated. Other unknowns continue to exist with the Toxkri. If we focus on the northern boundary, can we remain that certain of protection from the swamp?"

"General Chani, if I may be so bold as to interrupt?" stated Teeg as he rose in front of the assembly. "As all here know, I am entrusted with the pursuit and safekeeping of ... information for the kingdom's protection. If my king will allow it, I'll set forth some of that information now in order to illuminate our discussion."

"Proceed Lord Teeg," stated Leinor.

"Yes, we were beset by Malveel. Prince Eidyn has discovered as much. Yes, some of them traveled along the Toxkri's edge. It is the only explanation for these attacks. And yes a war is upon us. However, I don't think we are the nation in grave danger. My reports point elsewhere. As always, the puppets of Amird seek to strike this world at its strongest point. The target is once more Zodra and her people. For, as we all know, a defeat in the North is a defeat for us all. If Amird's servant Izgra and his armies smash the guard, the rest of this world falls to the Ulrog packs.

"Are we in danger? Certainly. Even here in our own streets. The enemy's servants are wily and cunning. They hide in the shadows and pounce when you relax. Those of us who are charged with determining threats to the kingdom have stumbled and this mistake has cost us the lives of those we hold dear.

"However, the question as to whether the Toxkri will protect us in the East can be answered with surety? Absolutely. My sources believe the Malveel skirted the edge of the Toxkri as it journeyed to the Nagur. It did not enter the swamp and certainly did not find a means to traverse its many dangers. I assure you, if any unnatural attempts to cross the Southern mountains and enter the Toxkri, I'll hear of it.

"The real threat rises once again in the North. A massive number of Ulrog are flooding the Northern Scythtar from the old Kingdom of Astel. They take positions all along the northern range. Ulrog packs step up their raids on the northern Zodrian villages and foray deep into Erutre land. Their targets are farms and orchards. They slaughter huge numbers of the Erutre herds. It is obvious they are trying to thin the supplies of their enemies. Once they build their numbers and depleted those supplies, they'll flood out of the mountains in force.

"The Keltaran giants begin to increase their raids on Zodra's western borders. At this time an attack by the Keltaran army would be devastating. As we all know, the Keltar and the Ulrog are mortal enemies and in the past the Keltar put aside their blood feud with the Zodrian Guard when the Ulrog launched major offensives. However, I begin to question many of the happenings in Keltar lately. The Guard cannot count on such generosity at this point.

"I believe the attacks by the Malveel were engineered to keep the Grey Elves locked in their wood and to engender fear of the outside world. We isolated ourselves for far too long. Our home is a beautiful place, but the world changes dramatically around us. Events are unfolding rapidly and the struggle between Order and Chaos is racing toward a climax. We have always ventured forth to lend aid to our allies. Now is the time to do so once more!"

A cheer of appreciation went through the crowd as Teeg bowed to the court and toward the throne. Ader smiled at the old Elf and Queen Eirtwin nodded her head toward him. Teeg returned to his spot next to Kael.

"That went well," whispered the Elf to Kael as he returned.

The court broke into small groups again and the conversation grew animated. The largest group formed around Paerrow and sought his opinion, but the distinguished Elf remained deep in thought.

"Who is Izgra?" Kael whispered to Teeg.

"A usurper on the ancient Astelan throne," answered the Elf.

"Where is Astel?" frowned Kael.

"Over the Mirozert Mountains to the East," smiled Teeg. "You do have a lot to learn, Kael."

The doors to the court opened and in stepped Manfir. The warrior's eyes were rimmed in red and his arms hung by his sides. His cloak remained shredded across the shoulder and covered in dried blood. The court went silent once more. Ader moved to the front of the platform and waved the man forward. Paerrow's concentration broke and he turned to Manfir.

"Welcome, Manfir. Perhaps now would be an opportune time to hear more on these matters from our northern allies. I am also eager to discover why Ader, yourself and your young charge have returned," said Paerrow nodding toward Kael.

All eyes once more turned to Kael. The boy's face flushed and his heart raced. Teeg rose and placed a hand on Kael's shoulder.

"My friend here suffers through quite a trying day. I'm a personal friend of his father and ..."

"Lord Teeg," interrupted Paerrow, "You're a master of information. However, many may attest to your commanding skill with disinformation. We're not children. If we are to assess our danger and assist in our response to that danger, we must possess all the facts. I beseech our sovereigns to allow the truth to be told."

Queen Eirtwin leaned toward her husband and whispered in his ear. Ader stood impassively at the front of the dais.

"Cousin Paerrow, you're a wise and sensible Elf," said King Leinor. "Your request will be granted. It is time to trust our people. Manfir, please inform the court all that has befallen you since you departed the Almar palace this morning."

Manfir bowed and held his place two strides inside the court's doors. All in attendance gave him their attention as he described the trio's departure from the palace stables. He quickly referenced their encounter with Diom and his unit at the Efer crossing.

"A brave soldier," interjected Paerrow.

Manfir related the journey through the Nagur. As he spoke his eyes remained fixed on Ader. The old trader stood stone still and never reacted to Manfir's comments. The discovery of the battle scene drew gasps from the crowded room.

"All of them dead?" questioned General Chani.

"All," replied Manfir.

"What of their attackers?" asked Chani.

Manfir glanced back toward the throne.

"Fled, presumably. Tracks led from the battle scene east into the North Nagur."

Kael turned to the dais and saw Ader standing there motionless. However, his hands moved to the top of his staff grasping it tightly.

"Those troops were sent to protect someone, were they not?" questioned Paerrow.

"Yes, Manfir. What of the boy Aemmon Brelgson?" asked Chani.

Kael's stomach lurched and tightened. He quickly looked down and tried to shield his face from all in the room. Teeg touched his arm and whispered in his ear.

"Steady boy. There is no shame in sorrow."

"The young man fell with the Elves," stated Manfir.

"My condolences, Manfir. The house of Manreel has lost a fine warrior," said Paerrow.

Kael's eyes shot up and he saw Paerrow bow deeply in Manfir's direction. His mind tried to go over what he just heard. Many of the older Elves were adding their condolences to Paerrow's. The chatter in the room built as the Elves assessed the news. Kael looked to Ader. The old man met Kael's gaze and remained expressionless. Kael's mind swirled with the bits and pieces of information he received. His anger grew. As more time passed he maintained less and less of a grip on what happened to him. Where was his Father? His brother was dead. Why were the Elves conveying their condolences to Manfir the tinker's son? More importantly, why did Manfir accept them? Kael flushed red. He hoped to go home, crawl into bed and cry for a week. Ader stared at Kael and adjusted his cloak. Teeg turned to Kael and whispered once more.

"Things are going a bit quickly for you my boy. Know that your best interests are kept in mind. Remain calm and quiet and all will be revealed later."

Teeg turned back to Ader and the old man resumed his granite pose at the front of the platform. He raised his hands and the crowd quieted.

"I too am interested in the information Prince Manfir brings. We separated after the burial of your brethren and I did not expect such a hasty return to Luxlor. Why are you here and what further news do you bring?"

"I proceeded to Kelky as you requested, Lord Ader. I met no trouble along the road and made good speed to the village. Brelg had departed for Zodra."

"What?" shouted Kael. "Why would he journey toward Zodra?"

"Kael Brelgson. Control yourself," said Ader sternly. "Continue Manfir."

Kael bit his lip and his eyes looked to the ground.

"King Macin called a meeting of all the lords of the kingdom. The Ulrog amass along the Scythtar Mountains. Keltaran giants raid the Western villages. They slaughter innocent folk and reports of atrocities filter back to Zodra."

"Brutalities by the Ulrog are well known and expected," stated General Chani "But the Keltar haven't committed such acts for centuries. They may hold a blood feud with the Zodrians and by default with us, but they do worship Avra as the Zodrians do."

"To trust in the scruples of the Keltaran, is to trust in the wind. They change as easily. I spent years along the northern and western battle lines and found no difference in the morals of the Ulrog, who serve the Master of Chaos, and the Keltar, who serve themselves. They're a people ruled by hatred and ..."

"Enough," chastened Ader "You're still young by my standards Manfir son of Macin and have as much to learn about holding your tongue as that boy."

Manfir bowed his head.

"My apologies, Lord Ader."

"So Macin called forth the lords of his land. He's a proud man and doesn't easily ask for help. The situation is escalating rapidly. How does this matter concern Brelg?" said Ader.

"Macin is nothing if not stubborn, my lord. The southern provinces of Zodra never assembled a governing body. The villages are too removed from the kingdom and run self-sufficiently. Village councils such as that in Kelky sufficed. Apparently, King Macin named Brelg a Duke of the Southern Provinces years ago. Brelg was unaware of this title until runners from the capital arrived requesting his presence."

Kael balled his fists and glared at Ader. The boy turned to Teeg and clenched his teeth.

"What in Avra's name are they talking about?" he hissed. "My father's an innkeeper."

"Patience lad," replied Teeg.

"War is upon us with the Ulrog, the Keltar, or both," stated Manfir. "Macin's forces are depleted and his supplies run low. The Zodrian Guard protects the South from these terrors and Macin finally intends to call on the Southlanders for help. As I said, he is a proud man and doesn't do this lightly. Brelg's right hand, Lieutenant Cefiz, remained at the inn to gather in Brelg's sons and bring them north. He informed me of these developments then departed for the capital. He carries with him the news of Aemmon's death."

Manfir glanced toward Kael. The boy's eyes were tearing again. Anger, frustration and sorrow washed over the boy. He longed to run from the room and north to Kelky. If he fell asleep in his old room, maybe he would awake to the world he knew before he stepped past the front gate of "The King's Service".

Kael was emotionally exhausted. His eyes darted between Ader and Manfir. His thoughts drifted to Cefiz and his Father. Has everyone deceived him for years? Kael was now beginning to question the identity of his own father.

Once more he flushed red. He glanced around at the faces staring and whispering. Finally, he looked toward the dais and met the calm, reassuring gaze of Queen Eirtwin. She stepped from the platform and approached him as the room buzzed and digested Manfir's news. Eirtwin slowly took Kael's hands and pulled him close.

"You are a beloved child of Avra," she whispered. "I know we have just met, but trust your instincts. In your heart, do you believe we care for you?"

The boy listened to her kind words and searched his feelings as he stared into her eyes. Kael nodded his head.

"Good," she said.

Kael found comfort in those eyes. He trusted this woman. She wouldn't betray him. His heart slowed and he regained a grip on his emotions. The queen leaned forward and kissed Kael on the forehead. The boy smiled at her.

"I also intercepted a runner from the Zodrian capital bound for Luxlor. I assumed his role and return to ask the Grey Elves for their council in this dire time. King Macin asks for a representative to be sent to Zodra," continued Manfir.

"I will go!" exclaimed Eidyn as he rose from General Chani's table.

"It appears this disease of loose talk is infectious, Lord Ader," stated the king as he frowned at Eidyn.

"I beg your pardon, father. I would be honored to be our representative to the Zodrian capital," said Eidyn lowering his head.

"You will be our representative," smiled King Leinor as he turned to Teeg. "And Lord Teeg shall accompany you to assess the situation."

Eidyn and Teeg bowed toward the king. Queen Eirtwin walked over to her son.

"Take care, my son. Amird's servants are in many places. The Lord of Chaos corrupts the mind and twists hearts. Be ever vigilant."

She leaned forward and kissed his forehead.

"News from the North grows as disturbing as the events that have taken place within the beloved Nagur, and it seems many things will be decided at this council session," declared Ader. "Since I'm a meddling old man, I can't allow meetings of such import to occur without my attendance. It's time for Manfir son of Macin to return home as well."

Manfir nodded his agreement.

"Finally, this boy must be returned to his father," said Ader motioning to Kael. "Therefore, he'll journey with us."

Kael's heart leapt. He felt a weight lift from his shoulders. Until now, events conspired to prevent his return to a normal life. Again his mind raced. He would travel all the way to Zodra to see his father, who was said to be some kind of baron or duke. Anxiety flooded his mind. Zodra was a long way off. What if they met another creature on the Nagur path? What if they were attacked in the open? What if there were others?

"Will Master Hilro accompany us as well?" blurted out Kael as he motioned to the hooded figure he saw slip into the room.

A rush of excitement swept the hall. The figure stood partially obscured by shadows and columns in a far corner of the court. The assembly spun in the direction Kael gestured. Those Elves nearest the figure bowed deeply and backed away. Only Paerrow stood upright and moved forward.

"Master Hilro?" said Paerrow as he lightly bowed.

"Ladies and gentlemen of the Elven court," said Ader in an attempt to politely draw their attention from the dark corner. "My brash young friend misspoke. Brother Hilro isn't in this room. My apologies for the shock that young Kael Brelgson causes you."

All eyes shifted between Ader and the large, hooded figure. Manfir took a half step in the man's direction before his body went rigid.

"Prince Manfir," smiled Queen Eirtwin. "In your haste to attend this meeting, I see you broke one of the laws of Luxlor."

"Pardon, dear lady?" questioned Manfir, snatching glances between the dais and the shadowed corner.

"It is known to all that weapons are not allowed in court sessions. Reason must prevail in places of diplomacy. I'm aware that it's quite an old rule and some may think foolish, but it was based on good sense. Your familiarity with my kingdom gives you quite a bit of latitude here. However, if you'd be so kind as to remove your weaponry," said Eirtwin turning to a page. "This good page will loyally safeguard your belongings."

Once again a murmur rose in the room.

"Does such a law exist?" a young woman near Kael whispered to her husband.

The Elf lord shrugged his shoulders then pulled his cloak tighter to his body, obscuring the view of a dagger's scabbard. Teeg smiled and nodded his head.

"Brilliant," whispered the old Elf to no one in particular "I should have recruited her when she was a child."

"My dear lady, I hope you don't think me capable of committing offense in your chambers?" said Manfir. "My sword has been sworn to your defense since my birth. Our houses' alliance has lasted centuries."

"It is not my protection I seek," returned Queeen Eirtwin. "When Leinor and I grant hospitality to a traveler, we also grant asylum and protection to our guests. These are strange times. You yourself state a time of war is upon us. Perhaps we need to return to the old laws. They were drawn up when conflict ravaged this world."

King Leinor stepped forward.

"The queen makes a valid argument. Diplomacy among great nations is the essence of what makes them great. Please remove your weaponry, Manfir."

"As you command, your highnesses," said Manfir bowing deeply.

The page approached the disheveled man and stretched out his arms. Manfir removed his broadsword and scabbard from his back and placed them in the page's arms. The young Elf immediately swooned under the weight of the enormous blade. Next, the warrior removed dual daggers from sheaths beneath his belt and piled them on top of the broadsword. He added various other daggers and cudgels from hidden folds of his cloak and robe. King Leinor snapped his fingers and another page stepped forward to assist the first. Upon completion, Manfir bowed once more toward the Elven rulers as the pages departed.

"It appears that you were sufficiently prepared for battle," smiled the queen.

"You are never prepared for battle with the servants of Chaos or the Keltaran savages, my lady," stated Manfir soberly.

"But are you ever prepared for peace, Prince Manfir? That is the question," demanded Ader.

Manfir looked questioningly into the old trader's eyes then spun to face the corner. Ader motioned the figure forward and it slowly stepped from the shadows toward the center of the room.

"Ladies and gentlemen of the Elven court, I introduce you to Granu, son of Grannak, heir to the granite throne of Keltar and Chief Abbot of the Monastery of Awoi," announced Ader.

Once again a gasp ran through the crowd. This time however, there was no bowing toward the figure as he moved forward. The lords of the Elven court stepped in front of their ladies. Many of the Elves in the room backed from the center leaving Manfir standing alone. The Zodrian prince stood his ground and once again his body went rigid. The huge Keltaran remained cloaked and hidden from view as he limped forward aided by a long staff. Manfir's eyes darted left then right, finally locking on a heavy candle stand buttressed to a nearby column.

The black robed Keltaran stood a full foot and a half over the head of Manfir. His shoulders were twice that of the Zodrian prince. The only parts of his body that were visible were his hands, huge, scarred and thick. Like the gnarled roots of an ancient oak tree, they radiated power. The Keltaran prince stopped within five feet of Manfir and slowly leaned forward, clutching his staff for support. One hand came free from the staff and grasped the end of his deep, cowled hood. Slowly he pulled the hood away.

Granu's head and neck were massive. The Keltaran were a people familiar with the rock and stone of their mountain homes, and Granu looked to be hewn from that stone. His strong jaw and high cheekbones gave him an angular, heavy look. His eyes were a deep, rich brown. Granu's most striking feature was the top of his head. It was shorn clean of hair and crisscrossed in scars and old wounds. An enormous hand stroked those scars absentmindedly as he stared at Manfir. He smiled and moved the hand to his waist. Without taking his eyes from those of Manfir, he bowed lightly.

"Well met Manfir, son of Macin," rumbled the giant's deep voice. "Granu, humble follower of Awoi, at your service."

Manfir remained stiff. Kael was reminded of a crouching cat. The warrior's eyes never left Granu. Without turning, he spoke to the rulers of Luxlor.

"If I knew your highnesses were taking council with dealers in death and murder, I would have sought a private audience for my father's request. It would save my nose from the stench of the beast who fouls this great hall."

Granu pursed his lips and slowly rose to his full height, one hand gripping his staff. His eyes grew dark and he furrowed his brow.

"In Keltar, when one is met with a bow or other sign of respect, we possess the good sense and politeness to return such respect."

"The last time I dropped my head to a Keltar, it was to avoid the battle-ax he aimed at it," snapped Manfir.

"Perhaps, if it met its mark, that ax would have knocked some manners into your skull," returned Granu, his voice rising, "or at least scattered your brains across the battlefield to save us from the poor manners you do possess."

"Alas it did not," growled Manfir "but my daggers found his belly before he instructed me on Keltaran etiquette."

"Perhaps I should take up the instruction where my brethren left off," snarled Granu raising his staff.

"Hold yourself, son of Grannak!" commanded King Leinor "I allowed you to enter my chambers with that staff due to your injury. If you take it up now as a weapon, you forfeit all rights of hospitality and my men will take you into custody."

Granu lowered the staff and bowed deeply to King Leinor and Queen Eirtwin.

"My apologies, children of the Nagur," returned Granu quickly. "The Lord of Chaos goads us all against what we know is right. May peace dwell in your house."

"And you, son of Macin," stated Leinor. "You're aware that any who enter my chamber are offered the hospitality and protection of my home. This is a place of open discourse and civility. If you cannot act accordingly, remove yourself to the anteroom and await your master there."

Manfir glanced at the old trader on the podium but Ader remained stony faced. Manfir addressed the king once more.

"In the house of the Elves, Leinor is lord. I will obey and ask for your pardon."

"It is given," frowned the king. "Now we must return to business. Prince Granu is an outcast from his people."

Granu raised his head and his stare challenged the room.

"A mutual friend contacted him and he made his way to Luxlor with the help of that friend," said Leinor.

Teeg's eyes shifted to Ader as Queen Eirtwin addressed Manfir.

"Granu believes he possesses information that may upset the plans of Izgra the Half-Dead. He wishes to be heard in the halls of Zodra and asks for our help in doing so. However, as we all know, the son of Grannak is a mighty prize for a Zodrian warrior. He asks for assistance from Luxlor," stated Eirtwin.

The room remained silent as Manfir glared at the giant. Queen Eirtwin allowed her statements to sink in to the crowd. Paerrow cleared his throat and approached the Keltaran prince. He stopped within two feet of the black robed monk. The stately Elf crossed his hands over his heart and extended them palms upward.

"The enemy of my enemy is my friend," stated the Elf "The Lord of Chaos does indeed set us forth against one another, but the courageous step forward and expose his treachery. I would like to suggest a course of action to the people of Luxlor, if I may."

"Paerrow the wise is ever our closest advisor," returned Eirtwin from the dais. "What do you propose, cousin?"

"Prince Eidyn and Lord Teeg are to be sent as our representatives to Zodra. Kael Brelgson must be returned to his father. Prince Manfir must return to his home in its hour of need. Lastly, Ader, the voice of Avra must always meddle in the affairs of this world," smiled Paerrow turning back to Granu. "I charge Granu, son of Grannak with a set of tasks that are in tandem with his own desires.

"You, Granu, will also represent us in Zodra. As a representative from this kingdom you are awarded the protection and rights given the Elven people by our allies to the north. I also charge you with the protection and well being of this boy upon his return to his father. In this way, you are bound to the fortunes of the Elves and the group with which you travel. You may serve your own agenda, but must also serve those of the group."

"Prince Granu, do you accept this proposal?" questioned Leinor.

Granu's eyes swept the room making contact with all who looked his way. Finally, they settled on Manfir.

"I will represent the Grey Elves in the Zodrian capital," affirmed Granu. "I swear this on the spirit of Awoi, the father of my fathers, and on the love of Avra the Creator and Life-Giver."

Granu turned and slowly walked toward Kael. The boy's eyes went wide as the huge man's black robe eclipsed the room from sight. Kael looked briefly to the dais as Granu approached. Ader, Leinor and Eirtwin remained motionless. Granu raised a gigantic hand over the boy's head and Kael flinched. A rumble started in the giant's chest as his hand hovered above Kael. He closed his eyes and swayed slightly to the rumble. After a few moments Granu stopped and quickly knelt before the boy.

"Kael Brelgson, I beseech Awoi the pure to ask our Creator to grant you safety in the tasks ahead. I, Granu son of Grannak, pledge what little protection I might provide to you on your journey north. I'm but a simple monk and carry no weapon or armor, but my staff and my body are pledged as a shield to you."

The room remained silent as all eyes locked on Kael.

"Granu, son of Grannak," stammered Kael. "I accept your pledge and I, uh, hope you aren't required to honor it."

Granu's face was hidden from all in the room save Kael and the boy swore he saw the dour giant briefly smile. Granu rose and turned to the room.

"It is decided then," stated King Leinor. "Eidyn, Teeg, Granu, Manfir, Ader and Kael Brelgson will depart for Zodra in the morning. The Grey Elves shall make ready to assist our allies in the North, or protect ourselves should the need arise. Do any here object to this plan of action?"

Paerrow looked about the room and returned his gaze to the podium.

"Nay my Liege. The people support this effort," said Paerrow.

"Excellent," said Queen Eirtwin. "Then the court is adjourned. All here know what is required of them. May Avra smile on your endeavors."

The assembly bowed to the dais and Elves filed from the chamber. Manfir and Granu remained in their positions.

"Prince Eidyn, I request that you tarry a moment," said Ader.

The Elven prince complied.

"I wish to illuminate you and the northern princes on a few rules," continued Ader as he stared hard at Manfir and Granu. "Lord Teeg, please escort Kael Brelgson to his chambers and see that he gets in no further trouble."

"As you wish," smiled Teeg.

Teeg and Kael walked toward the exit of the chamber as the others gathered by the throne. Manfir stood opposite Granu, his fists clenched and arms taut.

"The master intends to give several of his students the cane," whispered Teeg as they departed the council chamber. "They'll know their place before we leave for Zodra."

CHAPTER 10: BIRTH OF THE SERAPHIM

The duo strolled through the halls of the palace of Luxlor, with Teeg smiling smugly to himself. Kael wondered why the old Elf was so amused. Surely their situation was dire.

"I don't understand what makes you so happy," exclaimed Kael. "The world is on the brink of war!"

"All clouds are etched by a silver lining," stated Teeg. "You don't think that went fantastically?"

"Well, I'm not sure. Was it supposed to go at all?" asked Kael.

"It went exceptionally. I couldn't script it any better," laughed Teeg. "And that bit about you exposing Prince Granu as Master Hilro was fantastic. I mean, you threw everyone so far off balance, the shock of the prince heir of Keltar standing in their midst was an anticlimax. They almost took it as commonplace compared to your reference to Hilro. Think of it. The heirs to a pair of kingdoms that have been at war for thousands of years were standing a single yard apart. Amazingly, they didn't try to bash one another's heads in."

"Actually, I think they would have," argued Kael.

"Proud men cannot lose face easily, Kael. I guarantee both Manfir and Granu were more eager to hear what one another said than to kill one another. The killing starts once the information is gained," said Teeg.

"How do you know so much about the nature of men and the importance of information?" asked Kael.

"Information is my business. I hold a somewhat unique position in the kingdom," stated Teeg.

"What?" smirked Kael "Are you some kind of spy?"

"Absolutely not!" exclaimed a disturbed Teeg. "I prefer to call my duties information gathering. Spy! How preposterous!"

"Uh, I apologize," mumbled Kael.

"Besides," continued Teeg not listening, "the official title is Master of Spies."

Kael's jaw dropped and he stopped dead in his tracks, staring at the Elf as Teeg proceeded ahead gibbering to himself over the indignation of being called a mere spy. After a dozen steps Teeg realized he was alone and talking to himself. The old Elf quickly spun on his heel and addressed Kael.

"Come along. Ader instructed me to fill you in on certain things. You may ask questions and I will choose to answer some of them," said Teeg.

Once again questions flooded Kael's mind, but recent events dominated all else. He hurried to catch the old Elf and fell in beside him.

"Who is Manfir? I might guess, but I want to hear it," said Kael.

"Manfir is the heir to the throne of Zodra of course," stated Teeg. "He is the first child of King Macin of Zodra and his wife Queen Tay."

Kael shook his head from side to side and frowned.

"Impossible," exclaimed the boy. "I've known Rin for many years. Why would the prince heir to the most powerful kingdom in the world ride into Kelky three times a season in the guise of a poor tinker's son?"

Teeg hesitated.

"At this point," returned the Elf, "I'm not at liberty to answer that question. Ask another if you will."

Kael frowned.

"Who is Granu?" asked the boy.

"That I may answer," smiled Teeg. "Granu is the heir to the throne of Keltar. However, he was disowned and his brother Fenrel stands in his place. Granu also served as the Chief Abbot of the Monastery of Awoi, a prestigious position. The Abbot is the head of an order of priests who perform Keltaran religious rites. From what I gather, Fenrel disbanded the order upon Granu's banishment."

"Why is he here?" questioned Kael.

"You heard. He seeks asylum," replied an annoyed Teeg. "Do try to listen, my boy."

"No," challenged Kael. "Why is he here? I mean, he's the enemy. Keltarans are evil. We heard the stories of how they butcher women and children. Why would the Grey Elves give him asylum?"

Teeg looked hard into Kael's eyes and shook his head.

"Buried too deeply from sight in that village," mumbled the old Elf to himself. "Perhaps too deeply to become what he must."

"Please don't talk in riddles. This is all confusing enough," said Kael.

The Elf shook his head and smiled at Kael.

"I'm sorry, my boy. It's been quite a heady week. However, in order for you to dispel the confusion of which you speak, you must rid yourself of your preconceived notions and your learned prejudices. The Keltaran are no more evil than you, or your father for that matter. Men have waged war on men for centuries. 'Wrong' is a relative term. In the eyes of the Keltaran, fault lies with your people."

"But they come down from the mountains and raid villages and towns. Killing and stealing." protested Kael.

"They come down from mountains they were driven into centuries ago when the ancient Zodrian population grew and encroached on Keltar society," stated Teeg. "The Keltaran once were a flourishing community in the foothills of those mountains."

"But ... but they murder and steal," sputtered Kael.

"I know of occurrences of this type happening on both sides of the war," stated Teeg.

Kael frowned. Teeg was challenging the natural order of his world. Keltarans were bad and Zodrians were good. That is the way things are. Now, this elderly Elf was telling him some Keltarans were good and some Zodrians were bad. Why did they fight? What was it all about anyhow? Kael ground his teeth.

"Perhaps it might help you understand, if you knew the history of these peoples. Do you know anything about the Keltaran, other than they are murdering monsters?" asked Teeg.

"Some," said Kael weakly.

"We shall build on 'some'," said Teeg. "I'll give you a brief history of the Keltaran people and in so doing give you a small lesson in the greater problems of this world."

They quickly reached Kael's chambers and Teeg threw open the door and stepped inside. He walked over to one of the bookshelves in the room and pulled a large parchment from a recess. Near the bookshelf stood a white table carved from the same wood as the palace. Teeg unrolled the parchment and spread it on the table.

Kael looked down upon a map of the world. Some of the details were familiar, but others were unusual. The Nagur Wood remained relatively similar to what Kael saw on current maps. The Eru plains were the same although the Derolian forest looked much bigger on this map. The Zorim Mountains were readily recognizable. However, the wood running along the foothills of the mountains extended much further into Zodrian territory than Kael remembered.

"This is a map of our world from many centuries ago," said Teeg. "In those days there were no Erutre, just wandering tribes across the plains. Society did not exist as we know it. The Grey Elves had not come to this world and evil had no foothold in this realm.

Avra created this world. Man went forth and prospered, creating more order and beauty from the resources Avra supplied. Avra knew his supreme creation was clever and resourceful, but he determined to ensure their success. Therefore, he created the Guides, the Seraphim."

"The Guides weren't here first?" asked Kael.

"No," replied Teeg. "The Guides were created out of Avra's compassion and love for man. He anguished when men struggled. He pitied their failures. His compassion welled to the surface and out of it he created the Seraphim, Awoi and Amird. Their task was to push and prod man in the proper direction. The brother Seraphim roamed the world and helped man. They were teachers, counselors and healers.

"The brothers were long-lived, virtually immortal. When Avra dipped his hand into the life pool, he created the guides with a tremendous force of his will. His hand rushed through the pool and on either side a swirl of equal, powerful force was created. Their spirits spun in the pool strong and enduring. They lived for thousands of years.

"Just as Avra couldn't create man to be a slave, subservient to Avra's will, so he could not create the Seraphim as such. The brothers were instructed by their Creator then left to fulfill his wishes. They took different paths.

"Amird immersed himself in the culture of men. Pushing them toward fulfillment. Amird directed cultivation of the soil and spread its use. Amird helped men develop language skills and writing. He guided men toward using their minds to better themselves. Amird set men off on the right track with a hard shove and eventually they built speed, progressing forward on their own. The seeds Amird planted grew into art, literature and math. He truly was the father of the society men know today."

"But, Amird is evil. I mean, that's what the stories say," said Kael.

"Ah, again you refer to stories. Kael Brelgson you'll be much better off in this world if you start to believe, truly believe. Look around you. Do you honestly think this whole world just happened? How do you explain its existence? From the great Hdjmir Mountain down to a grain of wheat, the world is a most complex and beautiful place. Do you think it just stumbled upon itself?"

"I'm uncertain," mumbled Kael.

"Uncertainty is the springboard for faith, Kael. Will you stand on that platform forever, or take the leap and experience a deeper understanding of the world?" asked Teeg.

The boy looked down at his feet and fidgeted. Teeg smiled and put a hand on his shoulder.

"Take your time, boy. For now we'll stick with uncertainty and the possibility of faith. Now, where was I? Oh yes, Amird.

"Evil? Possibly. However, at this point in the lesson, he was simply the servant of a master he adored. All that he did was to fulfill the wishes of Avra. He worked hard, striving mightily to glorify his lord. Men flourished under his tutelage. Over a span of hundreds of years they moved out of their caves and huts and gathered in villages. Farms were planted. Societies formed and grew."

"Awoi held an extremely different take on man and the world. He recognized this world as unstoppable, a vast and ever expanding wildfire of newness. The world continually changes and transforms itself. Some of it is left behind and fades away as other parts evolve. An always advancing, improving world.

"Awoi looked at man and saw a creature capable of wonders. A being so infinitely advanced over all others, that he holds the power to create a course for all in this world. Awoi also saw a being ruled by desires and temptations, aware of so much around him, that he is also pulled by the power of Chaos. A creature possessing an equally immense ability to produce evil.

"Awoi felt his task was to instruct man in the ways of love, compassion and kindness and to show all men the task at hand. We are to glorify Avra through works of kindness, to hold those up who cannot hold themselves, to care for the weak and sick, to shelter those without a dwelling place. Awoi spent his time reaching out to the dispossessed and unwanted. Those wretched creatures left behind as the strong moved on. They were the projects of Awoi."

"Why did he do that? He would be forced to care for them. They were weak, a burden," interjected Kael.

"Not true, Kael Brelgson," returned Teeg. "Often, those who fall to the bottom and survive are the strongest among us. When you learn to survive in your most desperate hour, you learn how to truly live. Many of those Awoi helped rose to be leaders of tremendous spiritual depth and understanding. Men and women of compassion, who made their lives a testament to his principles.

Men and women who sacrificed all for the betterment of mankind."

"Then what happened to Awoi?" asked Kael.

"The unthinkable. Awoi and Amird led their separate existences. The world proceeded on its course for millennia. Then one day Amird and Awoi crossed paths. The brothers knew of each other's work but had not met for centuries. Awoi looked upon his brother's accomplishments with awe. Such progress. So many wonders. Man truly prospered with the guiding hand of his beloved brother.

"Amird privately smirked at his brother's successes and failures. To waste time on a man starving in the wilderness, while cities were springing up throughout that wilderness appeared absurd. One life meant nothing in the great scheme. Progress created casualties, such was the life bequeathed upon man.

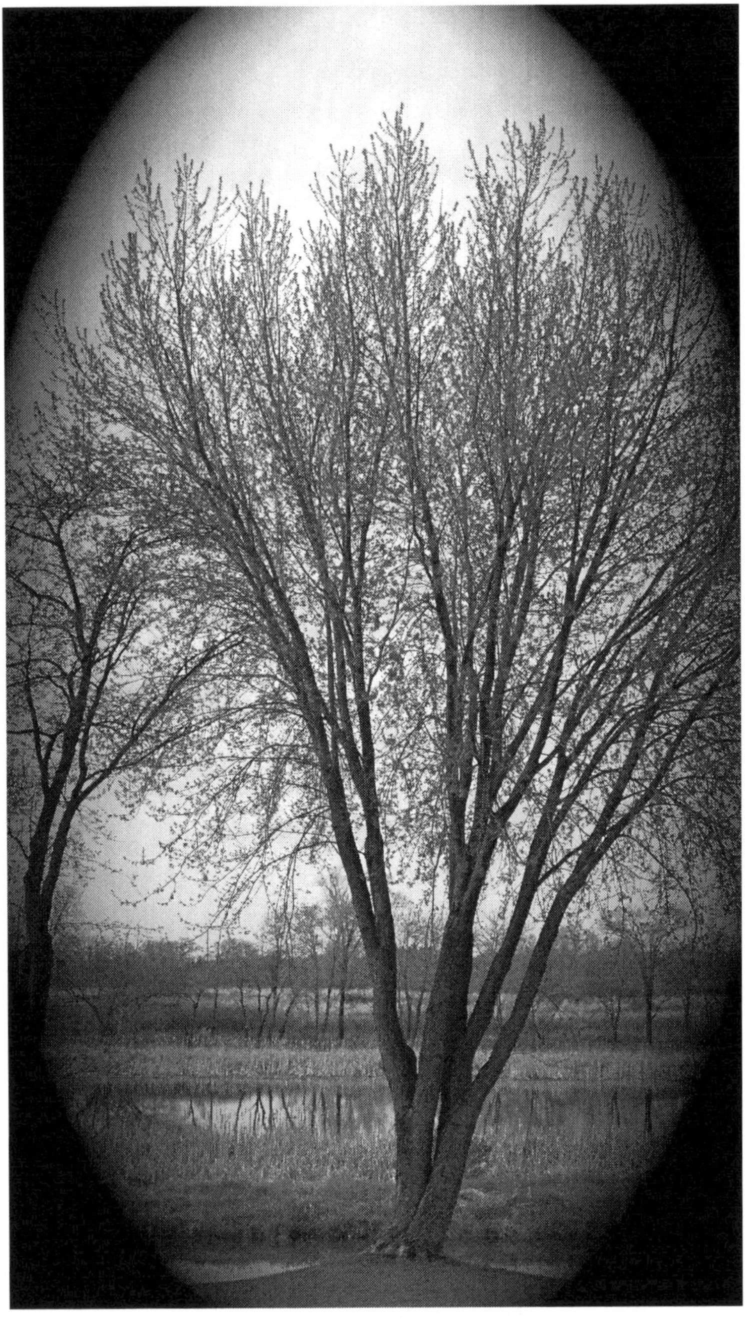

"The brothers spoke for days. Amird's confident talk heartened Awoi. Amird rambled on and on about his triumphs and basked in the adoration of his brother. Awoi saw the pride well up in his brother and it pleased him to make Amird feel good about his triumphs.

"One day the brothers were standing in a glade by the Northern Mountains. Without warning, Avra appeared to them. The brothers fell to their knees and praised their Creator. Avra bade them rise and walk with him. He asked them of the world and their work in it.

"Amird took the lead and described his progress with men. The building of societies and cultures. The nurturing of mathematics and language skills. The development of art and literature. Avra was quite pleased.

"The Creator turned and asked Awoi what he accomplished. The guide spoke glowingly of his attempt to instill a wonder and love of all things in people. His attempt to foster a culture of caring amongst men. Avra listened and again smiled in approval.

"The trio walked together as the two Seraphim basked in the glory of their Creator. Avra turned and spoke to the brothers. He praised them for their work. Their efforts were not going unnoticed. He then suggested that the two begin to work together more closely.

"Amird questioned his Creator, asking what benefit his great accomplishments might derive from Awoi's trifling. Avra corrected the Guide. The Almighty acknowledged the works of Amird but questioned their direction. Did they really glorify the world and create more beauty? Certainly many of them did. But almost as certainly they created a byproduct of sorrow for some inhabitants of this world. As cities develop and territories encroach on one another, battle lines are drawn. As men band together in societies, there are those who are different, outsiders to fear, mistrust and shun.

"Avra praised the work of Awoi. All of Avra's creations are beautiful in his eyes. No being is expendable as Amird suggested. Amird was told to think how beautiful all of his work becomes if the lives of all are improved, not just the strong and their followers. Avra departed the brothers with a blessing and left them to further their work.

"At first, Amird embraced this effort and tried to incorporate Awoi's work into his own. The Seraphim struggled to advance society but remain compassionate to the poor and lowly. However, Amird grew annoyed. He was used to quick successes and stunning advancements. Men in high places and of great power deferred to him, kneeling before him and seeking counsel. Awoi went unnoticed, happy to let his brother deal with such people. Soon, Awoi was coming to his brother to ask for favor.

"As a city outgrew its borders and encroached on a peasant's farm, the king's soldiers arrived to turn the peasant and his family into the street. Awoi went to his brother and asked for help relocating the family. When disease broke out in a region, Awoi went to Amird and requested supplies and food.

"Amird judged these efforts a waste of time. The strong survived and moved on. Amird felt his brother's efforts weakened the human race, adding weak bodies and weak minds to the population. His resentment grew. He reflected on his accomplishments. Avra created this world, but Amird in his wisdom and power pushed it to an apex. His vanity grew along with his hatred of his brother's compassion. Avra dared to chastise him and praise Awoi. Chaos and evil filled his mind. Power corrupted his spirit. He longed to be rid of his brother and rule these ignorant beings as they should be ruled. Man was only fit to follow orders. Amird would never be a party to another of Awoi's charitable causes.

"Avra was not seen again, and Amird pushed his brother aside. Amird involved himself in the development of all people and their leaders. Men made great advancements from their days of small villages and towns. Awoi, on the other hand, struggled to make men recognize the beauty in all Avra's creations. Many followed his example. Slowly, men found their hearts.

"One day, in the small city-state of Zodra, the queen gave birth to a child. The delivery of the child was very difficult, and the queen died. The king was heart broken. He adored his wife and fits of sorrow overcame him. When the child was brought to him, he was horrified. The girl child was huge and misshapen. The king recoiled in horror at the thing he blamed for his wife's untimely death. He told the midwives to take it from his sight and never to let him see her again.

"The child was housed and raised in the dank bowels of the castle. Kindly nursemaids cared for and taught the girl, but she was rarely allowed out of the innards of the huge castle. The nursemaids named the girl Gretcha, 'beautiful heart' in the old tongue.

"The king fell into despair. Despair turned to anger and abuse. He grabbed power and land, turning out those who did not bow to him and his tax collectors. Amird saw all this and determined to make Zodra the jewel in his crown. This king's misery made him ruthless. Ruthlessness led to advancement. Zodra grew in power and influence in the area. Councils or elders ruled many other cities. Soon they found it impossible to make decisions without first seeking permission from Zodra. Men of arms gravitated to the service of Zodra. Power drawn to even more power.

"Awoi learned of the girl in his travels through the lands near Zodra. On her seventeenth birthday Awoi visited the castle. He spoke soothingly to the king. He spoke of compassion and duty. He spoke of Avra and all the wonders the Creator bestowed upon the world. He spoke of a daughter being imprisoned for simply existing. He spoke of a girl with a brilliant mind and a beautiful heart alone in the world with no parents. A girl who sang like a bird and danced in the darkness of her world. The king was greatly moved. His anger turned back to sorrow and his sorrow to pity. He ignored his duties and sat in his chambers for days. The king was reluctant to face the girl. He still mourned his beautiful wife and he was ashamed at how he treated his daughter.

"Amird returned to Zodra to find his plans interrupted. He visited the king and found a man in a completely different mindset than the one he left behind. The king spoke of his duty to the people, his duty as a caretaker of their good fortune and their future. He questioned Amird as to how they could best serve the people, how they might improve the living conditions of all the peasants to prevent disease and starvation. Avra smiles on the compassionate.

"Amird was not pleased. He reminded the king that no one, not even Avra, prevented the death of his lovely wife. Amird reminded the king of life's trials and tribulations. Peasants were born into the world to serve. How could it be that his beautiful wife was taken from him while peasants bear handfuls of healthy babies in the squalor of their huts? Avra neither watches nor cares about this world. It's a trifle he's set before him, a toy with which to amuse himself. It's Amird who cares for the advancement of men, only Amird.

"Amird departed and left the king alone. The king considered all he was told. His pity turned back into despair. He wallowed in hopelessness.

"Awoi returned, unaware of his brother's visit. He found the king in a dark mood. The king refused to listen to his soothing words. In fact, the confusion he felt from the conflicting messages of the Seraphim added to his melancholy. He ordered Awoi to remove Gretcha from the castle. She was to be banished from the kingdom of Zodra. Awoi saw the king's dark mood for what it was. The distress would soon turn back to anger. The Seraph decided to save the girl.

"As Awoi and the Zodrian princess departed the city, women screeched and children fled from the sight of Gretcha. She was a full head taller than any man in the city and her powerful arms and legs rippled with muscle. Her features were pronounced and angular, as if her face were cut from granite. Awoi looked at the young woman and saw only her name, 'beautiful heart'.

"The pair traveled north. Whenever they stopped and tried to find a place for Gretcha to settle, people in the area eventually arrived and drove them out. Awoi feared for her safety and determined that they must find a place far from others. The Great Northern Mountains were uninhabited. The weather was harsh and the living hard, but Gretcha possessed enormous strength and fortitude. Awoi determined she would be fine and he planned to visit her periodically to insure her wellbeing.

"They built a cabin on the slopes of the tallest of the Northern Mountains and Awoi stayed with Gretcha for two years. He taught the woman how to hunt the mountain rams and the migrating caribou herds. He taught her how to find the edible mountain berries in the spring and summer. Awoi showed the Zodrian princess the tracks of the great grizzled bear and how to determine the passage of time since it made those tracks. Gretcha was extremely intelligent and a fast learner. She soaked in the world that was hidden from her in the dungeons of Zodra. Her naturally inquisitive mind propelled her knowledge and understanding of the world around her.

"As time passed, the hard life and harsh conditions of the Northern Mountains changed Gretcha even further. She added even more muscle to her frame, and her hair grew long and shaggy. When traders or trappers wandered through the area and came across Awoi and Gretcha, they fled in fear of the huge woman. However, all that Awoi saw was the beauty in her smile and the compassion in her heart. She was truly one of Avra's blessed creatures.

"When the two years ended, Awoi returned to his work in the name of Avra. He told Gretcha he planned to return within the year and reluctantly journeyed back to the world of men. Gretcha filled with sorrow, but knew Awoi must follow his calling. The Guide bade her farewell and departed, walking south.

"When he returned to civilization, he found it changed dramatically. As he approached small towns or villages, Awoi was challenged by armed troops. Often he was told there was no room for outsiders or strangers. Hospitality vanished. Many of the guards still wore the emblem of their land on their uniforms. However, the influence of the city of Zodra grew. Many soldiers wore the Zodrian emblem as well and paid tribute to her king for protection.

"After nearly a year of traveling, Awoi approached Zodra. As he reached the great city, he found it completely walled to outsiders. Guards ranged along fresh ramparts and called challenges to those who approached. Awoi was required to state his name and his business. After some time he, was turned away from the city.

"Undeterred, the Guide returned to the city day after day for a week and attempted entry. On the seventh day, Awoi called to the city walls once more and this time was told to wait. Eventually, a contingent of guards stepped from the gates and surrounded the Seraph. He was commanded to follow them to their king's high chamber.

"As Awoi stepped into the great hall of the castle of Zodra he was shocked. The throne was removed from its dais and placed in front of the platform's steps. The king, haggard and worn, sat hunched within it. An enormous marble bench was set upon the dais, and Amird lounged upon it, surrounded by young women. He frowned as Awoi entered the room.

'Did the gatekeepers not tell thee to depart, Awoi?' asked Amird.

'They did,' replied Awoi.

'Why didn't you follow the advice of your precious humans? Go now. I must attend to important business,' pronounced Amird.

'Amird, my brother, we must talk,' said Awoi.

'What of, a widow whose son has contracted a ragged cough? I cannot be bothered with such trifles. You think on the small scale, Awoi. I concern myself with nations and empires, while you worry over nothing. Be gone from me so I may complete my work,' demanded Amird.

'I leave you now, brother,' bowed Awoi, 'but as I go I ask you to think on whose work you are completing. His work or your own?'

Awoi turned and walked from the room. Amird arose and approached the king.

'He who harbors the beast that killed your precious wife stands before you and you do nothing? Are you a king or a peasant slave? Honor me and yourself by avenging the death of your wife!'

"Awoi walked through the city noticing the dramatic changes that overcame the population. Fear reigned in the eyes of all who dwelt there. Even the soldiers feared retribution for failure. The tension in the city was high. As Awoi tried to converse with those on the street, they kept their conversation short and quickly moved on their way.

"Awoi rounded a corner near the palace and was confronted by a troop of armed guards brandishing their weapons. The Seraph smiled and extended his hands, palms upward.

'I'm not armed and haven't raised a hand in violence my entire existence. What is it you good folk require?' questioned the Guide.

'You're to be taken into custody and killed if you resist,' answered their leader.

'I must continue the work of my Master. I've neither wronged nor harmed any here and request to go on my way,' said Awoi.

"The leader stepped forward and struck the Guide with a cudgel. Awoi fell to his knees and once again addressed the group.

'You are acting under the orders of your king. I forgive your transgression, for you are misled.'

"The leader struck him once more across the face and blood flowed from a large gash on his forehead. Awoi wiped the blood from his face and as he looked upward he saw movement on the castle's balconies. Amird stood above robed in black and scarlet, a smile on his face.

'Kill him,' shouted Amird, 'and discard his body outside the city for the buzzards to eat

Awoi lowered his head and sobbed. Not for the pain and outrage he suffered, but for the lost soul of his brother. The leader of the troop hesitated until he saw the Seraph crying. His wicked, twisted heart found no fear from a prostrate, defenseless man in the throws of sorrow. The leader moved forward smiling and raised his club. As he struck down toward the exposed head of Awoi a green light pulsed forth from the body of the Seraph. The club struck the light and bounced back as if striking stone. The leader dropped his cudgel and his arm ached from the contact with the light. He spun and ordered his troop to cut Awoi to pieces. Awoi rose and calmly asked the men to leave him in peace.

'I will not injure any here, but I cannot allow myself to be harmed,' stated Awoi.

The troops ran toward him and were struck by the green flame. They were knocked to the ground and many lost their weapons. Awoi looked to his brother on the balcony.

'I wandered the wilderness for centuries while you dwelt in the safety of cities. I learned to control my spiritual force to protect myself from the violence of nature. Neither beast nor storm harms me.

'Neither will your misguided servants. Please Amird, come away from here and talk to me. Something terrible takes control of you. I'm your brother. I love you.'

Amird was expressionless. He moved toward the balcony stairway.

'Perhaps, ... perhaps I am in need of good council, brother,' said Amird as he moved down the stairs. 'My duties consume and control me.'

Amird reached the ground and approached Awoi.

'Your first duty is the nurturing of man, not his subjugation,' responded Awoi. 'Come with me and we'll rediscover our mission.'

Amird's head sagged and he sobbed into his hands.

'You are right brother. I lose my way,' bellowed Amird. 'Please, help me regain control of myself.'

Awoi approached Amird and wrapped his brother in his arms.

'Amird, forces outside this world try to control you. Temptations wear you down. Remove yourself from this foul place and we will commune together in the pure splendor of Avra's world.'

Amird remained wrapped in his brother's embrace and sobbed into Awoi's chest.

'While you wandered the wild, I immersed myself in the matters of men. They possessed me. You learned to protect yourself from tempest and wild creature, but I learned something more useful.'

Amird lifted his head and his glowing red eyes stared into those of his brother.

'I discovered the perfect tools to motivate and teach men. Fear and Pain!'

Scarlet fire sprang from his body and engulfed Awoi. Unprepared for the assault, Awoi was badly burned. His body convulsed in pain, but he held the embrace of his brother.

'Think of the great goodness of your Creator, my brother!' cried Awoi.

Awoi screamed in pain and the green flame he used earlier sprang from his body. It struck Amird and sent him flying through the air. Awoi slumped to the ground once more. Amird landed on his back several paces away.

'Brother, what evil embraces you?' whispered Awoi, his head lowered.

Amird sprang to his feet.

'You! You and your Master try to force me to serve these pathetic creatures,' screamed Amird sweeping a hand toward the remaining soldiers. 'Amird serves no one. All will serve me, and this world will bow to my will!'

'You serve and do not realize it,' said Awoi. 'You are a slave to temptation and passions. Like a dog on a leash, you do the bidding of your master, Chaos. It corrupts your soul and seeks only selfish pleasures and empty promises.'

'A DOG!' shouted Amird. 'For thousands of years, thou art the only being I let address me in such a manner. I killed thousands who refused to follow my will. Avra praises your feeble work and finds fault with mine. You accomplished nothing in the millennia we existed. It is I who dragged these ignorant humans from the caves of their ancestors into the light of my knowledge. You are an obstacle in my path. Now feel the pain of this dog's bite!'

Amird raised his hands above his shoulders and threw his head back. His eyes rolled and his hands sparked and crackled. Crimson flame sprang once more from his hands and spread across his body. Within seconds he was a living flame. He lowered his eyes and glared at Awoi.

'Die, and pester me no further,' snarled Amird.

The fire sprang once more from his form and engulfed Awoi. Yet again the pulse of green power surrounded the kneeling Awoi and channeled the flames to either side of his body. Amird cursed his brother's name and advanced.

The red flame beat against the green wall and Awoi sweated from exertion. Amird bent low as he approached his brother and grasped the hilt of one of the soldier's discarded swords. Instantly the blade grew red hot and burst into flame. As he marched into proximity with the pulsating green wall, Amird slashed at it with the fiery sword. Each time he slammed the blade into the wall, Awoi clenched his teeth and winced from the pressure. Amird laughed and taunted his brother.

'You cannot hold forever, dear brother,' snarled Amird. 'You will gulp your last breath of Avra's sweat air when you can hold no longer!'

Amird doubled his efforts with the blade. He channeled most of the power of the flame into its razor edge. Each successive crash of the blade weakened the green sphere holding Awoi. Sweat covered the Guide and his breathing became labored.

'Amird, think on what you do,' gasped Awoi. 'You will forever be separated from our Master. What you do here today cannot be undone.'

'Avra is no Master of mine!' raged Amird 'He is weak and powerless, unwilling to force men to worship him. I, however, will force them. I have no intention of what I do here today ever being undone, even by Avra himself!'

The blade sparked and hissed, glowing with the fury of its owner. It crashed down once more into Awoi's protection, and rent a large gash in the wall. Amird howled in delight and his wild red eyes glared at his brother. Awoi begged him one last time.

'Show me mercy, dear brother.' cried Awoi.

The fiery blade leapt into the air and arced down on the prostrate Seraph. Awoi lunged up and out from the path of the blade, the troop leader's cudgel grasped firmly in his right hand. Amird's stroke missed its center mark but found Awoi's left shoulder and cut deeply into his arm. Awoi rose and the cudgel whipped into the back of Amird's skull with a loud 'thunk'. The scarlet flames vanished and Amird slumped to the ground unconscious. Awoi screamed in pain and staggered forward, falling to the ground. Blood sprang from his open wounds and spilled onto the dusty street. Awoi slipped into unconsciousness.

When Awoi awoke he was uncertain how much time had passed. The city was deathly quiet. Amird lay in the same position on the street, a small trickle of blood drying around his nose. The troop was gone and none of the city's inhabitants were visible. The Guide cried out for help, but none was forthcoming. He rose and walked to his brother's body, clenching his teeth and holding his aching shoulder. Awoi felt unsteady on his feet and blood still seeped from the deep wound. He knelt over his brother. Amird's body was warm. He lived.

Suddenly, an arrow crashed off the pavement beside him. Awoi leapt to his feet and called upon his spirit to protect him. A feeble, ragged wall of green light sprang up around him. He was in no shape to defend himself. He could not stand a second assault by Amird's mercenaries. He turned and looked at his brother one last time then fled from the city.

Awoi wandered north, using his skill in the wilderness to cover his tracks. He was losing far too much blood and was incredibly weak. Fever set in and along with it delirium. He wandered for days eating when he could. Days turned into weeks and his fever grew. Awoi knew not where he was or where he was going. The days and nights grew colder and the Seraph feared for his life.

One evening he climbed a steep ridgeline and the stress of the climb was too much for him. He fell to the ground unconscious. When he awoke, he started in fear. Silhouetted above him in the moonlight was a large bear. Awoi tried desperately to protect himself, but he was too disoriented and weak. He scrambled backward, shouting and flailing his arms. A kindly voice called out to him.

'Awoi. Be not afraid.'

Gretcha stepped forward and removed the animal skins she wore to fend off the coming winter.

'It is I, Gretcha. Have no fear. I will take care of you.'

Awoi felt relief flood his body. The savior became the saved. Gretcha's voice was the most beautiful sound he ever heard, his beacon in a storm of confusion. After weeks of struggle he finally relaxed. Awoi drifted back into a restful unconsciousness.

'I believed I lost you. When you didn't return within the year I knew something was wrong. You are a man of honor, and your word is your bond. Sleep now, Awoi the True. I will make you whole again.'

Gretcha stripped the bearskin from her torso and wrapped Awoi in its warmth. She scooped the Seraph up in her powerful arms and marched north toward their cabin.

For four weeks the giant maiden cared for the Guide. His fever rose in the first week but eventually broke and his faculties were returned to him. His shoulder was badly wounded. Gretcha bathed the wound daily and the gash closed and healed. However, the Guide was not able to raise his arm and it was all but useless to him.

Gretcha left everyday to pick mountain berries and occasionally hunt for game. Awoi grew to realize his deep love for the Zodrian princess. Her spirit was pure and her love immeasurable. She harbored no hatred or desire for vengeance even though she was so mistreated. Gretcha truly was a beautiful heart.

Awoi's health slowly returned, but his spirit remained weak. He was sure another encounter with his brother would result in death. Gretcha convinced him to stay hidden in the mountains and return to full strength before he left to try council once more. Two years passed. This time however, it was Gretcha who provided protection and sustenance.

One day in the early spring a hunched back old beggar struggled up the slopes toward their cabin.

'Hello, in the cabin,' called the beggar. 'Please spare a bite for an old man.'

Gretcha turned to Awoi.

'I will offer him some assistance, dear one,' stated the woman.

'Hold a moment,' said Awoi, 'I will go.'

Awoi exited the cabin as the old man entered the clearing.

'I saw smoke from your fireplace, friend,' said the beggar. 'I hoped to find someone of a giving nature and a kindly disposition.'

'You have, my friend,' began Awoi, 'We cannot offer much, but be welcome and we will share all that we possess. So as it should be with all Avra's creations.'

'So as it should be,' returned the old man.

Gretcha stepped from the cabin. Her powerful stride and large size startled the man.

'Be not afraid, good man,' said Awoi. 'Gretcha is of the kindliest nature and sweetest disposition of any being. Her size may intimidate you, but her heart is full of goodness.'

The old man recovered quickly and turned to the maiden.

'I was taken aback for I judged only a hermit or outcast like myself lived so far from all other mortal beings. I startled to see another step from such a small dwelling.'

'Ha,' laughed Gretcha smiling to Awoi. 'You are correct on both counts. A hermit and his devoted outcast live here together. That we found each other is a miracle.'

'We cheerfully offer you food and a warm place on the floor to sleep, but possess little more. Perhaps you desire someone to talk to as well? We are experts at listening to what troubles others,' said Awoi staring hard into the old man's eyes.

'A bite of food and a friend for conversation would be wonderful in these trying times,' stated the old man.

'I'm afraid we only have berries and some tubers to eat,' said Gretcha. 'I intended to hunt today.'

'Gretcha, my dear, we must offer our guest better than tubers and berries. If you intended to hunt, please go. I will hear our friend's story and perhaps render some comfort.'

Gretcha smiled and nodded. She entered the cabin and retrieved a short bow and small quiver filled with stone tipped arrows. Awoi smiled at her approvingly.

'Good hunting, my princess.'

Gretcha smiled and sprang down the path into the wilds of the Northern Mountains. After she was gone for a long moment, Awoi turned back to the old man.

'It's pure joy to spend time with someone so open and honest about her emotions,' reflected Awoi.

'She appears to be a remarkable woman,' said the old man.

'Honesty is a rare commodity these days. The world moves in a direction I do not favor,' stated Awoi.

'The world is what it is and we must shape ourselves around it, or it around ourselves,' replied the old man.

Awoi smiled and sighed. He placed himself across from the old man in the clearing.

'My world would be joyous once more if I truly believed you came here for council and assistance, my brother. But alas, I feel in my heart it is not the case.'

'Your heart leads you truly. I seek neither advice nor council from you,' growled Amird.

'You anger because I see through your ruse,' laughed Awoi. 'The guise of an old beggar does not suit you. You manipulate your appearance, but cannot change your true nature in the spirit world. I see your churning maelstrom there.'

'You are too proud, Awoi! You mock me and act above temptation. But we are not so unlike you and I,' barked Amird. 'I see that you too fall for the temptations of this world.'

Awoi stared at his brother with a puzzled expression on his face. Amird's anger turned to amusement.

'You mean to say the beast has not told you?' smirked Amird. 'She is with child you fool. You who are so observant. You missed that which is right in front of your nose. I saw it clearly as she stepped from the cabin. Its lifeforce is strong, like that of no other human. Half Seraph and half human. Perhaps when you are gone I will raise it as my own and make it one of my generals. It is the least an uncle can do.'

'You can raise nothing, for nothing grows under the whip of your oppression,' yelled Awoi. 'You know nothing of beauty or love, compassion or truth. Gretcha has lived on this world only a short time, yet she knows more of these things than you in your millennia of existence.

'Avra created us apart from men. It is true our spirits are different from those of men, but the Creator put us on this world in the bodies of men. Gretcha is no temptation because our bond is true. You live in lies, subjugating all into forced existence with you. Step into the light of truth and the world will show you what a beautiful place it is.'

'I care not for beauty you fool. I crave power. Beauty is a nuisance to production.'

'The butterfly is beautiful yet helps produce the sweet apple.' said Awoi.

'The hornet cares not for its looks and performs the same task. Yet, the hornet rules through pain.' came Amird's reply.

Awoi lowered his head and sighed.

'I grow tired, brother. I must rest. I'll not allow you to harm me. We were created with the same stroke of the painter's brush. Our powers are matched. To undo one is to undo both. Please leave me in peace.'

'It is true we were created together and our powers were matched. However, you live begging your existence off Avra and I surpass him, deriving my power from an ancient, darker source.'

Amird pulled a scimitar from the folds of his cloak. Flame leapt from it and the blade smoldered and sputtered. He cackled as he moved toward his brother.

'The last time I only crippled you. Now I will finish you!'

Amird slowly circled Awoi, sensing his power. Awoi raised his right hand and the green glowing light appeared around it. As Amird lunged toward him, Awoi spun away. The light spread from his palm and formed a wall between the men. Amird's sword met the wall and sprang back.

'I see you recovered a good deal of strength since our last meeting. No matter. I not only recovered, but have grown.'

Amird's eyes rolled into his head and he mumbled an incantation. His body burst into flames and the flaming sword he carried increased its intensity. Amird reached into the folds of his cloak and produced a second fiery blade identical to the first. He crouched low then sprang toward Awoi. The dual blades churned the air as the evil Seraph slashed again and again at his brother's shield. Awoi stood in his green shell, hand raised. He softly whispered prayers to his Lord, begging for the redemption of his brother. Sweat trickled down Awoi's forehead and each slash weakened the intensity of the glowing orb.

Gretcha was not too distant from the cabin when she heard voices rise. She returned and heard all. The woman crept to a spot behind a large woodpile. The revelation of her pregnancy angered her. Gretcha wished to tell Awoi under the right circumstances, and the opportunity had not shown itself. For him to find out in this manner was wrong. She watched the battle progress, stunned by the power of these two beings.

Amird pressed on with his assault. His supply of energy appeared limitless. As Awoi weakened, Amird sensed that weakness and doubled his efforts. The green wall thinned into tatters. Amird attacked the openings and each slash widened the gaps. Gretcha concluded two things. Awoi became vulnerable and would accept defeat rather than harm his brother.

The massive woman stood and grasped the handle of her ax, lodged deeply in a nearby tree stump. Amird eyed the green orb for a place to penetrate. Gretcha confidently stepped up behind him. Awoi stood covered in sweat, shoulders hunched, eyes closed, muttering prayers of protection. As Gretcha raised the ax the father of her unborn child looked up and their eyes met. He smiled softly to her.

'Goodbye, my love. We are done on this world.' whispered Awoi.

Amird howled in triumph. Both blades plunged through rents in the shield and found their mark in Awoi's stomach. The green orb immediately dissipated and Awoi fell to his knees, arms and head thrown back. Amird laughed, channeling more fire down the wicked blades as he twisted them in his brother's stomach.

'Nooooo!' screamed Gretcha.

Her broad-bladed ax crashed down on Amird. Gretcha's strength was that of five men and the ax penetrated the protective flame. It lodged in Amird's shoulder. The Deceiver cried out in pain.

Instantly, Awoi's head and arms sprang forward. His powerful hands locked onto his brother's wrists. Awoi wrenched himself forward, ramming the twin blades further through his own body. The brothers' faces nearly touched. Amird writhed in agony attempting to break free. Awoi stared deeply into his brother's eyes.

'It is time to return to our Master. Repent, and even now he will accept you to his bosom.' whispered Awoi.

'Never!' slavered Amird.

Awoi closed his eyes but his iron grip held Amird close. Awoi's body convulsed. Amird fought to break free. A green wall of light burst from Awoi and swept across Amird, scouring him of the scarlet flame and pushing it high into the sky. The bodies of both guides fell to the ground lifeless.

The flawless wall of green light pushed the sparking, leaping clutter of crimson flame toward the heavens. The auras hesitated in the sky, struggling with one another. The red fire abruptly fled from the green wall and fell to the earth, dissipating over many leagues of mountainous terrain. The green light stopped and swirled once below the clouds, then formed an orb and shot upward, out of Gretcha's sight and into the heavens.

Gretcha fell to her knees and buried her face in her hands. She sobbed for hours at the loss of her love. The brothers' bodies lay on the earth as they were created, side-by-side. The giant woman stood and walked to the fallen pair. She bent low and grasped the handle of her ax, wrenching it from the shoulder of Amird's body. She hefted the fallen Seraph onto her shoulders and carried him to the pile of readied timber. Somberly she tossed his body amidst the dried logs and set the entire pile aflame. Immediately the woodpile turned into an inferno, its dry timber hissing and popping in the cool mountain air.

Gretcha returned to her fallen hero. Awoi's body lay in a deepening pool of blood. The earth around the clearing was stained crimson. Gretcha gently lifted Awoi's body and carried it to their cabin. She stripped him naked and cleansed the blood from his body. She retrieved a white linen cloth and carefully wrapped him. Next, she set out for the mountain's summit. It towered over the other mountains in the Northern Range. When she neared the top, the Zodrian princess sought out a suitable cave.

The wind and snow whipped her face as she sealed the cave's mouth and departed the mountainside. She descended the mountain and traveled west, eager never to stare upon its horrible slopes again. The slopes that held the resting place of the only human who knew her for what she was, a lovely creation of her honored God."

"So Amird was destroyed that day, along with Awoi," stated Kael.

"His physical body was destroyed that day," returned Teeg, "but we are not solely made of skin and bone. Amird was a creature of special ability. He was a favored servant of Avra. When we leave the body we inhabit in this world, our spirit returns to the force from where it came."

"Where is that?" asked Kael.

"Why to Avra himself," said Teeg. "All men are creations of Avra. Avra takes them back to him when they pass over."

"So Awoi and Amird returned to the spirit pool of Avra?" asked Kael.

"Awoi returned, that is true, but Amird chose a different path," replied Teeg. "Amird's soul was meant to go to Avra, but since he rejected his Creator, his soul was banished from Avra's presence. The evil Seraph was without life and a physical presence on this world. His spirit however, was able to survive. He has lost command of it but it does exist.

"Amird's spirit is sustained by Chaos. The ever present power that tries to breakdown and corrupt all good that we accomplish on this world. Amird has become the essence of evil. His spirit moves through the lifeforce pool as a chaotic wave. He is unable to maintain his spiritual presence for long but he affects all he touches. Those who are strong in spirit are unaffected when he passes. Temptations and notions of evil are brushed away as soon as they arrive. Their strength resists the suggestions from Amird and Chaos.

"The weak willed fall easily into the trap of Amird. They are like the flame of a candle when Amird's spirit blows by them. Bending this way and that to his every whim, easily controlled. He sways them with unfulfilled dreams, lusts and passions.

"Amird believes that since he is able to affect others with the powers of Chaos, he will become all-powerful if he plunges the world into Chaos. If you are turned to the ways of Amird, you will help bring about more Chaos and evil. The more Chaos and evil in the world, the stronger Amird's foothold here becomes. One day he intends to use his army to challenge the Creator himself, stripping away control of this world."

"But ... but he's dead," said Kael.

"Again I ask you to put aside your notions of life and death. Amird lost his physical self on this world, but his presence and power are as great as ever. He influences minds and directs events through his hold over thousands of servants. Those who worship him, do anything for him," stated Teeg.

"What of Awoi? Why didn't his spirit stay to combat Amird?" questioned Kael.

"Awoi and Amird's time on this world ended. Awoi understood that and happily departed to join his Creator. Amird is the one who refused to obey."

"Well, what happened to Gretcha and her child?" asked Kael.

"Gretcha traveled west. She remained in the mountains and their foothills for fear of encountering people. Finally, she came to the lands where the Northern Mountains met the Western range. It was uninhabited, rough terrain. Ice cold winters full of stinging sleet, and summers as hot as any on this world. Gretcha built a cabin in the cradle of these mountain ranges. There she lived happily and gave birth to a child she named Hrafnu. Old tongue for 'memories'."

"Hrafnu the giant?" said Kael.

"Hrafnu the founder of the Keltaran," corrected Teeg.

"But he was evil," stated Kael. "He killed hundreds of Zodrians in the first Keltar wars. He started the feud with our people a thousand years ago. He was an outlaw."

"He was a man, Kael, just like any other. He dreamed dreams and held passions. All stories have two sides. A great ruler learns to hear both of those sides in order to make an informed decision."

"That may be fine for a great ruler, but this innkeeper's son is confident who the enemy is. The Keltaran are the enemy."

"As you wish," smiled Teeg.

"So Granu is a Keltaran prince?" questioned Kael.

"Yes," replied Teeg. "A direct descendant of Hrafnu."

The old Elf paused and considered if he should say more.

"That's enough for you to absorb in one day," said Teeg. "Perhaps we might resume this chat later and I'll answer more of your questions."

"No, please. I have so many," protested Kael desperately. "Like, why has my father been called to Zodra? What's this nonsense of calling him a duke? I need answers."

"And so you shall receive them. Slowly Kael, slowly. Be patient," replied Teeg.

"I'm tired of being patient. Too much has happened and too little explained!"

The door opened and in walked Ader.

"Tired of being patient. Is that what I heard?" laughed Ader. "I'm not sure you're aware of what true patience is, Kael. You worry over hours while I have sometimes waited centuries for a particular occurrence to take place. Relax, in due time all will be explained."

"I'm not sure I'm ready for due time," frowned Kael.

"You may not be ready, but we are," said Ader shaking his head. "No matter, we're off to Zodra in the morning. For now, I ask you to remain in your quarters and get a good night's rest. Will you do as I request?"

Kael lowered his head and stared at his shoes.

"Yes," he replied.

CHAPTER 11: DOWN THE WINDING STAIRCASE

Kael slept poorly. Questions ran through his mind. The encounter with Methra haunted him. What did he do, and could he do it again? Part of him was fascinated with the power he displayed. Part of him was terrified. He had felt so exhausted, frightened and angry all at once. He had let himself go, let his mind takeover. He was desperate to protect Ader, end the insanity of the last two days, and hurt the creature that killed his brother. These desires welled up and created whatever it was he hurled at the Malveel.

He tossed and turned in the night. When he felt he was finally giving in to sleep, the diffused light of the morning forest filtered into his room. Knowing he was about to embark on an exciting journey made him even more restless. Kael rose and dressed. He opened his door a sliver and stole a glance down the hallway. Perhaps he might find more answers this morning.

Eirtwin stood in the observatory staring East over the treetops of the Nagur as the rising sun splashed the canopy with light. Kael hesitated on the final stair of the tower and contemplated his decision to come here. After all, it may be the only solitary moment the queen was allowed each and every day.

"Why do you falter, Kael Brelgson?" asked the queen without turning.

"I ... I beg your pardon. I realized I might be interrupting a special time for you," replied Kael.

"You simply exchange one special moment for another," smiled the queen. "What is it that I can do for you? You knew I was here, so I assume you didn't come for the view."

"I," Kael hesitated. "I'm feeling a bit lost."

"And you hoped I might be able to help you find your 'way' so to speak?" asked Queen Eirtwin.

"Exactly," answered Kael.

"Ask me what you will, Kael, and if I am able to adequately answer your questions, I shall."

"Is my father really a duke?" asked Kael.

"Yes, and a rather silly first question I might add," laughed Eirtwin. "When the prince heir of the kingdom in question announces the exact thing in a room crowded with people, you can believe it to be true."

"I suppose," smiled Kael "Then how about the prince heir. Is he really the next King of Zodra?"

"Another silly question," frowned Eirtwin. "You must open your eyes and begin to see and believe that which is around you. I referred to Manfir as the prince heir in this conversation. Would I now say he was not?"

"No, I suppose not," mumbled Kael.

"Time is a rare commodity. Think before you speak," advised Eirtwin. "One day people will be counting on you to act quickly and decisively. Stumbling around before getting to the point might be disastrous."

"Yes, I'll try," said Kael searching his mind for the true questions it held. "Why did Ader and Manfir appear to me in disguise for so many years?"

"The forces of Chaos search for ways to destroy Ader and those who serve with him. Ader disguises his true nature to protect his allies from reprisal. This in turn protects mere acquaintances. Contact by anyone with Ader places their life in danger," stated the queen.

"Am I a mere acquaintance of Ader's, or am I an ally with more at stake?" asked Kael.

"You're learning," smiled Eirtwin. "I was vague. Presenting you with two alternatives to your question in hopes that you assumed the most favorable. Most would love to make a leap in logic that all that occurred is happenstance, bad luck. Those with insight and a keen intellect will pursue extra avenues and ferret out the truth.

"Yes, you are an ally. Yes, you have much more at stake, although, if you search yourself, you know this to be true. Your performance against Methra bears that out."

"If I'm an ally, then who is the enemy? Ader makes alliances with some strange folk. The prince of Keltar stood in your halls and nothing was done because of Ader," stated Kael.

"The prince of Keltar is an ally, or at least we believe him to be at this point," said Eirtwin. "Often, you must go on faith. Believe that which seems unbelievable."

"I would like to stick with what Manfir believes. Keltaran are evil. They are butchers. I'm unwilling to trust any of them," snapped Kael.

"Have you ever met a Keltaran before?" asked Eirtwin.

"Well, no." replied the boy.

"Again I caution you to be open and mindful of all that occurs around you. Past prejudices hold no bearing upon the future. To dismiss the help of a man such as Granu, without first interacting with and understanding him, is folly. You may destroy the most important alliance you enjoy," stated Eirtwin.

"What of your alliances? Why do the Elves side with Ader?" asked Kael.

"There is a distinct difference between good and evil. It is true that we are not from this world. However, it is also true that we are born from the same Creator. We are all servants of Avra and must fight against the forces of Chaos wherever we find them."

"What do you mean you're not from this world?" questioned Kael.

"We are from a different ... existence. We are just visitors here. Granted, we've dwelt here a long, long time, but we still consider ourselves visitors," smiled Eirtwin.

Kael looked puzzled.

"Avra's creation is not limited to this one world," continued Eirtwin. "He is the Master and Creator of many places. There exist levels of beings all fashioned for a different purpose. This world is but one of his realms."

"You are from a different ... world?" asked Kael.

The queen smiled and waved a hand out over the Nagur.

"Not a world as this is, but a world nonetheless."

Kael paused and reflected on all he learned. Avra, worlds created, races formed and evil rising. These issues were far too weighty for a boy from a small, backwards village. Forces greater than he imagined were at play. He wished to go back to his old life if he might, one day hoping to run "The King's Service" and let his father retire.

"How does all of this connect with me?" asked Kael.

"I told you I would answer your questions. I also told you that time is a rare commodity and a leader must get to the heart of the matter expediently. I'm afraid your time is up," stated Eirtwin glancing over Kael's shoulder.

Kael turned to see Ader standing at the top of the stairs. The old man bowed to Eirtwin and glanced at Kael.

"What am I missing?" he asked.

"A brief lesson," answered Eirtwin.

"Of what or whom I wonder," frowned Ader.

"Do not fret, Lord Ader, your wishes are being kept," replied Eirtwin.

"It's time we left, Kael," said Ader. "The others rose and prepared their mounts. I must return you to your father and attend to some pressing business in Zodra. If you finished your enlightening lesson with her majesty, I would like you to accompany me to the stables."

Kael nodded and headed toward the stairs. On an impulse he spun and knelt before Queen Eirtwin softly taking her hand.

"Thank you for everything," said Kael. "Your attention comforts me in a troubling time."

"Your visit delights me," answered Eirtwin. "Take care on the road ahead."

Kael and the old trader descended the stairs and headed toward the stables. They walked along in silence and Kael stared ahead lost in thought.

"You seem preoccupied," commented Ader.

Kael walked on without responding.

"I said, you seem preoccupied," repeated Ader a bit louder.

Kael blinked and looked to the old man.

"Oh, I'm sorry. I wasn't paying attention. 'Preoocupied'? Oh, ah, yes I guess I am," shrugged Kael. "It's Queen Eirtwin. Every time we speak I find myself questioning whether I'm being the best person I can be. She makes me want to do great things."

"She affects quite a few people in that manner," smiled Ader. "A remarkable woman."

They proceeded down the hall and exited the palace into the stable yard. An unusual party was arrayed across the yard. Manfir stood close to the stables stroking the neck of his mighty black warhorse. Eidyn and Teeg stood in the center of the yard strapping pouches to the backs of a pair of white stallions. The horses were outfitted with neither saddle nor reins. Just a simple lead and a light riding cloth adorned the Elves' mounts. Kael barely noticed the large figure of Granu standing stone still in the shadows of a large apple tree. The giant wore his black robe with the hood pulled up and over his head. His face was barely visible in the darkness of the robe. In his hand, Granu carried his enormous walking staff. As Kael and Ader stepped from the doorway, Ader's big gray stallion and Kael's chestnut trotted from the stables and approached them.

"It seems your little mare chooses you, not you it," laughed Ader.

Kael smiled and patted the beautiful horse's head. The stable boys saddled the mare and Kael's pouches were resupplied. He turned and greeted Teeg and Eidyn.

"Good morning, Lord Teeg," bowed Kael. "Good morning, Prince Eidyn."

"Since we'll be traveling companions, Kael, I prefer we also try to be friends," said Eidyn. "Ader and my parents vouch for you, and that is all I need to know. Please forgive me for our initial meeting. I don't regret exercising my duty, but I do regret getting our relationship off on a bad note."

"No harm was done and no offense was taken my Lor... er, I mean Eidyn. With all of the terrible things that are happening, it made sense for you to question anyone you encountered," returned Kael.

"Exceptionally gracious of you," bowed Eidyn.

"I suggest we get on the road," stated Ader. "Events in Zodra are progressing too quickly for my taste."

Kael moved over to the chestnut and pulled himself up. The leather saddle creaked and the metal buckles clinked. He watched puzzled as Teeg and Eidyn turned to their mounts. The horses remained unsaddled. Eidyn gripped his stallion's mane and threw himself onto its back effortlessly and more importantly noiselessly. A stable boy approached the prince and handed over a longbow and soft deerskin quiver full of lethal looking arrows.

The Elven boy approached Lord Teeg as the old Elf looked his mount over. The boy cupped his hands, bracing them against a bent leg. Teeg glanced at the makeshift stirrup and laughed.

"Boy, I was jumping onto the back of a horse a hundred years before you were born!"

The old Elf grabbed the horse's mane and deftly threw himself onto its back. He chucked the stallion's flanks with his heels and it pranced about the stable yard. Granu slid from the shadows of the yard's edge and moved toward the group.

"Do you require a mount, Prince Granu?" offered Eidyn amiably.

From beneath the blackness of the hood, Kael heard the deep rumbling reply.

"No, thank you. I fear your delicate animals would have a difficult time bearing my weight."

Eidyn protested, but was silenced by a warning glance from Teeg.

"I did not mean to offend," continued Granu. "I'm quite used to walking and will not slow you."

A snort from near the stables turned all eyes. Manfir stood smirking at the Keltaran and shaking his head.

"Do you wish to add a comment, Zodrian?" asked the hooded giant.

Manfir smiled and mounted his warhorse.

"I wouldn't slow for you if you were sinking in quicksand," snarled Manfir.

"Nor I for you, Zodrian. I'm glad you found this opportune time to delay us with your musings," stated Granu flatly.

Manfir clenched his teeth and edged his armored horse toward the giant. Granu rose to his full height, gripping the center of his staff.

"The forces of Chaos mobilize around us," grumbled Ader to himself. "Am I not burdened enough without the worry of you feuding children?"

The old man ignored the warrior's protests, gathered his robes close and turned as Tarader approached him. The horse dropped to its knees and the old trader straddled its back. Immediately, Tarader rose and trotted from the yard into the palace grounds. Lord Teeg smiled and followed suit.

Eidyn and Kael glanced from one another to the pair of glaring warriors then back again. Eidyn shrugged and the two young men chucked the flanks of their mounts and trotted from the stable yard.

Within minutes they passed through the ring of Almar trees and moved out into the city of Luxlor. A moment later the hoof beats of Manfir's huge black stallion echoed from behind. Kael stole a glance over his shoulder. The Zodrian prince sat ramrod straight and fought hard to prevent the stallion from breaking into a run as the animal tried to keep pace with the long stride of the Keltaran monk beside it.

The city was just coming awake as the forest sun filtered down to its streets. An old Elf walked along the streets carrying a jug. He deftly poured a few drops of thick liquid from the jug into some of the glowing glass jars that hung from trees lining the street. Almost immediately, the warm green glow from the jars faded. Kael greeted the man cheerfully, and the Elf's drowsy eyes lit up as he recognized the group. He returned the greeting and fervently returned to his work, smiling and glancing over his shoulder at the departing group.

They slowly made their way through the Elven city. Manfir moved to the lead, followed by Ader, Teeg and Eidyn. Kael trailed behind the Elven prince and glanced over his shoulder to see the dark figure of Granu steadfastly bearing down on them from ten yards back. Kael knew immediately that the Keltaran wouldn't be left behind, no matter the pace. However, Granu's hooded presence silently pursuing him through the woods frightened Kael. The boy couldn't shake the image of death chasing him all the way to the Zodrian capital.

After some time they arrived at the Efer. Kael remembered Ader's words from their previous crossing. He scanned the woods and easily spied the figures of expertly camouflaged Elves. This time however, he kept his discovery to himself. Once again, Diom lay near a fallen log surrounded by shrubs. The lieutenant went overboard in his attempts to conceal himself. So many leaves and twigs were stuck to his body that Kael judged he looked like a crazed porcupine. The boy worked hard to suppress a smile but then felt shame. Because of Kael's pride, Diom might endanger himself.

"Fonra, remove those buckles from your shoes. They reflect even this dull light. I discovered you easily," called Eidyn. "And Diom, you look ridiculous! Return to the palace and get a day's rest. I can't afford to lose you, but obviously recent events impair your judgment. Ilan, command of the squad is yours."

Kael's shame doubled. They moved out of hearing range from the squad and Kael eased his mount alongside Eidyn's stallion.

"It's my fault," said Kael.

Eidyn surveyed the boy.

"A warrior is responsible for himself in all matters," stated Eidyn soberly. "Most important of these is his own death. Excuses for poor judgment don't return the dead to the living. You're no more to blame for Diom's mistake than the lamplighter we passed in the city. Only Diom can take responsibility for Diom's error.

He'll see that the training he received in concealment was adequate and he'll return to that training. He'll be a better soldier for having this lapse in judgment now, not when harm might come to him."

The pair trotted forward in silence. Kael wondered what punishment Diom might receive from General Chani when the Elf returned to the city. When he looked up once more, Eidyn was staring at him.

"I can't help but muse over our first meeting," Eidyn commented.

"What about?" said Kael.

"You may refuse to answer me if you wish, but I must know a few things. Don't misunderstand me, Kael. I'm not a vain man. However, I am a proud one. I take great pleasure in my skills. I work hard to perfect them. When you're the heir to the throne of a kingdom, others hold you to a higher standard. I hold myself to that standard. I must know how you detected me in the woods," said Eidyn.

Kael bit his lip while he mulled over the events in the woods two days previous.

"Well, it was just a feeling at first," began Kael. "I relaxed against the tree and let my mind search for the sound of the Efer. I knew it must be close, but heard nothing during my trek. The more I relaxed, the more I allowed my mind to search for the sound of the river. Just as I sensed the sound of rushing water, I heard a loud crunch.

"It frightened me. I panicked and desperately needed to know whether I tricked myself or not. I searched for the sound to prove it a mistake, but heard even more noise. It was definitely footsteps, so I rose and sprinted toward safety. I decided my best course lie toward the river. It provided a barrier to interpose between myself and my pursuers. At least it would channel them into a narrow space."

Eidyn furrowed his brow and stared at the ground sliding beneath them. Kael hoped his information helped but wasn't sure he answered Eidyn's question. The Elf turned once more.

"I hope I'm not too presumptuous, but you may encounter a similar event in the future and I wish to instruct you on some basic rules," said Eidyn.

"Please do," replied Kael, happy not to offend the Elf.

"First, you committed a terrible error heading toward the river. You're fleet of foot and agile. To keep to the path is to hand the enemy a map to your position. Once you decide to flee, escape and concealment should be your goal.

"There is no shame in running, Kael, there is only shame in being caught. You were unsure whether the enemy on your heels could outpace you. If he could, the path is to his advantage. There were no obstacles to impede him. If he couldn't, he need only outlast you. No matter how far you outstrip him, you'll need to slow or stop. The enemy knows exactly where you are, the end of the path.

"Your enemy chose to pursue you. Therefore, you can assume he was confident he could kill or subdue you. If that were the case, your best option is a trek through the woods. You were unaware of your enemy's size, but again you can assume he was larger than you if he chose to pursue you. Therefore, the dense woods create a greater hindrance to your foe than to you. Also, your small stature increases the opportunity for concealment. The fox must give chase a hundred times before he finally lands a hare. Remember Kael, chance often favors the hare."

"Your instruction resounds with truth, noble prince," interrupted Granu, "but in reality the pursuer was neither larger than the boy nor confident he could kill Kael. By your own words you were puzzled by the boy's abilities. Perhaps Kael's best option was to turn and cut you down with the blade he possessed."

Eidyn reined in his stallion and swung to face the trailing giant. The remainder of the group halted as well. The Elven prince stared placidly at the dark figure and tension filled the forest air. Suddenly, Eidyn smiled and laughed.

"Quite true, my Keltaran friend. But at the time, that was my little secret!"

The company roared with approval and even Manfir cracked a smile as Granu threw a forearm across his chest and bowed deeply to the Elven prince. Eidyn spun his stallion around and winked at Kael as he headed back down the forest path.

"Lesson number two, Kael," whispered Eidyn. "Duty often compels us to attempt the foolhardy."

CHAPTER 12: THE COMFORT OF SLEEP

They cantered on. Kael grew weary. The monotony of the forest took its toll on the senses and lulled him toward sleep. Once more Eidyn moved close to Kael and spoke softly.

"Your earlier description puzzles me more than ever," said Eidyn.

"Why?" asked Kael.

"You say that you started to the sound of a large snap. Is that accurate?" questioned Eidyn.

"Um .. I ..er, know you are proud of your abilities Eidyn, but you must have erred and stepped on some dried twigs," apologized Kael.

Eidyn smiled and shook his head.

"No, my friend. It is you who are mistaken. I want to learn the technique you used in the woods the other day. It's not just any man that is able to hear an Elf shod in deerskin, tiptoeing on tree moss!"

"Tree moss," repeated Kael. "That's impossible."

"Impossible or not, I took one step onto a patch of tree moss and you heard it," laughed Eidyn.

"How could I hear tree moss? There is nothing to hear," said Kael.

Ader slowed and glanced over his shoulder. He frowned at the two men.

"If you look closely, Kael Brelgson, tree moss is made of tiny leaves and stalks. It's a plant like any other," stated Ader.

"Are you telling me I heard the snapping of tiny ..."

"I'm telling you that tree moss is a plant like any other. That's all I'm telling you. Conclude what you will."

Kael rode on lost in thought. He knew he was gifted with special abilities. He knew no one else in Kelky could do some of the things he could. But he never really put any of them to the test like he did on his first trip out of that sleepy village. He wondered if Eidyn toyed with him. Possibly a little embarrassment would help square them up after Kael almost eluded the captain of the guard. There was no way he heard the agile Elven prince lightly stepping on tree moss over fifty yards from his position in a dense forest.

All he did was let his mind reach out. He was tired and extremely relaxed against the tree trunk, just as he was now. Slumped in the saddle, plodding along in this monotonous forest. Watching tree after tree pass by with no change in their height or color. He let his mind once again reach out and explore the sounds around him. The buzzing of insects, the drip of sap, the calls of the birds and scurrying of small animal life.

Suddenly, he was aware of a soft padding sound, matching the pace of his group. Possibly more than one! He panicked and glanced at Eidyn. The Elven prince appeared unaware of anything. What should he do? Was it his imagination this time? All of the previous talk put him on edge. What should he do?

Ader slid in beside him. He looked hard into Kael's eyes.

"Let it go, Kael," said his friend, good old Jasper. "You are well taken care of here. Try to relax. That's it. Just drift off in the saddle. The chestnut will not let you fall."

Ader's words lifted a weight from Kael's shoulders. He felt comfort wash over him and the exhaustion from the last several days seep into his body. Within seconds, Kael was fast asleep in the saddle.

The chestnut jostled along the road to Kelky. Kael woke and blinked as the bright rays of the sun momentarily blinded him. The group was moving along the Great Northern trade route.

"That must have been restful," commented Teeg. "I never sleep in the saddle. I like to pay attention to what is going on around me."

"It ... just hit me," mumbled Kael.

"I'm sure it was better for you to sleep that leg of the trip," stated Teeg nodding behind the group.

Kael turned to see the edge of the Nagur retreating in the distance. Turning back, he pursed his lips and nodded his agreement. A wave of emotion caught him as they rode on. He fought with sorrow, anger and confusion. What was happening? He slowed the pace of the chestnut and let the group move slowly ahead of him. He was afraid he might cry and didn't want these hardened warriors to see him. As the imposing figure of Granu strode past the chestnut, Kael heard a deep chanting prayer from beneath the cowl.

After several moments gathering his thoughts and dealing with his pain, Kael looked up and nudged the chestnut to fall back in pace with the group. They crested a small hill in the road and to the East Kael recognized the grove of trees he and Aemmon used for shelter. Kael realized it was his last opportunity and reined his mount in on the crest of the hill. Slowly he turned to say goodbye to Aemmon. In the distance, passing clouds threw shadows across the edge of the ancient wood.

"Goodbye, Aemmon. I'm sorry," whispered Kael.

A splash of sunlight caught a small portion of the wood's edge. Kael's keen eyes picked out the tiny image of two figures moving along the forest's border. The distance was too great to determine specifics, but the smaller of the two wore dazzling white. The sun radiated off the clothes. The second, larger figure, wore the colors of the wood, dressed in browns and greens. The beam of sunlight was lost to the clouds and in an instant the figures were gone. Kael spun. All save Granu moved down off the crest of the hill.

"Prince Granu!" called Kael in panic.

The enormous figure wheeled and spun his staff in front of him. In two huge steps he stood next to Kael's mount.

"There on the edge of the wood. Do you see them?" asked Kael.

The Keltaran prince threw back the cowl of his cloak and scanned the horizon.

"What is it you look for, Kael Brelgson?" replied Granu.

The remainder of the party reined in at the bottom of the slope. They were too distant to hear the conversation between Kael and Granu. The giant shielded his eyes from the bright sun.

"On the edge of the wood, I saw two figures. They strolled along, slowly heading west."

"Were they human?" asked Granu.

"Yes."

"Did you recognize them?"

"No, they were too distant."

"Elves guarding the wood?"

"No, they were much too large."

"Foolhardy woodcutters?"

"The large one dressed as such, but the other wore a dazzling white robe."

"Unusual for somebody traveling through the woods. You can tell me nothing more?" questioned Granu.

"Nothing," stated Kael.

The giant stroked the stubble on his huge chin and stared toward the woods.

"I leave it to you, Kael Brelgson. If you wish to inform the remainder of the party, you may do so. However, know that the Elves are bound to king and country. They may wish to turn back and investigate. My gut tells me we should make haste. Events are speeding forward."

Kael stared at the Keltaran trying to determine a course of action. Certainly what he saw was important. The Elves would return, and the party would be severely delayed. Many other Elves patrolled the woods now. If these two travelers were up to no good, they would be confronted by General Chani's roving squads. Granu's stone face broke into a smile.

"The first of many important decisions you'll face, I wager," rumbled the giant.

Kael let a faint smile pass across his face.

"We better move on," said the boy.

They moved down the hill to the remainder of their group and fell into their usual positions.

"What was the delay?" questioned Manfir.

"Nothing," stated Kael. "I believed I saw something near the edge of the woods. However, upon further inspection, it may be a trick of the light on the trees."

Manfir narrowed his eyes at Granu.

"No matter," said Ader. "Remain vigilant Kael for you and Prince Eidyn possess the finest eyes in the group."

Teeg harrumphed and turned his stallion to move down the path.

"That is behind our estimable Master of Spies," added Ader smiling.

Teeg turned in the saddle, grinned and nodded in Ader's direction.

"So kind of you to say about such an old man," exclaimed Teeg.

The group moved north once more and the late afternoon slipped away from them. The land turned from the breaks and gullies Kael and Aemmon scrambled through, to the low rolling hills of the farmlands around Kelky. Eidyn fell in beside Kael.

"Did something alarm you in the woods?" asked Eidyn.

"Yes, I guess something did," answered Kael. "But I was overwrought and obviously needed rest."

Eidyn glanced toward Ader and Manfir riding twenty paces ahead.

"I ... I feel uneasy as well," stated Eidyn in a low voice. "I can't place it, but sense we're being watched."

Kael was uneasy ever since he heard noises in the woods and saw the two figures at its edge. He believed they weren't following his group, but the sensation of being watched was stronger than ever.

"I know Ader told us not to worry, but I'll strike a deal with you," said Kael.

"What do you propose?" responded Eidyn.

"We'll both stay as alert as possible. I'll share my impressions and feelings about the situation if you promise the same," offered Kael.

"Absolutely," came the reply.

CHAPTER 13: THE KING'S SERVICE

The journey dragged on for several more hours. In the distance the snowy peaks of the Zorim Mountains were set ablaze by the golden rays of the setting sun. Kael determined they never looked more beautiful.

"The King's Service" stood like a sentinel in the shadows of the early evening. A faint light glowed in the kitchen windows. The weary party led their horses into the stable yard and dismounted. As Kael wondered who burned a candle in the supposedly abandoned inn, the kitchen door swung open.

"Who goes there?" growled a shaky, old voice. "State your business or face my steel!"

A figure, backlit from the lighting in the kitchen, stood brandishing a cutlass.

"Hamly! Is that you?" called Kael.

The figure stepped from the threshold into the light of the moon. Kael immediately recognized the old man his father often employed around the inn to perform odd jobs and quick fixes. Hamly squinted in the moonlight, temporarily blinded as he stepped from the light in the kitchen.

"Kael?" said Hamly. "Cefiz told me you'd arrive soon. And who's that you travel with?"

"Weary wayfarers, sergeant," interrupted Manfir. "It's been a long ride. Did you keep the stove alit and the larder stocked?"

"I .. uh... Master Rin," mumbled Hamly as his eyes shot from face to face, "and Jasper, what a surprise to see you in Kael's company."

" 'Manfir' is sufficient sergeant. The boy learned many things on his recent trip. The least of which is my name and heritage. I take it Brelg ordered you to stay here and watch the inn?" said Manfir.

"I was told to remain at the inn and expect the return of Kael. I'm to report any unusual activity in the area," replied Hamly.

"And what is your report?" asked Manfir.

"No report. The area has been unusually quiet of late," stated Hamly.

"Are the stables stocked for our mounts?" inquired Manfir.

"Of course, sire," replied Hamly. "Flair!"

A boy a season or two younger than Kael sprang from behind the kitchen door. Kael recognized him from the village.

"Yes, granddad," said the boy eyeing the group nervously.

"Please, open the stables for these gentlemen, and see to their mounts," requested Hamly. "Leave Master Ader's giant thundercloud to itself, he'll find a stall to his liking. Also, take care with Prince Manfir's battle mount, he's high spirited."

The boy moved toward the stables. Upon hearing Manfir's title his eyes went wide and he bowed deeply, backing toward the structure.

"I'm sure such an able bodied young man can handle him," said Manfir, smiling at the boy.

As Flair backed into the shadows around the stable door he bumped into the huge figure of Granu. The boy let out a sharp squeak and nearly stumbled to the ground. Granu deftly caught the lad with his free hand and lifted him upright. Flair looked in awe over his shoulder at the giant and nearly stumbled into the stable door. The exhausted group let out a collective laugh that eased the tension.

Flair opened the stable door and returned to retrieve Manfir's mount. The black stallion was indeed proving difficult to lead and Flair struggled. Kael felt sympathy for Flair's predicament. He led his chestnut over to the Elves' stallions, gathered their leads and led them to the stables. Old habits were hard to break.

"Thank you," whispered Flair as Kael passed him.

"It's not a problem," smiled Kael.

When the young men returned from housing the horses, the entire group moved toward the kitchen. Teeg spun toward Kael and bowed with a flourish.

"May these weary travelers enjoy the hospitality of your wonderful home, Master Kael," smiled the old Elf.

Kael shot a glance at Hamly. He felt like a visitor here.

"It's the least I ... we can do after all of the things you've done for me," returned Kael.

Teeg threw an arm around Kael's shoulder and led him into the brightly lit kitchen.

"I was hoping you'd say that," replied Teeg laughing.

Once they entered the kitchen, Hamly immediately set about preparing dinner. It was late and Kael wanted to crawl into his old bed, but his hunger was too great. Flair flitted about the kitchen retrieving plates and cups as if he regularly worked at "The King's Service". Kael noted how the boy worked quickly and efficiently. However, Flair never took one eye off the imposing figure of Granu standing quietly in the kitchen's corner. Kael prayed that he didn't look as silly and fearful as the boy he now watched.

Within a half an hour Hamly produced a meat stew simmering in an iron pot and the group moved into the inn's common room. The largest table in the room was set with plates, cutlery and large pewter mugs. Ader dropped into the chair at the head of the table and removed his dusty shoes. Manfir wandered toward the front of the inn and surveyed the street outside. The remainder of the party took places around the old wooden table and discussed their trip. Manfir returned to the group to find the only available seat to Granu's right. He stopped and stood glaring at the giant. The group fell silent.

The giant's hood was thrown back and he was slowly spooning the hot stew into his mouth. His head never rose as he looked to his plate and methodically chewed the steaming food. Manfir stared down at the empty chair next to the Keltaran prince. Granu slowly munched his food.

"Sit down, son of Macin." stated Granu icily. "It's been a long journey and we're weary. None here are in the mood for your grandstanding. It's time to eat."

The room was filled with tension as Flair backed through the kitchen doorway carrying a tray loaded with brimming ale mugs.

"I'm also hungry and tired, but I'd as soon stand here all night than share a table with a murdering Keltaran," snapped Manfir.

Flair turned and inched toward the table striving mightily to balance the tray. Granu sprung to his feet sending his chair skittering across the stone floor and into the legs of poor Flair.

"Murderer? Who swept from the hills outside Volar and killed nine of our boys tending to a herd of goats?" boomed Granu as he turned on Manfir, fists clenched. "What kind of people lure another man's flock of sheep from their pastures, then beat and stone the man when he journeys to retrieve them? It is the Zodrians who journey further and further into our mountains and demand it as their own! Hrafnu moved us from you to save us from your aggression! Amird founded your nation on hatred and greed, and hatred and greed drive it!"

"How dare you accuse us," shouted Manfir. "I've seen your handiwork myself. Villages in the borderlands completely destroyed. The people beheaded and butchered. Men, women and children! Their bodies desecrated. The banners of the Keltar staked through them and flying from the buildings you didn't burn to the ground."

"You lie," growled Granu.

Manfir's body tensed and the giant moved forward.

"ENOUGH!"

Ader rose from his head position at the table. He moved to a spot beside the warriors. Kael's skin tingled as a faint green glow shimmered and spread around the old trader.

"I remind you of your pledges, gentlemen. I cannot allow this distraction to upset our plans. You must learn to deal with your prejudices and hatred. We can't afford a split in our group. Manfir, move to my place at the table's head and eat," said Ader.

"I can't sit ..," began Manfir.

"YOU CAN AND YOU WILL, ZODRIAN PRINCE!" commanded Ader. "Once again you forget your pledge. I had so little trouble from you over the years that I may have grown soft.

"Now! Now is the time when Amird's forces coalesce against us. And you, Keltaran Lord. You believe the Zodrians to be your enemy so completely that you blind yourself to the real danger. Now is when we must unite. Now, or you hold no hope and this world will be lost to darkness and Chaos!"

Flair's concentration was so utterly focused on the tray he balanced that he missed the entire outburst. Smiling he finally managed to reach the table and set the tray down. Ader quickly snatched two mugs from the tray and forced them into the hands of the northern princes. The Elves took his lead and helped themselves, passing a tankard to Kael. Ader lifted a mug into the air.

"To unity and brotherhood," shouted Ader.

The Elves raised their mugs high. Kael remembered something his father said when facing a particularly difficult chore.

"To a beginning of the end," mumbled Kael raising his mug.

Granu's deep, dark eyes looked into Kael's.

"To a beginning of the end," boomed Granu raising his tankard.

Manfir's eyes focused on Kael, and the hard lines of his face became even harder. He nodded toward the boy then raised the mug to his lips and emptied it. The others at the table followed suit and Manfir walked to the head chair and sat.

The meal lasted a full hour as Flair brought food and drink from the kitchen. Manfir would periodically rise from the table and go to the inn's windows. Ader stopped telling him not to worry.

It was getting late and the food and dishes disappeared. The ale produced a definite sluggishness in the travelers and exhaustion came down hard on Kael. Ader rose from his seat next to Granu and addressed the party.

"A long road lies ahead of us. I suggest you gentlemen find sleeping quarters and rest. We must maintain our wits as we journey ahead."

Teeg rose and moved to the stairway, followed by Eidyn. The Elves lightly ascended the flight without making a sound. Manfir mumbled something about checking the mounts and left through the kitchen. Granu rose and turned to Kael.

"I thank you for your hospitality, Kael Brelgson," smiled the giant. "You make your household proud."

He spun and climbed the stairway aided by his staff. Ader smiled to Kael.

"You forge an important alliance with the giant, whether you want it or not," stated the Seraph.

"An alliance against what?" questioned Kael. "I used to think he was what we needed alliances against, and now I'm not so sure."

"The world is a complicated place. It'll get much more complicated in the days and months to come. Just remember to trust in your instincts and do what you believe is right," said Ader. "It'll be nice to sleep in your old bed, eh?"

Kael smiled and nodded as Flair stepped from the kitchen with a broom. Hamly shuffled forward with a mop and bucket and the pair cleaned the floor. Ader turned and disappeared up the stairs. Kael thought it would be wonderful to crawl into his bed, but memories of Aemmon flashed into his mind. The room held only sorrow and guilt for him now. He walked toward Flair and put a hand on the boy's shoulder.

"You look exhausted," smiled Kael. "Let me do that. Everyone keeps praising me for my hospitality and I've yet to lift a finger."

The boy smiled wearily and looked to his grandfather.

"Well, the lad still has quite a few dishes to clean," said Hamly. "Six hands are better than four."

Flair handed the broom to Kael and disappeared through the doorway. Kael swept the floor as he heard the squeaky well pump in the kitchen. Hamly set his bucket down and mopped up. Kael wondered if Brelg struck a deal with the old man. Hamly was often around the inn doing odd jobs, but Brelg never employed him full time. The old man lived out west of the village on a small horse ranch. Hamly's daughter and son-in-law lived there as well with a brood of children. Kael saw Flair from time to time as the boy entered the village to pick up supplies. Kael wondered why the old man accepted the job. Hamly's ranch was small, but it produced exceptional livestock. Kael was sure Hamly didn't need the coin.

"Master Hamly, what did my father say when he left?" asked Kael.

Hamly stopped his mopping and looked to Kael. He carefully considered his answer.

"Ah, he needed to depart hastily and wanted a reliable soul to keep things here in order," started Hamly. "Cefiz followed 'im, so he called fer me."

"Don't you have responsibilities at the ranch?" asked Kael.

"Nothin' my son-in-law can't handle," stated the old man, then he glanced at the kitchen door. "But if he gets the call, it'll be upta the boy."

"The call?" questioned Kael.

Hamly looked down at the mop and shuffled his feet a bit. He struggled with his words and finally looked Kael hard in the eyes.

"The prince said you were told, but how much, I dunno," Hamly said half to himself and half to Kael.

"Well, I know my father was called to the capital for a meeting of the court," interjected Kael. "Trouble has begun, and we must put an end to it."

"Yes, rightly so," returned Hamly, his eyes narrowing.

"I ... I've a role to play," offered Kael. "Ader ... told me."

The old man's face relaxed and he smiled at Kael.

"Yeah, I've always known ya did. All these years I wondered and I guess it's come to it. Well, I served and am proud of it," said Hamly.

"Yes, uh, yes you did, and I suppose they'll reward you for it," prompted Kael.

"Never wanted any reward!" said Hamly quickly. "It was my duty."

"Duty?" asked Kael.

"Those of us who chose to come with Brelg. We were still in the Guard ya know. Fact is, I feel like I've always been in the Guard."

Kael's mind raced. What was the old man talking about? Hamly in the Guard? Was he referring to the Zodrian Guard. Certainly the old man meant the town's militia.

"Yes, you serve well. Um, the militia is helpful here," said Kael. "For what little they do in this quiet town."

"Ha! No militia in the South is built around such well trained military men," laughed the old man. "Why, when we first started to filter into Kelky, we took orders from that buffoon, Ipson the tanner. He was the captain of the militia then. The man didn't know which end of a sword to hold. At first, he was annoyed by your dad's suggestions, but after awhile he came around. You just can't ignore good sense."

"My father's suggestions?" questioned Kael.

Hamly laughed and shook his head.

"Good old Brelg. At first he played it real slow. He'd make a suggestion 'bout drillin' or trainin' and just act as if he stumbled onto a good idea. Ipson thanked him for the idea then acted like it were his own. Ya see, we intended to make the militia of Kelky stronger. It was important to get the village defended proper. We couldn't wait till the locals figured it out.

"Brelg sorta pushed it along. Pretty soon we were a pretty snappy unit. We weren't able to train much cause we were supposed to fit in. Act like regular folks. After a couple of years, more 'n half the militia were old Guardsmen. Some o' the locals couldn't keep up with our trainin' once Brelg got control from Ipson. Sakes, even Ipson himself dropped out, claimin' the tannery needed more attention.

"Don't get me wrong. Ipson was a good man, tryin' ta defend his village. But we held more important things in mind and he was kinda in the way. Some o' the villagers turned out to be real good men. Men you could rely on. Men you wouldn't mind havin' next ta ya in a tough scrape. Brelg hated ta do it but secrecy was important."

"Hated to do what?" asked Kael.

Once again a broad smile crept across the old man's face.

"We drummed some of 'em out, a course," replied Hamly. "Durin' trainin' some 'accidents' happened. A course nobody got truly, truly hurt, but a couple of the good uns needed to get a few bones broken. Once they was down, well, Brelg made sure they couldn't catch up to our trainin'. Some of them boys might have left the Hold as tops in their recruiting class if they were chosen for the Guard. Poor souls don't even know it. They got hurt and just stopped playin' soldier with the militia."

"The Hold? What Hold?" asked Kael.

"Why, the HOLD boy. The military barracks in the capital," said Hamly as he caught Kael's bewildered expression. "Where every recruit for the Zodrian Guard goes through trainin'."

Kael looked down at his broom in confusion. The old man's eyes narrowed and he shook his head.

"The ale must be workin' on your head, boy. The Hold in Zodra, where me an' yer dad were master drill sergeants."

"Drill sergeant!" exclaimed Kael.

Hamly stepped back with a mixture of surprise and shame in his eyes.

"Course I was a drill sergeant!" exclaimed the old man. "I know ya think awful highly of yer dad, but truth be told, I'm the one who taught 'im everything he knows. I'm the one who trained 'im and recognized the potential right away. I'm as proud as a father could be over Brelg Kelson!"

"Oh, that's right, you recruited him," said Kael, fishing for more.

"No, no. I never recruited him. He just showed up one day at the Hold. Demanded to be put to the test. We'll put anyone to the test if they ask. Most don't pass, and those that do normally don't make it past the first month of trainin'. Good old Brelg. Just a skinny lad, full of heart. He wouldn't say die. He passed the test and we found 'im a bunk. The other drill sergeants took one look at the lad and said he'd never make it. I bet a month's wages he would. I've always been pretty good at pickin' out the ones that'll make it. Somethin' in his eyes told me he would.

"Wish I'd never made that bet though. They was hard on the recruits that just showed up and took the test. They wanted you to be called like most of the Guard is. You know, a king's messenger arrives in the village and reads a couple of names. They hear about you, or a town elder nominates you. When you just show up, some figure you're a bit full of yourself and need to be knocked down a few pegs. It was worse for your old dad. He wasn't even from a village. Just a lad from the wilderness. He'd come from near the border. Livin' with his family by the seat of his pants. Tryin' to scratch out a livin' raisin' goats and sheep, while tryin' to avoid Keltaran raiders and Ulrog packs.

"Well, the other drill sergeants made that bet with me and figured it was easy money. Yer dad proved 'em wrong. They made it double worse for 'im while tryin' to take my months pay, but he would have none of it. He stuck it out all right."

"That's ... ah, when they made him a drill sergeant right?" questioned Kael.

"Sakes no, Kael! Yer old man was just a green recruit. He handled the toughest trainin' we threw at 'im but he still never seen a real battle. It was right to the front lines for Brelg and the rest of his group. He marched off to the Scythtar. I knew I wouldn't see many of those boys again, I never do. But somethin' told me I'd see Brelg.

"Three years later there he was, a sergeant of his own battle squad. He was covered in scars and looked twenty years older, but it was him. Walked right up to me on the trainin' yard and saluted. Told me I'd saved his life more 'n once out there. Ya know, things I'd taught him an the like. They'd promoted him in the field for saving the day not once or twice, but three times. Turned the tide with some pretty quick thinkin' when the Ulrog pushed the Guard up against the wall.

"He asked me to show him one more thing, how to teach. He'd become a leader of men, a natural commander, who men readily followed. He led by example, and those quick enough to keep up with him learned a great deal, but those who struggled got left behind. He realized he was wastin' good men by not teachin' them what he knew. The command assigned him to the Hold for a year to get a break. He was goin' at it pretty hard over those last three years.

"Well, I took him under my wing and taught him how to talk to the men. How ya get somethin' into their heads so it becomes an instinct. How ya get other men in a squad to know what yer thinkin' and suddenly yer all actin' as one. Brelg learned quickly. He transformed into one of our best drill instructors. Quite a few men thanked Brelg for savin' their lives with the trainin' he beat into them. Those were the days. The Hold churned out the best soldiers the world ever seen. Course, the General Staff needed somebody like Brelg on the front lines. After a year he returned to the Scythtar."

The old man's eyes took on a faraway look as his memory traveled back to the Northern Mountains. Kael was desperate to keep Hamly talking.

"When did my father meet my mother?" asked Kael.

Hamly came back to the present.

"Yanwin," sighed the old man. "A man couldn't ask for a better woman."

"Indeed, a fine woman," came a voice from the stairway.

Kael turned to see Teeg standing at the bottom of the stairs.

"Ya startled me, Master Teeg," said Hamly. "I didn't hear ya approach."

"Ah," smiled Teeg. "That is reassuring. If you did, I would be quite cross with myself."

"Were you there long?" asked Kael, his face reddened.

"Long enough to realize our good man Hamly took you places you've not been before."

Hamly took on a puzzled expression and Kael protested but Teeg cut him off.

"All things will be revealed shortly, Kael. It's of no great import that you learn some of them now. Lord Ader and I struggled over this for quite some time. Therefore, since you discover a few things about your father, I'll reveal your mother's story," said Teeg nodding to Hamly. "With Master Hamly's permission of course."

"By all means, Lord Teeg. It's yer job ta know these things anyhow. That way the boy will get the story straight," smiled Hamly as he turned to the kitchen. "I'll make sure the lad has done all right in the kitchen."

CHAPTER 14: THE ORPHAN'S WIDOW

Teeg strolled over to the table and pulled a seat out for Kael. Kael placed his broom against the table and sat down. The Elf lord slid into a chair across from the boy and crossed his hands.

"He's right you know. It is my business to know all things. If it's been written, spoken or even whispered, I'll eventually know it. I pride myself on the lengths I'll go to in order to obtain information," smirked Teeg.

The old Elf stared into Kael's eyes as if he were working on a puzzle. Slowly and deliberately he talked, delivering his monologue to an audience of one. He never looked for approval or reaction. He just stated the facts.

"Your mother Yanwin was the second child of King Macin and Queen Tay of Zodra," began Teeg.

Kael started in his seat. Teeg ignored the boy's reaction and the story unfolded:

A more beautiful woman in the kingdom you couldn't find. Talented in every way. Music, archery, poetry, Yanwin mastered all. King Macin was well aware of his daughter's gifts and smiled to himself realizing her worth. Many nobles and lords throughout the land desired to marry his daughter or arrange a marriage between Yanwin and their sons. Macin explored these proposals in search of the most advantageous. At first, the king suggested some of the more interesting proposals to his daughter. Princess Yanwin wasn't interested in marriage. She searched for more than becoming the symbol of connection and power these nobles wanted of her. Willful and stubborn, she refused the marriages her parents arranged.

To avoid the daily pleas and threats of her father, Yanwin broke from decorum. She spent long hours out of the castle, touring the city. She visited the market and often ventured out to the fields surrounding the city. She quickly became a favorite of the people with her easy manner and charm.

One day she strolled into the Guardian's Hold with her ladies in waiting and offered assistance. The offer was accepted and it became a daily routine for the princess and her entourage.

Often, the ladies broke from their chores to watch the recruits train. This was quite scandalous in the court of King Macin. Yanwin, however, didn't care about the conjecture of others. She arrived at the Hold one day to find Sergeant Brelg putting the trainees through their paces.

Brelg owned the reputation as a fine tactician who survived three tours of duty along the Scythtar. Battle plans and tactics fascinated the princess. The stories of the heroes of the Guard intrigued her. She boldly queried the sergeant on these subjects when he possessed a free moment. He readily answered any and all questions. She left the Hold invigorated by their interaction.

That evening Yanwin lay awake thinking about her day. This Sergeant Brelg was brilliant, a man of true intellect behind a rough exterior. He was so unlike the flippant barons and dukes her father paraded before her. Brelg didn't look on her as a princess of Zodra, but a woman of intelligence. He treated her as an equal. She asked questions and he answered in carefully prepared statements, not glossy, dismissive quips.

Yanwin returned day after day to the Hold. Sometimes, Brelg straightforwardly told her he was unable to answer her questions. The demands of the day were too great. Yanwin admired his honesty and sense of duty. She was a beautiful young woman and a princess of the realm. Many men tried to win her favor. Sergeant Brelg never once flirted with her. He remained respectful at all times.

However, through their conversations she noted he was keenly interested in her intellect. Her questions became more complex. Her knowledge of historic battles, both big and small, grew. After one particularly frustrating day with the recruits, Brelg told Yanwin she was his best student, one of the only compliments he ever paid her.

A petty handmaiden in Yanwin's entourage resented the princess. She went to the king with the story of the budding romance. Little did Macin know, the two were already deeply in love. He ordered Brelg and his troop out to the borderlands. The recruits weren't ready and Brelg knew it. He informed his superiors. They never responded.

The night before their departure, Yanwin went to the Hold. She was barred from entry in the evening, but noticed a familiar young man. Brelg had often told her to pay attention to this recruit during training exercises. Sergeant Brelg believed that one day this boy, Cefiz, would be a great warrior.

Once again Kael's expression showed shock. Cefiz? A great warrior? The boy fought hard not to question that description. He knew it might take the old Elf down a different path. He was interested in his mother and father and Teeg was giving him exactly what he wanted. The Elf lord paused for a moment to allow Kael to digest the news then pressed on.

Cefiz's prowess with weaponry was unequaled in his class. His strength and stamina surpassed by no one. His individual decision making during exercises was usually first rate. Brelg planned to make the young man the leader of his recruit class, but the boy lacked the humility to be a leader. His refusal to accept his losses and regroup to fight again was his downfall. Once a mistake was made in the field, there was no second chance. You were dead.

Cefiz's inflated ego extended beyond the training grounds. He saw the princess arrive day after day at the Hold. He noted how her attention never wavered from his every move. He convinced himself that she became infatuated with him.

At first he tried to dismiss the concept. Princess Yanwin was a noble and he just a soldier. All in the Capital knew of Macin's desire to marry off his daughter in alliance with one of the powerful houses of the court. However, as each day passed, the young man let the seed of possibility grow in his heart. He watched her as intently as she watched him. It was true that she was beautiful, but she was so much more.

The princess treated all as her equal. A kind word was always on her lips. She visited the wounded, freshly returned from the front, and offered them words of encouragement and praise. She read the lists of the dead as they were posted each month and she visited all of the relatives' homes. She was overwhelmingly compassionate to her father's subjects. Cefiz's own belief in her feelings for him and Yanwin's attributes tricked the man in love with her.

That night, on the eve of his departure to almost certain death, Cefiz was elated to see the princess approach him outside the gates of the Hold. Sorrow and fear hovered in her eyes and the young man mistakenly believed they were there for him. He would leave with the knowledge of her love in his heart.

How bitter a pill it must have been when the beautiful young woman begged the recruit to bring a message to Brelg? How he must have wondered what a fair maiden such as Yanwin could possibly see in the dour, scar covered veteran? However, the encounter saved many lives, for it was then and there that the young lieutenant decided never to let his ego get the better of him again.

Cefiz swallowed that pride and bade Yanwin wait outside. He marched to Brelg's chambers and knocked on the door. Brelg called for him to enter. The sergeant's eyes scanned communiqués spread across his desk.

'What is it, lieutenant?' questioned Brelg.

The lieutenant cleared his throat.

'Princess Yanwin awaits you at the gate, sergeant.'

Brelg looked up and eyed the young man.

'It's after hours,' stated Brelg in surprise. 'Training has concluded for the day. The princess is well aware that no ladies are allowed within the confines of the Hold after sundown.'

'That is why she stopped me at the gate and asked me to be her messenger,' stated Cefiz.

Brelg blinked and stared at Cefiz.

'What is she thinking?' said Brelg. 'It's the eve of our departure to battle. I ... I don't have time for this. Men's lives are at stake. I have work that cannot be interrupted. I need the men to commit to one another or all is lost. Please tell the princess I'm occupied.'

Cefiz nodded and turned to leave, then abruptly halted.

'May I speak freely, sergeant?' asked Cefiz.

Brelg felt relieved. Finally, this young man was about to step up and offer his leadership of the unit.

'Of course Cefiz, I desire your input on these matters,' said Brelg.

'To send the princess away would crush her. She defies her father, nay her king, to speak with you this evening. She risks all for you and you talk of battle plans. Have you no soul, no heart?' Cefiz's words spilled from his mouth.

Brelg stood at his desk stunned for several minutes. This arrogant young man dared to talk to him of heart and soul. What did this fool know of it? Princess Yanwin was the daughter of the king. Brelg was a loyal subject. He simply served her and complied to his office as a sergeant at arms when he hosted her at the Hold.

Yet Cefiz was right. Brelg's heart knew otherwise. He longed for her arrival everyday. Even on the days he knew they wouldn't find a chance to speak. If she was late, he fretted. When she was moody and dejected, he wondered what troubled her, but dare never ask for fear that she think he overstepped his bounds. He stood at his desk amazed at how foolish he was. As he assessed his feelings he was unable to deny them any longer. He loved this woman more deeply than he could ever imagine. His emotions in those few moments ranged from outrage to joy to intense sorrow, for he knew what must be done.

'Cefiz, I will let your comment stand as is. You're highly agitated. We leave for the borderlands in the morning. It's to be expected. However, my private affairs are just that, mine. No more will be said of this. Whatever the princess's interest in me, it's the diversion of a foolish young woman who bridles at the attempts of her parents to find her a suitable match. Return to the gate and inform the princess I'm unable to see her.'

'Sir, if you weren't my commander I'd call you out for that insult to a lady. The only foolish act she commits is to trust her heart to an ass!' spluttered Cefiz.

'Cefiz! Hold your tongue.... I can't .... It can never be. I.... I'm beneath her,' muttered Brelg shaking his head.

'Sir, go to her. Don't fear for this unit. I swear to you here and now it will hold. I'll do everything in my power to make this the best group of fighting men in the corps. At the very least say goodbye to her,' said Cefiz softening his tone.

Brelg flashed a weak smile and clasped Cefiz on the shoulder.

'I'm sure you will. I'm sure you will,' said Brelg and he stepped from the room.

Brelg's unit was sent to the heart of the fighting. Their tour of duty was to last a year but inexplicably stretched to two years. Ulrog raids from the Northern Mountains became more frequent. Ulrog raiders found a path through the mountains around Tar Hdjmir as well. Brelg's unit ranged the entire northern border. Often they went days without sleep. The fighting was endless. Their fame grew.

After two years Brelg was recalled to Zodra. As his troop journeyed home news of their return spread through the countryside. Town after town lined their streets to cheer the heroes. Flowers were strewn before the haggard soldiers as they plodded south toward Zodra. Zodra's people offered praise and thanks.

However, Zodra's king held no such favor in his heart. Macin's jealously and hatred of Brelg grew. The king ordered Brelg's troop to halt far from the city and return to the Hold only after nightfall as the capital slept. Brelg became furious. Many fine young men died defending the lands of Macin and his people and others in his unit bore the scars of battle.

Brelg refused to allow Macin to steal the glory his men. Half a day's journey from Zodra, Brelg set up camp for himself and sent his troop at double-time toward the city. His men arrived at the height of the afternoon market to their hero's welcome. The people cheered. Confetti flooded the streets. Children dashed amongst the warriors as they marched to the Hold. The men received the adulation of their people. Adulation they richly deserved.

Cefiz remained outside the city with Brelg until nightfall. The two soldiers silently packed their gear, entered the city and journeyed through the silent streets of Zodra to the Hold. In the shadows of the fortress, a unit of the king's guard milled about laughing and jesting. As the pair of warriors approached, the king's guard abruptly silenced and fell into formation. A short distance away Yanwin stepped from behind a pillar into the moonlight.

Brelg halted three yards from the unit, turned and bowed low to the lady. Yanwin smiled and nodded in reply. The troop edged forward. A leader separated from the others.

'In the name of King Macin I am to take you into custody Sergeant Brelg. You are to ...'

Cefiz stepped in front of Brelg. Two years of pitched battle against the worst nightmares Amird conjured had turned the eager recruit into a hardened and haggard warrior. Death hovered in his eyes. He drew two short swords and moved on the unit of ten men. They nervously backed away.

'Cefiz, save your steel for the Ulrog,' Brelg said calmly and fell in amidst the king's guard. 'Now is not the time to start spilling our brother's blood.'

The sergeant turned back to the lady.

'It is late and the streets of Zodra are no place for one so fair. My homecoming is complete,' smiled Brelg to Yanwin. He looked to the leader of the troop. 'Put your men to good use, soldier. Escort the Lady Yanwin back to the palace. You will find me in the Hold in the morning. Your duty can wait until then.'

In the morning Brelg woke in a cell in the bowels of the Hold. At noon he was led before King Macin and his court. A hum passed through the marbled room as Brelg and his guard approached the throne and bowed. The lords and ladies, dukes and duchesses averted their eyes as Brelg surveyed each side of the room.

'Sergeant Brelg, you deliberately disobeyed an order from your king. Explain yourself,' demanded Macin.

'Your highness, my men were in the throws of battle for two long years. To deny them the gratitude of their people is wrong,' stated Brelg.

'Do you dare call your king mistaken to his face?' growled Macin sweeping his arm across the room. 'In front of his entire court?'

'To his face, in front of this entire room or completely alone, I'll tell the man who issued that order he's an ass!' retorted Brelg. 'I'm a leader of men. However I cause disfavor, my men shouldn't suffer for it.'

A murmur swept the crowd and a few braves souls called out, 'Here! Here!'

'Silence!' shouted Macin. 'Brelg, you're far to valuable to the defense of this land and its people to throw into my dungeons for your arrogance and insubordination. You will, however, be confined to your quarters in the Hold for two months time. Upon which, your unit will return to his majesty's defense of the borderlands.'

The Duke of Ymril, whose nephew was a guard in Brelg's unit, immediately stood and interrupted.

'But your highness, that is far short of the usual furlough for returning guardsmen. These young men spent twice the time of any other unit at the front. Perhaps your highness might reconsider,' said Ymril.

'Two months time, Brelg!' shouted Macin flashing an icy glare at Ymril. 'And my dear duke, please return to your properties in the South on the morrow. Your quarters in the palace are dearly in need of repair and I cannot spare the room to accommodate you and your family!'

The Duke clenched his teeth and bowed to the king.

'With your majesty's permission, I'll take my leave to prepare the journey. Under such time constraints it will prove a difficult undertaking,' said Ymril.

'Permission granted!' snapped Macin. 'I grow weary. That will conclude the court's business for the day. Guards, you may escort Sergeant Brelg back to his quarters in the Hold and see that he complies with my wishes. The rest of you are dismissed.'

A close watch was kept over Brelg during his confinement. He was unable to leave his quarters and strictly forbidden from receiving visitors. His troops were allowed to return to their homes for several weeks. Cefiz remained at the Hold. He was allowed to meet with Brelg daily, often to bring him meals and consult concerning the troops' training. Unbeknownst to Macin or the guards, Cefiz also carried a steady correspondence between the sergeant and Princess Yanwin.

After two months time, Brelg's unit was ordered to the Pass of Hrafnu. More Ulrog than usual were traveling along the mountains through Keltaran held territory. Hunting Ulrog in Keltaran land was the most dangerous assignment a troop of Guardians had ever undertaken.

Macin ordered the unit to depart the Hold before sunrise on the morning of their sixtieth day in Zodra. The streets were empty as the unit's horses trotted toward the gates of the city. The only sound heard in the crisp morning air was the clink of their armor and weapons. A lone, hooded figure stood next to the empty guard post.

Brelg halted and dismounted. Yanwin threw back her hood and warmly embraced him. Soft words were spoken, and the soldier dropped to his knees. The princess bent low and cradled his head in her arms, whispering in his ear. Brelg took her hand and rising he kissed it. With a nod from Yanwin, he bowed, spun on his heels and mounted his steed. Smiling to her, he ordered the troop to move out.

Three years the unit roamed the borderlands protecting the villages and towns speckling the countryside. Their legend grew.

The king constantly ordered Brelg's unit into harm's way. The General Staff didn't countermand his orders, but they revolted in other ways. Brelg's units were replenished with the best recruits when their ranks thinned. Brelg was never without supplies of food and weaponry. Every village they passed took them into their homes and sat the troops at their tables. Often villages low on supplies shared the best of what they possessed with the unit. Blacksmiths and their apprentices put aside their plowshares and horseshoes and worked through the night repairing armor and short sword.

Macin never recognized the service or accomplishments of Brelg's unit. The heralds of Zodra never spoke of them, often reporting the happenings of other's lesser accomplishments. But in the pubs and marketplaces, stories of Brelg's unit circulated daily. The people referred to the unit as 'The Orphans.'

Yanwin wrote to Brelg when she was able. A training sergeant at the Hold was a comrade with Brelg. This sergeant made sure Yanwin received the names of recruits being sent to join the Orphans. These recruits never left the Hold without a packet of orders for Brelg and a letter from Yanwin.

After three years of constant battle, 'The Orphans' lost three quarters of its original members to injury or death, but Brelg and Cefiz held on, pulling victory from defeat on a daily basis. Yanwin grew in the favor of the people and when she traveled through the city a throng appeared around her coach. The princess tried to keep her life private, but the citizens of Zodra followed her every move. She took to wearing veils in order to protect her identity. The people referred to her as 'The Orphan's Widow.'

King Macin believed he squashed his daughter's interest in Brelg. He grew out of touch with the people. His confidants were unwilling to present stories about the people's love for his daughter and Brelg's unit.

However, one sly young colonel focused his eye on a seat amongst the General Staff. Colonel Ellow looked hard to find leverage with the king. He took charge of the supply line to the fighting troops and proved adept at confiscating food and supplies from the citizens of Zodra. Often, more supplies were confiscated than made it to the troops. Rumors surfaced surrounding a black market in goods and weapons.

Ellow's chance came one day when a young recruit was being prepped to join Brelg's unit. A change was to be made in the location of the supply wagons bound for 'The Orphans.' Ellow demanded to see the recruit's orders so he could change the rendezvous location. The colonel found a letter from Yanwin to Brelg bundled within the orders. Upon reading the letter, Ellow concocted his scheme.

Normally, Macin only met with members of the General Staff. Ellow knew this, but was desperate to present the letter to Macin himself. Ellow was clever and a student of the human mind. He spent his entire career intimidating and seducing. He knew the king would be in a rage. People were most open to the power of suggestion when they were at emotional extremes. Colonel Ellow sent a messenger to the king requesting a private audience, in order to 'protect the honor and reputation of the king and his illustrious family.'

After King Macin held court the following day, he sent a runner to Ellow's offices in the rundown river wharf area of the city. Ellow arrived at the court and was led before the king. Macin sat alone in his chambers.

'Colonel Ellow is it?' asked the king.

'Yes, your Royal Highness. At your service,' stated Ellow bowing deeply.

'Why is it I have never heard of you, Ellow? I'm aware of most of the officers under my command,' questioned Macin.

'I reside in what is commonly referred to as the "underbelly" of the city, your Highness,' snarled Ellow. 'The wharves.'

Macin's expression grew grave. Ellow quickly realized his mistake and his voice became like honey.

'A position as crucial as any in the defense of our great land, your highness. A position I possessed the honor of filling for seven years now. I toil long hours making sure the troops on the front lines receive the best, my lord. After all, it is they who put their lives on the line everyday to protect us from the beast and his bloodthirsty servants.'

'Yes. The troops are the backbone of this great land. Without their sacrifice there is no nation, no people and no king,' stated Macin.

There was a pause as Macin reflected on his troops and their sacrifice. Ellow sensed uneasiness in the king and a profound sorrow. This was not the emotion he desired. Snap decisions were never made by the depressed. He needed to ignite this prideful man.

'Of course, no nation or people amounts to anything without a powerful man of purpose at the helm. A man willing to force his people to make sacrifices for the good of their land. A king willing to make hard choices,' said Ellow.

'Quite true, Ellow. Quite true,' stated Macin snapping out of his reflection.

'Surely your highness is aware that his troops, those men sacrificing for his kingdom, don't always receive the best of these lands,' queried Ellow.

'Yes, these rumors filter back to me from the front. The General Staff hear complaints about the rations and armaments the front-line obtains. The Staff theorize that unscrupulous haulers create a black market for these goods. They have yet to act on their speculation.'

'Your Majesty, I'm involved deeply in the heart of these matters and duty compels me to break the news to your royal highness,' Ellow paused. 'The people are to blame. They lose faith. They no longer support our defense freely. They must be coerced, nay begged for the supplies of that defense.'

'What are you saying?' demanded Macin. 'The people aren't ignorant. They understand the import of their cooperation with the king's collectors. To shun the troops is tantamount to treason!'

'It's my duty to my brothers-in-arms that I reveal this devastating news to your highness. My commanders in your

General Staff shun admitting the weakness of the people. They wish you to believe they will stamp out this so-called "black market". Meanwhile our troops go hungry in the field. I don't blame the Staff your highness. They're soldiers, unused to dealing with matters such as this. War is their game, but wars are lost in the farm fields and warehouses of a great nation. A little waste here, a little hoarding there and a weak soldier with an empty belly dies from the chop of an Ulrog cleaver.

'Your Highness must create a new position on the General Staff. Someone must be commissioned to rally the people to the cause of the nation's defense. Someone must be given even greater power to commandeer the goods and services required for our troops needs. Someone must be able to contract trustworthy haulers and draftsmen to bring this lifeblood to our fighting force,' Ellow's voice grew. 'Someone with the unique knowledge to handle it properly.'

Macin sat quietly contemplating Ellow's words as the colonel constructed his plan. However, upon the last statement the king flashed a wicked smile.

'Colonel, your attempts to beguile your king for your own benefit, although quite bold, were also severely ill-advised. When my guards relieve you of your duty and throw you in...'

'Your highness, I beg you forgive me for the interruption,' stammered Ellow. 'As proof of my loyalty and trustworthiness, I present you with this document.'

Ellow held Yanwin's letter before him and bowed low. Macin was enraged by the interruption but paused to stare at the letter.

'Others continue the masquerade. Others let you believe what you will and continue to feed you lies. I must do their bidding. I'm a mere colonel serving generals. But when the honor of my king and his family is at stake, I can be silent no longer.' continued Ellow.

Macin slid the letter from the colonel's hand and slowly opened it. His hands shook as he read the contents. His eyes filled with rage as he read words of encouragement, loyalty and love. As he read, Ellow talked on.

'Brelg's unit is funneled the best and the brightest. Other troops go hungry while his unit feasts. Others make due with staff or bow, while his unit gleams with sword and armor. He boasts that he's subject to no king's laws or power by naming his unit "The Orphans", no authority binds him. The people pick up this name and chant it in the streets.

'He lays claim to your daughter by dubbing her "The Orphan's Widow", and the people chant that as well. Have you seen her? She hides her face behind a veil for the shame of it. Yet all along there are these letters. Letters that enthrall her to this man. Your General Staff knew of and sanctioned these activities. They care not for the honor of my king and his family.'

Macin's face boiled red. He crushed the letter, writhing in spastic contortions. Spinning around he foamed and spit as he shouted into the hallway.

'Summon the General Staff!'

Macin turned wild eyed to Ellow.

"You shall have your post on the General Staff,' he whispered. "And I shall have Brelg's head.'

Brelg's unit was recalled from the field. Messengers were sent to demand their return to Zodra within the month. The General Staff was subject to massive changes. Many of the top generals lost their positions and were imprisoned in the dungeons of the Hold. Others swore their loyalty to King Macin but lost his favor and their advice was shunned. Ellow became one of the king's most trusted advisors and he spread his lies about the faith of the people. The black market flourished as Ellow put greater and greater demands upon the people to produce. Crooked draftsmen drove their wagons out of the city in groups of ten or twenty bound for the troops in the North. Often, half of that group arrived, as the remainder filtered back into towns and villages, reselling goods to the people at inflated prices. Ellow's power and wealth grew.

Macin's anger smoldered as he awaited the return of Brelg. He opened his eyes to his city and didn't like what he saw. The people were jubilant with the news of the imminent return of their heroes. For weeks the women of the city gathered flowers and garland to decorate the gates. As the return of Brelg and his unit approached, an air of celebration swept the city.

On the thirtieth day since the decree went out for the return of 'The Orphans', Macin sat on his throne surrounded by his personal guard and the General Staff.

'Disobeyed,' shouted Macin, 'by my own soldiers. An example must be made of this unit!'

'Most assuredly, your highness. This type of thing will only spread,' commented General Ellow.

'Your highness,' said General Harnax. 'It's a long journey from the foothills around Tar Hdjmir to the halls of mighty Zodra. Scouts report heavy fighting in that area. A journey of that kind might take a good deal of time.'

Harnax was one of the few generals to retain his seat upon the General Staff. He commanded the Guard's cavalry units and was considered a brilliant tactician. Harnax was also renown as an honest man. If he believed a fight was unwinnable, he said so. However, if pressed to join that fight he complied immediately. His loyalty to king and country went unquestioned.

'Brelg's unit rides the best horse flesh I could find for them,' whined Ellow. 'He should've been here days ago!'

'My colleague has never joined the enemy in battle,' stated Harnax as he shot Ellow a withering glare. 'Therefore, I will forgive his ignorance on this matter. Brelg's unit is most likely hampered by injury. Their casualty rate is the highest in the corp. A situation that dramatically slows any return to Zodra. Additionally, they may ride the best "horse flesh" when it arrives at the front, but malnutrition and battle fatigue affect horse and rider alike. Those horses are no better than farm nags at this point. I beg your majesty to allow the unit more time.'

'Harnax, you have always counseled wisely. Therefore, I'll take your theory to heart and provide you with the task of proving its validity. You will saddle two of your best cavalry units and depart Zodra in the morning. You will seek out Sergeant Brelg's unit. If they deviate from orders or halt for worldly diversions in some town along the way, you'll judge them treasonous and cut them down where they stand,' declared Macin.

'But your majesty...' began Harnax.

'Harnax! Your place in this assembly isn't as secure as you think! Do not follow the lead of your former staff members and contradict me,' shouted Macin.

'Wise counsel, my lord. For treason and treachery are a disease that spreads,' returned Ellow as he smiled at Harnax.

'My lord,' came a voice from the table.

'Colonel Wynard, correct?' Macin asked the broad shouldered Zodrian.

'General Wynard, sire, due to your highnesses gracious promotion,' the general corrected. 'May I be so bold as to expound on General Harnax's reservations with this course of action.'

'Do you feel it necessary. Remember your predecessor, General Sturm, found it necessary to deceive me,' Macin snarled.

'I believe that General Harnax has your best interests in mind,' said Wynard.

'Go on,' sighed Macin.

'Your son, Prince Manfir, is a lieutenant in that unit,' stated Wynard.

'What?' screamed Macin. 'That cannot be! Manfir was to be assigned to the best unit in the corp. To learn by the side of the greatest minds this army produces. Sturm swore to me a year ago that he placed Manfir with such a unit and that the prince progressed tremendously. Treachery abounds! Harnax, you were here during that meeting, yet said nothing!'

Ellow saw an opportunity. He jumped from his place and shook a finger in Harnax's direction.

'This is how deep it runs your highness! Your most trusted advisors and friends. They betray this country to its very core,' he spun back to the king. 'Your son, aligned with a troop of outlaws and brigands. Stealing the wealth of this nation and leaving it defenseless in its hour of need! A purge is needed, a purge....'

THWACK!

The hilt of Harnax's sword slammed into the back of Ellow's head. The supply general fell into a heap on the marble floor. The cavalryman stood at the table boiling in suppressed rage. He dropped the sword at his feet. With clenched fists he moved to within a foot of Macin. The king's personal guard drew their weapons but Macin waved them off. Harnax halted.

'Macin you arrogant, blithering idiot, Manfir was posted to the best unit in the corp. Brelg and his lot are the greatest troop level tacticians we employ. "The Orphans" act as this nation's savior while you provoke more damage to the corps than any of its enemie,.' growled Harnax.

The general turned and pointed to four of the king's personal guard.

'You! Fall in beside me and escort me to my premises at the Hold. I'll remain under guard there until his Majesty determines my punishment.'

The aging general marched from the hall, hastily followed by the four stunned guards. As Harnax strode down the marble corridors of the citadel, a scout pushed past him and addressed the king.

'Your Highness, I bring you news,' shouted the scout.

'Out with it!' demanded Macin as he scowled at the retreating form of Harnax.

'Sergeant Brelg and his unit of Guardians approach the city. They will arrive within the hour.'

'Excellent. Wynard you will assume control of Harnax's cavalry units and station them just outside the gates. I want this wolf caged before he does any more harm to his country or king. My personal guard and the General Staff will join me up on the ramparts,' Macin ordered as he swept from the room, then added. 'And somebody attend to Ellow!'

The king and his staff rode to the gates of the city and pushed past the throngs of people moving through the streets. The news of the units return traveled like wildfire and the excitement was palpable. Children danced and sang as women braided flowers in one another's hair. Guard members stationed in the city brushed and straightened their uniforms. Garland and flowers were strung across the mouth of the gates and strewn before the entryway. Young men and boys laughed and wrestled calling 'The Orphans!' back and forth to one another.

Everyone Macin passed on his way to the gate, grew subdued and stopped their revelry. However, once the king was out of sight, their passion returned twofold. Macin leapt from his horse and climbed the rampart steps two at a time, followed by his entourage.

The city's wall was crowded with Guardians both on and off duty. They immediately snapped to attention at the presence of their king. Macin moved across an arching causeway that spanned the gate opening. There he found the sergeant of the guard, Sergeant Deling, and demanded a report.

'There's little to report, sire.' stated the sergeant. 'A half an hour ago several scouts alerted us to the return of one of our units.'

'And they haven't reached the city yet? This Brelg holds back to build the anticipation of his followers!' growled Macin.

The king looked down the outer edge of the city's walls. Wynard's cavalry units were stationed on either side of the gate.

'Wynard!' called the king. 'Move your units along either side of the road. These men will be treated as prisoners not given an honor guard!'

Wynard barked some orders to his men and immediately the cavalry swung out in front of the gates, lining both sides of the road. Macin paced the archway muttering to himself. The General Staff stood by silently as their eyes scanned the horizon. Ellow returned with a bloody towel clutched to his head. He scowled at the other staff members as he stepped in front of the king.

'A minor flesh wound your highness. I was caught unaware,' offered Ellow.

Macin strode past the general distractedly.

'Yes, yes Ellow. See to it,' said Macin with a flip of his hand.

A cry went up from the taller buildings just inside the gate.

'The Orphans! The Orphans return!'

The crowd roared in approval and pushed on the throng crowded just inside the gates. Macin spun and surveyed the horizon. Several leagues from the gate, the road rose to meet a small ridgeline. Swirling over that rise, a dust cloud grew. The crowd attempted to push through the gate and out onto the road. Others climbed the city wall and joined the soldiers on the ramparts. Macin turned on the sergeant of the guard.

'You will keep this mob under control or be relieved of duty, Sergeant Deling!' barked Macin.

The sergeant saluted and ran down to the gates ordering the soldiers to move the throng back into the city. The people climbed to the ramparts cheering. In some cases, soldiers reached down to help women and children reach the top of the wall. The windows of the buildings were jammed with wellwishers. A chant of 'The Orphans! The Orphans!' was picked up in the streets and carried to the parapets. The dust cloud grew thicker and larger but approached slowly. Ellow slid up behind the king's ear.

'He intends to bear down on the city in full glory, your highness. This loafer means to capture the imagination of the people and steal their loyalty. Supplanting you in their hearts,' whispered Ellow.

The roar of the crowd was nearly deafening as the dust cloud came within three hundred yards and shapes emerged from the haze. They moved slowly. Some on horseback and others walking. Loaded wagons creaked along amidst the riders and marchers. As the dust cleared, a hush fell over the roaring crowd.

Brelg led the unit, sitting atop a staggering warhorse, gaunt from undernourishment. Periodically, the sergeant turned the beast and ambled back amongst his troops shouting words of encouragement. The injured filled the wagons. In some cases, eight men shared the tiny carts with one another. Those marching were the most fit. Cefiz led his warhorse, which carried a severely injured comrade upon it. Fully two-thirds of the unit were injured or incapacitated in some way.

The city lay silent as the troops passed between Wynard's cavalry unit. A cavalryman sprang from his horse and threw the arm of a staggering soldier over his shoulder.

'You there! Get back in your ranks......' Macin's voice trailed off.

Wynard leapt from his horse and grabbed the other arm of a soldier being supported by a comrade. Macin said nothing. Brelg stopped the unit within tens yards of the gate. He sat swaying from exhaustion on his horse. Macin surveyed the group. Brelg looked older. His matted hair was streaked in gray. A grizzled, wiry beard covered his face. New scars marred his features. The heavy breastplate he wore showed signs of abuse. Dotted with dents, it also sported two large gashes near the right shoulder. Cefiz moved up to stand beside his commander. The defiant young man glared at the king and his General Staff. A wound caked in dried blood ran across his brow. Macin searched the group and found his son standing toward the back. Manfir held the tether of a draft horse in one hand. The other arm hung uselessly in a sling. Brelg stood in his stirrups and gazed up to the crowded archway. He saluted sharply.

'Sergeant Brelg and the 75th Lancers reporting as ordered your highness,' stated Brelg, using the official name of his unit.

Macin stood on the archway with his arms folded, chewing his lower lip. The crowd remained hushed during the long pause. Finally, Brelg found the sergeant of the guard standing amongst the throng at the gate.

'Sergeant Deling, I request permission to enter the city,' said Brelg.

Deling stepped out and stared up to the king. Again, Macin stood gazing distractedly at the scene below him. Ellow edged forward toward the king, but several strong hands from the General Staff locked onto his arms and drew him backward. Deling spun back toward his soldiers and barked orders.

'Asmir! Get to the infirmary and inform them we receive casualties. Lomin! To the Hold quickly and clear barracks three and four of its occupants! I want bunks and billets prepared for these men immediately,' said Deling as he spun back toward Brelg. '75th Lancers! Welcome home!'

The crowd roared in approval. Cavalrymen jumped from their steeds and relieved their weary comrades of their burdens. The throng pushed through the gate and lifted Brelg's troops onto their shoulders and carried them into the city. Brelg rigidly stood in his saddle, staring at Macin above. The crowd gathered up his soldiers and pushed past him back into the city. The king's eyes drifted toward Brelg and their gazes locked. Macin blinked, shook his head and spun on his heals toward the steps down to the streets below.

'I will see Sergeant Brelg within the hour in my chambers!' shouted Macin over his shoulder and he swept down the stairway.

Manfir refused to be carried away by the revelers as they swept out of the city. The troops in his cart were some of the more gravely injured soldiers in Brelg's unit and he was bound and determined to see they received proper care. As the rickety cart creaked through the city streets, women and children approached to lay bouquets of flowers in the injured men's hands and offer words of praise and encouragement. Often they turned to Manfir saying,'The Creator bless you, young man.'

The prince left the city the handsome young heir to the throne, and returned a hardened, weathered, unrecognized veteran of the border wars. Manfir finished helping the last of his injured mates into the infirmary and turned into the rapidly clearing streets. He stood trying to decide his next course of action. Should he return to the palace and report to his father, or return to the Hold with his comrades? He staggered down the near empty streets with no particular destination in mind. Now and again a man or woman passed him and smiled warmly, recognizing his tattered and bloody uniform. However, none greeted him as a prince of the realm. Weariness crept over him and he stopped and chuckled. A stranger and unknown in the capital city of the great nation he would one day rule. That was true irony.

A strange satisfaction came over him. A sense of freedom grabbed hold. Never before had he been able to walk these streets alone. Crowds had formed whenever he visited the market. His movements between the palace and the Hold always caused a stir in the streets. Young women rose to their feet when he passed and brushed their dresses flat with their hands. The people had greeted him warmly and he always returned the greeting with the same, but he liked this recent transformation. A soldier in the Guard. A warrior. A friend and comrade in arms.

Suddenly, he sensed he was not alone. Was someone there, listening to these reflections within him? His head shot up and scanned the streets ahead and behind. They were empty. Manfir laughed again and headed toward the Hold. After three steps, he noted movement in an alleyway to his left. An old man stood in the shadows leaning heavily upon a wooden staff. The colorful garb of tinkers covered the peculiar vagabond. A wizened, rough face with a weeks worth of snow-white stubble smiled at him from across the street. Manfir returned the smile and bowed his head. The tinker bowed in return and beckoned Manfir toward him. The young man felt oddly at ease as he accepted the invitation.

Brelg was given no time to wash the dust of the trail from his body or his throat. He arrived at the Hold and immediately set to making his troops comfortable and provided for. Officers were eager to greet him, and several members of the General Staff arrived to gather intelligence on the enemy. With minimal time left to fulfill the order of the king, he stepped from the Hold and grabbed a fresh mount from the stables. Within minutes he arrived at the palace and presented himself to Macin's aides.

Brelg was required to wait several minutes before he was brought before Macin. The sergeant rose as a page called him forward. The boy opened the doors of the king's chamber and announced Brelg's presence to the assembly. Macin sat on his throne at the opposite end of the hall. Brelg marched forward down a carpeted runway flanked by members of the General Staff and the leading nobles in King Macin's court. He halted three yards from the throne and addressed the king.

'Your highness, I present myself as ordered.'

'Very well, sergeant. I called you here to discuss what it is I'm to do with you,' said Macin shifting awkwardly in his seat. 'Serious accusations of misconduct were leveled against you. Are you prepared to face them?'

'Yes, Sire.' answered Brelg.

Macin glanced about the room, looking for support, then slowly stood and wrung his hands. Ellow kept himself invisible, hiding behind several larger generals.

'There are those who say you needlessly waste the supplies and manpower of this great land. The lifeblood of our people,' stated Macin.

'Yes,' stated Brelg as a murmur spread through the audience. 'The lifeblood of this great nation is being wasted.'

'You admit your treachery?' shouted Macin.

'Punish the traitor, your highness!' bellowed Ellow as he pushed through the generals. 'He's a coward and a traitor!'

A weary Brelg turned and smiled at Ellow.

'Sir, we haven't met, yet you feel familiar enough with me to hurl insult and slander in front of my country and king. I don't know you by sight, but information I possess allows me to make an educated guess. I'll wager you're General Ellow. Correct?'

'That's correct, Brelg,' snarled Ellow. 'And one bit of information I'm certain you possess is my rank in the Guard and my position as a trusted advisor to his Majesty King Macin III. You'll mind your tongue and address me with due respect.'

'Trusted advisor or not, if you're the same General Ellow whose mercenaries sell stores and weapons to Keltar soldiers, I'll gut you here and now,' said Brelg squaring off in front of the general.

Ellow immediately backed behind the generals, but they stepped aside to expose him.

'The lifeblood of this great nation has been wasted,' began Brelg. 'I'm a king's man, and will defend my homeland with my life, but I don't need to like the way in which we do it. A greater and greater tax is put upon the people to pay for their defense against Ulrog Hackle and Keltaran soldier alike. The burden on farmer, herdsman and tradesman is so great they barely feed their families. The people become slaves to the army, and the army becomes slaves to the battle with our enemy. The Ulrog enslave us simply by fighting us.'

'You admit defeat before we lose?' shouted Macin as a murmur filled the room.

'Absolutely not,' shouted Brelg. 'The fault doesn't lie with the farmer or the soldier but with others. I'll tell you the life of a soldier in the field. I'm allotted eight wagonloads of supplies, only to see three arrive at the rendezvous. New armor arrives that has obviously been scavenged from graves and old battlefields. My men are cut down by blades I swear were forged in Zodrian furnaces. I enter border towns to find draftsmen of questionable character spending freely at local taverns and boasting of their good fortune. Those cases where I prove materials went to the enemy result in immediate execution, but proof comes seldom and always too late.'

'You try to shift the blame,' snapped Macin. 'I'm informed on the best authority that you, Brelg, divert these wagons and hoard these supplies. You try to undermine this nation and its king, and poison the minds of those that love him .... it.'

'Sire,' said Brelg calmly. 'This information is false. Where it came from I can only surmise, but with all due respect, I don't possess so devious a mind as to perpetrate such a plan. To return to you bedraggled and filthy in order to cover a privileged lifestyle is possible. However, if you tour the infirmary of the Hold, you'll see troops with much greater problems than ragged clothing. Nine members of my unit alone have lost a limb in battle. Three are so malnourished they may not recover. A full two thirds of my force would be deemed battle insufficient in any other unit. To question the role that these men played in the defense of their country is an affront to their courage and honor!'

'Here! Here!' shouted many in attendance.

Macin's eyes scanned the chamber.

'Enough! Everyone save Brelg out!' he shouted.

The chamber quickly cleared. Macin dropped heavily into his throne. He clasped his hands and buried his face within them. Without looking up he mumbled.

'Brelg, what am I to do with you?'

'I'm yours to command, sire,' said Brelg.

'Ha! Were it that easy,' laughed Macin looking up. 'I force a situation in which I cannot win.'

'No situation is winless, sire. No outcome is predestined.'

The king's face fell into his hands once more then he pulled his fingers through his hair. He mumbled to himself and cursed. Brelg stood rigidly at attention. The king shot out of his chair.

'I refuse to let you marry my daughter!' shouted Macin.

'As my king commands,' returned Brelg bowing low.

'You're beneath her. She was meant for a man of position and alliance. I'll not allow her to marry a foot soldier!' screamed Macin.

'Yes, your highness,' answered Brelg.

'What do you mean "Yes, your highness"?' snarled Macin. 'Don't pretend that you're not ... involved with my daughter. Don't pretend that you're not keeping a clandestine relationship going against my will!'

'I pretend nothing, your highness. I'll not marry your daughter. You're my king, but you're first and foremost a father. If my heart were enraptured by the daughter of the baker and he forbade me her hand, I would honor his wishes. The blacksmith, the night watchman or a general in the Guards, the man's station in life matters not over his position as father. A father will always act in the best interests of his child and we must respect and honor that. We are nothing as a nation if we lose our honor, sire.'

Macin stared into Brelg's eyes. His face grew troubled. The king turned and looked through an open window at his kingdom.

'I see in your eyes that you truly believe what you say,' Macin's voice wavered. 'I ..... I betrayed you.'

Macin turned and fell forward onto his knees covering his face in shame.

'I ... I wanted you dead at the hands of the enemy,' confessed Macin. 'I hoped the Ulrog would remove you from my daughter's world. I sacrificed the lives of men to make mine easier.

'You talk of honor and respect. I own none of the former and deserve none of the latter. My actions trouble me and my thoughts betray me.'

Tears streamed down Macin's cheeks as he knelt before Brelg sobbing.

'When I ascended the throne I held a vision, Brelg. I dreamed of leading this nation into an era of peace and prosperity. My vision goes cloudy. I can't even foster that peace within my own household let alone within this realm. I harden my heart to the people, my soldiers and my family in order to do what is best for Zodra. I try to bend the will of those I love in my direction and instead drive all I care for away from me.'

Macin paused.

'I tried to murder you, Brelg,' mumbled the king grimly. 'I tried to murder you yet you stand here praising country and king. It's you who earned the right to wear this trinket, not I.'

Macin pulled his gold crown from his head and let it fall to the ground.

'I'm lost,' groaned Macin sobbing into his hands. 'Utterly lost.'

The doors to the chamber flew open and an old man dressed in colorful garb stepped before the king's throne relying heavily upon a huge staff. He stood squinting at the scene before him, taking stock of it. He waved a hand in the direction of the king's guard arrayed behind him and they immediately left the chamber. He stroked his white stubble with his free hand and nodded his head with a grunt of approval. Macin's eyes rose and he glared at the tinker.

'Old man,' sobbed Macin. 'I dismissed the court for the day. We do not seek your entertainment or slight of hand. Everyone leave me alone in my misery.'

'Macin! King of the Zodra! Commander of the Guardians and Protector of the Faith of Avra! Stand!' bellowed the old man.

Macin cleared the tears from his red-rimmed eyes and slowly stood.

'My heart is troubled on this day,' growled Macin. 'However, I'll not be spoken to by a simple tinker in this manner. You're lucky I wallow in self-pity at the moment and don't possess the heart to drag you to the...'

'In your family's two thousand year old grasp on the throne of this kingdom, I definitely noticed one similarity in all its members," said the old man cutting Macin off, 'they all talked far too much for my taste. You, sir, may be the worst so far.'

'What ... who are you?' sputtered Macin.

'As for Brelg forgiving you, he may do so. I can't control his actions. However, you should be asking forgiveness from a higher source. This kingdom is in disrepair. Men's lives sacrificed over vanity and greed. A daughter's life and love used as a bargaining chip for power. A people shunned and suppressed. Valor and duty ignored. Hypocrisy rewarded. You will one day be judged for your life and taken into the arms of your Creator, or shunned and cast out into the realm of Chaos. Do you truly repent, Macin? Will you really change?' asked the old man.

Before Macin answered, the old man stepped within a foot of the king and glared into his eyes. The tinker grew in stature as a faint green light hovered about him.

'It is deemed that you will suffer your penance here on this world. You just rediscovered a love for your family, a family that means everything to you. You will now lose that family. We shall see if you truly repent.'

The old man spun to Brelg.

'You're a unique man, Brelg. You're to become the caretaker of a little package. No more war. No more battle. It's time for you to settle down, and we think you chose the perfect woman. Prince Manfir awaits you at the Hold with instructions from me. He recently became my new protégé. I'll be along after I conclude some other business.'

Brelg hesitated, glanced at the king, then back to the old man.

'You do understand who I represent, don't you, sergeant?' questioned the tinker.

Brelg bowed deeply then rose.

'Yes, my lord,' replied the sergeant. 'I'll go at once.'

Macin spluttered a protest.

'Macin of Zodra,' interrupted the old man. 'The changes that are about to affect your life do not transform one fundamental fact. You are the ruler of this land and the steward of its good fortune. What you lose sight of is the fact that the people allow themselves to be ruled. It's the grace of the people that keeps you on the throne, for if you were truly a bad king they would have removed you long ago. I charge you with fulfilling the duties of your office to the best of your ability. Protect and nurture this realm and you shall restore honor to your household.'

Macin stood speechless, staring at the tinker.

'If that is all, your highness, I'll take my leave,' said the old man bowing to the king and turning.

'Who are you?' demanded Macin as the tinker reached the chamber's doors.

The old man slowly turned and smiled.

'Lately, I use the name Jasper. However, I go by many different names throughout the lands. The Borz Windriders call me Berbati. The Ulrog fear me as Hdi, or "little Awoi", and the Elves refer to me as Seraph or "Keeper",' the tinker paused. 'Zodrians however, usually refer to me as Ader, the voice of God. Good day.'

With that the old man turned and walked from the room.

"Just like that you told him all," came a voice from the kitchen doorway.

Teeg's eyes never left Kael as he smiled and responded.

"Not all, but a good portion. However, there's still so much for him to learn. Your sister and her husband's history are but a small part."

Kael turned to see Manfir framed by the kitchen doorway.

"So, now you know," said Manfir moving into the dining hall.

The Zodrian prince stood before Kael staring with his stony expression. A broad smile gradually crossed his face. A powerful hand shot out and grabbed Kael by the forearm. The boy was yanked to his feet and wrapped in the strong hold of Prince Manfir. As they embraced, Manfir whispered into Kael's ear.

"It's been difficult not being able to talk to you all these years."

The big man released the boy and immediately turned to Teeg.

"Ader may have your hide yet, Lord Elf."

"Wisdom is not the sole property of the Seraph, my friend. Occasionally, others must make decisions for themselves. Lord Ader would rather the boy sleep soundly on full knowledge than the half facts supplied by good man Hamly," replied Teeg.

Manfir glanced at the wide-eyed, confused Kael and laughed.

"If you think that boy will sleep tonight, you must redefine the meaning of wisdom!"

CHAPTER 15: RECRUIT

Manfir was correct. Kael lay awake for hours. Not only did the evening's news stun him, but the absence of his brother disturbed his sleep as well. He was so used to the rumbled snoring of Aemmon, that its absence unsettled him. After lying awake for several hours, Kael stole down to his father's room. He cuddled under the blankets of the oak four-poster and let his mind relax. The scent of his father on the blankets comforted him. He also detected the faint fragrance of his mother. Kael sobbed and drifted to sleep.

"... was already informed of his mother's identity. I felt it was necessary."

"Your feelings often contradict mine, Lord Teeg. No matter. What's done is done. I've kept things from the boy for so long, perhaps it becomes a habit," replied Ader.

Kael rose and approached his father's door, which was recessed near the main stairway.

"It seems our young earl switched sleeping accommodations in the evening," said Teeg. "Please come out and join us, Kael."

Kael slowly opened the door and entered the main hall. Ader and Teeg stood in its center and Flair busily cleared the table.

"You slept late, my boy," said Ader. "I was tempted to send Flair up to rouse you."

"Sorry," said Kael.

"However, upon hearing of your eventful evening," continued Ader, "I realized sleep may have become a rare commodity for you."

Kael stared at his bare feet and fidgeted. He knew Ader was upset and he felt guilty of the way he manipulated old Hamly. He desired to change the subject.

"Why did you call me that?" he directed at Teeg.

"Called you what?" asked the old Elf.

"Young Earl," quoted Kael.

Ader frowned at the Elf.

"You seem to take so much pleasure in revelations," growled Ader. "Please continue with them."

The Elf bowed lightly to Ader with a flourish of his hand.

"As the son of the Duke of Kelky and his wife, a princess of the realm, you are an earl," began Teeg. "I believe your proper title is 'Kael Brelgson, the honorable Earl of Kelky'..."

"all right then .." interrupted Ader.

"... fifth in line to the throne," said Teeg smiling.

"WHAT?" exclaimed Kael so loudly that Flair dropped a tray filled with plates.

"He said that you're fifth in line for the throne," sighed Ader, shaking his head.

"What throne?" asked Kael.

"My throne," came a hearty laugh from the stairway, "and I don't intend on letting it fall that far."

Manfir stepped lightly from the stairway and approached the group.

"Good man Hamly is nearly finished preparing our mounts. We tarry too long. It's time to move on," said Manfir.

"Quite right," replied Teeg.

Flair entered the room once more and set a plate full of eggs on the table.

"I took the liberty of making this breakfast for you, Kael. There are a few moments before grandfather finishes with the mounts," said Flair.

"Thank you," replied Kael, taking a seat at the table.

Ader, Teeg and Manfir left for the stables through the kitchen. When Kael finished his breakfast he brought the plate back into the kitchen and once again thanked Flair. The boy nodded and took the plate. Before turning to the washbasin, Flair hesitated and looked at Kael.

"Forgive me, Kael, but ... I couldn't help but overhear a good deal of what was said here in the last day. Is it true?" asked Flair.

"That depends on what you're talking about, and even then I might answer that I've no idea," smiled Kael. "Until I sit down with my father and ask a fair number of questions, I'm not going to fully believe anything."

"Well," puzzled Flair "I know one thing for certain. My granddad is as involved as any of them, and that means its the truth. Granddad's the most honest man I know. I hope that helps you a bit."

Kael laughed and clapped the young man on the back.

"It does Flair. It certainly does."

Kael walked from the kitchen into the stable yard. Ader stood by the gate to the yard engaged in an animated conversation with Eidyn. The young Elf pled his case concerning some weighty issue. Teeg stood nearby once again looking smug. Several horses were tethered in the yard, the Elves' stallions among them.

Near the stables, Granu stood scratching the nose of Tarader. Once more the Keltaran giant was covered from head to toe in his black robe. Just inside the stable door, Hamly stood staring distractedly at a pile of hay as Manfir conducted a quiet conversation with him. The old man shook his head and apologized. Manfir would have none of it. He smiled and clapped the old sergeant on the back. Hamly nodded and moved back into the stables as Manfir exited and walked toward Kael.

"Your chestnut will be saddled shortly, Kael Brelgson. If we're all prepared, we may leave then," said Manfir.

"Manfir," called Eidyn. "You're a military man of superior training. Why is it that our illustrious Guide, Lord Ader, refuses to use scouts? I'm fully capable and some might say quite gifted in this task. However, every time I ask, he refuses me."

Manfir looked from the Elf to the old man. Ader displayed a frustrated, perplexed look on his face. Teeg smiled and Eidyn's temper grew.

"We'll be in open country for a good portion of this trip. Ulrog range freely in the mountains and the Keltaran step up their raids. It only makes sense to post guards at our campsites and send scouts ahead of the party. I'm the logical choice," claimed Eidyn.

"I take nothing from your abilities as a superior tracker and scout, prince of the Grey Elves, but in my many years of experience with 'the voice of Avra', if he says your services aren't needed, then they aren't needed. Please, argue no more and heed his advice. Your strength and insight will be required down the road no doubt, so try to conserve them."

Ader smiled broadly and crossed his arms.

"Well said, Zodrian prince," called Ader. "And it only took me seventeen years to break you of the annoying habit of questioning my wisdom."

Eidyn shook his head in frustration. Kael smirked at the comical scene in front of him, men of great power and ability henpecking one another. Hamly exited the stables leading the chestnut. The horse was expertly groomed and saddled. Kael felt pangs of guilt as the old man led the horse toward him. He felt the need to apologize for misleading Hamly.

"Master Hamly, I'm sorry I let you believe..." began Kael.

"No matter, Kael my boy. No matter at all," replied Hamly as he adjusted the chestnut's reins. "I've begun ta talk a bit much in me old age. Need to keep my flapper shut, I do. Just can't help talkin' bout things. Runnin' a horse ranch hasn't been near as excitin' as my days in the Guard. I like to let the memory roam if ya know what I mean?"

"Yes, I guess I do. I'm truly sorry," said Kael.

Hamly shuffled once more and stared toward his feet.

"Head up, Sergeant Hamly!" called out Manfir from the back of his warhorse. "No harm was done, and your tidbits were nothing compared to the floodgate opened by the 'Master of Spies'."

Teeg smiled as was his habit, and bowed deeply. Ader grumbled something about 'chatty Elves', and Hamly stood tall in front of Kael's mount. Even the ominous presence of Granu let out a low rumbling chuckle. Manfir nudged the black stallion in front of the old man.

"Did you saddle the extra mount as I requested, sergeant?" asked Manfir.

"Yes, sir," replied Hamly.

"Flair. Did you gather your things?" called Manfir toward the kitchen.

The young man sprang from the doorway. He carried a small bag of clothes, a sack of tools and a short cudgel. Hamly spun to Manfir.

"What's happenin'? Where's the boy off to?" asked Hamly.

"Aemmon wasn't the only boy I hand picked for the Guards, my friend," smiled Manfir.

The prince tried to hold a straight face but could not keep a broad grin from spreading there. Hamly looked puzzled.

"The boy is too young, Manfir. He isn't eligible."

"He'll be eligible by the end of the season, sergeant. The king calls upon many to return to duty. Brelg left to join in consult with my father. I think young Flair would find his call earlier than his birthday. Besides, I would rather he accompany us now, than journey by himself in a fortnights time," replied Manfir.

"But his parents, they haven't been told," stated Hamly.

"Would you do me that favor?" said Manfir.

Hamly scrutinized Manfir. They stared at one another for over a minute. Finally, Hamly shook his head.

"If yer only doin' this cause the boy is my grandson, it's no good. You'll just get 'im killed," said Hamly.

"You know me better than that, my friend. The Guard only takes the best. Of course bloodlines play a part. However, Master Flair possesses what it takes. Now will you tell your daughter for me?"

Hamly pursed his lips then let out a yell and threw his hands in the air.

"Wahoo! I knew ya had it in ya boy!" said the old man as he ran over and bear hugged Flair. "I never pushed for ya with any of 'em, but I hoped they'd notice ya! Well I'll be. Never thought I'd see the day. Your dad's gonna be awful proud! Wish he stood here now. Stay a moment and gimme that thing."

Hamly snatched the cudgel from the boy's hand and ran into the inn. He was gone a few moments before he returned carrying a wool blanket. He stopped in front of Flair and threw open the blanket revealing a cutlass and scabbard. The weapon was obviously cared for over a number of years.

"Granddad, I can't take your sword. I'm not ..." began Flair.

"Oh, go on boy. I don't use this 'un much anymore. All I'm gettin' good for is runnin' errands and such. A recruit for the Guard gets looked upon a lot better if he shows up with a proper sword."

The old man turned to Manfir.

"Your highness, I've shown the boy a thing or two, but if ya don't mind, do ya think ya might give him a few tips on the way. I'd certainly appreciate it."

"Done," replied Manfir.

A huge smile beamed back at the prince from the old man.

"Well, we must be on our way," interrupted Ader. "Hamly, with Brelg gone, your son-in-law becomes the commander of the militia in this area, correct?"

"Yes, sir. He does," replied Hamly.

"Then you may tell him of your grandson's good fortune, but the usual rules apply concerning our movements and whereabouts. Understood?" said Ader.

"Understood!" said Hamly with a sharp salute and a wink for his grandson.

The remainder of the group mounted their horses and Hamly swung the gate wide open. As they passed, the old man saluted once more and Kael noticed Hamly's lip quiver as Flair saluted in return.

The group quietly rode down the main street of town. Manfir took the lead as the hulking form of Granu strode silently in the rear. It was early and many of the inhabitants of the small village were in their beds. Kael laughed to himself. The stable boy, sneaking from his own village with princes and lords. What would they make of it? Perhaps that's why they were sneaking, so no one would think of it.

They passed the last structure in town, Daz the weaver's shop. His old dog Trig sprang from beneath the porch and barked at the group as they slid by. A withering look from Granu sent the dog yipping back under the porch. They moved into the countryside and Manfir increased the pace. The horses began a light trot.

"We will try to get some distance between us and the town while the morning air is cool. The horses will need to slow under the noonday sun," stated Manfir.

After several minutes at this pace, Kael stole a glance backward. The town disappeared beneath a ridgeline and Granu fell behind as well. Manfir never turned to check on the status of the lone footman of the group.

Nearly an hour later, Manfir reined in the black stallion and slowed the pace to a walk. Kael was afforded the opportunity to look around. The boy was never this far to the north of the village before. The country was relatively the same as that around Kelky, rolling hills broken by ridgelines gave way to sporadic fields and meadows. The grasses grew high throughout the region making fine cover. Kael noted how much recent events changed him. He no longer looked at these rolling grasslands as cattle pasture, but as battle lands, a place not of beauty, but of danger. His anxiety rose.

"Truly remarkable country," came a voice to his left.

Kael turned to find Granu quietly walking beside him. The Keltaran's head was almost level to Kael's.

"You were able to keep up?" said Kael, his eyes widening.

"I have hiked many leagues through the thin air and up the steep slopes of the Zorim Mountains. This is but a stroll to a Keltaran," stated Granu.

"I saw you falling behind?" questioned Kael.

"Although the leaders of this group choose to leave issues of security to unseen forces, I desire a more tangible feel for the situation. Let them believe that I can't keep up. I will cover our rear," smiled Granu.

Kael heard a chuckle from just ahead and realized that Teeg slid backward in the group and rode just ahead of Kael.

"Our spy master is quite efficient at his job, don't you think, young earl?" asked Granu.

"Ah, yes, I guess he is," nodded Kael. "Please, don't give me a title. I'm sure I'll never get used to it."

"Responsibility is the most difficult of all the tasks Avra puts before us, Master Kael," said Granu. "How we respond to our Creator's challenges determines who we are. I exercised no choice in being born to the house of Grannak. However, how I respond to this challenge is what my Lord will judge. You too are called upon to face your life, not to hide from it. How will you respond?"

Before Kael was able to answer, the big man slowed and allowed the group to distance from him once more. Kael looked up to notice Teeg moving forward to his space beside Eidyn. The boy rode on left with his thoughts.

The hours passed as the sun hit its apex and slid toward the horizon. Fatigue set in as the riders spent long hours holding themselves in their saddles. They crested a small ridgeline and Kael saw travelers ahead of them moving north. The travelers were on foot and in no particular formation. As Kael came closer to the group he saw the distinctive clothing of farmers and herdsmen. Kael was nearly on top of the group when he saw Teeg steal a glance over his shoulder to the south. Kael followed the Elf's gaze back down the road. Granu was nowhere to be found.

"Our large friend knows well the prejudices of these country folk," stated Teeg.

The travelers stepped from the road to let the riders slowly pass. Manfir reined in when the black stallion stood amongst them. The men couldn't possibly recognize the prince, but his bearing and outfit told them all they needed to know.

"Good day to you, men of Trimble. Wherefore are you bound?" asked Manfir.

A burly, balding man in herdsmen garb stepped forward and bowed quickly to Manfir.

"We're bound for the capital, my lord," said the herdsmen. "And you?"

"We're bound for the capital as well," said Manfir. "Aren't you Nyven the cattleman?"

The broad shouldered man smiled and his eyes narrowed as he studied Manfir.

"Yes, I am," said Nyven. "Have we met, my lord? Surely I'd remember such a fine gentleman as yourself."

"I normally conduct our business," came the reply from Ader.

Nyven stepped forward and inspected the old man.

"Ho! If it isn't wily, old Jasper. How fare you?" asked Nyven glancing back to Manfir. "And by gum tis Rin. I didn't recognize you outside your tinker's garb. Times must be good for you, by the look of the mounts you ride. They must be worth a king's ransom!"

"They are, my friend. They are. You have always possessed a keen eye for animal flesh. How go your herds in the fields around Trimble?" answered Ader.

"Quite well. I added fifteen head to my count this season. It forced a good deal of work on me. I was prepared for it, but now comes this business," said the cattleman as he pointed a thumb over his shoulder to the north.

"Are the militia of Trimble called north?" asked Manfir.

"Yes." replied Nyven. "I sent a runner to the king to explain my situation. Every year the Guard commandeers more and more of my stock. I don't mind supporting the troops, but how can I produce if all of my men are called up? Who'll tend the herds?"

"Macin called the whole militia forward?" asked Teeg.

Nyven hesitated and inspected Teeg. The cattleman noted the Elf's mount, clothing and confident stare. He nodded his head and proceeded.

"Yes indeed, Lord Elf. My runner returned and informed me two thirds of the men should march north. Not only are my herds poorly tended, but Trimble is poorly defended even if she is in the heart of the country," said Nyven. "I left good men behind, but it worries me."

"Why didn't you stay?" mumbled Kael.

"What's that laddie?" asked Nyven.

Kael turned red and glanced about.

"I said, why didn't you stay? Your herds are obviously important and must be tended," said Kael. "Who better to care for them than their owner?"

"The king, in his infinite wisdom, demanded two-thirds of my men. No less," frowned Nyven. "A man doesn't send another to face danger in his stead. I wouldn't send these fine boys in harms way unless I was willing to go there myself."

Kael turned a brighter red and stared at the ground. He needed to learn a lot about soldiering and honor. Prince Eidyn looked to Manfir after the disparaging remark concerning King Macin. The prince's countenance remained stony.

"I might ask if you're called as well, good man Rin, but the company you keep leads me to think otherwise," said Nyven waving a hand toward the Elves and the two young men.

"I was called, in a manner of speaking, Nyven my friend," smiled Manfir. "I accompany these honored representatives from the Elven people in hopes that King Macin will accept their aid in these troubled times. I must also attend to duties of my own, for the sad truth is, even the aid of the Elves may not save my father's kingdom in its hour of need. All able bodied men, prince or pauper must arm themselves."

"That's for certain," rambled Nyven looking to Teeg and Eidyn. "The support of the Grey Elves is a blessing in these times. The stories we hear from the North concerning the trouble in your father's king....."

The big man stopped and swung his head back toward Manfir. The Zodrian prince turned the black stallion and headed up the road.

"His father's what?" asked Nyven in confusion.

Ader sighed and a knowing look passed between him and Teeg.

"Come, Tarader," said the old man as the huge gray turned and followed Manfir's stallion.

"Tarader?" mumbled Nyven as his eyes went wide and his jaw dropped.

Teeg slid down from his mount and with a slight bow approached Nyven and his men.

"Good day, gentlemen. I am Lord Teeg, emissary of his majesty King Leinor of Luxlor ...." began the Grey Elf Lord.

Kael turned to Flair and the pair chuckled as they turned their horses and passed by the stunned cattlemen. As Kael proceeded north, he listened to Teeg's fading and formal voice.

"... Prince Manfir just gave you a delicate bit of information, and one that you should keep to yourselves. His whereabouts and that of Lord Ader, and I assure you Lord Ader is real, are a tightly held secret. Now, I'm quite certain of the loyalties of every man here. Jilk, you and Trawney lived in the Trimble area for years. You perform admirably as both herdsmen and militiamen. .."

"Do you think they'll talk?" Flair asked Kael.

"...because it's my job to know these things. I might tell you what you ate for breakfast if I desired to..."

"Would you, if someone you never met in your life knew that much about you?" laughed Kael.

"... refer to me in my unofficial title as the Master of Spies....."

The boys laughed again and rode on.

The group resumed their steady march northward. Shortly, Teeg rejoined them. Ader reined in beside the Elf and the pair talked quietly. Teeg showed no signs of concern over the revelations made to the herdsmen. Ader appeared satisfied. As Ader moved to rejoin Manfir at the head of the group, Teeg turned and winked at Kael.

"I'm a master of human nature as well. Those men are all of impeccable character. They never miss work or shirk their duties. They're true to their wives and serve their Creator in words and deeds. They're as trustworthy as men can be. No, we'll experience no trouble from the men of Trimble," said Teeg.

"How do you know so much about everybody and what they do?" asked Kael.

"It's my job," answered Teeg. "If it were my job to bake bread you would taste the most exquisite bread ever to cross your lips. If it were to build houses, they would stand for a thousand years. I perform at my highest level in all I attempt, in order to honor my Creator and his graciousness."

"What if you're uncertain what your job is?" asked Kael.

"Then my job is to listen for his calling and open my heart and mind to the possibilities," said Teeg. "Travel through life experiencing the variety of paths he sets down before you. You'll know when the right one presents itself. To serve your Creator and your fellow man is true happiness."

Kael gazed down the road. Lost in thought once more. Wondering what his calling might be.

Several leagues down the road a large black figure stood atop a small hill. The group approached. Kael's sharp eyes immediately determined who stood there.

"Granu, son of Grannak awaits us," confirmed Eidyn.

Manfir gazed at the figure ahead then scanned the horizon in both directions. Kael and Flair sensed the prince's uneasiness and scanned the horizon as well. Ader put a hand on the soldier's shoulder.

"Don't trouble yourself, my boy," said Ader. "I swore to you that he is true, and so he is."

The group reined in near the giant.

"I believed we left you in the broken lands north of Kelky," said Manfir.

The large, hooded figure stood motionless and silent.

"Hail Granu, son of Grannak," called Teeg. "Your decision to avoid contact with the militia was wise. I doubt they would take kindly to a Keltaran strolling through their lands."

Granu threw back his hood and exposed his shaved scalp to the fading sun.

"Hrafnu taught,'You find trouble or let it try to find you'," stated Granu. "I prefer the latter over the former."

Manfir grunted and frowned at the name. He moved his stallion down the road.

"We may continue down this route into the village of Quay, or make camp in a small grove to the west of the road just ahead," said Granu. "The former may provide the comfort of a small inn or tavern, but undoubtedly draw the attention of more than a handful of militiamen. The latter will provide all the shelter we need and keep prying eyes from our business."

Manfir spun his stallion to face the giant.

"You want me to follow the orders of a Keltaran on matters of security, here in the open lands?" snapped Manfir.

"No," said Granu mildly. "I want you to hear the advice of a man wise to the prejudices and fears of the world. It's to our advantage to move through the town in the early hours before it's fully awake. Fewer of the inhabitants will lay eyes upon us and fewer tongues will wag. We're not here to impress the country folk with our credentials."

"What? No one is here to impress anyone! I spent seventeen years in the role of a mute, mindless..."

"Prince Granu makes sense, even though he uses little tact in making his point," interrupted Ader frowning at Granu. "Prince Manfir deserves neither your accusations nor your jibes. None save I witnessed his sacrifice over these many years."

"Forgive me Ader, favored of Avra," said Granu bowing lightly.

"And you," Ader sighed turning to Manfir. "I can't spare energy separating the two of you. I never misled you, so hear me now. Granu is pledged to us and his intentions are honorable. The man offers a sensible suggestion but you are so misguided by hatred, you refuse to see its merit. Leave your enmity here on this road. We can't afford to let it separate us when it matters most."

Manfir remained tense for a moment and gnawed his lower lip. Finally, his shoulders drooped and he bowed his head toward Ader. He glanced in the Keltaran's direction but Granu already forged ahead and the group followed him off the road into the grasslands. They moved in a northeasterly direction for some time and finally came to a small grove of pine trees growing near the edge of a low bluff. Amidst the pines lay a clearing. The soil was soft, sandy and covered with pine needles. Fifty yards from the grove, a creak tumbled over the bluff and cascaded into a shallow pool. The group reined in and dismounted.

Flair set to work. He gathered in the Elves' mounts along with his own and Kael's chestnut. He led the horses to the pond and tethered them near food and water. Granu entered the grove and began splitting wood with a hatchet he retrieved from Flair's tool sack. Kael noticed Manfir stop and appraise the campsite.

"The cliff will protect us from the rear, and the tree line makes excellent cover for the Elves and their bows if need be," muttered Manfir.

"Cover from whom?" asked Kael.

Manfir came out of his deep concentration.

"What is that Kael ... uh, oh yes," said Manfir. "I'm simply assessing our choice of campsite."

"Why?" asked Kael. "We're still in Zodra."

"You'll learn, Kael. Always set up camp as if you'll slumber in the heart of the enemy's territory. It's a good habit and one that may save your life one day. Not all of the servants of Chaos stand across the border with blades poised to strike. Some stand in the halls of this kingdom and will shove a knife in your back as they cower behind you for protection.

"This site has merit. The cliff and trees keep us hidden and the turbulent air and pine boughs will diffuse the smoke from our fires. The mounts will find food and water, yet be nearby for protection. We're far enough from the road so that anyone foolish enough to use it at night will not stumble upon us. It's a good place to hide."

"My people were good at hiding before they were forced to become good at fighting," came a voice from inside the grove.

Granu stepped from behind the pine trees and approached Kael and Manfir.

"Come into the clearing. It's almost dark. I've sent the Elves in search of fresh meat. Their eyes do not fail them in the darkness as ours do," said the giant.

Manfir clenched his teeth and followed Kael into the grove. Flair was still working on the horses.

"Flair," called Manfir over his shoulder. "Only a quick rubdown tonight. You need your rest as well as the horses."

"Yes, sir!" replied the boy.

They ate in silence, each man lost in his thoughts. Kael marveled at the diversity of their group. What did he get himself into and where would it end? He hoped its conclusion would come when he was delivered to his father, but a voice inside him knew better.

Would he be allowed to join the Guard as well? Would he be called to fight in the North against roving packs of Ulrog? Would he be sent to the frozen slopes of the Zorim Mountains to battle ax wielding Keltaran raiders? He surmised that this is what Teeg called opening yourself up to the possibilities.

CHAPTER 16: WAVES IN THE POOL

Sulgor entered the dark chamber slowly. His last meeting with Izgra left him reluctant to face the Half-Dead with less than positive news. The black hooded and heavily robed warlock stood near an arching window that looked west toward the Mirozert Mountains. Izgra's gaze never left the sun as the glowing ball of flame dipped toward the snow capped peaks.

"What news do you report?" demanded the Half-Dead.

Sulgor kept low.

"Methra the Worm and Quirg returned to the nothingness of Chaos," replied Sulgor.

"As I stated," said Izgra.

Sulgor quickly moved on.

"However, the Worm accomplished his mission," growled the beast. "Methra eliminated the two Elven messengers bound for the horsemen."

Izgra remained silent.

"He and Quirg returned to the Nagur path, drawn by a powerful spirit moving through the ancient wood. Reports from Luxlor confirm a battle," added Sulgor.

"The fools," grumbled Izgra. "All know the Caretaker dwells in the wood. His spirit alone would draw Methra like a moth to a flame."

"Methra was aware of the Caretaker," snarled Sulgor, taking small pleasure in the success of his brethren. "However, there was another."

Izgra spun and faced the Malveel King. Sulgor shrunk low as candlelight displayed a glimpse of decaying flesh beneath the warlock's cowl. Red eyes bore down on the beast.

"What did you learn?" demanded Izgra.

"Two boys entered the wood, bound for Luxlor," replied Sulgor.

"Boys?" questioned Izgra.

"They are of the proper age," returned Sulgor.

"Go on," demanded the Half-Dead.

"The pair hovered near the wood's edge for a time," continued the beast. "Methra and Quirg were drawn to their location. When my brothers arrived, the boys split and only one remained. Our servant in Luxlor was unable to determine exactly what took place, but the remaining boy was eliminated."

Izgra turned back to the window and gazed west.

"I felt it," said Izgra, his voice rising in pleasure. "A wave as this boy's spirit passed. He held great power. Quirg fell at his hands."

Sulgor sensed his master's triumph and took great satisfaction in deflating the warlock.

"Methra did not kill the new Seraph in the wood," stated the Malveel.

Izgra spun and the red eyes flashed. The Half-Dead's hands rose, charged with the red flame of Chaos.

"What are you saying?" snapped the warlock. "His spirit was full of power, he must have been the Seraph."

Sulgor backed away, immediately regretting his small pleasure.

"He was not," growled the beast. "Our contact in Luxlor assures me the dead Zodrian boy was not the Seraph. The other was our target."

"I felt the dead boy's passing," snapped Izgra. "How can this other be the one?"

"I do not know, my lord," answered Sulgor keeping low. "The heirs to the three thrones flock to his aid. They accompany him."

The flames around Izgra's hands flickered and faded as he digested the news.

"The three shall raise the one and place him on the throne," quoted the warlock. "The verse of the Scribes."

Sulgor nervously eyed his master. Izgra hesitated a moment longer then turned on the Malveel.

"It means nothing," snapped Izgra. "The Scribes' ravings may be interpreted myriad ways."

"Word has spread throughout the Elvish rank, he has begun to grow in his abilities. Already he begins to accomplish what others cannot. He is no longer shaped by the world, but begins to exercise his powers to shape it around him."

Izgra's hands clenched forming bony fists.

"We cannot allow him to learn more," shouted the warlock.

"Appropriate measures are being taken, my lord," said Sulgor. "Your servant in Luxlor sets a plan in motion."

"Do the Elves harbor the boy?" demanded Izgra.

Sulgor's lips curled into a wicked smile. As much as he bridled at the control of this warlock, the Malveel Lord still took great pleasure in the successes of their ultimate master, Amird.

"The fools act as always. That which we desire most is quite often that which they protect the least," snarled Sulgor. "The boy is being moved toward Zodra. He is surrounded by a powerful, yet small group of allies."

Sulgor sensed the smile beneath his master's hood. Izgra reveled in the news for only a moment then took control.

"Our servant in Luxlor does well, but cannot be solely relied upon," snarled Izgra. "So we know the boy's description and those who travel with him?"

"Yes, my lord but ... " began Sulgor.

"See to it, Sulgor," screamed Izgra. "I want the boy and his escort dead! The Scribes' prophecies toy with me. I cannot allow this threat to become a distraction from the triumphant return of our lord. Chaos will reign once again!"

Izgra spun and retreated from the chamber. Sulgor bowed low and watched the warlock depart.

"One last thing, my lord .... " said Sulgor.

Izgra halted without turning.

"Ader Light Wielder accompanies the boy," continued the Malveel. "Our asset believes Methra was lost to the Guide, but was unable to verify this."

Izgra paused.

"Methra would have died at the hands of the Light Wielder a millennia ago if not for Amird's interference in the battle," snarled Izgra. "Our good graces allowed him to serve Chaos and the purpose for which he was made a thousand years more than he should.

"Ader made a mistake by calling attention to himself. He emerges from the shadows at a most opportune time. Kill the old Seraph when you kill the new. Their deaths will be double the triumph," said the black figure as he disappeared behind the curtains of the chamber.

CHAPTER 17: THE BLACKSMITH'S APPRENTICE

In the morning, Kael was once again the last to wake. The clearing was filled with the hazy gray of predawn. A mist hung in the air. Flair had saddled their horses and given each the remainder of the rubdown he was forced to forgo the night before. One thing was for sure about Flair. He was a hard worker. Kael knew Hamly's ranch produced quality horses, and now he knew why. Flair worked himself to the bone to make sure these horses were properly cared for.

Flair led the chestnut over and helped Kael into the saddle. Eidyn tossed an apple to Kael and the young man deftly snatched it out of the air.

"Cold rations this morning, my friend," said Eidyn.

"Anything will do," smiled Kael.

Manfir put his heels into the flanks of the black stallion and the group moved forward. They wound their way around the brambles and thickets that populated this area of Zodra. It was tricky riding in the semidarkness before sunrise. The group climbed a small embankment and stood on the Great Northern Trade Route. Manfir surveyed the road in either direction. Kael saw no one on it. The big man turned to the group.

"We will arrive in Quay within the hour. I suggest Granu ..." began Manfir.

Kael turned to survey the group as well. Granu was not amongst them.

"It's disconcerting when the lone Keltar in our collection slips away like that," grumbled Manfir to Ader.

"Disconcerting? I call it self-preservation," returned Ader.

Manfir led them down the road toward Quay. It seemed a short span indeed before they came upon the outlying structures of the town. A large dog howled at them from a nearby farm. The smell reminded Kael why hog farmers always built furthest from the town center. Recent events were so foreign that the familiar smell of hogs comforted him.

They passed a few more small farms and an old mill set against a creek that wound into the countryside. Kael noted how early it was. None of the farmers were working outdoors yet. The sun left the eastern horizon and a sliver of sky shown underneath it.

Finally, several hundred yards ahead, Kael saw a cluster of buildings and a few people moving amongst them. The group slowly made its way into town. They passed the local tannery and waved a swarm of flies from in front of their faces. The blacksmiths shop stood across the road and his apprentice, outfitted in a heavy leather smock stood at the bellows stoking the fire blazing hot for the day's work.

The boy looked up as the group passed. Kael noticed how the young man appraised them and their mounts. A satisfied look passed over his face and then he looked to the horse's hooves. The boy stepped from the blacksmith's shed.

"Master Elf! Are your horses in need of any shoeing? Your young master's mount carries his front left awkwardly," said the boy pointing to Eidyn's stallion.

Teeg reined in and the group followed suit.

"Perhaps you should take a look, my good man. We would hate for him to pull up lame while far from the nearest town," called Teeg.

The boy smiled and approached Eidyn's white stallion. He bowed low as he came close.

"Is he of a good nature, my lord?" the boy asked Eidyn.

"The finest," smiled Eidyn.

The apprentice nestled in next to the horse's left forearm. He grabbed the stallion's leg and lifted it back.

"What news in these parts, my friend?" asked Teeg amiably.

"Little news here," replied the boy. "We're too far from anything important for anything worth talking about to happen. It looks as if a stone shard is lodged under the shoe."

The boy removed a small pry bar from a sack tied to his waist and worked it into the white stallion's shoe.

"What of business then, is it slow?" questioned Teeg.

"Now that's a bit different. Business is good," smiled the boy as he looked up to Teeg.

"Brisk eh?" said Teeg. "Why so?"

The boy grunted a few times as he worked the pry bar under the horse's shoe.

"Unusual amount of travel on the road," stated the boy. "Plenty of people heading north."

"People?" said Teeg.

"Men mostly. Some riding and some walking. Those riding often require a bit of work on their mounts. Those walking need plenty of other things repaired. Plenty of shoddy workmanship down South. Reattached three skillet handles this week. They don't take kindly to setting on the flame of an open fire. You can't control the heat that way. Handles just pop off," said the boy. "Plenty of sword repair as well."

"Sword repair? Someone looking for a battle, master blacksmith?" asked Teeg.

The boy blushed and glanced back at the shed.

"Uh, I'm not the blacksmith," stammered the boy. "The smith is, uh, still asleep in the back. If you're nervous, I'll call him up to work on your mount?"

"No, no. Don't bother him. I'm sure he is a busy man. Your services are more than adequate. But what is this of a battle?"

The boy smiled with the compliment and worked on the horse's hoof.

"Oh, lots of those moving north are members of the Southern militias. King Macin called them up and they're bound to obey. Many of those swords haven't seen duty in years. Took me fifty turns of the sharpening stone to take the rust off of some of them." said the boy.

"Fifty turns! Ho, those were old blades. Heavy in rust eh?" laughed Teeg. "Any other unusual travelers on the road?"

The boy halted his work and looked up at Teeg once more. Kael noted a difference in his expression. He no longer looked at the group as customers he might help in return for a bit of coin. It was as if he now recognized the group for what it was. The boy's eyes narrowed and he answered slowly.

"No... just the usual merchants and tinkers, my lord."

The boy glanced at Ader with some uneasiness. After a moment of silence the old man smiled at the boy and addressed him.

"You look uneasy, lad. Did you begin work on an empty stomach? Never a sound idea," smiled Ader.

"Forgive me, my lord, but you look familiar to me. I apologize for my impertinence, but have we conducted business in the past?" asked the boy.

"Two summers ago you purchased the leather hide used to make the forging bellows from me. You just began working as Boon's assistant," smiled Ader.

The boy's eyes drifted off and a look of recognition entered them.

"Master Jasper?"

"Excellent memory, lad," said Ader.

The boy turned to Manfir and nodded.

"And your son, Master Rin. I apologize for not recognizing you, but you changed your station in life dramatically. Such beautiful mounts. And where is the old nag and cart?" the boy asked Ader.

"The nag is put out to pasture, and the cart is no longer needed," replied Manfir.

The boy appeared stunned to hear Manfir speak.

"And in the company of Elven royalty. Things certainly changed for you," stated the boy. "Congratulations."

The apprentice bent over once more smiling and shaking his head. He was obviously pleased with the good fortune of Jasper the tinker and his son Rin. Teeg's face grew into a broad smile and Kael knew immediately the old Elf was planning something.

"Tell me, my boy, any unusual weaponry amongst the travelers?" asked Teeg.

"Not too much," replied the boy as he forced the stallion's shoe away from the hoof. "Mostly blades with the usual Southern style. Not much sophistication. I saw a few dozen arrows made by the river folk, very distinctive heads of steel. Some cutlass from the Erutre. I assume the owners bartered for them. The Erutre keep a good deal of contact with the Southern towns that border their lands. A few unusual crossbows, but people make them all different ways anyhow."

"You're gifted with a keen eye for detail," smiled Teeg. "A good deal of information to be gained by noticing the weapons a man carries."

"More than not it'll tell you where a man has been and whether he keeps coin in his pocket," smiled the boy.

"Coin?" asked Kael.

The boy turned to Kael and nodded.

"A poor farmer or merchant doesn't retain money to spend on the mending and maintenance of a weapon," explained the boy. "If he's traveling, he ought to keep a weapon in its finest condition in order to protect himself. If he doesn't, he's either an addlebrained idiot or too poor to get it done. Since I pick out the addlebrained idiots once I talk to them, I'm able to determine which ones simply can't afford it."

The boy clenched his teeth and applied pressure to the stallion's hoof. The pry bar popped and a rock shard shot from beneath the horse's shoe and landed on the street.

"There we go," exclaimed the boy. "That'll take the pain out of his step. Hold here a moment."

The boy stepped into the blacksmith's shack and returned with a bucket of water. He washed down the hoof and scrubbed out the area that held the rock.

"You don't want him to get infected," he commented. "He should be just fine."

"It was the ring on my young friend's hand?" interrupted Teeg pointing to Eidyn.

The boy stood, wiped his hands on a rag and for a moment looked confused. Comprehension crept across his face.

"His ring, my lord?" smiled the boy.

"Come, come Master Hindle. How did you know we were Elven royalty? We might be any two Elves traveling on our good King Leinor's business. Messengers. Military men. Craftsmen sent to Rindor. You knew we were royalty," stated Teeg.

"The young prince wears the crest of the House of Leinor on his ring finger," stated Hindle. "I'm a blacksmith's apprentice. I notice beautiful metal work immediately. Tis quite a remarkable piece. I wager it was given to Prince Eidyn when he came of age."

Kael and Flair looked at one another in astonishment. Ader coughed loudly and Teeg just beamed.

"I did not tell you my companion's name," smiled Teeg.

"You didn't need to tell me. Your companion is young by Elven standards. There is only one heir to the throne of Luxlor, and only he wears the crest of his family on his hand," stated Hindle. "In turn, I never gave you my name, Master Elf. How did you come upon it?"

"Tis my business to know many a place and those who are important to those places. I daresay I was required to search my memory for the blacksmith's apprentice in Quay, but you moved yourself to the top of the list in this small town," said Teeg turning to Ader. "A remarkable boy don't you agree, Lord Ader?"

The old man grunted and nodded his approval. Hindle cast a probing glance over the old man and Manfir. He was unable to reconcile the pair from what he knew of their past. Teeg interrupted his deliberations.

"Well, my boy. We must be about our business. Is the stallion's shoe set?"

The boy smiled and returned his gaze to the horse's shoe. Hindle produced a small hammer from the sack tied to his waist and hammered the shoe back into place.

"What do I owe you for such fine work, young man?" asked Teeg.

The boy hesitated and swept his gaze across the group once more.

"However much it pains me to pass on some coin," frowned Hindle. "I'll charge you nothing. I'm not a knight or prince of the realm, but I too am Zodrian. I never stood toe to toe with an Ulrog pack, and I don't expect to. However, I'm thankful to those who do and I wish to contribute to the fight in anyway I can. Instinct tells me you're important, far more important than I might imagine. Therefore, I render my services happily and free of charge. May Avra bless your proceedings."

Hindle bowed deeply and stepped back from the group. Teeg quickly glanced to Ader and the Guide nodded.

"The town of Quay requires a bit of competition in its sleepy streets," stated Teeg. "While your master, Boon the blacksmith, spends most of his day sleeping, and the remainder swilling ale, you do the work of the blacksmith of this village. Perhaps a new blacksmith's shop is needed here."

The old Elf deftly produced a small sack from the folds of his riding cloak and tossed it to Hindle. The young man caught it and from its weight and feel knew immediately it was filled with gold coin. He shook his head vigorously and walked back toward Teeg.

"I can't accept this in good conscience," said Hindle holding the sack toward Teeg. "I didn't earn it."

"I never said you earned it, my boy!" laughed Teeg. "But you will."

"Pardon?" questioned Hindle.

"You're a bright young man full of initiative and honesty. Just the sort of lad deserving of a benefactor, don't you agree?" asked Teeg.

"Well, I ...uh.." stammered Hindle.

"Exactly! This town requires a skilled, and might I say sober, artisan to supply them with their forged goods. Master Boon hasn't provided this service for some time. The only quality work to come out of his shop is yours, my boy. Therefore, certain powers are determined that you be given every opportunity to advance yourself."

Upon hearing "certain powers", Hindle glanced at Ader. Kael wondered what Teeg was up to. Hindle's eyes narrowed and he smiled.

"And what must I do in return?" asked Hindle.

"Why nothing, my boy. Absolutely nothing. Simply offer the quality goods and services this community requires to grow and prosper," smiled Teeg and he paused. ".... and maybe a few other chores."

"Such as?"

Teeg's smile and flippant manner disappeared.

"Continue to keep your keen eyes open. Merely what you do now. Observe. Maybe a bit of conjecture. Ask some innocent questions during the course of a conversation. Remember what you learn. Lastly, report that information to me."

Hindle became as serious as the old Elf.

"These things I can do, and would do for my crown. But I know naught of you, Lord Elf, and though your companion's ring tells me he is of the royal Elven house, he is no master of mine. Why should I do these things?" asked Hindle.

"Because this ring asks it of you," came the reply from beyond Teeg.

The young man looked past the Elf to see Manfir sitting on the back of his giant black warhorse. His hand clasped a chain hung about his neck. Dangling from the end of the silver chain was a large ring. Hindle inspected it from a distance and smiled.

"My prince calls me to do his bidding and I will obey," said Hindle bowing once more.

"You may never face an Ulrog pack, master blacksmith, but when you do the things Lord Teeg asked of you, you serve as well as any Guardian of the realm. An army does not support itself. All who serve are heroes," stated Manfir.

The village stirred as the group stood in growing sunlight.

"What of Master Boon?" asked Hindle. "He works me hard, but pays the wage agreed on and teaches me a skill. He was once a fine craftsman."

"Master Boon is a good man," said Teeg. "He simply loses sight of what life is about. Once you establish business, he will need employ. No doubt the townsfolk will come to you over him. Try to help him if you may, but remember, you are the master now."

Hindle's face remained serious and he bowed to Teeg in acknowledgment. Teeg turned to Ader and Manfir.

"I will hold here a moment while you move on. I have further instructions for our young friend. He'll need an effective way to transport his information. The town wakes and we must depart before too many eyes fix on our strange troop," said Teeg.

Manfir nodded and turned the midnight stallion down the road.

"Fare you well, Master Hindle," called the Zodrian prince over his shoulder.

The horses trod slowly through the city as shutters swung open. Townsfolk moved into the street and called greetings to one another. Several heads turned and followed the progression of riders. Some of the inhabitants called out greetings to the weary travelers, and others narrowed their eyes and stared.

"Any increase in our speed merely calls attention to us," said Manfir. "So many men pass through this town lately that five more will be of no account."

"Perhaps not my friend, but I'm sure the presence of an Elf is a rarity," returned Eidyn as he smiled at a pair of scruffy boys shadowing the troop.

The boys laughed and ran ahead of the riders throwing a tightly wrapped ball of cloth back and forth. Kael smiled at the memory of he and Aemmon doing the exact same thing through the streets of Kelky. Only a few years ago, when he and Aemmon were the age these boys were, Kael caught a tongue lashing for spooking the mounts in the stable with such a ball. When Kael looked over to Ader, he noticed the old man fidgeting on Tarader's back. Perhaps it really was difficult for the Seraph to ride bareback constantly. Kael turned his gaze back up the road and saw one of the boys standing against the outer wall of a not too distant building. When their gaze met, the boy instantly disappeared behind the wall.

Kael longed to be that boy's age again. A few chores and obligations to meet sometime during the day then freedom and no worries. He feared he might never attain that freedom again.

"We're almost through the town. Let's pick up the pace in order to reach the walls of Ymril this day," said Ader. "The further north we move the riskier it is to spend the evening outside city gates."

Manfir nodded his assent and gently tapped his heels into the black stallion's sides. The big horse snorted and began a light trot. The remainder of the party did the same and the group moved on in a slow rolling cantor. They reached the edge of the town and departed as the blue sky filled with the gray smoke of morning cook fires.

CHAPTER 18: THE MERCHANT AND THE MENACE

Manfir led them north for several hours. The cool breezes of the morning disappeared and were replaced by the beating midday sun. As they crested a small hill Eidyn called ahead to Manfir.

"Perhaps we should hold here a moment."

The big man reined in the black stallion, and gazed back south. After a few moments, Teeg came into view. The troop waited for his arrival. Kael realized they abandoned Granu and didn't make plans to reunite with the Keltaran prince. Surely they outpaced him. Teeg's stallion jogged up the hill.

"How fare you, my lord?" asked Eidyn.

The old Elf's usual smug smile crossed his face.

"Quite well. What a remarkable young man is our new blacksmith. As clever as any man I've met. Explain it to him once and he understands. What a find in the tiny village of Quay. I've instructed him to contact my cousin, Lord Paerrow, with his reports."

"An excellent choice," stated Ader.

"Yes. He volunteered to oversee my affairs while I am away," replied Teeg. "Master Hindle will provide Lord Paerrow with crucial information concerning this whole area."

"That is good, Lord Teeg," said Manfir. "Now that you rejoin us, I may increase our speed. We'll need to rest the horses shortly, then make a push for Ymril by nightfall."

"What of Prince Granu?" asked Kael. "With his injury he'll never catch us."

"If he doesn't rejoin us, he doesn't rejoin us. I do not care," stated Manfir.

"Don't worry about Granu," whispered Ader to Kael. "He's quite a remarkable young man himself."

The group formed up once more and set off north. Manfir increased the pace and the horses worked up a lather. Manfir kept the group at this speed for nearly an hour. As the road wound up out of a small ravine, the riders faced a long flat plane. In the distance, Kael spied a slow moving cart heading in the same direction. As they came closer, Kael noticed a single man driving it.

When the group came within fifty yards of the cart, the driver reined in his horse and pulled to the side of the road. He was short and powerfully built, the only hair on his shorn head curled in a bushy black mustache under his nose. He wore a heavy flowing brown robe and leather gloves covered his hands. Sweat ran down his shiny bald scalp. As the group crept closer, the driver's hand slipped inside his cloak and the other rose in greeting.

"Good day to you, gentlemen," called the stranger. "How fare you this fine day?"

"Excellent, good sir," called Teeg. "And yourself?"

Kael noticed that Ader and Manfir always deferred to the elder Elf in these matters. Teeg possessed a way of disarming people. They immediately became talkative around the old Elf.

"A good deal better if I might escape this heat," said the trader running a glove over his shiny bald scalp.

"Ah. The sun is unusually hot today," said Teeg "But at least her presence keeps bandits from the road."

"Aye, that's true," nodded the trader. "What brings an Elf lord to this north bound road?"

"On my king's business I'm afraid. No lord here," said Teeg pointing to himself. "Just a tired old messenger heading to Zodra with correspondence for King Macin. My son and I were lucky to be able to join these militiamen heading that way. Safety in numbers you know."

Kael shot a glance at Eidyn, who smiled innocuously at the trader. The family ring was gone from his hand and his military garb replaced by a simple cloak and trousers.

"Tis good advice, my friend. These are troubled times and news of late concerns me. I wish this old nag could keep up with your fine mounts. I find comfort in your company."

"Fear not, my good man," smiled Teeg. "We rode hard for a good bulk of the day and our mounts require a respite. We need to water and feed them near the next brook. We shall do the same to ourselves then move on toward Ymril. If you're truly inclined, you should join us. What news troubles you so?"

"Keltaran. Roaming freely in Zodrian territory," exclaimed the trader. "That troubles me. The giant brutes overran several of the western villages, slaughtering all who oppose them. The stories are too brutal to repeat. My hands quake at the idea of it."

"Keltaran you say? Down from the mountains and in the western wood?" asked Manfir eyeing Ader.

"Worse than that Master ....?"

"Rin," replied the Zodrian prince, then turned and pointed at Ader, "and my father, Jasper. We travel from Kelky in the South to serve with our two attendants in the army of our king."

"Well, your help is needed, Master Rin. All the king's men must heed his call. Even your father may be put to some good use," said the trader.

Ader scowled deeply but quickly recovered and addressed the trader.

"Whatever his kind majesty requires of me," said Ader in a feeble voice. "Are you called up as well Master ...?"

"Tepi. I'm Tepi from Cagson. And no, I'm not called. His majesty understands the important service traders provide to the public," stated Tepi with his chest puffed out. "With the war escalating, shortages of food and goods grow. We help alleviate the pressure on the citizenry by servicing those needs. I travel from Quay, where I delivered necessary food and supplies."

"You mentioned trouble worse than Keltaran roaming the western wood," said Teeg. "How so?"

"We usually face those abominations lurking along the borderlands," stated Tepi. "But they become so bold as to ride out onto the breaks and prairies of our great land, attacking villages deep in our own territory. I wager this road itself is no longer safe from them."

"Surely the king dispatches units from the Guard to protect the road?" questioned Manfir.

"None can be spared. Ulrog packs flock from the Northern Wastes and hammer our borders. Without constant reinforcement, the Ulrog will push out of the mountains. At least these are the stories I hear," said Tepi.

"What of the tribes of the Eru plains?" asked Eidyn. "They're allied to the Zodrian Guard."

"Ah, the horsemen are few and far between. They come when their lands are threatened. Even then, they simply move their herds deeper into their own territory to protect them," said Tepi.

This time, Eidyn and Manfir's eyes met. Kael noted the deep concern shared by the men, and the sharp-eyed Tepi noticed it as well.

"I don't give counsel where it's not requested," said the sweating bald man to Manfir. "But four more militia men and a pair of Elves won't make a difference in this conflict. You appear to be level headed gentlemen. Save yourselves and return to your homes in the south. The king won't miss you, and your aged father can finish his days in a rocking chair as opposed to under the edge of a Keltaran battle-ax."

Ader's face grew red and he smiled at the trader.

"That may be the way to save ourselves from the bloodshed now," said Ader with disdain. "But what of the future. In my short time left, the Ulrog may not advance to Kelky, but what of the lives of these two young men? Do we run now only to see the enemy eventually arrive on our doorstep?"

Tepi smiled dismissively at Ader, and turned to Manfir.

"Your father holds the sentiments of an earlier time. The world changes. The crown conscripts an army for such matters. Let those who train partake in the bloodshed, and those of us skilled in other matters go on with our lives." stated Tepi as his eyes bore down on Manfir.

"Your advice is noted, although it was not requested, Master Tepi," stated Ader in a strong voice. "We will answer the call of our king. If you wish to join us on the road, you may."

The trader's eyes bore down on Manfir.

"Then you must do as your father says," said Tepi in a cool steady voice.

"I must," replied Manfir.

The prince spun his horse northward and began a light trot up the road. The others in the group quickly fell in behind him. Tepi glanced back and forth across the roadway and put his whip to the old nag pulling his wagon. The beast snorted and lurched the swaying wagon forward.

After twenty minutes at this pace, Kael noted a telltale depression in the road about a half league ahead. A stream crossed at this point.

"We'll break from the road ahead and water the horses to the east of it," said Manfir.

After several minutes they were within fifty yards of the shallow stream. Manfir reined in and turned to the east. Another hundred yards from the road a small grove of trees grew close to the stream's side. Manfir motioned to the grove and the group headed that way, Tepi's wagon bouncing behind them. Kael was happy to see Manfir choose a shady area for them to rest. As they wandered through the thickets and brambles that grew beside the road, Kael thought he saw a figure sitting in the shade of the grove. Just ahead of him, Eidyn drew his bow and notched an arrow. The young men glanced at one another nervously.

"Your injury hasn't affected your speed my friend," called Teeg into the grove.

The black form awakened from a slumber or trance and grabbed the tree it leaned against for support. It grunted and pulled itself to its feet. There, with his black robe covering him from head to toe, stood Granu. Kael knew it must be the Keltaran, for no man in these parts stood that tall.

"It's difficult to travel while avoiding the road, but I felt it best," said Granu as he removed the cowl which covered his face.

Ader made a quick hand motion and the giant halted as Tepi's cart clanged into the grove. The trader glanced about the area and gasped when he spied Granu.

"Who .... who've we run into here?" gulped the trader.

"A mutual friend and servant of my people," stated Teeg offhandedly. "My master, King Leinor, spared his life once and the brute became indentured to my kingdom."

"Is ... is it dangerous?" exclaimed Tepi slipping his hand inside his robe once more.

"You may consider the Keltaran a brutal race, Master Tepi, but their word is their bond. This fellow hasn't seen his homeland in fifteen seasons, and is true to his service. If he was not, Leinor would put him to death," lied Teeg.

Tepi relaxed, but his hand never left his robe.

"What's the thing doing here in the wilderness all alone?" asked the trader.

"He's an excellent servant and bears almost any burden I require," commented Teeg. "But he does tend to upset the locals when we travel in these less than, shall we say, civilized locations. I often order him to jump ahead of us and wait. In this manner, no one gets upset. A worldly man like yourself must realize how these small villages get ugly when the townsfolk are upset."

Tepi relaxed even further and winked his assent.

"They're a backward folk these Southerners," laughed Tepi then shot a glance to Manfir. "No offense, of course."

"None taken," returned Manfir eyeing Granu. "We don't take kindly to outlanders."

"Nor do you treat them kindly," stated Granu.

"Not when they enter our lands armed and full of bloodlust!" shouted Manfir. "Master Tepi, inform our Keltaran servant of the deeds of his people this very week."

"I might, but it loathes me to talk to the creature," smiled Tepi.

"You may not wish to talk to me, but you will not refer to me as a creature in my own presence. I'm a man, and a better one than some here I might add," growled Granu.

Tepi took a step backward and shrunk beneath the giant's withering glare.

"Lord Elf," sniveled Tepi. "Did you hear that? Your servant threatened me. Do you control it or not?"

"Murder and butchery on a massive scale," exclaimed Manfir with fists clenched. "My people suffer at the hands of yours. Women and children! Barbaric!"

"This is a mistake. Slander spreads. My people aren't capable of this deed!" said Granu moving toward Manfir.

"Capable and willing!" shouted Manfir advancing on the giant. "I hold you personally responsible for these atrocities!"

"Yes! Yes!" squealed Tepi in a frenzy. "Now is the time! Now!"

"Enough!" yelled Teeg. "Nothing is to be done now. The Keltaran is under my protection and that of my king. I'll hear no more of revenge."

Granu and Manfir glowered at one another across the grove. Tepi narrowed his venomous eyes at the old Elf and spat on the ground. Granu broke eye contact with Manfir and turned to Teeg.

"I am yours to command. Do you require anything, master?" asked the giant.

"Of course you imbecile," snapped Teeg. "These horses will not water themselves! And make sure they're well fed this afternoon. We have a long journey ahead of us."

The giant bowed and gathered the reins of the Elf's horses in his hands. Teeg and Eidyn dismounted and the other travelers followed suit. Flair immediately tended to the remaining horses, and Kael gathered wood for a small fire. The remainder of the group stretched out on the ground under the shade. Muscles were stiff and backsides sore from many hours in the saddle.

Kael wandered to the southeast of the grove in search of firewood. His mind wandered over the day's events. These men were so unusual, able to switch their personalities on and off to suit the situation. They acted like actors in a huge play.

Who was the real Teeg? The tottering, helpless old Elf; The cunning provider of information to his crown; The arrogant, flippant member of the Elven court. Kael was unsure if the man truly was any of these. They all confused him so. Ader; Crusty, clever old trader; Powerful, controlling statesman; Mouthpiece of the Creator himself. Manfir; Silent, brooding commoner; Outspoken prince of the realm; Fierce, fiery warrior.

He even confounded himself. Son of an innkeeper; an earl; a Guardsman. Was he himself something he was unsure of? He knew he was different from the others. He was always different from Aemmon. The memory of his brother brought a tear to his eye as he looked out over leagues of scrubland.

Awareness startled him. Something or someone was among the grasses. He concentrated and picked up sounds of movement thirty yards ahead and to the left. His heart raced. Was it a prairie deer, hiding amongst the thickets? Langre cats prowled these ravines and breaks. Did he stumble into one? He backed away slowly and reached into his tunic to draw his blade. As he stepped backward he bumped into something behind him and his heart leapt. Strong arms held his shoulders and a voice whispered in his ear.

"Remain calm."

Eidyn stepped to Kael's left and carefully unslung his bow. He notched an arrow and took a bead on a thicket thirty yards in front of the pair. Kael saw no movement, but was sure something hid behind the bushes. The bowstring creaked as Eidyn slowly drew the arrow backward. Eidyn loosed the arrow at the exact moment a figure flashed from the thicket and into the shadows of another. The Elven archer quickly notched another and drew it back. The voice of Ader broke the silence.

"Prince Eidyn, now is not the time for sport! Return to the grove and rest yourself."

Eidyn and Kael turned to the old man in surprise. Out of the corner of his eye, Kael saw another flash as the figure behind the bush retreated even further from the men. Kael was sure it would never be caught now.

"Ader," said Eidyn. "Something stalks us from the brambles."

"We're not in need of food, Eidyn. Leave the creature be and come back to the grove," said Ader calmly.

"But Master Ader," interrupted Kael. "I don't think it's an animal. I believe it's a person."

"Nonsense. Eidyn would know instantly," Ader turned to Eidyn. "Do you think a person is stalking Kael from the scrub out there?"

Eidyn hesitated a moment and then looked to Kael.

"I've been uneasy ever since we left Luxlor. Perhaps the discovery of the bodies of my kin upsets me, but I feel watched and trailed on this journey. I can't confirm whether the creature was a prairie deer or a person. Whoever or whatever it was, it reacted with amazing speed and cleverness. The shaft of my arrow barely left my bow when it was on the move," said Eidyn.

"I too feel uneasy on this road," said Kael. "I feel eyes upon me."

"Perhaps the Keltaran are in alliance with some group we're unaware of," came Tepi's voice from just inside the nearby grove. "Perhaps they scout and shadow the roads, planning an assault on the kingdom."

The squat, bald trader stepped from behind a pair of trees and approached the trio. He wore his flowing robe of thick brown wool. His hands were still covered in heavy leather gloves and he sweated profusely.

"The day the Keltaran decide to assault the kingdom of Zodra, they'll not need to scout the realm," laughed Ader. "There's one way and one way alone to assault Zodra. Bring everything you have to bear upon the capital city. Keltaran warriors won't bother with the outskirts of the remote town of Ymril."

Tepi sneered at Ader and turned a honey sweet smile to the young men before him.

"The old always consider the old ways as the right ways. Those of us in a more contemporary mind are willing to accept all possibilities," smiled Tepi.

"Humph!" chortled Ader as he turned and strode toward the grove. "I suggest you gentlemen return to camp. And Eidyn, please leave the prairie deer to their dinner!"

Tepi waited until Ader was out of sight then turned to the remaining men.

"Don't listen to old fools and their old ways. We're in a time of war, and no quarter should be given to the enemy. I understand this Keltaran is a servant, a thing I've never heard of, but he should be kept on a tight leash," said Tepi to Eidyn. "One day that staff he carries just may break your neck."

"I don't fear him, Master Tepi," stated Eidyn. "But I will heed your advice and take care."

The Elf made his way back into the grove.

"Elves. Arrogant and useless," said Tepi shaking his head. "You're in a troop of fools young man. Best for you to go home and let them kill themselves."

"I'll stay with my master," said Kael.

"Suit yourself," said Tepi as he turned and trudged back into the grove.

Kael did not want to return with the trader. The man troubled him and the boy preferred to wait. Kael turned and looked back over the scrubland stretched out before him. His thoughts wandered over the possibilities Tepi presented. It would be nice to go home and forget all this nonsense. The army was there to protect the people. Why was he traveling north toward danger? He longed to see his father, but Brelg would surely return to Kelky once his business was done? Kael was lonely. He missed Aemmon.

As he stood thinking, he swore he heard the faintest of whispers out among the thickets.

"Get out of my head and leave me be!" shouted Kael as he spun and tromped into the grove.

CHAPTER 19: LED THROUGH DARKNESS

 The group lazed in the grove for an hour. The horses were watered and munched on the long grasses that grew next to the stream. Tepi refused to unharness his carthorse, so Flair did it for him. Flair also provided dried beef to the travelers, even offering a share to Tepi. The trader turned his nose up at the boy and retreated to a shadowy corner of the grove to eat his own provisions. Granu kept well out of sight, down by the stream. Finally, Manfir rose and scooped his saddle up with one hand.
 "We spend far too much time here. We must be on our way," said the Zodrian prince.
 The group gathered itself together and mounted their horses. Flair harnessed Tepi's carthorse while the trader grumbled about the delay. However, the remainder of the group waited patiently and soon all were on their way. The assembly made its way back to the road and turned north. Granu trailed in his usual place. Tepi's nag found it difficult to keep pace with the group, but every time the cart fell back toward Granu, the sweating trader whipped the horse mercilessly to garner speed.
 The sun slid toward the horizon once more and progress was slowed. Tepi unexpectedly found a great deal of compassion for his cart horse and frequently halted to water the nag at a roadside brook or stream. The land was full of such streams. Everywhere Kael looked, the land rolled out toward the horizon with small breaks and ravines. To the west the plains elevated at an almost imperceptible rate to the mountains beyond. To the east, they slid toward the grasslands of the Erutre. Essentially, Zodra was an enormous washbasin, collecting the runoff from the mountains to the west and north. Hours of similar, unending landscape passed before them.
 They splashed through a rock strewn, shallow stream and Tepi shouted for a halt. Kael turned to see the trader throw his

hands up in frustration. Manfir reined in his stallion and the party halted.

"Master Rin, I'm afraid I fouled a wheel," called Tepi.

"This fool will be the death of me," grumbled Ader as he shook his head.

Surprisingly, the bald headed trader heard the Guide.

"Perhaps, if you weren't in such a rush to get yourself killed in battle, I wouldn't have run pell-mell into these rocks, old man. Haste makes waste," said Tepi.

"Perhaps, if you drove with both eyes on the road, instead of on the Keltaran, you would have missed such hazards," snapped Ader.

"I don't delude myself as to who my enemies are," growled Tepi.

Kael edged back toward the stream and saw Tepi's right front wheel splintered between two of its wooden spokes. The wood appeared rotten and worn. Granu strode up to the group.

"What's wrong? That nag drinks more than a battalion of Keltar warriors," said Granu

The giant knelt near the wheel and inspected the break.

"Hold your tongue Keltaran, and keep your paws off of my cart," snapped Tepi.

The trader showed surprising agility as he jumped from the seat of the cart into the stream with a splash. Water sprayed into the Keltaran's face. Granu wiped himself clean with the sleeve of his robe and calmly backed away from the cart.

"As you wish, Master Tepi," he said.

Manfir rode back to the stream and shook his head.

"That wheel won't hold for another league," said Manfir. "And I'm sure you don't keep a replacement handy."

"It takes room away from my goods," whined Tepi.

Manfir looked about the landscape and spied a tall, lonely elm.

"Perhaps we'll be able to mend it quickly and get back on the road. The elm should provide some timber," said Manfir.

Flair was already on the move. The boy galloped to the tree and dismounted. He tied his horse to the nearest thicket and produced a hatchet from a bag on the horse's side. Tepi stared at the wheel and shook his head.

"Master Tepi. Get that cart over to the tree. We must prop it up and remove that wheel," commanded Manfir.

The trader snapped out of his brooding and glared at the Zodrian prince. He slowly climbed back into the cart and coaxed the old nag over the rocky surface to the tree. Kael unhitched the nag. Tepi leapt down as Manfir used his sword to gouge a hole in the ground near the wheel of the cart. Flair cut a sturdy thick post about a yard long. The boy came over to the cart and stood ready with the post.

Manfir grabbed an edge of the cart next to broken wheel and heaved upward. He strained on its weight and it slowly rose. The cart hovered over the ground for a moment and Flair fixed one end of the post in the hole. Flair tried to wedge the other end under the cart to keep it propped in the air. However, Manfir did not lift the cart high enough. The prince glanced over his shoulder at the group standing behind him. Granu mumbled something and threw back his hood. The fading sun shown on his scarred head as he stepped forward and threw a shoulder into the cart. Immediately, it rose high in the air and Flair slid the top end of the post beneath. The two men let the cart settle onto the post and stepped away.

"How long, Master Flair?" puffed Manfir.

"Two hours for a proper job," replied Flair.

"How long for a repair that will get him to the next village?" asked Manfir.

"Less than half that time," said Flair.

"As quickly as you can," said Manfir patting the boy on the back. "The rest of us might as well take a break."

Flair worked diligently on the cart's restoration. Kael had never watched a wheel repaired so he stayed and helped the young man with any requirements. In Kelky, they brought their damaged carts and wagons to Jemer the blacksmith. Often, small towns employed men like Jemer, who wore more than one hat out of necessity. Blacksmith, wheelwright, carpenter, mason, Jemer did it all.

Flair lived on his grandfather's ranch. The ranches were normally self-sufficient and young men like Flair were taught any number of skills. Kael was certain Flair performed all kinds of tasks on request.

After an hour, Flair sufficiently restored the wheel. Manfir inspected the work and was quite satisfied. Flair cut strips of green wood from the elm and bent them inside the wheel frame, supporting it from the inside out. It was lucky that the wood was fresh and pliant. The group gathered up and once more made its way north.

Manfir attempted to increase the pace, but Tepi lagged. The sweaty trader complained and worried his wheel might collapse. The temporary repairs created a hitch in the wagon's turn. Every time the wheel reached the affected area, the cart jumped and rattled. Tepi grumbled about his aching back. Kael grew annoyed.

"Why don't we go on and just leave him to his business?" whispered Kael to Teeg.

"Courtesy, my boy," answered Teeg. "When you're out on the open road, you try to help others. We offered him our companionship and he accepted. To leave him now is quite a breach of good faith."

"But he's in no danger," replied Kael. "Those repairs will last all the way to the Northern Wastes, if he were inclined to drive there. He simply slows us down."

"I know you're anxious to see your father, but whether this Tepi is an ass or not, we promised to travel with him," said Teeg. "We will not be with him long."

The sun crawled down to the horizon and Manfir's expression became grave.

"We'll not make Ymril today. The journey requires several more hours and unfortunately the sun is setting. Clouds will hide the moon tonight, creating a dark evening. I don't wish to tempt the fates and make a horse lame while stumbling through this darkness. Delays cost us a warm bed and a hot meal," frowned Manfir. "We'll pull off the road ahead and make camp once more."

They traveled for several more leagues and found another brook spilling through the countryside not far from the road. Manfir led the group to a clearing near a wide field of tall, wild grasses.

"We find both water and food here for our mounts. There is less protection for us from the elements and anything else, but I don't think we'll find any better," said Manfir.

"Agreed," said Teeg. "The land is similar to this all the way to Ymril. We will find no better."

The group pulled into the clearing and set up camp. Flair and Kael quickly built a fire and the young cattleman stewed some meat within minutes. Eidyn and Teeg cared for the horses. Ader walked to the far side of the clearing and surveyed the horizon as the sun passed beneath it. Tepi parked his cart awkwardly in the middle of the clearing. The fat trader once again agilely leapt from its seat with a blanket in hand. He stomped toward the fire and looked into the pot in which Flair prepared the meal.

"Call me when it's ready," demanded Tepi.

He walked to his cart and ducked underneath it, curling into a ball under the blanket. Within minutes the sound of his loud snoring filled the campsite. Granu took several water flasks from the saddles of the horses and disappeared into the tall grass in the direction of the brook. Manfir pulled some maps from his saddle and studied their contents near the fire. The sun set and the light from the fire danced inside the darkness surrounding their little enclave.

Kael and Flair sat near the fire and talked about their day as they prepared the meal. Kael looked toward Ader and saw the old man standing near the tall grasses. The field grew so high it nearly reached the old trader's head. Ader stood gazing into the distance softly humming to himself. Kael felt the uneasy sensation he shared with Eidyn earlier in the journey. He suspected that he was being watched. Kael stood and tried to survey the grassland about him.

The darkness was impenetrable. A light breeze played off the grasses and the light of the fire touched their golden stalks.

Kael approached the old man and Ader stopped humming. He turned to the boy.

"Is the meal prepared yet?" smiled Ader as he swept past Kael.

"Uh, it will be shortly," replied Kael.

He stood watching as Ader ambled to the fireside and complimented Flair on his hard work. Kael turned back to the tall grasses and stared into their shifting wall. The uneasiness crept over him once more. Teeg and Eidyn finished with the horses and moved to the fireside as well. Manfir stood a few paces from Tepi's wagon sharpening one of his daggers and the heaving lump under the cart informed Kael that Tepi continued his slumber. The boy quietly approached the swaying wall of grass and slipped inside.

CHAPTER 20: THE LESSONS OF PREJUDICE

Immediately he was plunged into darkness. The soft seed stalks of the wild grasses brushed one another just over his head. He still sensed someone or something just beyond his sight. Kael slowly picked his way through the field. He tried to create as minimal a disturbance as possible.

He heard a small noise to his left. Was it a light laugh? What was out here? He moved in its direction. Once again he heard a small noise in front of him. He picked his way through the field. Here and there Kael passed small scrub trees that spread their branches several feet above the deep pasture. The field thinned under these trees, creating small, empty pockets in the sea of grass. The spreading trees stood like dark islands rising above the waves.

The wind whipped. The stalks ahead parted for an instant. Was that a small figure darting ahead of him?

"Hey! You! Stop!" ordered Kael. His call was lost against the wind.

Kael increased his speed and worked his way left. No one was there. He moved ten yards further and came to one of the scrub trees. Its canopy created a void of darkness beneath. Twisted branches and a gnarled trunk were barely visible under the canopy. Kael stopped and sat with his back to the tree trying to concentrate on his surroundings. Perhaps he would be able to sense movement once more. He let his heart slow and controlled his breathing. He reached out for any sound to alert him to the figure's whereabouts.

"Are you afraid?" came a husky whisper from directly behind the boy.

Kael started and shot a glance over his shoulder to the opposite side of the trunk. A blackness, deeper and more tangible than that created by the tree, hovered just beyond his reach. The twisted trunk of the scrub tree obscured the figure.

"No," lied Kael.

"It is foolish not to fear the unknown. Fear is healthy, as long as you control it," said the voice. "You are curious? You want to know what shadows your group?"

"Yes," replied Kael.

"Curiosity is also healthy, when tempered with caution," chided the voice. "Fools let their curiosity lure them to their deaths. The wise man uses caution as his aid. Time reveals all."

"What are you, foolish or wise?" asked Kael in return.

Kael heard a rustling and noted movement inside the blackness. It fell away like a curtain and Kael looked into the visage of Granu Stormbreaker staring at him from behind the gnarled branches of the tree. The Keltaran giant crouched under the tree with all but his face completely covered by his black robes.

"I'm neither foolish nor wise, for I'm a servant of my Creator and my path was chosen for me. If my decisions seem foolish to some, so be it, as long as they conform to the wishes of the Master," murmured Granu.

The duo stared at one another for a while. Finally, Granu's face broke into a wide grin.

"Are you afraid now?" whispered the enormous man.

"No," lied Kael once more.

"I don't believe you, but that is the correct answer," said the giant keeping his voice low. "What are you doing out here?"

"I saw .... or maybe heard someone in the tall grass. I tried to discover what it was," replied Kael.

"Hmmm, interesting," said Granu. "Did you see someone or did you hear them? Surely you know if it was one or the other. If it was a person why did you say you tried to discover 'it'?"

"I ... I am not sure. I guess I heard it first and followed it into the grass. As I followed it I thought I saw someone," said Kael frowning. "I might ask why you are perched under this tree?"

"A valid question," answered Granu. "I was returning with flagons full of water..."

The giant pulled several water skins from beneath his robes and shook their contents.

"... when I was distracted by the sound of movement in the underbrush. I followed its course and tried to surprise it by running ahead and lying in wait. After several moments you skulked through the grass and sat there opposite me," smiled Granu.

"I didn't skulk, I was tracking," grumbled Kael. "Nothing came past before me?"

"Nothing."

Kael shook his head in dismay.

"It was right in front of me. Not more than three paces. I almost captured it," said Kael.

"Whatever it was, it was playing with you, Kael Brelgson," said Granu.

"How so?" asked Kael.

"When I returned to the clearing with the water, I entered from the north and made a wide circuit through the clearing to its south side. I like to get a feel for a place. Learn its strengths and weaknesses. I heard movement to the south of the clearing in the grass. I suppose that is where you entered. I tracked the movement east. I followed from in the clearing as the movement turned to the north, then once more to the west.

"Your phantom led you in a circle around the campsite. I passed this tree when I strolled from the brook earlier and knew exactly where to hide when I reentered the tall grasses. You sit on the opposite side of the camp from where you entered the field."

"I ... I wasn't paying attention to my path," said Kael.

"An example of how your curiosity might endanger you. Your mystery creature led you where it wanted. You must exercise caution. Strength lies in numbers, Kael Brelgson. When you have numbers at your disposal, use them," stated Granu.

"I wasn't afraid," said Kael sulkily.

Granu shook his head back and forth with a wry grin on his face. The absurdity of the scene struck Kael. This giant man crouched in a ball under a stunted tree. His disembodied head grinning at the boy and floating in the darkness created by Granu's cloak and the moonless prairie night.

"Why do you grin at me so?" asked Kael.

"It is humorous for me to think that you were unafraid of the unknown, yet are so obviously afraid of me," smiled Granu. "A creature of unknown origin coaxes you into the tall grasses and toys with you, but your true fears lie here in front of you. On the other side of this tiny tree."

"That isn't true, I'm not..." defended Kael.

"The Keltaran aren't the monsters you're taught about, Kael," replied Granu.

"I never said .."

"Prejudice is taught. Hatred is learned," interrupted Granu. "All of Avra's creatures are born pure of heart. We aren't born with hatred in our hearts, but with the potential for hatred. The forces of evil and Amird plant the seed when we are most vulnerable. If it's watered with the anger and hatred of others, it will grow. Why do you fear my people?"

"You come from the mountains and murder Zodrians and destroy our villages and towns," replied Kael defiantly.

Granu smiled once more.

"Have you ever spent a winter in the mountains, Kael?"

"No," came the reply.

"It's cold, bitterly cold. We own huge herds of mountain goats and sheep. We breed and raise this stock. It is our life, our means of sustenance. They provide food, clothing, and milk. They often seek the valleys to find forage and shelter in the winter months. We must head into these valleys to gather our wayward herds. Often, your people claim these animals as their own," said Granu.

"That is no excuse to raid and pillage villages," interrupted Kael. "Perhaps these villagers were unaware this stock was yours."

"Believe me. In the beginning, every effort was made to provide this information. The stock is branded. Their horns are often clipped to prevent injury. There is no mistaking a Keltaran sheep for a wild ram. Your people look down on us as no more than savages. To steal from a savage is no sin. We're less than human and treated as such," replied Granu.

"I thought you Keltaran were the superior ones. Lords of battle. War over peace. You raid our villages to steal," snapped Kael.

"I'm not the first person to tell you to look past what you're taught and expand your vision. I'm sure I won't be the last," stated Granu. "Would you like to hear the same story from a different point of view? Would you like to hear the story of the Keltaran and then judge history with a more open mind? A ruler happily gathers information, for you cannot rule from a position of ignorance."

Kael bit his lip. The others might wonder where he went. However, to sit here and steadfastly defend his people, when he was acutely aware he never really considered the conflict, was wrong. He showed his own ignorance if he refused to hear the Keltaran out.

"I'll listen," said Kael.

"Good," said Granu. "The mother of my people was a maiden named Gretcha, a Zodrian princess."

"I know of Gretcha," said Kael proudly.

"So," smiled Granu. "You already begin to see things from a different perspective."

"Uh, yes, I guess I do," said Kael.

"What do you know?" asked Granu.

Kael quickly recounted all he learned from Teeg concerning Awoi, Amird, and Gretcha. As he finished, Granu smiled.

"An even-handed telling I must say," said Granu. "I will further your education on this matter."

Hrafnu was no ordinary child. He possessed even greater size and strength than that of his mother. It was said that he could fell a full-grown oak with three swings of his ax. His intelligence was supreme as well. He studied the habits of the mountain rams and goats and soon tamed and bred great herds. Mother and son were never in need. The world outside their peaceful valley continued on its way and the mother and child lived a simple, happy existence.

When Hrafnu was old enough, Gretcha told her son all she knew of the world. She told him of the Zodrian kingdom and the cities and towns full of people to the South and East. Hrafnu grew interested and longed to see such places. Gretcha told

Hrafnu how she and her son were different from the rest of the human race. She told him of people's fear and ignorance. Hrafnu heard and understood.

The boy grew into a man. Gretcha taught him everything that Awoi taught her. Hrafnu learned to track the great grizzled bear and what mountain berries were edible. She taught him how a snowdrift might become a shelter during the fiercest storm, what herbs cured common ailments, how to make bows and arrows, tools for cutting lumber and shaping it. Often Hrafnu improved upon the knowledge he acquired.

One day Hrafnu returned to his valley from hunting. He noticed the chimney of their cabin produced no smoke. As he entered the cabin he saw his mother lying on her bed. She looked gray and ill. He knelt beside her bed.

'Mother, what's wrong?' questioned the alarmed man.

'I'm dying, my so,' replied Gretcha smiling.

Hrafnu hung his head and sobbed. The old woman ran a hand thru his thick hair.

'Do not grieve, my love. I lived a long life. Much longer than most,' said the old woman. 'I go to join your father in the hands of Avra. This is a day I longed for.'

'I.... I won't know what to do. I'll be lost without you,' cried Hrafnu.

'No, you will be set free without me, my gift. For that is what you are, a gift from your father to me. He knew he would leave me, so he gave you to me in order to fill my life with joy and happiness. My days were blessed from the day you were born. Now you must enter the world and make your mark.'

'How am I to do that?' asked Hrafnu. 'What am I to do?'

'I don't know, my son, but Avra will guide you. Stay true to what I taught you and you will triumph. You are special, over all other humans. Remember that.'

Gretcha spoke the truth, for she was nearing one hundred years of age and her son neared eighty, yet he bore the look of a man in his twenties. He inherited the long life of his father and lived for centuries.

'I go now to spend an eternity with my love,' whispered Gretcha. *'Live a good life and know that we wait for you to join us.'*

The old woman gave a long sigh and breathed no more. Hrafnu's head fell into his hands and he sobbed deeply.

The giant buried his mother in their valley and resumed his life. Years turned to decades and he saw and spoke to no other being. He grew lonely. Hrafnu reflected on the life of his mother and father. He wanted desperately to honor the way they both lived. He determined to contribute to the world the way his father contributed. He left his valley and went out to view the world.

Amird's control left its mark on the kingdom of Zodra. The city grew rapidly. This growth required more land and more supplies to sustain the great metropolis. War and conquest became the focus of the kingdom. Power struggles within the city were the norm. Assassination and murder reigned in the court of the castle. As Zodra's power grew, so too did the scope of her reign.

This is the world Hrafnu encountered as he emerged from his valley. After trekking hundreds of leagues from his home, Hrafnu came upon a scene of chaos. Zodrians had raided a small mining village the night before. The men and boys from the village tried to defend their homes, but the Zodrians slaughtered them and pillaged the town.

Hrafnu stepped from the woods to find the smoldering remains of this tiny village. The women of the town were gathering the bodies of their husbands and sons and dragging them away for burial. Children roamed the streets crying. Hrafnu knew his size and appearance would frighten the villagers, so he promptly fell to his knees, lowered his head and extended his palms upward. Nevertheless, many of the women and children fled in terror.

'In the name of Avra, I come in peace and seek only to help.' shouted Hrafnu.

One young woman was a strong believer in the ways of the Creator. She watched Zodrians butcher her entire family while she hid in a cellar corner. The young woman could stand no more. She walked confidently into the village street and called to Hrafnu.

'You come too late creature. All is gone. Nothing remains. All that is left for you to take is our lives, a commodity of scant value that we shall surely lose as the bitter winter approaches. Be gone from us and leave us in our endless sorrow.'

Hrafnu's heart filled with sadness for these women and children. The bold young woman spoke the truth. With no supplies, the winter surely would take most of them. Hrafnu determined to follow in the footsteps of his father.

'I carry no weapons and am not a violent man. I offer my services to you. Anyway in which I might help, I shall. I can help you rebuild your homes. I am proficient with medicines and herbs and may be able to heal the injured among you. Anything you ask,' said Hrafnu.

'If you wish to help, then bury our dead!' scoffed the young woman.

Dozens of bodies lay throughout the village. Hrafnu rose and calmly moved forward. Those who lingered to hear the conversation fled and hid in what remained of their homes. The young woman stood steadfast as Hrafnu approached. He bowed low to her.

'As my lady command,' said the giant.

Hrafnu worked for the remainder of the day and half the next, stopping only to eat and drink a small meal from his supplies. Dozens of graves were dug at the end of the town. Hrafnu reverently carried the fallen bodies of the townsmen and boys to the graves and set them to rest. He said a small prayer over each and commended their souls to Avra.

When Hrafnu laid the last body to rest, he knelt in the new graveyard and bowed his head in prayer. When he looked up, he was face to face with the bold young woman.

'I do not know where you come from, friend,' said the woman, 'but your heart is full of kindness. Thank you for helping us in our hour of need.'

'Tis what Avra calls on us all to do for others,' said Hrafnu.

'What is your name?' asked the woman.

'I am Hrafnu, son of Awoi.'

'Bless you Hrafnu, son of Awoi. I am Uttren,' said the woman.

Upon seeing the task complete many of the others lost their fear of Hrafnu and emerged from hiding places. Soon, with the help of Uttren, Hrafnu was binding broken limbs and applying healing herbs to cuts and bruises. He stayed in the village for a week and the women learned his gentle nature and kindly manners. All who knew him lost their fear of the giant. On the seventh day Hrafnu addressed the villagers.

'Winter approaches. If I read the signs properly, it will be harsh. You stored no food, cut no wood. Hunting will become difficult as the herds wander further south. There is not enough shelter standing to house all of you. You told me the soldiers came before. They will come again. You must leave, or you will all die.'

'And go where, Hrafnu? A group of women and children alone in the wilds? I and several of the others can take care of ourselves, but what of the children? You accomplished so much for us, but your suggestion holds no merit. I would rather the whole of us huddle in one small building than wander the wilderness,' cried Uttren.

'I know of a solution to your problem,' said Hrafnu. 'Come with me, to my home. It is two weeks march from here.'

Hrafnu described his valley. He talked of its clear streams full of fish, the great herds of mountain rams he tended, the immense lodge he built after the death of his mother, rooms full of wool, mountains of stacked firewood.

'I offer you life, and ask for nothing in return,' stated the giant.

The group left the next morning. It was a hard march on the children, but with Hrafnu's help all arrived safely. They settled in shortly before the onset of a particularly nasty winter. It arrived early and stayed late. The group held strong in Hrafnu's lodge, supported by his vast storehouse of food and supplies.

Three years passed and the women remained. Life was good in Hrafnu's valley. Every summer the giant roamed the outskirts of Zodrian territory and tried to help the orphans of war. Men, women and children received his kindness. Often he returned to the valley with those in need. His people accepted the needy and the population grew.

After the third summer, Hrafnu returned to his lodge. New buildings stood throughout the valley. The herds grew and winter corn was ready for harvesting. The residents greeted Hrafnu cheerily. He entered the lodge and sat at the great table, weary from a long march. Uttren entered and asked all others in the lodge to depart. She sat opposite Hrafnu and stared at him.

'Uttren, I was away too long this summer. I miss the valley. How fare you?' said Hrafnu.

'Not an unpleasant looking man. A bit oversized, but no one is perfect,' stated Uttren to herself. 'Yes, it is what it is.'

'What did you say?' questioned Hrafnu as he raised a tankard of cold ale to his lips.

Uttren snapped out of her deep rumination. She stared at Hrafnu but this time directed her comments to him.

'We are to be wed after the harvest, Hrafnu son of Awoi,' stated Uttren.

'WHAT?' spluttered Hrafnu, spraying ale across the room.

Uttren stood and put her hands to her hips.

'I said "We are to be wed after the harvest". Did you not understand or does the concept not appeal to you?' demanded the woman.

'No .. I ... uh.' mumbled Hrafnu.

'Listen to me, Hrafnu,' growled Uttren. 'I have overseen this valley for three summers now. When you are gone, I rule in your stead. I order work details. I decide when to harvest the summer crop. I decide when the sheep are to be shorn. I choose which ewes to slaughter. I settle all disputes.

'I am of marrying age and I want to bear a child. If you neglected to notice, there are not many men to choose from in this valley. You are kind, generous, and provide for all I shall ever want or need. Besides, I love you and can think of no other man I would rather share my bed. We will be wed or I will leave the valley.'

Hrafnu stood and bowed. A broad smile crept across his face.

'We will be wed, fair Uttren,' said Hrafnu.

'On the day we met, you asked me to order you and you would do anything I asked,' replied Uttren. 'You remained faithful to that pledge for three years. I will order you no longer, my husband.'

Uttren rose and for the first time bowed politely to Hrafnu. She too allowed a broad smile to widen upon her face. She spun and stepped lightly from the lodge into another beautiful day in Hrafnu's valley.

Uttren bore Hrafnu many children. All of the children mirrored their father's size, strength and intellect. Years passed and the population in the valley grew. Hrafnu traveled less and less, for the demands of his own lands called for attention. Many of the people he ruled harbored hatred for the Zodrian kingdom, but Hrafnu preached tolerance. Many lost loved ones at the hands of Zodrian raiding parties, but Hrafnu emulated his father and forgave. When Hrafnu reached one hundred and eighty three years of age, Uttren died. The giant buried her in the valley next to his mother and mourned her the rest of his life.

Hrafnu's longevity and that of his offspring molded the look of his people. Some of his sons outlived three wives and fathered many children by all of them. The population in the valley grew. Some of his sons took their families to neighboring valleys, but maintained close ties with their father. All of Hrafnu's people deferred to their father's judgment on important matters. The kingdom of Hrafnu spread along the foothills of the Western mountains.

Zodra also grew. The city now stood as the capital of a great and spreading nation. Surrounding cities were referred to as the capitals of the provinces. The monarchy gave dukes and barons a share of power in order to keep the nation unified. Their early brutality faded as time took them further and further from the influence of Amird. The citizens of Zodra bridled at the life of fear they lived under. Uprisings in the provinces and at home caused reform. Often, particularly harsh or unpopular rulers were thrown out of the castle, and a respected duke was installed in his place. In this way the royal family of Zodra changed many times over the years. Peace and civility ruled the kingdom.

As Zodra grew, and Hrafnu's people spread across the land, it was inevitable that they should come in contact. Stories of giants roaming the mountain lands spread throughout Zodra. For years the Zodrians reported these sightings and myths sprang up concerning the race of giants. Boastful woodcutters and miners embellished their peaceful encounters with Hrafnu's people and the fear of the giants grew. More and more of these encounters turned violent. Hrafnu's people quite often ran from their attackers.

Hrafnu preached peace. He was the first of my order, a teacher in the ways of Avra. He coaxed his people to show patience and turn from their attackers. Many of Hrafnu's people died from encounters with the Zodrians. Often they were unarmed and unskilled in the ways of warriors. They were simply cut down and paraded through Zodrian villages as trophies by their attackers. Again, in order to build their image, these attackers embellished the fierceness of these giant, peaceful shepherds.

Hrafnu prayed and agonized over the fate of his people. He was a follower of his father Awoi and his Creator, but he was also the leader of a people. The population grew and a clash with the Zodrians was inevitable. Some of his sons called for war to protect themselves. They armed themselves with crude weapons.

Hrafnu decided to avoid disaster. He convinced his burgeoning population to head further into the hills and mountains. The valleys held too much danger. His people were already great trekkers and the strains of hiking through the mountains held no consequence for them. When encountered by Zodrians, the Keltaran merely climbed the nearest slopes and disappeared from view. The Zodrian cavalry were unable to follow and would not give chase on foot even if they could. The Keltaran found safety in their mountains and learned to love them.

Hrafnu's eldest son, Netur, was as peaceful a man as Hrafnu himself. Hrafnu saw the beauty of his wife in the eyes of his eldest son. Netur however, also displayed his mother's single-mindedness. He was a stubborn, independent man. Netur was one of the first to leave Hrafnu's valley decades before when the population grew too large to be supported by the limited resources. Hrafnu blessed the move and wished his son well. The men kept in contact and Netur respected his father's wishes on all things. They fiercely loved and respected one another.

When Hrafnu sent word to the outlying population of his intention to move further into the mountains. The son considered the advice of his father and although he found it to be sound, he could not follow it. He lived in the foothills surrounding his own valley for half a century and could not bear to leave them. His clan was tied to the land and loved it.

Hrafnu moved high into the mountains. One of his scouts discovered a narrow gorge that opened into a wide valley. Jagged peaks surrounded the valley and a stream, born from the snows of the mountain peaks, wound through its lush green grass. Hrafnu surveyed the land and acknowledged its merits. It was large enough to support his herds and growing population. Water was plentiful. But most importantly, it was secluded and remote from the eyes of Zodra.

The powerful hands of his people cut huge slabs of stone from these mountains and fashioned a stronghold to protect themselves. Thus was Keltar born. The Mountain City. A place of refuge and peace.

Hrafnu kept close contact with his son and periodically asked Netur to change his mind. Netur never did.

One summer a runner was dispatched to invite Netur and his people to join in the three hundredth birthday celebration of Hrafnu. The runner returned with grave news. Hrafnu's beloved son and grandchildren were slaughtered. Their homes were burnt to the ground and their livestock stolen. The Zodrians committed their worst once more.

Hrafnu threw himself into a fit of sorrow. The Zodrians took his first-born child, his closest connection to his beloved Uttren. He was inconsolable. After a night, his sorrow turned to rage. He leapt from his chair in the great meeting hall and called for his cloak. The giant stormed from the hall and stopped before a great woodpile used to fuel the lodge's huge fires. His people gathered about their raging ruler as he wrenched an ax from a massive stump.

'Once, long ago, an ax was wielded in anger to protect a loved one. It smote the shoulder of the evil Amird and helped send him from this world. So shall this lowly tool of civilization be used once more,' cried Hrafnu. 'Evil has no place in this world. The righteous are charged to banish it!'

He strode from his fortress of seclusion to cheers from some of his people and gasps from others. This was not the kind, *gentle purveyor of peace, the wise ruler of compromise. This was a powerful demon consumed in a fit of rage. Several of his sons ran to their homes and pulled weapons from hiding places. They fell in line behind their silent father and marched for two days to the valley of Netur. There they found the scene of carnage. Netur and his people lay rotting in the sun, the buzzards feasting on their bodies.*

'These Zodrians don't even afford us the decency of burial!' cried the giant. 'How many of theirs have I interred in my Creator's earth? How many have I prayed over as I roamed their borders? But my children are less than animals to them!'

The giant stormed into the midst of the valley hacking at the carrion eaters gorging themselves. His sons built pyres and Hrafnu prepared the dead. The pyres were set afire and burned for hours as they consumed the children of Hrafnu the Peacemaker.

The colonel of the Zodrian cavalry had set up camp a day's ride from Netur's mountain valley. His soldiers swilled ale and stuffed themselves on Netur's slaughtered livestock. They laughed and told stories to one another of their great conquest. As always, the unarmed thirteen year old, cut down from behind as he fled the cavalry, turned into a seasoned Keltaran warrior, armed to the teeth. The ale helped contribute to the tall tales, and shortly even the tellers believed them.

When the colonel spied the smoke from the funeral pyres rising in the distance, he turned to his men.

'It seems we didn't finish the jo,.' called the colonel slurping wine from one of Netur's silver goblets. 'We must rid our great nation of this infestation. These creatures must be hunted down and destroyed!'

The Zodrians filled with bloodlust and rallied to their leader. They mounted their horses and stormed back toward Netur's valley.

Hrafnu and his sons scoured the valley searching for survivors through the rest of the day and on through the night.

When none were found, he returned to the remnants of the village. The funeral pyres still smoldered and filled the valley with a ghostly gray haze as the sun crept over the horizon. Hrafnu called his sons about him and turned toward the morning sun. He and his sons knelt in the center of the smoking village with heads bowed and asked Avra for guidance. Instantly, the Zodrians rushed into the valley howling. They pushed their mounts hard toward the handful of Keltaran kneeling in the grasses. Hrafnu turned his head to face his sons.

'Stand true and do not run. Revenge has been handed to us this day and we will take it. Rally to me and we will give no ground and no quarter to this enemy!'

The Zodrian horses charged down the long valley. The armor on both horse and rider glistened in the dancing light of the new sun.

'Death to these beasts!' cried the Zodrian colonel.

The cavalrymen cheered and howled in approval as they rapidly closed the gap on the handful of Keltaran. Hrafnu rose. The cheering stopped as the cavalry beheld a man unlike any they had ever seen. Hrafnu stood a foot taller than even the largest of his children. A wild mane of red and gray hair cascaded from his head and beard and spilled down over his shoulders and chest. Huge corded muscles, worked hard everyday for three centuries rippled under the ram skin he wore. The smoke from his children's funeral pyres rolled over him as he slowly lifted a giant ax with one hand and laid it calmly in the other.

'Stay in your ranks,' nervously called the colonel. 'One dog wishes to nip at your heels and you balk!'

Slowly Hrafnu's six sons rose to their feet. Axes and huge hammers were raised to their shoulders. The charge came on, but thinned as some riders held back.

Hrafnu calmly spoke to his sons and they fanned out beside him. The cavalry charged headlong into the Keltaran line.

'For Zodra!' cried the colonel as he slashed a cutlass toward Hrafnu's head.

Hrafnu's ax shot into the air, held aloft by one powerful arm. The steel of the cutlass rang as it met the ax head. The blade spun from the colonel's hand and stuck in the ground in front of Hrafnu. The giant laid the shoulder of his free arm hard into the armored breastplate of the colonel's charging horse. The mount was driven hard off course and Hrafnu shifted his weight into the beast. The horse went down in a heap as Hrafnu raised his ax. The colonel spilled from the saddle and rolled across the valley floor. He quickly sprang to his feet. The wine's effects were completely washed away by the surge of battle.

    'Zodrians to me! Zodrians to me!' cried the colonel as he squared off against Hrafnu. 'Cut down their leader and the rest will flee like their kin before them!'

    Hrafnu's sons were trading blows with multiple foes as they too heard the colonel's cry. Horses rushed in from all around to hem Hrafnu in. The son of Awoi saw none of it. His rage was fixed on the man in front of him. Spearmen charged in on the giant as he slowly approached the colonel. One swing of his ax split spear and man alike. More riders rushed in, only to find their mounts thrown to the ground by massive hands. Hrafnu's steel shod boots tread the life out of several. Still he advanced on the colonel who cautiously backed away.

    Hrafnu's sons were heavily engaged, but saw the battle shift to their father, who was methodically drawn away from them. Gnard, the third of his children, called to his brothers.

    'Men of Keltar, to your father!'

    The sons of Hrafnu drew a line and hacked their way foward. Hrafnu took no notice. Two riders blocked his way to the colonel. Hrafnu spun his ax and held out the handle lengthwise. The handle was as long as the height of a normal man. The giant lunged forward knocking pikes from his path and levered the handle under the necks of both animals. With all his strength, Hrafnu lifted and pushed the stallions backward. The riders were thrown from their mounts, and the horses sprawled to the ground.

With the giant thus engaged, the colonel saw his chance. He darted forward and plunged his short sword toward Hrafnu's belly. Hrafnu saw the maneuver but was unable to avoid it. He spun his torso, but the edge of the blade found its mark, slicing hard against his ribs. Blood sprayed from the wound as Hrafnu swept the steel ax head down hard on the colonel's helm. Helm and head split in two. The colonel dropped to the ground lifeless. The sons of Hrafnu broke through the Zodrian line and rallied to their father.

Hrafnu's sons encircled him and inflicted heavy damage on the enemy. The Zodrians broke and fled. Hrafnu roared in agony. Blood streamed from his wound. Many of his sons received damaging blows as well, but none perished. The Zodrians formed rank at the far side of the valley. A young captain calmed his men and turned to assess the situation. There, lying across the valley, scattered about Hrafnu's group, lay over half of their rank. A roar echoed to him from the enormous beast wounded by his colonel.

'These valleys are the lands of my people!' bellowed Hrafnu. 'Those who trespass are in forfeit of their lives. Zodrians, you drove my mother out. You helped kill my father. My son's ashes are scattered to the four winds because of the evil hand of Zodra. NO MORE! My children will suffer at your hands no longer. Return to your city and spread my word. Leave my people in peace and you shall possess peace. If you choose to challenge us, you choose death!'

The young captain looked to his bloodied troop and made a wise decision. He turned to his sergeant.

'These Keltaran as they call themselves, rise from their slumber. I fear for our people. We must leave this place to protect our homeland from their wrath.'

The captain returned with his troop to Zodra. He was summoned before the king and relayed the story of the battle. Many believe he reported accurately all that took place. The captain warned his king of the ferocity of the Keltaran. He advised the king to allow these people to live in peace. The king weighed the captain's advice and found it full of wisdom.

However, there were those in the king's rank that did not want peace. They twisted the words of Hrafnu. They focused more on his threats and his challenge to the sovereignty of the king. After all, these lands were claimed for the Zodrian crown by his majesty's emissaries. These nomadic mountain tribes held no claim over the land. The mountains must contain riches untold. Why else would a people choose to live in these frigid wastes? The king was swayed. He outfitted a great army and determined to sweep the mountains clean of the Keltaran.

Hrafnu was not idle. One battle is all the giant needed as a lesson. Just as he quickly improved on all his mother taught him, he was a quick study in battle. He recognized both his peoples strengths and weaknesses against the Zodrians. Their size and strength were a clear advantage. Their limited numbers were not. If the Zodrians attacked in great numbers, the Keltaran would be overrun.

Hrafnu returned to his valley and fortified his city. His people went to work immediately. The walls around Keltar grew higher and thicker. Windows were filled in with mountain granite. The furnaces of the great mountain city were busy as well. Hundreds of axes were produced and distributed to the men of Keltar. Hrafnu was pleased with the success his simple tool produced in battle. The ax was a symbol for his people. Used everyday to help them subsist in their harsh environment, but equally effective as a weapon.

After several weeks, Hrafnu surveyed the progress of his people. Young men trained in the streets with their weapons. Hrafnu's sons stood as captains over these men. No jealousy or power struggle stood in their way. They were a people committed to the defense of their land. Hrafnu was pleased. He stayed in his city and waited patiently.

The Zodrian king took several weeks to marshall his forces. Horses were commandeered from surrounding ranches and a great army was assembled. They ventured forth two weeks to the day of the death of Netur and his people. The king saw them off with orders to rid Zodra of the threat from the mountains.

Hrafnu was true to his word. If the Zodrians entered a valley that was home to his people, they were set upon. Often they found nothing of value in the valley and decided to set up camp. In the night the Keltaran came. Down the steep cliff sides of the valley. Over ridgelines the Zodrians believed impassable. Raiding parties swept down and ran off the Zodrian's tethered horses. Keltaran silently eliminated Zodrian outposts.

Sometimes the battle was met. Once the Zodrians left horseback, they were at a huge disadvantage. Hundreds of Zodrians lost their lives in the surprise raids conducted by the Keltaran. The Zodrians developed tactics to combat the Keltaran raids, but their numbers were already significantly depleted. Then their fiercest enemy arrived.

Winter came to the lands of Hrafnu and his people. Bitter cold swept down the mountain passes. The Keltaran struggled with the temperatures, but the Zodrians were no match for them. Hundreds of horses and riders perished in the frigid climate. Those who survived were too weak to protect themselves from the sporadic Keltaran raids that followed winter's onset. The general staff withdrew the army to the safety of the capital. This was the beginning of a hundred years of bloodshed between our peoples.

Zodra stewed in her losses, frustrated by the harrying attacks of the Keltaran fighters. Often, Hrafnu and his people disappeared from the mountain valleys when the Zodrian army marched forth. The army scoured the mountains for months and never found a single Keltaran. Winter arrived and the army dragged itself back to the capital after weeks in the saddle.

Summer after summer the Zodrians rode forth. Summer after summer their frustration grew as their soldiers fell in battle or spent months from home with no victories to report. This was Hrafnu's genius. He demoralized the enemy at the same time he defeated them. Keltar was stocked with a year's provisions. If they chose, the Keltaran could outlast any foe. Winter was their greatest ally.

No Zodrian ever looked upon the mountain city. It lay deep in the saddle between the Scythtar and Zorim Mountains. When Keltar was founded, peace was the objective. However, as fate decreed, Hrafnu's choice was also perfectly suited for defensive warfare.

The entrance to the valley was incredibly narrow with steep sides of broken shale. The footing was treacherous. A thousand foot cataract spilled from the glacial peaks behind the fortress into a deep pool at the back of the city. The pool overflowed into a rushing stream that washed through the center of Keltar then charged through a wrought iron break in the walls of the fortress. Once free of Keltar, the stream wound through the remainder of Hrafnu's valley. It provided fresh water during any siege if need be. The walls of the valley met the walls of the city. The shear faces of the Zorim Mountains ensured that no enemy could attack the city from behind.

For a hundred years the Zodrians and the Keltaran were engaged in a neverending dance of war.

"You act as if the Keltaran never lost battles." scoffed Kael. "But I know songs of great Zodrian victories."

And victories there were for your homeland. Kael, I don't pretend that my ancestors were untouchable. They suffered great losses throughout this century of warfare. Zodrian generals contrived schemes to defeat the Keltaran. They developed armor and tactics to defend against the heavy axes of their mountain cousins. Slowly, Hrafnu's sons were taken from him. His bitterness grew.

Can you imagine a life of near immortality? Hrafnu wasn't only long lived, but his strength and cunning made him virtually unbeatable in combat. Wife gone. Sons disappearing.

His great grandchildren turning into old men and women around him. Hrafnu's life work changed into protecting his people instead of spreading the word of his father and his Creator. He despised the Zodrians for making this life for him.

However, the Zodrians changed as well. The influence of Amird was a thing of the past. Men arose from the common folk of Zodra and took their place among the leaders. Manreel was such a man. The son of a small landowner, he rose from amongst the ranks of the cavalry. His prowess on the field of battle grew. First, he rose to the command of a small unit. This unit distinguished itself. They lost few men in battle, and turned back many of the Keltaran attacks. Soon, more and more men were assigned to the unit and it grew.

Manreel was an intelligent man. He studied his victories and noticed a pattern. When the enemy engaged him, one truth always shown through. If he retreated into Zodrian territory, the Keltaran never followed. His men regrouped and found respite from any fight. He kept his units close to the borderlands. If his superiors ordered him to engage an enemy force, he waited until the enemy moved close to the border. Other generals struck deeply into the heart of Keltaran territory, only to find their exit hampered and harassed the entire way out. Often they were cut to ribbons, unable to retreat.

Others in the general staff hinted at a lack of courage amongst Manreel and his men, but those who fought beside him knew otherwise. When the battle was met, he rode prominently in the front rank. If ordered to attack when outnumbered, Manreel attacked. Caution was not cowardice.

All knew of Hrafnu's challenge from years before. All considered it a boast by the giant. Manreel studied his words and saw them for what they were, a statement of fact and a veiled proclamation of peace. The Keltaran only attacked when the Zodrians entered disputed land. This land lay uninhabitable for either side in the conflict. Leagues of fine grazing land lay empty.

Manreel came to a conclusion. Why wage war at all? The Keltaran lived in a secret, undetected mountain fortress. The

Zodrians spread south along the open plains. Were these foothills worth all the bloodshed? The young colonel went to the king with a bold plan to stop waging war with the Keltaran.

King Debold remained unsure. Years of bloodshed and bitterness clouded all save Manreel's vision. Manreel asked the king's permission to form a protectorate to ensure the safety of the homeland. They were to adhere to one purpose, keep Zodra free from invaders. King Debold agreed and thus the Guard of Zodra was born.

Did you ever think about that, Kael? Your precious Guard, the pride of the entire country, was formed as a stay at home army. An army to protect, not conquer.

"I never considered the name," admitted Kael. "I guess that makes sense. They guard us against invasion."

Ah, then how did such a force spread across our world? Why does that force find itself deep in Keltar territory? Things have changed since the days of Manreel.

So, the king granted Manreel's request. A force was formed under the young man's command. Their tactics were pure. They remained within the original borders of Zodra. They confronted any and all invaders who crossed these boundaries. They aided their brothers in the army when it did not pull them too far from their task of protection.

Many of the General Staff scoffed at the force. They charged Manreel and his Guard with avoiding the real fight. Manreel's force found more time to drill and practice. More time to improve technique and plan. The general army grew into a ragged force of farmers and ranch hands pressed into service by the crown. Manreel's forces were polished and professional warriors. Their skill with weapon and horse were unmatched in the kingdom. Time and again they rescued members of the regular army struggling to escape the borderlands with their lives.

Manreel's plan was true genius. The people of Zodra felt safe within their nation. The enemies of Zodra stayed clear of their borders. The Keltaran remained true to the pledge of Hrafnu. Highwaymen and robbers disappeared from the kingdom. A new threat to the north was emerging, but was not yet known to the people. Within Zodra's borders, things grew peaceful and comfortable. Peace is a powerful tool, Kael. Much can be resolved and accomplished with just the promise of a bit of peace.

The people doubted the purpose of their war with Keltar. The Zodrian kingdom was rich and protected. The people were well off. What did they require from Keltaran lands? The regular army grew to respect and cherish Manreel's guard. Guardsmen were the elite fighting men in the kingdom, but they were also champions of peace. They pushed Zodra toward peace.

However, with any brilliant plan, there are always those who will subvert it for their own glory. The General Staff was comprised of such subversive men. They saw no glory in an army pledged to safety and protection. They only dreamed of conquest and plunder. Surely the Keltaran were hiding something in their frigid mountains. Rumors of gold and precious gems circulated about the Zorim Mountains. These lands needed to be taken in order to discover the secret of their wealth.

Others in the General Staff came from a family history of soldiering. There appeared to be no honor in the plan Manreel proposed. These men lost fathers and grandfathers to Hrafnu and his people. Revenge held a razor sharp claw around their hearts. They couldn't abandon the fight merely for the safety and happiness peace brought to their nation. Personal vendettas meant all the world to them.

Manreel's fame and wisdom grew. Many agreed with his plan and saw the merit of it. The king himself issued fewer and fewer raiding parties into Keltar territory. Life settled in Zodra. Fewer young widows and fatherless children walked her streets. However, the General Staff would not be denied. Luck, be it good or ill, found its way to their doorstep.

One day a young Zodrian soldier was separated from his squad during a border skirmish. He wandered for days in an attempt to avoid the Keltaran and return home. On the third evening he stumbled into the entrance of a narrow gorge hidden by an overgrowth of brush and timber. He followed a moonlit stream up the gorge and into a broad valley. The valley stretched up into the heights of the mountains. At the far end sat a fortress of iron and stone. Its broad face held a wrought iron gate. On either side of the gate, heavy stone stretched to the valley walls. The frightened soldier slipped back out of the gorge and eventually carried the news back to his superiors. Keltar was a secret no more.

His news was just what the General Staff hoped for. The young man brought proof that a Keltaran metropolis thrived in the mountains. A keep filled with untold riches. King Debold was informed that the area was well known for producing gems and precious metals. Earlier raids to this area confirmed traces of such riches.

The General Staff also exaggerated the size of the Keltaran stronghold. They portrayed it as a city whose only purpose was to consolidate Keltaran power and build an invincible army. Manreel's policies of tolerance had allowed the enemy to secretly build its strength. The day would arrive when an unstoppable Keltaran army of tremendous magnitude would sweep from the mountains.

Manreel protested these notions. Surely the Keltaran lived in such a city for centuries. When they disappeared from the valleys of the Zorim, where did they go? If the city were constructed to consolidate Keltaran power, it must have been achieved years ago. In fact, the discovery of the city bolstered Manreel's theory. The people of Hrafnu simply wished to be left alone, peacefully penned in the small valley with their flocks. They were harmless to the kingdom of Zodra. The best response was to leave them be.

The king listened carefully to both arguments, but the temptation of a huge source of wealth and power within his grasp was too much. Amird won again and the Zodrian army prepared siege engines and weapons of destruction.

Manreel only shook his head and promised to protect the kingdom's borders while the army was away. The General Staff scoffed at Manreel and his Guard. The army would show the Guard what true soldiering was all about. They would bring riches and power to the kingdom while ridding it of its biggest threat. Vengeance for years of death and destruction would be brought down on the Keltaran.

Hrafnu and his people were not passive in their own defense. The Keltaran maintained a system of spies to monitor the activities of Zodra. Do not forget that our peoples are cousins, Kael. Not all of my brothers and sisters are born with the size and look of our patriarch. This was even more apparent in the early days when Hrafnu still took in the outcasts of Zodra. Those of our people who might blend in with the Zodrian population, frequently journeyed to the borderlands and the capital itself.

The news was everywhere. The king intended to destroy the Keltaran threat forever. The heroes of the Zodrian army pledged to strike a secret fortress. They intended to stab deep into the heart of Keltaran territory and reduce this stronghold to rubble. They would drag the monster that spawned this race from his city and execute him for his crimes against Zodra. The Zodrian kingdom would move into the mountains and never again fear its Western boundaries.

Hrafnu heard news of the construction of siege engines, and the imminent battle. As always, he hung his head in sorrow, but only for a moment. Years of battle and loss hardened his heart. He no longer wept for the losses of his enemy. He no longer considered the Zodrians as blood of his blood, and children of Avra. He was obliged to protect his people.

Hrafnu took council with his remaining sons and grandsons. All agreed. This Manreel and his Guard had held out a hope for peace. Hrafnu had prayed that the man's words were heeded. However, now that they were disregarded, a problem arose for the Keltaran. The partial peace that lasted over the last decade allowed the Zodrian army to bolster their number. The Zodrians commanded an army the likes of which Hrafnu and his people never faced. This army was aimed at the heart of Hrafnu's land. They marched toward Keltar's women and children, its flocks and fields.

If the Keltaran harassed the Zodrian army during its approach, they were sure to damage the Zodrians, but not stop them. If the Keltaran were to meet the Zodrians in open battle at the foot of the mountains, they would surely perish, overwhelmed by sheer numbers.

Hrafnu grew bitter over the years, but not stupid. His only defense had been and always would be the blessed winter. Within weeks the first bitter blasts from the north would arrive. Howling winds and ice storms would blow down the valleys. No tent, blind, or tree line would offer protection from the icy hand of the North. Any army on the road at this point would be subject to the harsh treatment of the weather, a much tougher foe than a Keltaran raiding party.

For years Keltar lay undetected in its valley. The key to success was to leave the ravine without fortifications. The city itself held enough to confound any enemy that stumbled upon her. However, no army stumbled. A ravine entrance thick with gorse bush and choking trees was all the Keltaran required to be overlooked for a century of warfare. However, the ravine would go unnoticed no longer.

Hrafnu called for his stonemasons and carpenters. It was time to plug the hole into his beautiful valley. His plan called for a tower to be built on each side of the ravine's opening. The towers would be attached to the walls of the canyon, fifty strides from one another. Across those fifty strides the masons would erect an impenetrable wall of stone and iron, with a gate no army could penetrate. Once more Hrafnu's brains won out over his bitterness.

The Zodrians required time to complete their siege engines, and even more time transporting them West. Hrafnu would take advantage of this time to seal them off from his precious city and her people. When the Zodrians arrived, they would be forced to form their massive army up in front of a tiny defensive position. The Zodrian strength, massive numbers, would be wasted in an attempt to focus on so small a target. Only one or two units could attack the gate at a time.

Hrafnu believed this tactic would slow the Zodrians so significantly that even if they did breach the gate, the ensuing battle through the ravine and eventual siege of Keltar would waste the remainder of the fall. The Zodrians would be stuck in the mountains, low on provisions as the winter arrived. As long as Hrafnu's army held the gate for several weeks, no Zodrian would ever set foot in Keltar.

It was a good plan, and should have worked to perfection. Hrafnu gambled that the Zodrian forces would move together to the battle. Keltaran harassment of Zodrian raiding parties was well established. The cavalry needed to escort the siege machines to protect them.

At first, Hrafnu was correct. The Zodrians completed their siege engines and slowly drew them through Keltaran territory while the cavalry patrolled the perimeter. For days the group moved toward Keltar. However, a Zodrian scouting party secretly moved to the ravine. There they discovered the work of Hrafnu's masons.

The gorse were cleared from the opening. Two mighty towers stood on either side of the ravine. Midlevel on the towers a massive wall spanned the opening. The Keltaran dug a deep, wide trench in front of the wall. They diverted the Cliebruk stream into the trench and icy water swirled and surged at the wall's base. A massive iron gate, recently forged in the furnaces of Keltar, lay resting against the wall. Winches and pulleys were bolted into the ravine in readiness to hoist the gate into position.

The Zodrian scouts recognized the horrible miscalculation of the General Staff. The Keltaran had used the Zodrian delay to their advantage. The scouting party sprung to their horses and rode hard to inform the staff. The siege engines were still a week away from their destination. However, the cavalry would be able to reach the ravine in little over a day's ride. If Zodra were to grasp any hope, the cavalry must break from their escort of the siege engines, ride to the newly constructed gate and halt its completion.

The General Staff agreed with this assessment. The cavalry prepared to depart. However, the General Staff were familiar with Keltaran tactics and feared a trick. They sent riders to the border to contact Manreel. The Staff ordered the young colonel forward to protect the siege engines and their personnel.

Manreel agreed that the fight was at the gate. Delivering the siege engines unharmed was crucial to the plan. Without the cavalry escort, the men manning the engines became vulnerable to an enemy force. Manreel knew his duty and rushed to their aid.

The Guard's cavalry pushed their mounts to the limit in hopes of reaching the ravine within a day's time. Manreel took up position with the siege engines as they crept toward Keltar. The gate was near completion as the exhausted cavalry arrived. The busy Keltaran masons and carpenters threw down their tools and took up arms. The Keltaran workmen marched out to meet the Zodrian threat.

The narrow ravine entrance afforded the Keltaran giants the best possible fighting ground. The Zodrians would be forced to charge their mounts into the tight opening. The Keltaran armed themselves with long handled axes and pikes. The Zodrians would find it difficult to make contact using only their short sabers.

The groups stared at one another for several minutes. The Zodrian leader accomplished his mission. Work on the gate halted. However, he was acutely aware that every passing moment allowed the Keltaran the chance for reinforcements. If he and the Zodrians were pushed back from the gate and work resumed without harassment, all was lost. He determined to take the gate and push into the ravine to secure it.

The cavalry officer ordered his riders to form into groups of fifty. The Keltaran, on the other hand, formed into a wedge, two men deep. Those in the front rank crouched low with heavy headed axes at the ready. The back line extended long pikes over the heads of the men in front.

The Zodrian cavalry leader lowered his sword and the first line of fifty shot forward. The turf churned under the steel shod hooves of the Zodrian mounts. A second wave of fifty sprang forward a few moments later. The horses' breath steamed in an unusually chilly morning air. The first wave raised their shields and lowered their heads. They crashed hard into pike, ax and Keltaran. Riders spilled from their horses, skewered by the sharp tipped pikes. The Keltaran wedge faltered, but held. Horses with and without riders spun from the wedge and bolted from the ravine along its walls. The second Zodrian wave hit the Keltaran wedge.

The second wave fared as the first. More riders spilled from the saddle and several Keltaran fell under the hooves of the charging stallions. Once more the wedge held, but now its members were bloodied and injured. Horses raced along the ravine walls back out of the valley to form up in the rear of the cavalry. New waves of fifty took the forward position and waited for the signal from their commander. He lowered his saber and once again they leapt forward. Armored horses slammed into the wedge and the sickening sound of grating metal and breaking bone could be heard. Bodies lay strewn about the ravine's opening, and the wails of the injured carried down the valley. The Keltaran made a brave stand, but the shear number of horsemen made their task nearly impossible.

Runners arrived in Keltar to inform Hrafnu of the battle. The ancient giant grimaced at the news. Once again the Zodrians destroyed his hopes for peace. The giant gathered his remaining sons about him and they headed to the gate. When he arrived, Hrafnu scaled its wall to better assess the battleground below. As he stood on the wall, he watched his courageous masons and carpenters face the sixth charge of the Zodrian cavalry. Their numbers were thinned and the dead and wounded lay bleeding across the ravine's mouth. The gate beneath him lay on its side, ready to be hoisted into position. The masons were just hours away from completing their task. He determined not to be cheated. These Zodrians would not enter his valley. The gate would hold.

The General Staff remained with the siege engines, the strength of their upcoming assault. Manreel's cavalry circled them. The young colonel and a group of retainers trotted forward to scout the terrain ahead. Zodrian messengers from the battle appeared with news. The cavalry engaged the enemy and intended to take the ravine.

The Zodrian colonel was a warrior at heart. He knew how the best laid plans of generals meant nothing once the fight raged. The conquest of Keltar would not be fought against the walls of the mountain city, but in the narrow ravine that hid it for centuries.

The battle at the gate was disastrous news for the Zodrian General Staff. Their intentions were thwarted. Even if the ravine gates were taken, the journey through the narrow passage would be a bloody affair more suited to foot soldiers than horsemen. Every step the cavalry progressed toward Hrafnu's city would be paid for with massive Zodrian casualties. Zodra's strength lay in her cavalry and the open spaces. This campaign turned to folly.

Manreel analyzed the situation. Once again Hrafnu appeared to choose peace. If his intentions were so murderous, he would have set upon the Zodrians at night while they camped. Ambushes would have been set to take advantage of the

Guardsmen when they were off their mounts. The Zodrian cavalry would have been separated from the siege engines through diversion. The engines would then have been burnt where they stood.

This giant proved time and time again his deep understanding of tactics. Hrafnu's choice was obvious. He refused to fight. Hrafnu intended to finish his gates before discovery and allow the Zodrians to expend all their energy for naught.

Hrafnu planned wisely in all things but one. The giant falsely assumed the Zodrians would not separate their forces. The General Staff followed a rulebook of tactics established through centuries of rigid tradition. They believed in one way to encounter all situations. Hrafnu did not perceive the desperation of the generals. Years of peace eroded their standing in the eyes of the public. Their power waned as Manreel's notion of peace took root. When faced with the devastating ruin of their plans by the gate, they broke from their hallowed tradition. They gambled all and separated their forces.

Ironically, it was Manreel, the champion of peace, who allowed them to roll the dice of chance. Without Manreel's Guard standing ready to protect the siege engines, they could never have split forces. Confident in his ability to protect the engines, their decision was both desperate and sensible. Their strategy to force their way down the ravine to Keltar, however, was not. Manreel was correct as usual. Capturing the gate was one thing. Running the ravine to the valley was quite another. It could never be done.

The young colonel made a quick decision. He countermanded the General Staff's orders and commanded the cavalry to pull back. Hrafnu could keep his valley. The General Staff could prosecute him for insubordination later, but he would save the lives of most of these men. He sent the cavalry's messengers back to the staff and left with his retainers to order retreat at the gate.

Hrafnu turned to a messenger and ordered reinforcements. These arrogant Zodrians would lose many good men trying to force their way down his ravine. It would be a bloodbath. Why were they so ignorant? He determined to retrieve his brave masons and ironworkers and finish the gate. With the gate intact, Zodrian and Keltaran alike would live. There was no alternative. The eighth wave of Zodrian cavalry turned from their charge. The remaining Keltaran scrambled to regroup their thinning number. Hrafnu smiled at his beloved sons and stepped to the edge of the wall.

'*Zodrians!*' *bellowed the giant.*

The field below silenced except for the moans of the injured.

'*Why don't you leave us in peace? In all of my years, you have done nothing but murder and plunder. I was patient in the ways of my Maker. Patience that lasted the lifetimes of normal men!*'

The giant's eyes went wild and angry. He clenched his teeth and growled.

'*My Maker leaves my heart, and what remains is a cold, dead stone. You will die here today, as will all Zodrians I encounter! Peace is for fools! Now is the reign of death and destruction!*'

With that, the giant stepped onto the parapet and leapt. A causeway spanned the swirling trench of frigid water twenty yards below. The stone rang out as Hrafnu's steel shod boots slammed onto it. The giant landed in a crouch and touched one hand to the granite surface. He remained for a moment poised like a mountain cat ready to spring as his hand caressed rock hewn from the mountains he loved. He slowly rose and moved into the ravine's mouth with fists clenched.

Even at the age of three hundred, he was an impressive figure. His long, wavy red hair cascaded like flame over his exposed shoulders and down his back. A vest of black sheepskin was tightly bound to his torso. A jerkin of heavy deerskin draped to mid thigh, and the steel shod boots, made of mountain ram's hide, were bound by thick cords up to his knees. Powerful, knotted muscles rippled on every portion of his body and his sweat steamed in the chilly morning air. He marched forward like a fiery demon stepping from the pits of Chaos.

Hrafnu approached his masons. The Zodrian cavalry reformed. The giant's right hand moved over his head to his back and drew out the massive heavy-headed battle-ax that hung there. The other hand drew forth a broadsword most men needed two strong arms to wield. Hrafnu held it like a dagger.

His sons scrambled to the scaffolding behind the wall. They were desperate to protect their father. It might take the reinforcements some time to arrive. Hrafnu stepped amongst his fallen men. He turned to those who still walked and barked orders.

'They will sing songs of your bravery for centuries my children. Return to the gate carrying the fallen. Complete the work you started and protect our people. I will take care of the flies that bite and pester us.'

They stared at him blankly for a moment.

'GO! NOW!' roared Hrafnu.

Those who were able grabbed their fallen comrades and hauled them toward the causeway and safety. Hrafnu's sons met them and dragged many to the temporary safety of the wall. Hrafnu stood alone amongst the dead and sneered at the Zodrian cavalry

'You interrupt my plans for peace once more. Now your people will never see peace. I remove my pledge. Borders and laws do not matter to you, so they will hold me no longer. Once I gut you, I will gather my troops and march on Zodra. All will fall before my ax. Women, children, all Zodrians will pay for my centuries of sorrow!' howled the giant madly. 'The day arrives Zodra, and you are ill prepared for the horrors Hrafnu will inflict!'

Hrafnu rammed the broadsword into the frosty ground in front of him and firmly grasped the battle-ax with both hands. He raised it high over his head and clenched his teeth. The Zodrian line was poised to charge, yet sat motionless with fright. Their leader's saber lay limp by the side of his stallion.

'Come to me, yapping dogs of Zodra! I grow weary of your cowardice!' shouted Hrafnu.

The Zodrian colonel's saber snapped into the air. He snarled and slid his horse in line with the next charge.

'For king and country!' shouted the colonel as his saber slashed downward, its tip aimed at Hrafnu's heart.

The steel shoes of the Zodrian stallions pounded the ground, reverberating through the canyon like thunder after a brilliant lightning strike. Riders spurred their nervous mounts ferociously. These were battle-hardened horses, but even these beasts never beheld the like of Hrafnu. He stood wild-eyed in the center of the field howling and bellowing for the riders to come.

The giant stretched to his full height, considerably higher than that of the masons and carpenters who stood in the ravine earlier. He hefted the ax once more with a single hand, and the other retrieved the broadsword. The Zodrian riders converged upon him. His shoulders were above the horses' craning heads, and with a sweep of his great ax, three riders to his right were cleanly taken from their seats and thrown to the ground. His left hand deftly drew a plane with the broadsword an inch above the horses. Three more riders were cut from their mounts.

Quickly, the giant spun to his left and hemmed in the riders who passed him against the ravine's walls. In the confusion, the riders on the opposite wall and retreated. They had made their run and were returning as ordered. These riders didn't turn to see the colonel and a dozen of their mates trapped by the huge reach of Hrafnu.

Horses slammed into one another as the colonel tried in vain to form the small group into a line. Hrafnu marched directly amongst the fighting force, hacking and slashing. Riders dropped from their horses dead or wounded. The crazed stallions kicked and jumped, throwing men from their mounts and trampling them.

The remaining cavalry across the field sat frozen in horror. Their orders were clear. They were to make a run at the Keltarans, inflict as much damage as possible, then return to the rear of the line. Once the bottleneck in the ravine cleared of Zodrian cavalry, the next two lines were to be sent forward at the colonel's command.

However, the next line of cavalrymen was unsure who was in command. They were not aware that the colonel and his men were unable to break off their attack. They waited in vain for their commander's return.

Hrafnu saved the colonel for last. The Zodrian officer was thrown from his horse, and as Hrafnu approached, the colonel lunged with saber extended. The giant flicked it aside with his broadsword as the battle-ax swept through the colonel, cleaving him in two. Hrafnu spun and hurled insults across the ravine as riderless horses raced past the remainder of the stunned Zodrian cavalry.

The giant's sons ran across the causeway to aid their father. Hrafnu waved them off.

'Return to the gate. There are not enough masons to finish the work. You must provide the muscle they need.'

His sons complied. Pulleys and winches hefted stone and mortar into place. Minutes passed as the giant glared across the ravine's opening. Minutes turned to hours. The Zodrians bickered over command. Several unit leaders saw the situation as untenable. Even if they gained the gate, they could never reach Keltar. Others cared nothing for the gate. Here stood the enemy of their people. What glory would come to the man that delivered a fatal blow to Hrafnu? The horror they witnessed in the loss of their colonel was passing with every minute. Their confidence built as they reminded one another that it was only one man.

Hrafnu leaned on his ax and stared across the valley. Every moment the Zodrians waited was a moment closer to the gate's completion. He grew restless. The taste for blood grew in his heart. Years of vengeful ambitions were being fulfilled.

Amird's grip grew stronger on Hrafnu. The Zodrians would pay for the deaths of all of the children he lost in this struggle. He turned to see the iron gate swaying from dozens of ropes. It would not be long now. The gate would fit into its hinge posts and his city would be safe.

'I grow weary of your cowardice, Zodrians,' cried Hrafnu. 'Ride forth, or go back to your dung pen of a kingdom!'

The Zodrian leaders saw the same developments as Hrafnu. Their cowardice and hesitation forfeit their chance to capture the gate. Several riders hurled insults back to the giant and the cavalry line grew restless. A shield slipped from the saddle of a rider in the front rank, spooking the mount next to him. As the horse reared and lunged forward, the men on the far ends of the line concluded the charge was called. The heat of the moment carried events. Horses bolted forward from all sides of the line. A charge of cavalry surged into the ravine.

Hrafnu smiled and swept up his ax and blade. The uneven line of horsemen came barreling down on him. Once more Hrafnu defied his age. The great ax cut huge swatches through the approaching Zodrians. The broadsword deftly picked rider after rider from their mounts. As the giant decimated the front line, a second charged forward. When he was unable to swing freely, the giant simply threw a shoulder into the nearest stallion and bowled the cavalry line over. Wild-eyed horses fell kicking madly. Riders tumbled to the ground. Ax, broadsword and steel shod boot systematically dispatched those scrambling for safety. The melee of mounts and riders worked to Hrafnu's advantage. The Zodrians were unable to reach Hrafnu over the horses that surrounded him, but the giant's long reach inflicted more and more damage.

Line after cavalry line assaulted the giant. The Zodrians scrambled to form fighting units. Once a small line was patched together, it charged back into the mix. The bloodshed continued unabated.

"Have you ever heard a song by the Delvin scribe Iorg, describing the scene that day, Kael?"

"No," replied the boy.

"It portrays a decidedly Zodrian lean, but I believe it to be quite a fair study of events. The Scribes prefer accuracy over all else in their histories. Would you like to hear it?" asked Granu.

"Yes, of course," answered Kael.

Granu's eyes closed and he searched for the words. The prince's voice softened as he sang the lines of "The Battle of Keltar Gate".

Jumping down from towers bound
Neath a wintry sky
Hrafnu sneered and drew his ax
To kill here or die

The riders came in waves of two
And broke upon his beach
Twenty died from his cruel ax
None escaped its reach

Turning round with wild howl
To face the onslaught of his foe
Twenty more were put to death
Fighting toe to toe

The news soon came to Manreel's ears
He winced, the death toll high
And riding forth he drew his sword

To kill here or die

Hrafnu heard the thunderous hooves
And stayed his bloody game
Cries arose from all about
The dying, maimed and lame

Giant eyes narrowed upon the sight
Of Manreel on his steed
Hrafnu grit his teeth and ventured forth
To commit an evil deed

"Ho! Hrafnu!" shouted Manreel
"I journey to your den.
I should have come here long ago
To stay this waste of men!"

"Manree," snarled the fiend
"Flatter yourself not so.
I travel forth to greet you,
And make you next to go!"

"Travel on," waved Manreel
Then raised his fiercesome blade
Hrafnu thundered forward
Across the open glade

They met upon this open glade
Earth encased in snow
Hrafnu swung his weapon
Manreel blocked the blow

Hrafnu spun and thrust his ax
Manreel's horse did wheel
The Zodrian hero disappeared
From air ripped by steel

"Ho, Hrafnu!" cried the Zodrian
"You tarry with your blow.
Your age has made you sluggish,
dull-witted, weak and slow."

Manreel spoke in hearty boast
But knew his words untrue
The day would not be won by strength
Only skill and speed might do

His warhorse was his best defense
Against the giant's brawn,
Dunrave's flanks were armor sheathed,
Steel glittered in the dawn

Manreel drew the steed about
Charging hard to Hrafnu's front,
Its steely chest slammed forward,
The giant caught the force full brunt

Horse and giant stood immobile
Neither gave up ground
Manreel's blade slashed downward
Its mark was never found

Hrafnu gathered all his strength
And raised the horse on high
Slamming Dunraves to the ground
Manreel lying there nearby

The giant should have finished him,
Yet his rage knew no bound
He threw his arms on high
Shouting, "Vengeance is found!"

Manreel rolled upon the snow
And scrambled to his blade
Hrafnu spun to meet him
His smile slow to fade.

"No armored beast supports you now

fair Zodrian leader of men.
Methinks no longer do you boast
Having 'journeyed to my den'."

"Hrafnu! Dark powers control you
And hatred twists your mind.
Vengeance consumes you,
And makes your heart go blind."

"You disgust me mortal creature,
to issue soft words now.
Judgment day is here for you,
See the sweat upon your brow."

"The sweat of battle is truly there
Yet fear will not be found.
I fight for king and country
to them stay honor bound."

Hrafnu roared and swung his ax
Manreel leapt and rolled
The giant's ax clove frozen earth
Locked solid in its fold

Manreel stopped at Hrafnu's feet
No room to use his sword.

Hrafnu raised an iron boot
Laughing, "Manreel I grow bored."

The iron boot rushed downward
Toward Manreel's helmless head.
If not for quick action
The Zodrian surely would be dead.

From neath his cloak he drew
A dagger forged in Elven fire
And praying held it o'er head
His fortune now so dire

Hrafnu came down upon this blade
With all his force and weight
Steely spike rent iron boot
Sealing Hrafnu's fate

The hilt glanced Manreel's head
And wedged against the earth
Manreel was saved
Hrafnu's howl held no mirth

The giant lost his footing
Falling toward the snow
Manreel snatched his weapon

Readying the fatal blow

As Hrafnu fell, Manreel rose
His blade did spin and slash
Hrafnu's body was exposed
There opened a mortal gash

The Keltaran king lay dying
Manreel's worst was done
The giant lay in disbelief
His battles always won

Those arrayed across the gate
Shuttered their mountain hold
The Zodrians cheered their hero
His courage shown so bold

Manreel stayed the joyous cheer
He held his hand on high
Stepping toward his terrible foe
Who lay waiting there to die

Manreel knelt beside the giant
Cradling his shaggy head
No mortal man is now aware
Of between them what was said

The giant howled in agony
Holding hands up to the sky
"Father, today I am not your child
Today I killed and died!"

CHAPTER 21: TO EACH HIS OWN

Granu's eyes remain closed for a moment. Kael sat lost in thought. The story of Manreel was always that of a glorious hero, a man who fought evil and destroyed it. Now, Kael was confused. If he were to believe this version, Hrafnu was not evil at all. When Hrafnu met Manreel on that open field, the giant was a man driven to the depths of hopelessness and misery. A man pushed harder and further than any man was ever pushed. Wouldn't Kael give in to hatred and despair so much earlier than Hrafnu had?

The pair sat in silence for a long while. The history of the world as Kael knew it had just drastically changed, and the judgments he held were changed with it. The murmur of approaching voices interrupted the boy. Granu's hand signaled Kael to remain silent. Someone spoke just inside the clearing.

"... telling you the giant murdered the boy. Where else might he be? The beast is no good. When he shows himself, you must deal with him. You are the only one in the group keeping him from murdering us all in our sleep! He will do his worst then flee to the hills, back to the scum that spawned him in those forsaken mountains," snarled Tepi.

"I do not trust him, and prefer to see him chained and caged than with that staff," snapped Manfir.

Kael shot a glance at Granu. The giant let out the smallest of sighs and frowned.

"But I gave my word to the Elves to treat him as an ally, and that I shall do," added Manfir.

"Elves? Out-worlders and trespassers," hissed Tepi. "They own no rights and no say in the business of men. They act in their own best interests. If it doesn't benefit them, they care not. They would sacrifice all of Zodra if it meant one extra coin in their pocket!"

"You don't know them, Tepi, and therefore do not know what you say," stated Manfir.

There was a moment of hesitation before Tepi spoke again.

"Perhaps you're correct, Master Rin," Tepi offered sweetly. "You are probably right."

"I deal with the Grey Elves quite a bit and assure you of their intentions," said Manfir.

"Yes, well I do not and bow to your superior experience," came the trader's hypnotic voice. "You're a man of true power and intellect. You see things more clearly than others."

"Yes ... I uh..." stammered Manfir, "like to think I ..uh"

"Grasp the situation," offered Tepi's voice melodically. "You are in control. You are a master of fate. A man not to be toyed with."

"Yes ... that's correct," mumbled Manfir.

The hair on the back of Kael's neck stood on end. He watched Granu's face. The giant's eyes narrowed and his expression turned grim.

"However, you grow weary of your responsibilities. You carry such a heavy burden," continued the sickly sweet voice of Tepi.

"Yes," came the soft reply.

"If only you might lay your burden down at someone's feet. Let them carry it for awhile," sang the voice. "Let someone else decide, someone else worry. Wouldn't it be nice to let someone else relieve you of the burden, it's so heavy?"

"Yes," slurred Manfir.

Granu's huge arm swept out and clasped Kael's collar. The giant ripped the boy from his feet and propelled him through the grasses. The long, thin leaves whipped Kael's face and he tried to protect himself from their sharp edges. In an instant, Kael hovered in the air three yards from the pair in the clearing. Manfir stood in front of Tepi with shoulders slumped and head hung low. Tepi stood over the Zodrian prince looking larger than Kael recalled.

Granu burst from the grasses behind Kael and his deep voice echoed in the clearing.

"I found the boy, he was lost in the field," boomed the giant.

Manfir's head snapped up and he glared at Granu. Tepi threw his cloak about himself and shrunk into it. The trader slid into the night shadows back toward the main encampment.

"What in Avra's name were you doing, Kael?" slurred Manfir.

Kael shot a glance over his shoulder at the placid face of Granu. The giant betrayed no emotion. Kael turned back to Manfir as Granu set him upon his feet.

"I ... I heard something in the grasses, and went to investigate," stated Kael.

"Without letting anyone know! What were you thinking?" snapped Manfir.

"I went in a short distance, but before I knew it, the grasses were over my head and I lost my bearings," pleaded Kael. "I panicked. Then I saw Granu's face looking down at me from above the field."

Manfir's eyes narrowed and he stared at the giant. The Zodrian prince appeared exhausted.

"I'm in no position to command, but it might be helpful if your Keltaran friend kept us informed of his whereabouts," Manfir whispered through clenched teeth.

"I held no time to inform you, Master Rin. My search called for all of my attention. I noticed the boy step into the field from across the clearing and knew it could come to no good. I focused on his entry point and followed. If I reported to you, as a servant might a master, I might skew my bearings and lose the boy. The grasses are like the waves of the sea. One wisp of the wind and what was, is no more," said Granu calmly.

Manfir eyed him suspiciously, then turned and marched toward the encampment. Kael glanced at Granu and saw a grave expression cross the man's face. They followed Manfir into the camp.

Kael woke to the noise of Tepi rummaging in his cart. The young man opened his eyes and noticed most of the group still wrapped in their bedrolls. On the opposite side of the fire lay Granu. The giant's big frame rhythmically heaved up and down, but Kael was sure the giant's eyes were slightly open, watching Tepi. Flair quietly moved about the encampment trying hard not to wake any of the men.

Kael rose and softly asked Flair if he required any assistance. Soon, the two young men built the fire up and boiled a pot of water for tea. Flair amazed Kael. The young ranch hand woke early and followed the brook to a pool it formed about a half league from the encampment. The young man hooked several nice trout and now sizzled them in a small pan over the fire.

Shortly, the entire group roused themselves and readied for departure. Tepi wandered over to the fire eyed the trout critically and devoured half of the meal before returning to his cart.

The group doused the fire and started on their way to Rindor, the river city.

"Master Tepi, I am sure you will find someone to service your cart in the village of Ymril," stated Ader abruptly.

"Ah... yes, that I can," said Tepi. "When do you anticipate our arrival there, good friend Rin?"

Manfir lifted his head and wearily looked at Tepi.

"Pardon," said the Zodrian prince.

"I say when do you anticipate our arrival in Ymril? " smiled Tepi.

"Oh, uh I'm not sure. Uh Ymril is ..." mumbled Manfir.

"We'll not be going to Ymril," cut in Ader decisively. "We'll push on through to Rindor."

"Not to Ymril?" exclaimed Tepi. "Why, that makes no sense. It's the next town along the trade route. A warm bed and fresh food are what we all need. Master Rin, surely you see the logic in that?"

"Uh, yes, that sounds satisfying. A warm bed," said Manfir.

"Of course, we'll hear no more of this pushing ourselves. It's far too great a journey for one day. All the way to Rindor, the old man talks nonsense!" laughed Tepi.

Ader's eyes narrowed and he studied Tepi intently.

"Of course, if the Elves and their slave wish to continue on. So be it," continued Tepi sweetly. "Those outlanders must conduct business with the crown. The rest of you merely rush to your deaths. Why hurry?"

Kael felt the hairs on his neck tingle as they did the night before. Ader's mouth tightened and his eyes bore into the trader.

"Perhaps good man Tepi is correct..." stammered Manfir.

Ader turned Tarader hard and faced the group. The giant horse blocked their path. The old man rose high on the back of the mighty stallion, towering above the other members of the party. The early morning sun struck him full in the face and his grave expression stopped everyone in their tracks.

"Ridiculous," stated Ader firmly. "Rin. It's time for you to shake the cobwebs from your head. We will stick with our plan, and this ... trader ... will leave us at the crossroads to Ymril. We travel on today, hard. Rindor by nightfall is our goal and with Avra's help we will make it so!"

Manfir's shock set him upright and rigid in the saddle. His eyes were wide and fully alert. Ader's jaw was set hard and his gray eyes bore into the Zodrian prince.

"Of course, we'll travel on as you say," stated Manfir. "There's much to be done and scant time to manage it. My apologies."

"Apologies accepted," said Ader as he spun on Tepi. "At the crossroads you will part with us. Until that time you will remember that you are a guest in this traveling group. You will stop when we stop and go where we go when commanded to do so. If you do not like these rules, be gone with you now!"

Tepi shrunk into the seat of his rickety old wagon, shifting the reins of his horse between his fingers. Ader spun his mount back down the road and the horse trotted forward. The remainder of the group hesitated, still in shock from Ader's outburst. Kael looked about him wondering what to do. His eyes met those of Granu. The giant stood in the road just behind Kael's mount smiling in deep satisfaction. He slapped Kael's mare on the rump sending her trotting after Ader. The rest of the group roused from their shock and continued down the road.

They traveled for hours. Periodically, Manfir or Ader called for a stop to rest, feed and water the horses. Ader took the lead during this leg of the journey, talking to Manfir constantly. The Zodrian prince became more alert after this encounter.

Tepi kept his cart to the back of the group and tried to call as little attention to himself as possible. Kael noticed Tepi distractedly talking to himself. The cart's continual hiccup jostled the bald man.

After hours on the road, the travelers came to a fork. A crude sign was fashioned onto a post near the right hand road. The sign simply read "To Ymril". Ader reined in and looked over his shoulder at the group.

"We made a good pace today. I do believe that if we push on we'll reach Rindor just after nightfall," The old man paused. "Unless there are any objections?"

All remained silent and Kael stole a glance at Tepi. The trader sat in his cart covered in his robes, sweating profusely. He simply stared at the reins.

"This is where we say goodbye to you, Master Tepi. Ymril is not nearly so far down the right fork as our journey to Rindor. You should arrive within the hour," stated Ader.

The trader looked up and a wicked smile crossed his face.

"Old man, you lead your compatriots to their death. You think I'm an ignorant gypsy, wandering through these lands full of hate and prejudice. You don't know one grain of what I am. While you rot on the foothills of the Scythtar, I'll be raised far above all men!" snarled Tepi.

The trader raised his arm and his riding whip mercilessly snapped on the back of his old nag. The horse lurched forward and trotted down the road to Ymril as the red faced trader cackled. The old cart rattled and shook as it bumped down the road.

"I sense Master Tepi will one day come to a bad end," stated Teeg.

"It'll come none to soon for the rest of the world," added Eidyn.

Tarader once again headed north along the Northern Trade Route. This time however, the group was able to improve their pace without the straggling presence of the trader and his cart. Kael found the pace refreshing. The breeze created by their trot cooled him slightly and the concentration required in the saddle took his mind from the foreboding sense of doom Tepi placed there. Conversation in the group started again. Even Flair chanced a discussion on horsemanship with Eidyn. The loss of the trader lifted a brooding cloud from the entire company.

The ride to Rindor took less time than Ader suggested. The sun was near to setting as the group passed homesteads. Kael saw small cottages and huts set here and there on rolling hilltops a half league from the road. Goat pens and corrals were erected near the homes. The occasional dog barked in the distance as the group trotted down the road. The area reminded Kael of Kelky. Good people set in the middle of good land, just trying to make a life for themselves. People unaware of the larger world about them. People just happy to be left to themselves and the land they worked.

And why shouldn't they? Why did things like war and disease poke their heads into the happy lives of these people? Kael's thoughts wandered to images of his mother. She was so happy when she were alive. They lived a simple life, and that's all she ever wanted. If Kael knew then what he knew now, would he have seen it differently? No, he was sure his mother, the daughter of the most powerful man in Zodra, was content. They were just another of these families, happy in their lives. Happy to be left to themselves and the life they chose. Happy until she was taken from them. Now his brother was gone as well.

"To each his own." said Teeg riding close by Kael.

"Uh, pardon." mumbled Kael, waking from his reflection.

Teeg nodded to a small cottage in the distance. A pigpen was set thirty yards from the home and a few cows roamed a nearby hillock munching on grass. A large dog raced from under the porch and pulled up on the next hilltop. Its bark was barely audible in the distance.

"I said 'To each his own'," restated Teeg.

"What do you mean?" asked Kael.

"All of us are born into our own situation, as it were," answered Teeg. "We all can't choose who we are to be and how we want to live."

"Why not? Why can't we decide to be and live a certain way?" said Kael.

"Any number of reasons Kael. The first and foremost being that our Creator may not want it that way. Another may be that the powers of Chaos may want to intrude on your plans," added Teeg. "What about the desires and needs of others? They may not be evil, but their intents and desires may conflict with yours."

"Its not fair. People should be allowed to be left out of it!" barked Kael.

"People cannot be left out of it, Kael. It's about everyone, not just some of them and some of us. There are those who pretend they are not involved. They bury their heads and dismiss it all. Yet one day it comes to you. One day you are called upon, sometimes in a small way, and sometimes in a big way, but you are called. If you cannot meet the challenge, you fail. The Creator makes it easy to follow him, Kael. Search your heart, know what is right and act. That is all he requires," said Teeg.

"But what if I don't feel like acting? What if I feel like I'm not the one who should be acting?" questioned Kael. "How do I know what my job is?"

"As I said, my boy, it'll come to you. We're all born into a situation. Our lives may take us many different places, but our true nature always rises to the top," answered Teeg. "Your father was never meant to be a shepherd's son. He could have stayed in the foothills of the Zorim, chasing wolves from his flock, but something called him. Your mother could have married some fool of a courtesan, probably a titled baron with wealthy land possessions, but she did not. She followed her heart."

"But my mother escaped. She left responsibility. When they moved to Kelky she was able to run and avoid it," stated Kael.

"Ah," smiled Teeg. "You think that story I told you is about your mother escaping? Running from a controlling father and the responsibilities of a kingdom?"

"Well, isn't that what she did?" questioned Kael.

"OF COURSE NOT YOU DOLT!" shouted Teeg.

The remainder of the party turned to stare at Teeg and Kael. The old Elf's eyes bore into the boy.

"We are having a lesson. Please attend to your business gentlemen!"

Eidyn smiled at Manfir.

"That was me, not so long ago," smiled the Elven prince.

Teeg resumed the discussion.

"Do you honestly believe walking away from a life of privilege and power to run an inn in the middle of nowhere AND raise two small boys is an escape from responsibility?"

"Well, I thought .." began Kael.

"No, you didn't think!" snapped Teeg. "I don't find a problem with you feeling sorry for yourself, Kael. We all do it now and again. But don't let it start to cloud your perception of reality! Don't let it tell you that you're the only one who sacrifices. You've been a part of this struggle for a short time. Some of us have been waging this war for hundreds of years. Some of us lost loved ones, just as you lost Aemmon. Some of us know what it's like to release a normal life, a carefree life and accept a life of struggle."

Kael bowed his head, squirming in the saddle. He reflected on Hrafnu once more. He contemplated Awoi and Gretcha. He pondered his father's years in the Guard. He thought of Cefiz. He glanced forward to Manfir. So many scars crisscrossed the big man's arms and face. Teeg, as perceptive as usual, continued.

"Those scars are what you receive for joining the struggle. Even a man as stoic as Manfir wouldn't lie to you. He would admit that each and every scar caused him pain. But would he give them all back, to avoid the fight? I think not. The struggle will wound you. It may even kill you. But if the fight is worthy, that is enough," said Teeg. "You wear your first scar. The loss of your brother will stay with you a lifetime. Just as the rain will cause an old wound to ache, so will memories of your youth cause your brother's memory to ache in your heart. Live with your scars. Know there will be more to follow, but never never question whether they are worth it."

Teeg turned forward and trotted ahead to join up with Eidyn. Kael was left with his thoughts. Thoughts of doubt and sorrow. Thoughts he decided to deal with.

The troop cantered along and night fell over the rolling hills around Rindor. The road rose to the crest of one of these small hills. Kael's sight fell upon Rindor. Two leagues down the road stood the river city, bathed in moonlight. The Ituan River flowed deep and wide at this point in its journey from the Zorim Mountains to the Toxkri Swamp. Its spinning, rolling currents pushed around an island at the river's widest point. Set atop this rocky island stood the city of Rindor. Massive stone slab after massive stone slab rose straight out of the flowing waters and stretched into the clouds. Not a single square yard of the island was left without structure. Martins and terns wheeled around the parapets feasting on the flying insects of nightfall. Their darting figures resembled a star shower as the moonlight caught their plumage and lit them in the night sky. The shimmering water rolled past. Kael felt his heart race at the beauty of the city.

RINDOR

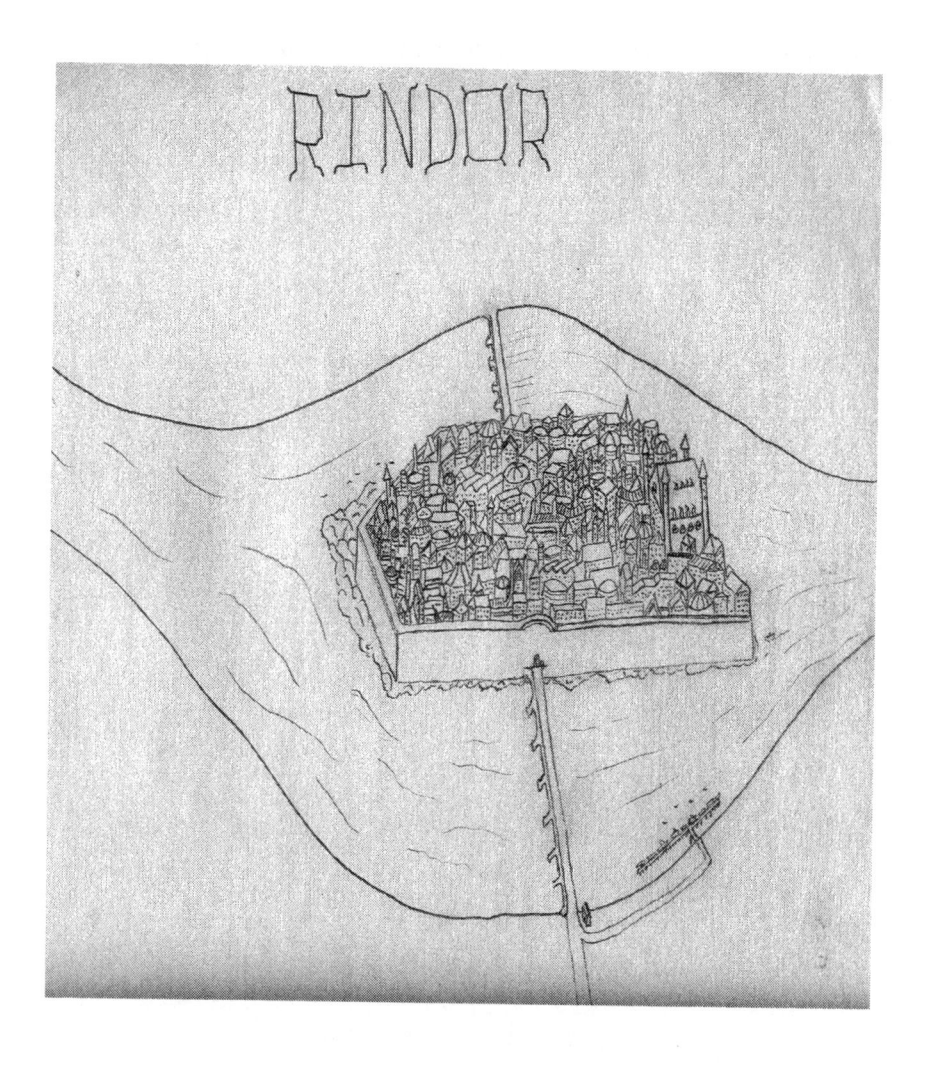

"The duchy of Rindor awaits gentlemen," said Manfir smiling. "Perhaps a warm bed and a good meal will take some of the ache out of our bones."

The group trotted down the road at a much livelier pace with that suggestion fresh in their minds. As they approached the river, they came to a long bridge. The bridge spanned the river from the south shore to the island. A large guard post sat next to the slightly arching bridge. Windows glowed with candlelight in the early evening. A guard stepped from the post and blocked entry to the bridge. He held a large trident nearly as tall as himself. The guard quickly surveyed the travelers and his eyes nervously shifted back to the guardhouse. He dipped the trident's pointed tines slightly forward and spoke loudly.

"Stand your ground! What brings so many riders to the doors of Rindor this night?"

Kael glanced through an open window and saw other uniformed soldiers throw gaming cards down on a table, clutch similar tridents and scramble to the post's doorway. Several soldiers burst through the door at once and took up position behind the spokesman. All of them nervously fidgeted with their weapons.

Ader edged his huge stallion to the front of the group and a look of compassion and understanding spread across his face. At first, the soldiers appeared uneasy about the presence of Tarader. However, once the old man spoke, their tension melted away. His voice was steady, calm and reassuring.

"I will wager your day is a long one?" smiled the Seraph. "Mine feels like an eternity. The open road treats old bones poorly."

Ader rubbed the small of his back as he hunched over.

"Aye, it is a long and tiring day," returned the spokesman. "Many folk travel the road."

"A sign of troubled times," sighed Ader. "People uprooted. Armies forming. Men called to battle. What are simple folk like you and I to do?"

Kael watched the spokesman and others in his group turn to one another and acknowledge their agreement with the old man.

"Tis true. We were just discussing the troubles over a game in yon house," said the spokesman pointing to the guard post.

"Most assuredly Rindor will find herself embroiled in the troubles, as all great nations do," said Ader shaking his head sadly. "And you poor gentlemen will find yourselves as embroiled as your homeland."

"You may be right sir, you may be right," nodded the spokesman.

The others in the group shook their heads in agreement. That's when Kael felt it. A tingle on his neck. The slightest raise of the hairs on his arms. A breeze of power misting over him. He calmed himself, closed his eyes and focused.

The boy became aware. Aware of the stream of power gently flowing from the old man. Unlike Ader's display in the Nagur Wood, this use of his power was subtle, invisible. It washed out over the Rindoran soldier and the group arrayed about him. It delicately pushed and prodded their feelings.

"An old man shouldn't be out on the road at night, but the command of my crown forces me," frowned Ader. "I'm loyal to my king and must obey. We are called to Zodra and to Zodra we must go."

"Yes, the life of a soldier is hard," agreed the spokesman narrowing his eyes at the group. "But we are honor bound to our duty. You arrive at Rindor at a late hour, in force and heavily armed. I cannot allow you to enter the city."

Ader's arm swept across his traveling companions.

"You call this ragged group a force," smiled the old man. "This collection threw itself together on the open road in order to protect itself. An intelligent man such as yourself surely understands the logic in that."

Kael felt the power from Ader intensify and flow out over the group. An even greater feeling of calm swept over him. He felt genuinely good about the situation they were in. These men were their friends and caused them no harm. All was fine here.

"This is true," nodded the spokesman smiling. "Tis foolish to travel the open road alone."

"Caylit, there is no threat with these travelers," called a soldier from behind the spokesman. "Let these good fellows be on their way and we'll return to our game."

The spokesman shook his head and cleared his mind. The smile quickly faded from his face with the challenge to his authority. He eyed the travelers once more.

"I've a want to allow you to pass, but the odd nature of your group calls me to question myself. How comes an old man, two young boys, a man with the look of a hardened veteran, a pair of Elves, and a ..." the head guard halted.

He edged forward toward Ader and scrutinized Granu. The Keltaran giant stood at the back of the group hunching down behind Eidyn's stallion. Kael was amazed at how such a big man made himself so unnoticed.

As the guard slowly moved past Ader the old man raised his hand slowly.

"My nephew, a bit slow," said Ader touching a finger to the side of his head. "I was saddled with the poor boy after his parents perished from the red fever years ago. He has no caretaker. I can leave him with no one as I ride to war. As you see, he is a man of no small measure, but as gentle as a kitten. I'm afraid I will lose him on the battlefield."

A wave of empathy swept over Kael. He almost believed Ader's story himself and was overwhelmed with sympathy and sorrow for the plight of this old man and his addled nephew. Surely the boy would be lost on the northern battlefields. The spokesman frowned and nodded at Granu.

"A sad state. Avra challenges us all in our own way," frowned the guard.

"Yes, he does. Perhaps Rindor will be the last place he sleeps in a warm bed and eats a decent meal. We are to be sent to the battlefields immediately," said Ader.

"A soldier's life is hard," mumbled the guard seeming to come to a decision. "The least we can do as an ally of the crown is to provide that last meal and bed to the troops who protect us with their lives."

"Here! Here!" came a few calls from the group arrayed behind him.

"You may pass," stated the head guard. "Foran! Signal the gatekeeper."

One of the guards ran to the post and removed a lit candle. A small, wooden deck on the back of the guardhouse faced the river. The soldier strode over to a series of posts set into a rail. He touched the candle to the top of seven posts. The heads immediately sputtered and caught fire. Seven torches guttered in the night.

"We must wait for acknowledgment," said the guard.

Kael searched through the darkness across the river to where he assumed the bridge ended. After a short wait, the boy saw a light appear in the distance. A lone torch was lit in reply.

"Go now and find rest and comfort in the citadel of Rindor, my friends," said the guard. "If you stay to the right as you enter the city, you will come shortly to 'The Singing Mermaid'. Tell them Caylit sent you there. Tis an excellent establishment if I do say so."

"He must," added a soldier behind the head guard. "His father-in-law owns it."

Caylit scowled, then clapped the fellow on the back and laughed as they turned to reenter the guard post.

"Fare thee well, old man. May Avra smile on you," called Caylit over his shoulder.

"Oh, I can assure you He does," whispered Ader to himself.

CHAPTER 22: BRIDGE TENDER, GATEKEEPER

The group moved out onto the bridge and began their journey over the Ituan River. The horses' hooves sounded out the pace on the heavy timbers forming the causeway. Kael stared in amazement at the structure beneath his feet. He estimated its distance at three hundred yards or more. Rolling black water surged and swirled below them, pounding the stone moorings of the bridge. However, Kael felt none of this assault as he trotted above the torrent on his sturdy mount. It was as if he were riding on solid ground, not a bridge. The structure stretched to a width of at least five yards. Several members of the group rode abreast with plenty of room to move. Fish jumped in the river below and Kael noted several small boats moving in and out of its currents.

"The fishermen find better luck in the evening, and the catch is fresher for the morning market," commented Manfir from off to Kael's right.

Kael turned to see the Zodrian prince smiling and looking down to the waters below.

"What is it they fish for?" asked Kael.

"Oh, mostly river cat and some pike," smiled the prince. "But the good ones luck into an occasional urgron. They are the prize."

The comment caught Eidyn's attention and he peered over into the water below.

"Urgron? What are they?" asked Kael.

"A rare delicacy," answered Eidyn. "The lords and ladies of the Rindoran court pay a pretty price for an urgron. Especially one that is in season."

"In season?" questioned Flair.

"The fish is a delicacy in its own right," replied Manfir with a twinkle in his eye. "But the true delicacy are the eggs a female lays. They are prized by the nobles."

The Zodrian warrior eyed the swirling currents and eddies of the water below them.

"What do they do with the eggs?" asked Flair.

"Why, eat them of course!" exclaimed Teeg.

"Ugh!" replied Flair contorting his face in disgust.

The group chuckled.

"What do they taste like?" Kael asked Manfir.

"Oh, I've never tasted them," answered the big man.

"I just thought you, um, you were staring at the river and I thought .." started Kael.

"Fish eggs, Kael?" laughed Manfir. "I agree with my good man Flair. Ugh! A nice game hen, or mutton leg are my fare. But fish eggs?"

The entire group chuckled once more as Manfir continued.

"No, the true treasure of the Urgron is not in eating it. The true treasure lies in catching it," said Manfir dreamily. "You truly don't know happiness until you stand silently on the banks of the river in the summer moonlight, casting a line for the Urgron."

"Why is that?" asked Flair.

Manfir smiled at the boy.

"Solitude."

"Pardon?" replied Flair.

"Solitude. Sweet solitude. Just you and the Urgron. If you're lucky, maybe just you for awhile."

"I don't understand," said Kael. "You want to catch it, don't you?"

"Eventually, I suppose," smiled Manfir. "But the true pleasure of fishing is the silence. The chance to let the worries of the world wash away down the river and leave you for awhile. Escape. Let the water calm you, and your thoughts escape to your dreams."

Kael saw the head of an otter poke above the midnight surface of the river. The animal chirped a call and splashed back under the flow. As Kael stared at the water he understood what Manfir meant. The constant roll of the river soothed him. He desired nothing more than to stand on the edge of the bridge and rest, watching the river slide away underneath him.

"State your business for the record book."

A hunched old man stood fingering through the pages of a leather-bound, raggedy old book. The book lay on an easel set just to the right of the massive gates of Rindor. A torch guttered in a wrought iron holder set into the granite of the city walls. The light from the torch played across the book and illuminated the ink stained hands of the old man as he frantically tried to turn it to the proper page. His wrinkled face was framed by wiry white whiskers both above and below. He screwed his face into a sour expression and spit a mass of chewing juice on the decking at his feet.

"Darn pages keep sticking together," mumbled the old man glaring at the book.

"Is there really a need for that Gency, old boy?" asked Teeg.

The old man squinted in the failing light at the riders in front of him. He grabbed the torch from the wall and walked amongst the riders. As Gency approached Teeg, the Elf smiled pleasantly to him. The bridge tender's eyes widened and he quickly glanced at the rest of the group then to the gates. When he was satisfied no other Rindorans were present he turned back to Teeg.

"Why, uh Master Elf, how is it you know my name?" stammered the old man pathetically, as he eyed Kael and Flair.

"Gency, please," pleaded Ader. 'We are tired and hungry. I will come to the gates tomorrow and we shall talk. The lads in this group are fine. Everyone knows everyone else. Just open the gate and let me get to a bed."

The old bridge tender fidgeted and frowned in exasperation.

"Well how am I to know who is one of us and who is not?" grumbled Gency to himself as he turned and shuffled to the gate.

The torch spilled its light onto a small hole cut in the gates facade. The hole sat three yards above the decking of the bridge and a light chain ran through it. On the end of the chain was affixed an iron ring. Gency tugged hard on the ring. A bell sounded hollowly as Gency muttered to himself some more. The group waited. Nothing. Gency frowned deeply then tugged on the chain once more. The bell rang again.

"Weneth ya old fool! Open the forsaken door!" shouted Gency.

Ader turned to Teeg and a smile played between them. Gency stood nearest to Kael and turned with an exasperated expression.

"The old fool has got the easy part of the job. Just open the gate when I ring. That's all! I'm the one that sits out here in the rain and snow, freezing to the bone some nights. Its enough ta ...."

A loud "clank" sounded within the gate and it slowly creaked inward.

"Now if ya want me to take the outside agin, all ya has ta do is ask. I never asked ta come inside," said Weneth as the gate swung wide open. "I'm not used to the darkness inside the walls. It lulls me ta sleep. I was used ta the moonlight and the rushing of the river. Now its just silence and darkness. Good evenin' Master Ader."

Ader nodded at an old man almost identical to Gency, who slowly pushed the gate to the wall.

"Evening Weneth. How are the bones?" said Ader as he edged Tarader into the city.

"Not so bad," replied the old man as he continued. "Never wanted to come inside. Never asked to come inside. I like the wind on my face and watchin' my river roll by. The bones weren't so bad."

The old gatekeeper stopped for a moment as the troop passed. He glanced at Manfir and lightly bowed.

"How goes the fishin' my boy?" asked Weneth.

"Eh?" said Gency squinting at Manfir. "Oh! How are you my boy? Didn't recognize ya."

"My bones may have gone brittle in the rain and snow," laughed Weneth turning on Gency, "but you've lost your eyes years ago, reading all night in the darkness with naught but a wee candle."

Gency frowned at his brother.

"I haven't cast a line in the water for years, my friend," smiled Manfir to Weneth. "One day soon I hope to. When that day comes, you must teach your brother about our arrangement. Even with his failing eyesight I'm sure we could become profitable again."

"I'm sure I'm fully aware of yur arrangement. Don't ya remember who let ya out every evening?" said Gency in mock disappointment.

"Then a fifty-fifty split is still acceptable?" smiled Manfir as the group moved into the city leaving the brothers at the gate.

"Fifty-fifty?" shouted Gency at his brother as Ader and the group moved down the street to the cities interior. "You told me it was sixty-forty all those years ago. You old cheat!"

"I told you it was sixty-forty and did not lie," Kael heard Weneth laugh. "I just didn't tell you who got the sixty and who got the forty!"

The group rounded a bend in the city street and the old men disappeared from view, their argument faintly heard in the night air.

The street before the group looked like a canyon. Buildings rose straight up on either side. Dozens and dozens of feet above their heads, rooftop met rooftop and tower joined to tower to form the canopy of this massive block of stonework. Here and there where the moon's glow reached through the maze of rooftops, it splashed its light on the mist-dampened cobblestones of the river city. The horses' hooves echoed down this canyon of granite and the group headed through the city.

"What was that all about?" Kael asked Manfir.

"When I was a lad," smiled Manfir. "I used to love to go down to the river and watch the fishermen. Often, I wandered up and down the river for hours. Sometimes I threw a line in the water and sometimes just explored. My mother grew worried by my long absences. When she discovered what I was doing, she forbade it. I was but a lad and the prince heir to the throne of Zodra. She feared for me. Exposing myself to the rough and tumble world down by the wharves was not the way a young prince should occupy his time.

"So, as any inquisitive boy might, I grew more determined by her refusals. At night, I slipped from my quarters and came to the gate. Weneth and Gency were younger then. They both held a soft spot for a boy looking to do mischief. I stole through the gate and fished the night river."

"What deal were you referring to?" asked Flair.

"I never truly discovered the habits of the Urgron," said Manfir. "At first I played at fishing. However, after reeling in a few nice specimens of pike, I quickly developed a passion for it. I was bound and determined to catch an Urgron but they eluded me. They are intelligent, solitary creatures. Hard to pin down. They move throughout the river where they please. They are the royalty of the currents. No predators but man.

"Often you think you hook one, only to find it steal your bait. Extremely frustrating. After months with no luck, I grew bitter. As I trod across the bridge after one particularly frustrating evening, I noticed Weneth staring at me with a silly grin."

'What is so humorous?' said I.
'You, young prince,' said Weneth.
'How so?' said I, furrowing my brow.
'I have never seen a lad take such displeasure in his mischief,' laughed Weneth. 'I wonder how the kingdom will fare under such a serious, driven ruler? Catching the fish is but a small portion of the pleasure of fishing. Standing amongst the beauty and majesty of Avra's creation is the true joy. Watching the waves roll by and feeling the wind on your face. Hearing the call of the nighthawk and the hoot of the great owl. Watching the moon drift from horizon to horizon. These are the pleasures of fishing.'

I lowered my head and considered his words. He was right, but I was as determined as ever. Weneth laughed and added.

'But it would be nice to catch a fish now and again.'

We both smiled as the night watchman patted me on the back.

'I might help you in that department, my young prince,' said Weneth. 'Answer a question. What is my job?'

'You're the night watchman of the citadel's bridge,' said I in confusion. 'The bridge tender.'

'Turn and look about you, my friend,' instructed Weneth 'What do you see?'

I turned and surveyed the world from Weneth's vantage.

'I see the bridge stretching back to the shore. I see a small outpost. I see the moon and clouds. I see the river churning under the bridge,' said I.

'Go on,' said Weneth.

'I see the moonlight on the water. I see a small fishing boat moving under the pilings of the bridge. And another by the shoreline...

Weneth cut me off as he rang the bell to open the gate.

'I stand at this post from dusk till dawn,' said he. 'I see where they catch 'em, and where they don't. I see where the tricky ones get away and leave a good man grumblin'. I see where the pike are schoolin' and the river cat jumpin'. Each night when Gency let's you out, just hover here a few moments and I'll let you know where to dip your line in the water.'

The city gate swung open and Gency poked his head out. Weneth smiled and patted me on the back.

'Now off to bed with you,' he said.

The next night he informed me of a school of pike hanging under one of the bridge's pilings. Sure if I didn't reel in a dozen within the hour. The next night the rivercat were feasting on fresh water mussels at the bottom of an eddy near the far shoreline. I battled several into the boat. As I passed Weneth with my stringer full, he smiled with pride.

Several weeks later he sent me after an Urgron that ran the shallows along the citadel's walls. A few skiffs attempted to land the fish to no avail. I pushed my skiff into the strong current and rowed to the spot. Weneth signaled by candlelight when I reached the area. For two nights I tried to land that fish, but found no luck.

Then on the third evening, my line plunged into the water. The moon waned and scant light reached the river through the cloud cover. I found it difficult enough to see my hand in front of my face let alone the strong creature I battled under the oily black of the running river. I fought the beast for three quarters of an hour. My arms ached from tugging and spooling the line around a gunwale on the small boat. Finally, the Urgron thrashed to the surface, scaring me half to death. Its big body slapped and whipped the river's surface into froth. Far in the distance I heard the whoop and holler of the watchman as he surveyed the scene with delight. As I strained to lift the beast from the blackness beneath me, I heard Weneth call out.

'Use the gaff ya fool! You'll break the line!"

I never landed such a fish, and held no inkling that its girth might snap my corded line or sturdy pole. One hand fumbled in the boat as the other strained with the thrashing creature. My hand came across the handle of a short gaffing stick. I quickly hooked it into the side of the Urgron and hauled the monster aboard.

The walk back across the bridge was a trial as I buckled under the weight of the beast. As I approached Weneth I expected to see the man beaming at me. However, he stood with lips pursed and head downcast.

'Look at this beauty!' said I delightedly.

The watchman barely looked at the monster.

'Aye, tis a beauty.' he acknowledged softly.

'That was one of the grandest moments of my life,' I said with exhilaration.

He smiled and slowly nodded.

'What in heaven's name is the matter?' I exclaimed

'I apologize,' said Weneth. 'My excitement got the better of me.'

'What are you on about?' I laughed.

'I did not mean to call you a fool young, Prince Manfir,' said he, hanging his head lower still, 'but I stand here many a night dreaming of casting a line and catching a monster such as that. The fear that you might lose him right next to the boat overcame good judgment. Many apologies.'

I laughed heartily and told him I cared not. 'Twas the heat of the moment. Weneth rang the bell. As Gency opened the gate, the doorkeeper's eyes went wide at the sight of my catch. On my return to the castle, I passed the fishmongers' booths. The idea of returning with my catch to the palace did not seem right. News would surely travel within the walls that the queen's son caught a grand Urgron. My mother would be none to happy with my antics. Therefore, I slid in behind the fishmongers' booths and found the man the palace purchased most of their fare from. I negotiated a fair price for my catch and he was happy to accommodate me, knowing he would sell it to the palace for a profit. We agreed to keep my activities a secret and if I were to continue, he would buy all I caught. Ironically, the next evening we dined on my own grilled Urgron.

Late the next evening I had tremendous luck with some schooling pike Weneth had seen jumping near a sandbar mid river. As I returned to the gate I stopped and produced a medium sack of coins from beneath my belt. I held it out toward the watchman.

'What's this?' exclaimed Weneth.

'I didn't throw that beast in the trash you know,' I laughed. 'Geleg the fishmonger paid a good price for it.'

'Well....' stammered Weneth pointing at the bag. 'That's yours. You caught the monster.'

'Tis true, I pulled the line to the skiff, but it was you and your knowledge that showed me where to go.'

'No, no I can't,' replied Weneth.

'This fool insists,' I demanded. 'It's not proper for me to profit off of another's knowledge.'

The reminder of his indiscretion and his desire to share in the glory of the achievement prodded Weneth into acceptance. He smiled broadly.

'I knew you'd get that one. It toyed with many a boat throughout the week, but I knew you possessed the patience to play it just right.'

I smiled and once again handed the bag of coins toward him. His hands shot up once more pushing them away.

'I'll share in the profits, but not take them all. The fish was your catch. You deserve the most. I'll accept a seventy-thirty split.'

'I wouldn't have caught the beast without you. Besides, I wouldn't even be on the river without the help of you and your brother. Gency deserves a cut as well. Fifty-fifty.'

'That silly bookworm. He's taken to reading the night away by candlelight inside that blasted gate. He neither enjoys nor appreciates this beautiful river. He isn't even sure what you're about as you sneak out at night,' grumbled Weneth.

'Nevertheless, he is a part of this and deserves a share,' said I.

'Sixty-forty,' frowned the watchman. 'We'll take twenty parts each.'

I smiled as a plan formed in my head. I was the heir to the throne of Zodra, a duke of Rindor. My family's wealth was almost countless. I had no need for the money, nor a want for it. However, this goodhearted man would not accept more than his share. I negotiated the price with Geleg, so only I knew the contents of the purse.

'Done!' I exclaimed. 'I agree to a sixty-forty split. I will deliver your share to you each evening after a sale.'

I quickly counted out some coins and handed them to Weneth. He gaped at the sum as I laid it in his hands. It was more than three months his salary. He thanked me profusely for the coin and I returned to my quarters after first visiting Geleg.

This arrangement lasted for the three summers I visited Rindor in my youth. I daresay it was quite profitable for all concerned. I satisfied a young man's urge to rebel against my parent's orders, and satisfied my love of the sport. Weneth and Gency purchased land together South of the city. Their sons and daughters work a profitable ranch the two men purchased with the extra coin they received.

"What plan did you put into play against the watchman?" asked Flair.

Manfir smiled as the group arrived in front of "The Singing Mermaid". A crudely drawn sign depicted either a mermaid diving beneath the waves of the river or an otter. Kael wasn't certain. As they dismounted, the prince continued.

As the end of my third summer in Rindor approached, I knew I wouldn't be returning for a fourth. My education at the Hold was to begin in my fourteenth summer and I would spend the entire year in Zodra. One evening as I returned across the bridge I smiled and tossed a small sack to Weneth. The watchman's normal grin was gone.

'I never need to go into the markets, for I leave all of the supply gathering to my wife,' said he. 'I sleep a good portion of the day away in order to be alert in my city's service.'

'It's admirable that she takes the full task upon herself,' said I in confusion. 'Why do you tell me this?'

'My wife is ill,' he replied.

'I'm terribly sorry,' I returned. 'Is there anything I can do? Is it serious?'

'It's but a small thing. However, I needed to make a visit to the markets.'

'Yes, and ..' I prodded.

'I'm not a man of letters, but I've a meager understanding of numbers.'

The watchman dumped the contents of the small sack into his hand and slowly counted the coins. When he finished he looked up to the crescent moon floating in the cloudless sky. He calculated figures in his head, abruptly stopped and frowned.

'I'm quite cross with you,' he stated. 'How long has this been going on?'

'I don't know what you're talking about,' I exclaimed defensively.

'Well,' said the watchman. 'I stopped by the fishmonger's booth yesterday. I wished to see that Urgron you caught last evening in the light of day. Twas a fine fish.'

'Yes, it was,' I returned.

'Unless I'm mistaken, it seems that master Geleg is selling his fish at a loss to himself,' frowned Weneth.

I stood in silence for a moment staring at my feet and fidgeting.

'Manfir, the backbone of every man is his integrity, his honesty. Knowing you've been fair in your dealings allows you to expect fairness in return. We were to split the proceeds sixty-forty.'

'Ah, but I did!' I exclaimed smiling. 'I just never specified who was to get the sixty.'

Weneth furrowed his brow and frowned once more.

'Are you telling me this entire time you've been givin' me sixty parts of your profit?' asked Weneth.

'Per our agreement,' said I and quickly cut off further protest. 'Weneth, I'm the heir to the throne of Zodra. I require nothing. What use might I find for this coin? You stand here year after year serving the citadel. You deserve it. Our arrangement will come to an end shortly anyhow. I must leave for Zodra at the end of the week and attend training at the Hold for my next several summers. Please accept that you were misled, but deserve even greater rewards than this.'

'I proudly do my job for the price agreed upon by the stewards of the city. I never expected more. I can't repay you. The coin was used to support my family and can't be retrieved. However, I'll hold myself indebted to you, my prince,' said Weneth bowing lightly.

'I'll accept that,' said I smiling.

I reached up and tugged on the chain. The bell sounded and a moment latter the huge gate swung open and I marched into the darkness of the city at night. From behind me in the darkness I heard Weneth softly call out.

'Take care, my boy. The patience you learned on the river will serve you well on the battlefield.'

I never returned to fish the river.

CHAPTER 23: THE SINGING MERMAID

The group entered the cramped lobby of "The Singing Mermaid". The horses were tethered to a series of posts set out front. Granu remained with them in the shadows of the street. A small cluttered desk sat unattended near the front door. Past the desk and through the lobby sat the smoke filled common room. A small bar stood on the right side of the room and several rough looking characters leaned against it, chatting to one another over pints of ale. Teeg stepped into the room and all went quiet.

"What can I do fer ya, Master Elf?" asked a rotund, balding man pouring ale from a tapped keg.

Teeg surveyed the room quickly and pointed to a large empty table in the corner.

"That will do nicely. The horses on the street need housing. Seven billets in your establishment are required. I need that table full of whatever hot fare you serve, and an equal measure of ale to go with it," said Teeg as he produced a small pouch from beneath his belt and threw it to the landlord.

Quick as a cat the landlord's hands shot out and snatched the bag from the air. He hefted it for a moment then smiled.

"Of course, me lord," said the man. "Briny! Get out here and set up the corner table."

A greasy haired young man poked his head through the swinging doors that led into the kitchen. He surveyed the crowd in the common room for a moment then disappeared.

"Send the wash boy to Hentil's stables and secure a number of their stalls! Tell Hentil the usual deal applies!" bellowed the landlord as he filled mugs retrieved from a wall.

A crash was heard off in the kitchen and Kael imagined several employees scurrying about to fulfill their employer's wishes.

"Woman! Can you not see we entertain paying customers?" continued the landlord.

Kael followed the man's gaze to a sultry woman at a far table. The woman smiled and slowly stood. She smoothed her tight dress over her voluptuous body and sauntered forward. Auburn hair cascaded over her exposed shoulders. Kael flushed slightly as the woman brushed past him.

"I don't think our old friends will mind if we take our time getting the rooms ready. They're hungry and will spend some time at the table," purred the woman.

"Eh, old friends?" said the landlord squinting at the group in the darkly lit and smoky common room.

The woman glided past a smiling Ader and slid up tight against Manfir.

"Hello, Rin," she whispered through pursed lips. "You never said goodbye the last time you were here."

"Rin?" said the landlord as recognition crept across his face. "And old Jasper too. How fare you?"

"My father never sees past the man with the fattest purse," said the woman. "Your Elven friend blinded him as soon as he tossed that coin across the bar."

"Now, now, Lete. There's no need to be mean. I was looking after the interests of my new customer," frowned the landlord. "It's not often that we receive guests of such high station."

A few of the men at the bar grumbled disapproval.

"Oh, you know what I mean," growled the landlord to his regular patrons as he rubbed the thumb and index finger of his right hand together.

They laughed and nodded their heads at the gesture. Manfir stood stock-still and rigid as Lete tightly circled and inspected him.

"You look no worse for the wear," she commented. "A few more scars and a few more lines in the face, but as handsome as ever."

"Vetic, your daughter has gained weight," said Manfir softly to the landlord.

Lete stopped in her tracks, and a few men at the bar winced. Vetic looked about the room as if trying to find a means of escape.

"But as in all things," continued Manfir. "She uses it to enhance her already formidable assets."

The room remained quiet for a moment. Even the unflappable Teeg looked for a rock to hide under. Lete let out a deep, soulful laugh and stepped away from Manfir. She spun slowly in front of him, throwing her head back in laughter and lifting her arms to the ceiling. The dress remained taught against the curves of her body.

"This is the new version of Lete. More of me to love in all the right places."

Manfir remained expressionless. His eyes inspected the woman.

"You mean the married version, don't you?" commented Manfir.

The woman stopped mid spin and the smile fell from her face. Her arms came down and she folded them in front of her bosom.

"Life moves on with or without some people," she humphed. "You came in through the south gate?"

"The head guard of the south post, your husband Caylit, has an important position," replied Manfir flatly.

"I suppose," said Lete as she absentmindedly glanced at her feet and wrapped a finger around one of her long curls.

"I'm sure the fact that every visitor from the south gets referred to your father's inn is purely a side benefit of your nuptials?" deadpanned Manfir.

Vetic coughed and dropped one of the mugs he was polishing.

"Hold your tongue!" snapped Lete. "I love Caylit and married him out of love. If you think for one moment I'm ... I'm using that good man..... You're mistaken! You waltz back in here after two years and... and think you can judge me!... You think you know what it's like to struggle to make ends meet. You .."

Lete's arms waved wildly in front of her and she once again advanced on Manfir. The Zodrian prince stood as rigid as before. Lete waggled a finger in his face and her tirade carried on. She smacked Manfir on the chest. The big man wrapped her up in his arms, lifted her from the floor and quickly kissed her.

"Congratulations," he said dropping the stunned woman back onto her feet.

She stared at him puzzled for a few moments more.

"Wha... what did you do that for?" she asked.

"I congratulated you. Isn't it customary to kiss the bride after a wedding?" said Manfir.

Lete looked bewildered.

"Why did you walk in here and pick a fight?" she asked cautiously.

"I wanted to know if you truly loved the man. My accusation assures me you do," smiled Manfir. "You are a tough woman to read, Lete. The same cool exterior no matter what's going on underneath. The only time I've seen a crack in that facade is when you truly care about something. You must love the man deeply to defend him with such passion."

The barmaid blushed, fidgeted and stared at her shoes.

"I do," she whispered.

"I wish you great happiness," Manfir whispered back as he lightly kissed her forehead.

"I will see to your rooms," said Lete as she smoothed her dress once more and proudly walked to the stairway.

As Lete strode up the stairs, Briny emerged from the kitchen carrying a platter of roasted game hens. A boy followed with a pot full of boiled potatoes. Vetic filled the table with mugs of ale, bread and butter.

"Come gentlemen," said Teeg. "Let us take some respite here at the table."

The group remained for a moment more and Lete disappeared from view up the stairs. They moved to the table and filled in around it. The bar's patrons settled upon the woman's departure. They chatted once more and enjoyed their ale.

Kael was ravenous. He immediately tore into the game hen in front of him. The others were equally hungry and followed suit. After a moment, Kael noticed the swinging doors to the kitchen slowly open and Briny back out with a tray of vegetables. The young man stepped away from the doors and they remained open as the light from the kitchen threw itself onto the wide-eyed servant. The patrons at the bar continued in their revelry and saw nothing. However, Kael glimpsed a huge figure, covered in black slide past the gawking cook and glide silently up the stairs.

Briny watched Granu disappear from view then he slowly made his way to the table. Briny's eyes still registered shock as he silently picked up a plate full of food and turned toward the stairs. Teeg's head was bowed over his food as he tore into the game hen, but he chuckled as the serving lad turned.

"Don't forget some drink as well, my good man. He gets irritable if his thirst is not quenched," stated Teeg.

Briny gulped hard and quickly retrieved a mug of ale. The servant walked to the stairwell as if walking to the gallows. When he too turned on the landing and disappeared from view, the entire table laughed. After a few moments into their meal, Kael turned and addressed Manfir quietly.

"I'm confused. If you're the heir ..." Kael coughed and glanced about the room. ",...if you are who you are, why did you spend so much time in Rindor?"

"I'm officially a duke in the realm of Rindor," stated Manfir. "I hold title and possessions in these lands."

"What? How can you be a duke in a land you will one day rule?" whispered Kael perplexed.

"Quite true, Kael. Quite true," said Teeg smiling, "but our friend here holds many titles."

Manfir frowned at the old Elf and turned back to Kael.

"Rindor is a bit of a strange situation, Kael. It's not actually a Zodrian possession."

"What do you mean by 'not actually?'" questioned Flair.

"Rindor is a city state. What I mean by that is, Rindor governs itself, with plenty of input from Zodra when she will take it," answered Manfir.

"Take it?" said Kael.

"Please do start from the beginning, Teeg," groaned Ader. "You and our illustrious Rindoran duke always seem to start in the middle and finish at the beginning."

The old Elf arched an eyebrow and looked crestfallen. He turned to the young men and took on the air of instructor once more.

"When Zodra expanded and dominated this part of the world, they ran into Rindor," began Teeg. "'Twas not the impressive citadel you see here today, but a mighty enough fortress stood here to give the Zodrians a moment of pause. A formidable wall stood encircling the entire island and a large village thrived within.

"The river provided the perfect defense. No bridges existed then, and the only means of visiting the city was by barge or riverboat. Siege engines were useless against the city. They were unable to affect the wall from the shoreline, and no barge or river craft could bring them close without braving the current and battle from the island. The Rindorans are master boatsmen and made quick work of any watercraft that attempted to breach their city's defenses.

"The Rindorans could not be starved out. The river is the source of their food. They simply put to water in small craft at night and replenished their supplies. Attempts to thwart this harvest resulted in more Zodrian deaths. Zodrians are not much for boats."

"So," continued Manfir. "The Zodrian army bypassed Rindor, sending messages to the Zodrian king that it was unconquerable. The army left several units encamped on both shorelines and a siege of the city began. It lasted for months.

"The Zodrians would not be denied. The king, I believe it was Nyox the second, held parlay with the Rindorans. A treaty was struck. Quite a brilliant plan actually. The Zodrians agreed to return all the land around the river to the control of Rindor. The King of Rindor was considered a duke in the kingdom of Zodra and the Rindoran lands would be his duchy. All tax and tributes in these lands were assessed as any other duchy in the Zodrian kingdom. The duke took his part and the kingdom theirs. However, there was one small exception. The city proper remained an independent entity. On this island, the ruler of Rindor is still the king. He has sovereignty over all others here, even the king of Zodra."

"Do you mean to say that Macin, your father, is required to bow down before the Rindoran king?" asked Kael.

"Absolutely," replied Manfir. "The treaty stands. You will never find my father anywhere near Rindor."

"He's never been here?" asked Flair.

"The last time his father was here, Macin was getting married," smirked Teeg. "I wore a glorious silver doublet."

"What?" questioned Kael. "King Macin was married in Rindor?"

"Both kingdoms held suspicions and fears," continued Manfir. "Did the other hold to the bargain? Were they being compensated fairly? Rindor moved all commerce within the city walls in order to avoid Zodrian taxation. The Zodrians, in turn, taxed the land instead of the sales from a harvest. This way they ensured their share. Rindor complained bitterly during seasons with drought and frost. Tensions rose as the game persisted.

"Eventually the two houses found a way to ensure loyalty. Every so often, as the houses grew further and further apart, a Zodrian prince or princess was married off to a Rindoran. It has been going on for centuries. Our houses are entwined."

"Our Rindoran duke's father, married the sister of the wife of the prince heir of Rindor," smiled Teeg.

Flair blinked and shook his head in consternation. Ader frowned at Teeg and the Elf let out a sigh of exasperation.

"It is quite simple. When Macin was slightly older than Kael is now, he was invited to a royal wedding in Rindor. He was not the King of Zodra then, so he happily attended. Corad Kingfisher, the prince heir of Rindor at the time, married Lucyn, a beautiful young woman from one of the powerful Rindoran houses. Her family was the wealthiest in Rindor and second only to the Zodrian royal house in wealth within that kingdom.

"Prince Macin represented the royal house of Zodra at the wedding. There he saw Lucyn's younger sister, Tay. He was smitten," continued Teeg. "Macin knew through his station and power he might demand the young woman's hand in marriage, but Manfir's father is no fool. Shrewd men never take by force what they might win with minor effort. Macin was handsome, witty and the heir to the throne."

"Some say he was rather funny in those days," said Manfir distractedly.

"Yes, he was," recalled Ader. "A young man with a limited idea of the responsibilities ahead of him. Hardly a care in the world. In fact, when Macin courted Tay, Corad grew angry with him. Never serious. Never willing to talk of the world. They might have cemented the bond between the kingdoms even further if Macin did not treat his future brother-in-law with such disdain. They grew ever apart and competitive."

"So the rulers of Rindor are your...?" began Flair.

"Aunt and uncle," finished Manfir quietly. "I will one day rule Zodra, but will always be their nephew and subject within the walls of this city."

"Manfir also owns much of the land to the northwest of the river. Lucyn and Corad have a son, but he is younger than Manfir. Therefore, his grandfather's lands fell to Manfir. Our friend is the wealthiest Rindoran in the kingdom. When he rises to the throne of Zodra, he will be the wealthiest man to have ever lived," smiled Teeg.

Manfir scowled at Teeg, but the old Elf waved it off and pressed on.

"Our friend tends to neglect his duties. With great wealth also comes great responsibility. I employ good people to keep his interests in line," laughed Teeg. "Quite easy actually. A small legend has built up over Manfir's ability to check on his interests even when he has not been seen in a dozen years. The tenants on his land are treated better than any others in the kingdom yet they cannot even recall what their benefactor looks like."

The group extended their conversation about Rindor and the surrounding lands for some time. Kael and Flair were fascinated by the talk. Kelky was their world for so long that the everyday happenings of a city like Rindor were fascinating. Vetic paused by the table and informed the group that the entire third floor was at their disposal.

"It seems that the room at the end of the hall has been occupied by a member of your party,...ah... who was too tired to take his meal in the common room," said Vetic clearing his throat. "Some of you gentlemen will need to double-up I'm afraid."

"Not a problem," said Kael slapping Flair on the back.

The young ranch hand smiled back. The food disappeared and several rounds of ale were swallowed when Teeg rose.

"Ah, I find that I cannot continue our chat through such heavy eyelids. If you will excuse me, gentlemen," said the Elf bowing.

Eidyn excused himself as well, and soon the men retired to their rooms. Kael and Flair took a room with two bunks. As they lay down to sleep they talked briefly of their day. Kael was sure the boy was as astounded by all that happened as he was. Shortly after their conversation ended, Flair snored loudly. Kael lay in his bunk thinking and drifting in and out of sleep.

Suddenly, his sharp ears picked up sounds of movement in the hallway. Kael silently stepped from his bunk and moved to the doorway. The boy leaned against the wall and opened the door a hair's width. His keen eyes discerned a figure at the hallway's end. The light of the moon bathed the figure in a faint glow. It slid something into the folds of a long overcoat. The moonlight caught the glint of steel. Kael suspected the man came from the common room. The coat was a fisherman's slicker, and the broad rimmed hat and boots were of a type the wharf workers at the bar sported. The smell of fish and oil hung in the air of the hallway and seeped into Kael's room.

The man turned and walked purposefully down the hallway toward Kael. The boy felt frozen with fear and uncertainty. With a good deal of effort Kael took a half step away from the door. Through the slit in the doorway, Kael's eyes remained fixed on the character approaching him. The figure's head was cocked slightly forward with his hat obscuring his face. As he stepped within a few feet of the doorway, his hands shot into his pockets and he abruptly halted. In a flash he produced two small objects.

Fluidly, tinder was struck and put to the bowl of a large pipe. The heady aroma of strong tobacco filled the hallway and the bowl glowed red. A gruff, heavily accented voice whispered toward Kael's hiding spot.

"Let me be about me business lad. Yee have had a long day. Get ya ta bed."

The figure took a deep draw on the pipe, flaring the bowl and sending a warm orange glow about his face as he looked up at the slit in the doorway. The weary, dirty countenance of Teeg stared at the boy. The old Elf somehow grew a week of stubble in an hour. A small silver ring hung from an earlobe surrounded by dirty, oily hair. Smudges of tar and oil covered his hands and face and he appeared to be missing a tooth.

The Elf paused then winked before he proceeded down the hallway and out into the night of the city. Kael felt oddly reassured that someone like Teeg, the Master of Spies, was on his side. At least he thought Teeg was on his side. The boy threw over the latch on the door, then returned to bed and fell fast asleep.

CHAPTER 24: SUMMONS

"OPEN IN THE NAME OF THE KING!" shouted the voice in Kael's head.

"OPEN IN THE NAME OF THE KING, I SAY!" echoed the voice.

"Kael, wake up," whispered a much more familiar voice. "Get up. What should we do?"

Kael's eyes let the morning light slowly bleed in. He was not used to the ale, and it made it difficult for him to gain his bearings. The fuzziness cleared and Kael saw Flair standing over him pulling on his trousers.

"They say they're soldiers," said a bewildered Flair. "Should I open the door?"

Kael nodded, stood and put on his own clothes. Flair threw the latch and let the door swing open. A large man stood in the doorway. He wore a tight fitting leather garment fitted with a silver breastplate. A design embossed on the breastplate showed two huge fish swimming around an island castle. He sported a helm whose crest resembled the spine of a great fish. Across his shoulder was hung a heavy steel net and in his hand he carried a large spiked trident.

"Your presence is required at the castle. Retrieve your goods and personal belongings and we will escort you there," stated the soldier.

Kael saw a door on the opposite side of the hallway swing open. The soldier in front of that door took a step back as Manfir scowled and stepped into the hallway. The prince was fully dressed, and his broadsword was slung across his back. A heavy beard had grown during their time on the road, and he obviously found no time to bathe yet. The soldier in front of Kael spun and approached Manfir.

"You will surrender your weapons to my men. They are not allowed in the presence of his majesty," said the captain forcefully.

"What does this concern?" asked Manfir.

"A troop of heavily armed mercenaries entered our kingdom in the dead of night and hid itself in one of our," the captain paused, "shall we say, more questionable establishments."

Kael heard a loud cough as someone near the stairwell cleared his throat. The boy stepped further into the hallway and looked past more soldiers. He saw the landlord's head peering over the top step. Vetic gave another loud grunt of disapproval and disappeared from sight. The soldiers tensed as Manfir edged further into the hallway.

"His majesty wishes to know your business," stated the captain.

Ader opened a door further down the passage and stepped into the hall smiling.

"Obviously, his majesty is interested in hosting our Elven emissaries in a more appropriate venue," stated the old man cheerily.

As if on cue, Teeg and Eidyn stepped from their doorway in full court attire. An impeccably groomed Elven courtier replaced the oily dockworker from the previous evening. Eidyn was also resplendent. The Elven prince's ring was back on his finger.

"Now that we have escorted our Elven guests to their destination, we will turn them over to your care and his majesty may discern their business as he wishes," said Ader.

"You and your troop performed admirably, my good man," said Teeg producing a small pouch. "Your protective services are no longer required. I mistakenly assumed Corad Kingfisher was aware of our impending arrival."

The Elf tossed the pouch to Ader and stepped forward to fall in amongst the soldiers. Ader slid the pouch into his pocket and bowed deeply. The captain took on a bewildered look and hesitated as Ader turned to retire to his room.

"Sir!" called a soldier from the end of the hall.

Kael's eyes surveyed the end of the passageway. The hall ended with a small window that looked over the backyard of the inn. Alleyways ran off in different directions through the maze of the city. A soldier stepped from Granu's room and addressed his commander.

"This room has been used, but stands empty at this early hour."

The captain turned from the soldier and addressed Ader.

"The report stated seven travelers were to be brought before his majesty, and I will do my duty. Whether you are a protective escort or not is immaterial to me. There will be no debate. Turn over your weapons and gather your things quickly. We leave immediately!"

The captain turned and issued orders to his men. Ader's face tightened and he nodded to Manfir. The Zodrian prince drew his blade and handed it hilt first to the nearest soldier. Kael drew his dagger and turned it over as well. Several Rindorans took station by the window and others remained in the hallway ensuring the group gathered their things. When all was ready, they marched down the stairs and assembled in front of the inn. Teeg mildly protested the need to drag his good serving men with him, but the captain remained deaf to the complaints. As they formed up in the street, Kael spied several soldiers scouring the narrow alleyways about the dirty inn. He wondered where Granu hid himself.

The group marched across the slick, wet cobblestones of the river city. The streets were laid in no particular fashion. At times, the men turned a corner to almost walk directly into the doorway of a building, only to quickly turn again. Some streets traveled for a few blocks in one direction, then turned and headed back the opposite direction for an equal distance. A few early risers were about the city and with each step, the gray dawn brightened into daylight. Kael lost his sense of direction in the maze of streets.

The group stepped into a large plaza. They made their way past booths and stands being set up by scores of people. Most of the Rindorans stopped to view the odd procession as it swept through the market place. Their interest was only momentarily captured however, as their chores called them back to work. Kael's face broke into a smile as he noticed an old man unfurling a canopy with the words "Geleg's Fishery" scrawled across it. Kael noticed Manfir run his hands through his hair, briefly obscuring his face from the old man as they passed. It was not necessary. Geleg the fishmonger glanced at the group then immediately turned to his booth.

Kael was about to turn his attention back to their route, when something caught his eye. Two small figures darted from behind Geleg's booth across an open walkway to the space behind the nearest booth. They jumped from booth to booth keeping pace with the troop. Storage areas kept them hidden most of their journey across the marketplace. Also, their speed and stature made them a blur as they sprinted between open spaces. Soon, they advanced ahead of the group and Kael lost sight of them altogether.

The marketplace ended in a row of towering shops and inns. A small opening in a corner of the square funneled travelers onto a twisting street between the buildings. The group continued their march toward the opening and Kael saw two boys run from behind the nearest booth. The boys laughed and rolled a wooden ring back and forth between them. The group passed and the boys stopped and stared. The captain smiled and nodded to them and they bowed in return. As the captain returned his attention to the street, one of the boys fidgeted with the wooden ring in his hands. Kael noticed Ader studying the boys intently.

The group passed between the buildings and moved down the city street. Recognition struck Kael. Had he seen that boy before? Where was it? On the road? In Kelky? He spun to look at the boys, and the spot in the square where they had stood was empty. Kael searched the square beyond but within moments it was lost from view.

The street wound for several hundred yards. The group halted in front of a giant granite structure. Stonewalls lay buttressed to one another reaching up into the sky. The only ornament for gray rock was more gray rock. Parapets opened onto balconies that Kael could not see.

This experience was quite different than Luxlor. The Elven palace stood in an open clearing and Kael was able to view it from a short distance and get a feel for its beauty. Here, he turned a curve in the road and was on the place, a few feet from its massive foundation. The palace of Rindor was a huge gray rock like the island it sat upon.

A short flight of ten stone steps led the group into an alcove in the granite wall. Two soldiers in similar attire to their escort stood at attention in front of large wooden doors bound in iron. As the captain of the escort approached they saluted and opened the doors for entry. The group swept up the stairs and past the doors. A wide alabaster hallway stretched out in front of them. Beautifully embroidered tapestries lined the walls of the hallway. Small ornately carved side tables were placed strategically up and down its length. Each table held a stunning sculpture of porcelain or blown glass.

"Not much from the outside, but like most people, her true beauty lies within," whispered Manfir as he walked next to Kael.

Kael smiled back at the prince. It was then that the boy was struck by his friend's appearance. Shaggy, unkempt hair hung to Manfir's shoulders. His dark beard nearly obscured his features. His traveling cloak and clothing were dusty and stained with sweat. The Elves were the only presentable members of the bunch.

The group walked into a round room no bigger than the common room at "The Singing Mermaid". A number of plush chairs were arranged in a circle about the room. On the opposite side from the doorway sat a man and a woman. The man wore a uniform similar to the guards, except that the breastplate and helm were of a golden hue. Additionally, the helm upon his head displayed a much more pronounced crest.

The woman was of uncommon beauty for her age. She wore an alabaster colored gown of gauze and lace. Fresh water pearls draped the nape of her neck and formed a delicate tiara on her honey colored hair. The group entered the room and the man and woman stood.

One of two guards placed by the entry to the room stepped forward to inquire their business. Teeg quickly slid to the front with Eidyn in tow.

"Teeg Fin Ciar, the Grand Duke of Luxlor and Eidyn the prince heir of Luxlor, with their protective entourage, here upon their Majesty's request," stated Teeg.

The man in the golden breastplate hushed the guard as the servant tried to announce the group. He waved the wayfarers and their escort into the meeting room.

"Step forward so we may speak," announced the king.

Teeg strode forward purposefully, attracting all eyes. Kael noticed how Ader and Manfir tried to stay inconspicuous and let Teeg and Eidyn lead.

"Greetings, Corad Kingfisher. The bounties of the great river remain kind to you these many years," stated Teeg bowing.

"Greetings, Lord Teeg," returned Corad. "I might compliment you likewise, but the ravages of age never travel amongst your people and the compliment would be lost. You also have changed little in lo these many years."

"We all change your Majesty, on the outside or the in," said Teeg turning to Lucyn. "Yet your bride is blessed by Avra and mirrors the image I remember from my last visit, upon your wedding."

The Elf Lord swept forward and bowed to one knee before the queen. He lightly took her hand and pressed his lips to it. She returned the gesture with a nod of her head.

"You jest, Lord Teeg, you have not changed on the inside much either," smiled Lucyn. "As I recall upon your last visit, you were the essence of decorum and the height of flattery, and you remain so."

"Or shall we say your last 'official visit'," corrected Corad with a cough. "For if my information is accurate, you have visited our island quite a few times since the day I was blessed with the hand of Lucyn."

The queen smiled back at the king, then both turned penetrating eyes on the Elf as he rose. Teeg arched an eyebrow and stroked his chin.

"Your Majesties hold me at a disadvantage. It is true that your island is a polished gem amongst the rushing waters of the Ituan, but it is quite difficult for me to make such a journey in my old age. The days of my wayfaring youth have sadly passed me," frowned the Elf.

Corad scowled and turned to his wife. From beneath one of the gauzy waves of her sleeve, Lucyn produced a small parchment. She slowly unrolled it and perused its contents.

"Hmmm, let me see," murmured the Queen. "Ten months ago you passed through the Southern gate as Demrol, a tinker. You took lodging at the 'Broken Plow' and journeyed on through the north gate three days later."

She paused and glanced at the old Elf, letting her words sink in.

"A year before that, you arrived with a performing troop and spent three days in the square fascinating both children and adults with your slight of hand. Your tenure was short-lived however, and you left the troop once more through the north gate. An interview with the troop's leader revealed several interesting facts. Shall I expound?" asked the Queen.

"By all means," smiled Teeg.

Kael noted that the Elf truly enjoyed himself.

"You joined the troop in Quay. The leader stated that you interviewed with him by producing several of his own personal belongings, of which he was unaware of their disappearance. He was astounded by your abilities and immediately signed you on. He admitted that you added a good deal of profit when the troop arrived in Rindor either through your performances or, shall we say, through your ability to work the crowd while its eyes were occupied elsewhere," Lucyn paused once more.

Teeg cleared his throat and frowned.

"When one assumes a role, one must immerse themselves fully," mumbled the Elf.

"Shall I skip the details of your brief dalliance with the lovely contortionist of the troop?" asked Lucyn.

Teeg's eyes shifted quickly to Eidyn then back to the Queen.

"Lucyn please, decorum, decorum," groaned Teeg.

The Queen smirked and nodded her head in agreement.

"Six months before that you passed through after visiting my nephew's properties in the north. After attending to his business there, you entered the city and lodged at "The Singing Mermaid". Once again, after three days you departed...."

Forgive the interruption, your Highness," begged Teeg. "But you make it shockingly clear that you are well aware of my movements in and around the realm of Rindor. I am nonplussed, and extremely impressed I might add."

"It is I who am extremely impressed," countered Corad. "For a man who finds it 'difficult' to journey in his old age, you get around fabulously!"

"I too am impressed," stated Lucyn. "I watched your performance in the square. Most entertaining. The red hair and long beard were amazing. If I had not seen you so often, I might not have recognized you."

"Seen me so often? I did not perform for your majesty during that visit. 'Twas simple street folk and merchants in the crowd," said Teeg.

Lucyn smiled with deep satisfaction.

"Come, come Lord Teeg. The Master of Spies isn't the only person able to manipulate their appearance," laughed the Queen.

Teeg frowned and searched his memory.

"The washer woman with the bundle of clothing balanced on her head," offered Lucyn.

Teeg's face registered recognition and he turned a deep shade of red as he rolled his eyes in embarrassment.

"Corad was never informed of the slight of hand you performed on my backside as I thanked you for the performance and passed by," laughed Lucyn.

"What?" exclaimed the King.

"Now, now Corad. As the grand Duke of Luxlor says, 'When one assumes a role, one must immerse themselves fully'," laughed Lucyn as she patted Corad's shoulder.

"Your Highness," exclaimed Teeg grimly. "My deepest and most humble apologies."

With a flourish and a wave of his hand, the old Elf bowed deeply and once more kissed the queen's hand. He arose still clasping her hand. A devilish smile played across the Grand Duke's lips as he looked into Lucyn's eyes.

"Something amuses you, Lord Teeg?" Corad stated curtly.

"Why yes. I am absolutely enchanted," laughed Teeg.

"Strange," stated Corad "It seems to me that my wife holds you at a distinct disadvantage. She is aware of your forays into our kingdom. She monitors your business and activity. She keeps tabs on you, and until now you were completely unaware. In short, she outfoxes the fox. What amuses you so?"

Teeg let Lucyn's hand go and turned to face the king with the same smile still playing across his face.

"A job well done," stated Teeg. "In my business, a business of information and supposition, it is quite rewarding to discover you have successfully completed a task. I feel particularly good about a certain task that was put before me years ago. I might go so far as to say I am quite smug over the results."

"And what task might that be, Master Elf?" asked Corad.

"Your marriage," stated Teeg matter-of-factly.

The room became deathly quiet as Corad reddened. Lucyn arched an eyebrow and pursed her lips. After a moment the queen addressed the smiling Elf.

"And how, pray tell, did our union figure into a task of yours?" asked the Queen.

"Oh, it did not 'figure in' to a task of mine," smirked Teeg. "It was a task of mine."

"Preposterous!" blurted Corad. "Remember whose hall you stand in, Lord Elf! I am a man of patience and virtue, but I will not tolerate a slander against my wife's good name."

"Ah! No slander was intended, my lord," smiled Teeg. "However, the facts are the facts."

"Explain yourself!" barked Corad.

"Your Highness was a young man of … an independent nature, if you will," stated Teeg happily. "An accomplished warrior. A well-read, learned man. A scholar. A man living life to its fullest. However, you lacked a grounding influence. You attacked life yet displayed no subtlety whatsoever. Myself, and a group of associates, felt you needed such an influence in your life. A partner to cover the areas of character that were, for a better word, deficient."

Corad scowled at the Elf and Lucyn put a forefinger to her chin and studied the Grand Duke.

"Your introduction was arranged," stated Teeg. "I was in charge of finding you a suitable partner. A task I was loath to perform. Not my area really. However, like all of my duties, I dove in headlong. I scoured the kingdom for a young woman I felt would round out the character of the royal house of Rindor. My assets pointed to the wealthy house of Everd. I observed Lucyn Everd for over a year before I judged her the perfect choice.

"'Twas difficult to determine the statesmanship of a young woman based on the inane list of choices and decisions she must make everyday. They certainly don't match the difficult choices she will help to make as a monarch. However, often the trivial choices we make in life are the true indicator of our character. I reported to King Leinor and the others that the match was found. A woman of staggering beauty, but with her most valued assets in here."

Teeg tapped a forefinger to his head.

"Ridiculous!" scoffed Corad. "You mean to tell me the King of the Grey Elves had a hand in my courtship of Lucyn? I don't believe it."

Kael kept his eyes fixed on Lucyn. Her husband blustered on, but the queen remained poised and thoughtful. Kael noticed the ends of her lips begin to slightly turn upward.

"Actually, today is a bit of redemption for me," said Teeg beaming once more. "I predicted that Lucyn would step into an analytical role within Corad's reign. I knew her intelligence to be great and felt she would become a trusted advisor to your majesty. Her organizational skills would truly benefit you."

Teeg turned and frowned at the queen.

"Sadly however, my predictions did not come to fruition," he said. "Lucyn and Corad were wed, and the beautiful young maiden assumed the role of loving wife and doting mother. She showed no interest in helping run the kingdom and spent days performing the innocuous tasks of the wealthy upper class. I was crestfallen. The report I issued to my associates was so positive, that missing the mark by such a great distance was nearly intolerable. It has been a nagging thorn in my side for lo these many years, until this day. I do not like to make mistakes."

Lucyn's mouth crept even higher and she studied Teeg.

"This is utter nonsense," spluttered Corad glancing to his wife for reassurance. "Lucyn and I met by happenstance in the market. Complete luck. She hardly ever came to the island. Her estates were too distant. I happened to be down in the market by my parents request..."

"Ah, yes. I know you were," smiled Teeg.

"And my lady in waiting ...." started Lucyn.

"Her name was Gia," added Teeg.

"...demanded that we buy new linens," continued Lucyn smirking. "She just had to go into the capital for them. They needed to be a certain type and quality. We were required to go immediately. No delay."

"She tended to overplay her part a bit," laughed Teeg. "Subtlety was not Gia's strong point."

Lucyn fought hard not to smile or laugh outright. Corad furrowed his brow and stared at the ground.

"I will be immensely pleased to return to my associates and inform them that not only did my predictions come true, but Queen Lucyn surpasses even my extremely enthusiastic expectations. Running a full blown intelligence operation, and an active member of that operation," stated Teeg smugly.

"I take extreme offense in your government meddling in Rindor's affairs. I have a mind to ban your people from our realm and King Leinor shall...." shouted Corad.

"Corad?" whispered Lucyn.

The King stopped abruptly and turned to her.

"Do you love me?" she asked smiling.

"Yes," he stated softly.

"Do you trust me?" she asked.

"Completely," he answered.

"Then why does it matter how we were brought together?"

Corad searched her eyes.

"It does not," he stated.

The couple looked into one another's eyes, and Lucyn finally allowed a broad smile to play across her face. With her eyes still locked on her husband, she addressed Teeg.

"Corad was sent to the marketplace to oversee a reordering of the booth spaces."

"Precisely," stated Teeg.

"That order came from his father," said Lucyn.

"Correct," said Teeg.

"You never meddled in Rindor's business did you, Lord Teeg?" asked Lucyn.

"Absolutely not. I conducted their business for them."

Recognition crept into Corad's eyes as he gazed at his wife.

"My parents..." he began.

"Were just a few of my associates," finished Teeg.

Corad frowned and pursed his lips.

"I feel manipulated," he stated.

"I couldn't be happier with the outcome of your machinations," said Lucyn. "But I must admit that I too feel manipulated."

"Ah the human heart. Such an unrivaled mystery," laughed Teeg. "It can have exactly what it desires yet still possess enough doubt to question how it was achieved. Forgive me if I think of you as a pair of silly fools but that is certainly what you must be. You do not doubt one another's love for a moment, but you doubt how it was founded. What matter how you met? The here and now are all that matter. Do you think for one moment I could force either of you to love the other? I might as well try to catch sunbeams!

"If either of you didn't love the other, the union never would have been met. I knew Lucyn was a perfect match for you, but not for matters of the heart. Your introduction was facilitated, but your love was your own, there for you and you alone to admit or deny. I hoped the fire would spark, but who is truly to know the fickle ways of the heart."

"Were you a part of this group of 'associates', Lord Ader?" asked Lucyn unexpectedly as she turned to face the old man.

"Ader?" questioned Corad. "What's this all about?"

Lucyn broke away from her husband and moved toward the Seraph.

"Come now, my lord. To my knowledge you haven't visited our island for a lifetime of men, but that is certainly who you must be. Captain Caylit is a fine officer, and no other being could manipulate him so easily," stated Lucyn.

"Leinor will be informed that Lord Teeg may have performed his task too admirably," stated Ader flatly.

"Now I'm informed that one of the mystics enters my land unchallenged. What next?" scoffed Corad.

"Mystic?" mumbled Ader and clenched his teeth.

"Oh, and there may be more surprises to come, my love," said Lucyn slyly, "but we shall see, we shall see. Our guests must first inform us of their intentions for visiting our lands."

"We bring intelligence and an offer of support from my family to the crown of Zodra," stated Eidyn curtly.

Kael noted uneasiness in the young Elf's demeanor. Certainly, he was upset with being ignored throughout the conversation thus far.

"Ah, yes," said Corad glancing at the Elven prince. "The prince heir travels in his family's name."

"We bear news of attacks perpetrated in our lands and fear an Ulrog offensive is imminent," said Teeg.

"My information suggests this as well," stated Lucyn. "However, I am relying on information gleaned from Zodrian sources. I do not employ assets near the Scythtar."

"It's a subject of much debate between us," added Corad. "Is this yet another in the long line of skirmishes between the Ulrog and the Zodrian or is there a shift in strategy."

"It is obvious that there is a higher authority manipulating the Ulrog horde at this point," said Ader. "They begin to scheme and plan. Their tactics become more complex and refined. They develop an intricate communications system and use it to attack in unison. It's apparent that they are being controlled by an extremely intelligent command structure."

Corad's face remained stony and cold. He glared at the old trader and Kael felt the doubt within his mind. Lucyn remained passive and studied Ader. Her musings were unreadable.

"What says the son of Grannak on this matter?" questioned Lucyn abruptly.

All in the party remained quiet and still. Kael knew to display any emotion over Lucyn's knowledge might betray their companion. Lucyn's eyes turned icy and Kael finally noted anger in the beautiful woman's expression.

"I know where this conversation is heading gentlemen! I know what you will eventually ask of Rindor's wives and mothers!" snapped Lucyn. "Do you honestly believe we will respond to any requests without all of the possible knowledge at our disposal?

"The lodger at the end of the hall was your companion. His description, or what little was seen of him, is like that of no other man in the kingdom. He was undoubtedly a Keltaran, and the minute information I am able to extract from that wild realm tells me the prince heir to Keltar has been banished. Lord Ader seems to attract this type like moths to a flame. Now answer my question!"

"My Lady is well informed..." began Teeg. "However, we have not...."

"He brings news of doom," broke in Ader grimly.

Teeg glanced to the old trader and a knowing look passed between them. It was time. The old Elf lightly bowed and allowed the Seraph to step forward and take center stage with the rulers of Rindor.

"War, Lucyn. Not just the skirmishes that cost Zodra hundreds and thousands of good men's lives while the waters of the Ituan roll peacefully past your island. War! An army of such magnitude amasses on the roof of this world that when it crashes down upon us none will be spared.

"Your island will be no match for this force. The Ulrog breed, build and prepare for this battle every moment of every day. The Ulrog tear all of the resources of Astel from the earth and build toward this conflagration. They fashion mountains of weapons for mountains of Ulrog.

"The people of Hrafnu continue to feud bitterly with the Zodrians. However, without them, the Zodrians might have been overrun years ago. By waging their own battle against the Ulrog, they protect the flank of their hated cousins. In the west, Ulrog raiders are held in check and forced into the Northern Mountains by the Keltaran.

"What are the consequences of a Keltaran shift in this policy? What will happen if the Keltaran decide to retreat to their mountain home and allow the Ulrog to pass through unimpeded? Worse yet, what are the consequences if the Keltaran decide to forsake their Maker and join the forces of Amird and Chaos? These are the questions that Granu son of Grannak put forth to the lords of Luxlor and will put forth to the house of Zodra. The Abbott of the order of Awoi calls for the children of Avra to unite and save this world from the forces of evil."

Ader allowed his words to settle upon the rulers of Rindor. Lucyn returned to a passive, contemplative expression, while her husband displayed skepticism. Ader broke the silence.

"Lord Teeg did perform his task admirably. You are quite an insightful woman, your highness. I come to make a request of you, and you are well aware what it is," said Ader. "I ask you to form the Spear of Rindor and send it to the aid of Zodra."

"What?" exclaimed Corad jumping from his chair. "You must be joking!"

"No, I'm quite serious," stated Ader.

"You expect us to assemble the only protective force this city maintains, and send it off to a foreign war?" gasped Corad. "We would be defenseless!"

"Would you rather face the enemy with allies at your side, or alone in the coffin these city walls surely would become?" asked Ader.

Corad turned to his wife and threw his hands in the air.

"Am I mad? The Elves sneak into our city under cover of darkness, dragging with them a renegade Keltaran prince and this vagabond of a mystic," said Corad flipping a finger in Ader's direction. "And the lot of them demand that we purge our city of its fighting force and leave it naked to the whims of any opposing army!"

The Rindoran King spun back toward the Seraph.

"There's a saying that my family passed down through generations. 'When Ader knocks on your front door, death slips through the back,'" barked Corad. "I'll not turn my men over to you to be slaughtered for the Zodrians."

"Nonsense!" shouted Ader. "I understand your trepidation. However, the fact remains, the Rindoran Spear is needed and must march north."

"They 'must' and will do nothing of the kind!" shouted Corad. "We enjoy a long history of peace. Rindor was a peaceful fishing community. Peaceful yet well protected. Our founders understood the wicked heart of man. They fashioned this city as a haven from that evil. Envy and conquest drove Zodra in its quest to overrun us. If not for peace and the skillful use of diplomacy, we might still be under siege today. We will not sacrifice Rindorans for a foreign war."

"You continue to claim this a foreign war, but if not for the Zodrians, this war would be on your doorstep. You avoided this fight for many years. Generations of Rindorans have been spared while the sons and daughters of Zodra are lost. Tis time to throw your lot onto the table," demanded Ader.

Corad looked to his wife once more but she remained seated, offering no counsel. She stared at the old man and assessed the situation. The king spun back toward Ader and shook his head.

"No. Our treaty with Zodra calls for an immediate member of the royal house to request the type of aid you seek. Macin and I don't communicate. He is a stubborn old fool. We'll not expose the kingdom based on the ravings and requests of a magician and his mercenary soldiers," said Corad.

"Then I will make the request, uncle," boomed a voice from the back of the group.

All eyes turned to focus on Manfir. The Zodrian prince stood tall and folded his arms.

"What? What is this all about?" blurted Corad.

Kael watched the smile begin to creep back onto Lucyn's face.

"Ah, now the plot truly thickens," whispered the queen.

Manfir stood rigid in front of the inspection of his uncle. His dirty, oily hair hung past his shoulders. A grimy, dust stained traveling cloak draped across his shoulder. The beard he grew on the open road obscured his features. Corad walked toward Manfir and slowly circled him.

"What befalls you, boy?" said the King with disdain. "You look atrocious. I didn't even recognize you."

"This boy becomes a man, and sometimes the tasks a man endures make for a difficult life," stated Manfir.

Lucyn rose and approached her nephew. He bowed low and accepted her hand, giving it a tender kiss.

"Did you know it was him, my dear?" asked a perplexed Corad.

The queen nodded her assent.

"Why didn't you tell me he..." began Corad.

The queen held up a hand silencing her husband.

"My dear, look at the man. Look at the life he chooses. He gives up all that he possesses and all that he is in order to follow some cause of the Seraph. The value of this cause I cannot divine, but his passion is true, his belief resolute. He has been gone from us a long time now. It was his choice to divulge himself, not mine."

Lucyn addressed her nephew.

"You changed. Is your life that hard?" asked the queen.

"At times," replied the warrior.

"Do you make this request of your uncle with a clear conscience?" asked Lucyn.

"I do not make a request," stated Manfir. "I put forth a demand."

Lucyn's eyes narrowed and she glared at Manfir. Her husband turned bright red and the queen rolled her eyes at her nephew.

"What are you saying, boy?" coughed Corad. "Remember to whom you speak! In this city I am your king and you are my subject. You skulk into this land in the dead of night as a mercenary. Announce your presence to no one. And now that you do, you take on the trappings of a foreign ruler. A Lord and Master, not a loyal, loving nephew. While you stand here before me, you are a subject of this land!"

"Anywhere I stand, I am a servant of Avra," said Manfir. "The needs of his people are foremost in my mind. If I must use my position in a foreign land as a means to protect them, so be it."

"Avra! Ridiculous!" scoffed Corad. "Why do you make this demand of me? You abandoned Zodra sixteen seasons ago. Word is you fell out of favor with Macin and the people question your courage. Where were you these many years? Some say you run from your duties. You galavant about the world on the heels of this charlatan, performing faithful duty to a Creator who cares naught about you."

"ENOUGH!" boomed Ader. "Corad Kingfisher, you are a blasphemer and a nonbeliever! Your ancestors treated me with disdain and contempt, but it will be tolerated no longer. I left your kingdom to its own devices over the centuries because you were protected and on the path of righteousness. You do not believe in our Maker but thankfully do not stray into the net of Amird and the masters of Chaos.

"You WILL honor the request put before you! The Spear will march north, and I will finally trust you. Send our escort about their business and clear the room of your attendants. I will confide in you as a sign of good faith."

Corad reddened and blustered once more, but Lucyn put a gentle hand on his forearm. He looked into her eyes and calmed once more.

"Information wields more power than any spear, my love," said Lucyn. "If the Seraph wishes to part with some, it is of little cost to clear the room."

Corad nodded.

"Captain Lintos, return to your duties. Thank you for the expedient exercise of your task this morning," stated Corad.

"At your command," returned the captain and he spun toward his men. "Guard, form rank in the hallway!"

The escort streamed into the hall, formed rank, and marched toward the exit. Lucyn whispered to several attendants behind her seat. They too exited to the corridor and closed the doors behind them. When all was quiet, Ader addressed the monarchs.

"Many years ago, Manfir son of Macin left his kingdom. He put aside his worldly possessions, his title, and some might say his duty. He put aside aspirations of glory, dreams of honor, and plans for revenge. He took his life and turned it over to a greater cause. Why?" began Ader. "He answered a calling. I was but the voice of that calling, not the message. Avra called upon him to protect something, something crucial to the fight against evil. Something Chaos fears and hungers to destroy.

"Events in the world are coalescing. Amird plots his restoration to this realm. He returns backed by the full Chaotic power of the darkness. Millennia passed and the struggle between good and evil crept forward. However, it creeps no longer. It flies. It sprints.

"We face the destruction of human life on this world. Do not fool yourselves. This war is not meant to last forever. There must be a victor, but you must make the choice to save yourselves. I cannot do it for you. If you do not accept this challenge, surely all mankind will be wiped from the face of this earth."

Corad turned and faced his wife. His steely jaw was set and he searched her eyes for the guidance he always found there. Lucyn bowed her head. Her breath stayed regular and steady as a look of serenity shown on her face. Her eyes rose and met those of the Seraph.

"The signs are there for all to see. I did not want to believe but I knew it was true. A great war approaches and many will be lost. Word from the Eru is dark. Their riders are harassed in the northern marches. They are kept off balance and running. When they try to defend one location, another is set upon. They request assistance. We are silent.

"Derolian woodsmen give my people reports of Ulrog Hackles massing along the mountains. The woodsmen fight when they are able, but each month the Ulrog numbers increase. Our people complain of a lack of timber from the Derol. We hear the Derolians plight, but we are silent.

"The cries of my Zodrian cousins are the loudest. Blade and armor return from the North with no man to outfit. The death toll grows greater every month. A generation of young men is being robbed from them. Macin clenches his teeth and fights on. He asks nothing of us, but we know the despair they face, and we are silent.

"It is time for our silence to be broken!"

She turned to Corad and took his hands in hers. She bowed down before him and looked up into his eyes.

"We have been happy lo these many years my husband and my king. I served you loyally and faithfully our entire marriage, as you have do so for me. You are my bastion, my rock. Change is hard and sacrifice even more difficult. It is our time. I have seen it clearly for many years now, but held my tongue. I did not want to lose you.

"However, Lord Ader is right. We can sit idly by no longer. If we do, we will be the last standing, surrounded in a world of Ulrog. We must take up arms and fight at the sides of our brothers and sisters to the north."

Corad stared down into her eyes a moment longer. Slowly he pulled her up till she was wrapped in his arms.

"I would stand toe to toe with the Demon Lord of Chaos to protect you, my love. If you have kept me ignorant of your knowledge, it was out of love for me. If you say it is time, it is time."

Corad turned to Ader.

"We may not see eye to eye on our beliefs, mystic, but you may command my trident at the head of the Rindoran Spear. We will march north at the request of Manfir, son of Macin, heir to the throne of Zodra."

The Rindoran King stepped forward and held a hand out to the old trader. Ader enveloped it with his own hands and smiled his assent.

"Now you must tell me of this secret weapon, this thing that the Lord of Chaos fears so. What weapon is so mighty that it frightens the Master of Fear?" asked Corad.

Ader turned and faced his troop. He held a steady, calm smile on his face and winked at Kael as he wrapped an arm around the boy and pulled him forward.

"Corad Kingfisher," said Ader and he turned to the queen. "Queen Lucyn, meet Kael Brelgson, titled prince of Luxlor, heir to the broken throne of Astel, ... and my grandson."

"WHAT?" exclaimed Kael.

CHAPTER 25: REVELATIONS ONE

Kael sat on a window seat in the ancient towers of Rindor staring through diamond panes of thick leaded glass at the river hundreds of feet below him. Eddies and currents churned and swirled on their way past the rocky outcrops of the river island. Fishing boats, tiny from this distance, moved in and out of these currents searching for schools of pike and the lone, prized Urgron. Clouds drifted past, painting the river and countryside in shadows. Kael closed his eyes and took a deep breath. Confusion, shock and anger exhausted him. He wanted a full day of sleep. The weight on his chest grew so heavy. He needed his father.

After Ader proclaimed him the heir to a kingdom he never heard of, as well as the old man's grandson, events moved rapidly. Corad and Queen Lucyn intensified their focus on the young man. They fired questions at both Ader and Kael, occasionally shooting disbelieving looks at Manfir. The Zodrian prince stayed stoic as usual. Ader delayed their questions by requesting accommodations in the castle. Attendants were sent to collect their belongings at "The Singing Mermaid". Teeg and Eidyn were dispatched to track down Granu, the errant member of their party, and bring him to the castle as discreetly as possible. Flair and Kael were led from the meeting chamber to a set of rooms high in the castle's towers. Kael wanted to protest, but was so overwhelmed by these new revelations that he was unable to act. He spent over an hour staring at the river below when there was a knock upon his door.

Kael wandered over and slowly drew it open. Ader stood in the hallway, hands clasped behind his back rocking on his heels. Kael scowled at the old man.

"What do you ...?"

Ader's right hand shot up, cutting off Kael's words.

"You have every right to be angry. You have every right to be upset. You have every right to ask questions," announced the old man. "But first let me say, all knowledge that was hidden from you was for your own good. Your mother and father hoped for a normal life for you. I tried to fulfill that wish."

"They gave me a normal life," exclaimed Kael. "It wasn't until you got involved that it turned..... ABSURD!"

Ader frowned and took on a hurt expression. He struggled with his feelings. Finally, he closed his eyes and sighed.

"In the past hour you were thinking. In that hour, if you reflected on anything I said in the meeting room, one conclusion certainly reared its head," Ader opened his eyes and smiled at Kael. "If my claim of kinship to you is to be believed, then Brelg and Yanwin are not your true parents."

Kael clenched his teeth and glared at the old man.

"ABSURD .... I say it again, ABSURD!" shouted Kael. "I don't possess a clue as to what is going on, but I know who my parents are."

"Calm yourself, my boy! I don't tell you this to hurt you. I fought against this moment your entire life. Do you think it pleases me to shatter your world? I spent years protecting the fiction that is your life. I knew I would expose that fiction one day. Events force my hand. Today is that day."

Kael spun and stomped to the window. He looked back down at the rushing waters of the Ituan River and clenched his teeth once more. He folded his arms in front of him, his body rigid with tension. He refused to face the old man. Perhaps Ader would simply go away and with him all of Kael's troubles.

"I don't want to hear another thing," he whispered. "Whatever was hidden from me in the past, and whatever the future holds, I know one thing. My life isn't 'fiction'! I know who my mother is, and I love her. I know who my father is and he's waiting for me now. All I care about is seeing him. Once I find my father, I hope to put all this behind me."

Ader sighed and leaned heavily upon his walking staff. Silence hung in the room for a long moment.

"I'm sorry, my boy. I didn't mean to imply that those you care for are merely players in a troupe banded together to hide you. Their love for you and yours for them is as true as any love. You are simply an innkeeper's son from the Southlands. That's all you ever knew. We are truly just the sum of our experiences," said the

Seraph. "However, that was a chapter of your life. For good or ill that chapter is closed. 'Twas not my doing, but now that it's done, I can't afford to allow you to indulge in fanciful notions. You will never return to your old life, no matter what the future holds. Your father will never return to his old life."

"Why not? By whose decision?" growled Kael to the river below.

Ader frowned and sad eyes scanned Kael's hunched shoulders.

"As much as I might wish to indulge you, Kael, unfortunately I cannot," said the Seraph softly. "This isn't just about you. It's not just about Brelg and Yanwin, or Mester and Wist for that matter. The future of the world hinges in the balance. In order for your kind to succeed, many sacrifices must be made."

"Who are Mester and West?" muttered Kael.

"Mester and Wist," corrected Ader curtly. "They're your parents, Kael, the couple that lovingly brought you into this world. A woman who held you in her arms upon your birth and cried tears of joy. A man who proclaimed a joyous new era of prosperity for his kingdom upon the birth of its new heir. I don't deny for one moment the place in the hearts of Brelg and Yanwin for their eldest son Kael, but don't belittle the love and sacrifice of your true parents."

Kael turned. He furrowed his brow as he struggled with his emotions. He didn't want to hear this nonsense, but a part of him craved it. He was angry with Ader for all his recent deception, but trusted him. So many conflicting feelings.

"Go on," mumbled Kael lowering his head.

Ader moved toward the boy and led him to the window seat. Kael sat and once again stared at the hypnotic flow of the river below him. He calmed and let the old man speak.

"Astel was once a thriving kingdom to the East. It lies through the Derol forest and over the Mirozert Mountains, quite a journey from here. Astel was a kingdom of rolling hills and sporadic forests. The lakes were filled with fish and the forests with an abundance of Avra's creations. The palace sat on a bluff overlooking a lush valley.

"The DeHarstron family founded Astel and they ruled it for centuries. The kingdom was renown for producing great thinkers and artisans. The power of the mind was valued above all other commodities. Not the least of these thinkers were the DeHarstrons themselves. War was banished as an inefficient and unnecessary means to resolve conflict. Famine was eradicated through cultivation and irrigation techniques. Medicines were developed and studied to defeat disease. The poor were provided for and the aged cared for. In short, Astel transformed into a model of Avra's hope for his children.

"Do not mistake me, however. There are some things that even the greatest of societies cannot control. The Ulrog roamed the frozen wastes behind the Scythtar Mountains. Occasionally, they accomplished the difficult journey through the mountain passes and swept out to attack Astel. 'Twas nothing like the harassment of the Zodrians and the Eru, but it was enough to force Astel to maintain a trained fighting force. As with all studies performed in the kingdom, the army produced superior tacticians and brave fighting men.

"Mester was a fine example of the best of Astel. He truly was a great thinker, an architect, a philosopher and engineer. He improved the road system and developed ways to strengthen the fortifications. He was also an excellent military man. The Ulrog population grew and their forays into Astel intensified. Mester led the Astelan armies against huge bands of Ulrog raiders. He systematically decimated their numbers.

"In his twenty-third year he traveled to Luxlor on a diplomatic mission. He spent a season in the White Almar palace. There he met the fair Wist, fourth daughter of Ilver Admir and Alel of Forend. He fell in love and remained in Luxlor for two more years wooing the hand of the queen's sister."

Kael's eyes left the river and met the Ader's.

"The queen's sister?" said Kael puzzled. "That means..."

"...you are half Elven," stated Ader.

"What?" replied Kael with shock.

"No secrets anymore, Kael. All will be revealed. But I must ask a favor of you. Will you heed sound advice if given?" said Ader.

Kael's attitude softened. Whether it was truth or fiction, the Guide was finally giving him answers. Kael was hungry to hear more.

"I'll heed your advice, if I agree that it's sound," stated Kael.

"I suppose that's as close to a 'yes' as I should expect," stated Ader. "I'm willing to reveal all to you. Anything you ask I will try to answer, but..."

"Just as I thought," interjected Kael. "A condition to this 'truth telling'."

Ader frowned and shook his head.

"Don't become surly, my boy. I've dealt with kings and generals for centuries. I'm not prepared to coddle a surly adolescent after all these years," said Ader.

"Sorry," apologized Kael as he eyed the river once more.

Ader cleared his throat and pressed on.

"As I said, I'm willing to answer all, but I ask you to take your time. The revelations are there for you to discover, but please digest them slowly. Your past and the implications for the future are too great to rush through. Emotion and heartache are there. Joy and knowledge as well. Do not rush through what you need to learn and lose sight of why you are learning it," said Ader.

"Why am I learning it?" asked Kael.

Ader stroked his chin and smiled at the boy.

"To discover who you are and to decide who you wish to become," said Ader.

The boy sat for a moment weighing Ader's words. Already he felt overwhelmed by the information he uncovered. Each question that popped into his head generated a hundred more. Each possible response revealed a hundred more possibilities. Ader was right. He mustn't rush down a raging river of questions. Instead, he must digest the information that is to be given him and determine the important next questions.

"So," began Kael cautiously. "Tell me about this woman, Wist."

"Your mother?" said Ader as he searched for words in the river below.

Kael held up a hand, pausing the conversation.

"For now, let us just call her Wist," said Kael softly.

Ader smiled and nodded his head at the boy.

"As I said, Wist was the daughter of Ilver Admir. Ilver was an Elven woman of great beauty and standing in Forend. She held the confidence of kings and queens for centuries. She bore four daughters, Wist was the youngest," said Ader. "When the Elves discovered the world rift, Wist traveled with her sister and her sister's husband through the breach into our world. She was so loyal to Eirtwin, and followed her anywhere."

"Eirtwin?" said Kael in shock.

"Your mother's sister," smiled Ader. "It took all my counsel to dissuade her from wrapping you in her arms and doting on you like a child. I daresay you might have been a bit confused if the ruler of the Elven people treated you like a new born babe."

Kael stared at Ader in disbelief.

"Do close your mouth boy. It is a bit disconcerting."

Kael shook his head and blinked hard. Once again the answer to one question flooded his mind with dozens more.

"If Eirtwin is my ... my aunt," Kael nearly choked on the words. "Then Eidyn is .."

"Your cousin," concluded Ader. "Although I must admit he is a bit older than you. Nearly a century to be exact."

Kael fell backwards against the framing of the window seat. He felt dizzy.

"I believe you're not truly an Elven prince. I may have exaggerated a bit in our meeting with Corad and Lucyn," continued the Guide. "Your title is something more along the line of a Viscount, but I never paid any attention to such trifles. If you are interested feel free to ask Teeg."

"What about Eidyn?" asked Kael. "Does he know this information?"

"Our young Elven heir is learning things as we go along, just as you are. He knows you possess unique ... ah, we will call them gifts, but he is truly unaware who you are. Events progressed rapidly following your birth and news from Astel was quickly cut off. Only a select few know you were even born." said Ader.

"Well, I don't know how to exactly react to that. Should I be glad or sad?" said Kael frowning.

"It depends," answered the guide.

"On what?" asked Kael.

"On who exactly knows, and how much they know," added Ader. "Once again, Kael, don't underestimate the importance of what was accomplished by an old soldier and a disowned princess. Not to mention loyal followers like Cefiz and Manfir."

"Well ...." spluttered Kael. "What was accomplished? Why did my parents give me away? Did they even know my father and mother ...er, Brelg and Yanwin ... oh whatever, you know what I mean! And if there was a good reason, why didn't I simply go to live with relatives?"

"Normalcy," stated Ader.

"Huh?" blinked Kael.

"Normalcy, Kael. Your parents wanted you to be protected but also to live a normal life. A request that baffled me at first. I could offer you all the protection any of the great realms might muster. By a simple command a tower would be built, guards posted. Of course the enemy would know your location. Even the most loyal of realms contains a traitor or two. There would be attempts on your life. Security would grow ever tighter and more restrictive. Maybe you would be allowed to wander in the woods or the market once in awhile. However, they would be cleared first and guards posted everywhere. Does this sound normal to you?" asked the Seraph.

"No," answered Kael.

"Do you think you would have been normal under those circumstances?"

"No," answered the boy once more.

"Of course not," exclaimed Ader. "That is when I saw the solution. Anonymity. Just a village boy from the country. Someone the enemy considered a nobody, from nowhere. A place so unimportant in the struggles of this earth, that it goes by unnoticed and unchanged. Thank Avra for Kelky!"

"Queen Eirtwin said that even the smallest hamlet and everyone in it contributed to the whole. All were important," said Kael.

"Your aunt is a wise woman, Kael. That is the difference between Order and Chaos. To Chaos, only the powerful are important. The rest are expendable. Sacrifices to the advancement of their domination," stated Ader. "Chaos cannot conceive of someone such as yourself not living in the heart of power and fame."

Kael smiled and shook his head. Ader's eyes met his and they exchanged a chuckle.

"What do you find so amusing?" asked Ader.

"You called the queen of the Grey Elves my aunt. I don't think that will ever sound normal to me," laughed Kael.

"I suppose not, but you will find so much more to grapple with as time goes on," stated Ader.

"Why?" asked Kael. "Why am I so important?"

"Ah. This is what I was afraid of," said Ader. "You go to put the cart before the horse. You must learn who you are before you learn why you are."

"What?" blurted Kael shaking his head. "You all talk in riddles."

"What I mean is, you begin to delve into your ancestry. You are discovering where you come from and the people who brought you into this world. There is much to discuss on both topics. Both are topics of history and fact. Both give you a solid foundation to discuss who you are.

"However, why you are is a topic concerning the future. You have obviously done nothing of note in this world yet, so why you are so important must happen in the future. The future is unknown and open to theory and conjecture. Let us stick to and discover the facts about who, and then I will deal with the why. Agreed?" asked Ader.

"Agreed," nodded Kael and he added. "Why did you call me your grandson?"

"Because that is what you are, my boy," announced Ader. "Well in a manner of speaking."

"Why is there always a condition with the answers you people give?" grumbled Kael.

"We are unusual people and the usual rules don't apply to us. We must answer cautiously," laughed Ader. "Centuries ago the people of the Astelan plains called me Ader the Hartstrong. It was a title of respect to my longevity I suppose. They were a wonderful group of nomadic hunters. Quite civilized really. In fact, more civilized than many of our societies today. I spent many years with them, nurturing their society, trying to help them achieve their full potential."

The old man stared at the river now. His eyes took on a faraway look.

"That is when I met my wife, Loriad. She was a chieftain's daughter. Smart, pretty and athletic. Frankly, the type of woman I met throughout my life countless times. Special, but not so special if you know what I mean," laughed Ader. "However, I soon realized that Loriad was different. At first I puzzled over what drew me to her, but then my eyes opened.

"She was a person of profound wisdom. Others deferred to her on all matters. What appeared cloudy, cleared with a few insightful words from her. When there was strife, she calmed discord with the most logical and fair of all choices. I had grown accustomed to telling men and woman alike what to do, but found myself happily laying some of those burdens at her feet. She was a blessing to me."

The Guide stared at the swirling water of the river, lost in reminiscences. Kael remained silent, too nervous to pull Ader's reverie away from a time of happiness. Finally, the old man snapped out of it. He turned to Kael.

"She died in her sleep after forty-eight seasons of marriage. I mourn her passing everyday," said Ader.

He stared into Kael's eyes for a moment.

"Every so often I see her, in the face of one of our descendants. A smile, a gesture. I see her now in the way you try to keep your face passive. Your furrowed brow," smiled Ader. "You are the seventeenth generation born into the line of our union, Kael. I have watched you all grow up and die as I toil on this earth. It is both a blessing and a curse."

Sorrow washed across the face of the Seraph.

"Over the years, our descendants assumed the throne of Astel. Generation after generation received the gift of Loriad's wisdom. It was only natural that her children's children claimed leadership. I sometimes spent decades away on the business I was created for. Often I kept my visits private. Over the centuries the Astelans let my memory turn from history to myth.

"The people revered the family for its accomplishments, not a tenuous connection to a traveling mystic. Astelans changed my descendants' name to DeHarstron. You, my boy, are Kael DeHarstron, the only child of King Mester DeHarstron and Wist Admir, true king of Astel."

There was a knock upon the door. Ader and Kael's eyes remained locked on one another for a moment. Finally, the Guide turned and called out.

"Please, enter."

The door swung open and Teeg stepped into the room smiling merrily.

"Hmm," mused Kael. "If I didn't know better, I would swear you two contrive these interruptions."

Ader laughed and patted Kael on the back. Teeg took on a look of indignation then smirked.

"You're right," stated the Elf pausing for effect. "You don't know better."

Kael gave a halfhearted frown then smiled at the old Elf. His mood lightened greatly. At least now he was starting to get answers.

"Did I interrupt a particularly interesting chapter of "The History of Kael Brelgson"?" asked Teeg.

"Apparently, it's 'Kael DeHarstron', " announced the boy.

"Ah yes, then it was rather interesting," said Teeg. He turned to the Seraph. "I'm here to inform you that our rogue Keltaran prince was found by Eidyn. He is here now, under extreme protest I might add. I would appreciate it if you would go speak with him and calm him."

"Where did they find him?" asked Kael.

Teeg smirked and shook his head in disbelief.

"Eidyn tracked Granu's movements through the entire city. The giant hid under piles of manure in Hentil's stables. He remained there even as Rindoran guards searched it numerous times. He was trod on by horse and soldier alike and never budged. Reeking of dung, he exited the stables and made his way in broad daylight through alleyways to the north wall. Not a soul caught sight of him. I find it almost inconceivable that so ... so large a man may travel unnoticed!" said Teeg.

"Lord Teeg, you of all people should know the stealth of the Keltaran. They spent a good part of their history hiding. They are accomplished in the matter," stated Ader.

"True, true," returned Teeg shaking his head. "But if I were a washer woman dumping the mornings dirty water into the alley and a shadow the size of a house passed me, I would certainly question what I just saw."

"Is a washer woman in your repertoire, Lord Teeg?" joked Kael.

The old Elf stopped abruptly in confusion, then smiled and tugged an earlobe.

"On occasion," laughed Teeg. "But only if I find time for a close shave in the morn."

The trio burst into a hardy laugh. Ader turned to Kael.

"Are you satisfied for now and willing to digest what you have learned? I will stay and continue our conversation if you wish?"

Kael pursed his lips and deliberated. Ader was trying his best to appease the boy. Kael wanted so much to continue their talk, but knew he must live in the present as well.

"I was given plenty to think about. You might as well attend to Prince Granu. I shudder to think what might happen to the walls and occupants of this palace if he becomes any more agitated," said Kael smiling.

Ader patted the boy on the back once more and he and Teeg stepped from the room closing the door behind them. Kael returned to his seat by the window and once more stared through the beveled glass at the river sliding by beneath him. A calm settled over him. Slowly his heavy lids closed as he sunk into the thick cushions arranged on the seat.

CHAPTER 26: THE BLACK OBELISK

Guttering torches cast odd shadows on the walls of the dank chamber as Sulgor crept forward in search of his master. Usually, Izgra sensed the Malveel Lord's approach and stood waiting for him. This time however, the beast found the chamber empty, Izgra's dais deserted. Sulgor moved forward. The heavy, black velvet curtain hanging behind the dais shifted in the sluggish currents of air pushing through the open balcony of the chamber.

Sulgor stopped. A barely audible hiss and buzz emitted from behind the curtain. Sulgor was drawn to the oddly familiar noise. The Malveel desperately strained to hear more. Dare he move forward? Izgra was clear concerning the curtain. None were to look past its blinding darkness.

The Malveel growled. Was he not Sulgor the Magnificent, first of the Malveel? Surely when the Deceiver returns, he will once again place Sulgor at his right hand.

The Malveel lord moved forward and slid his scaly head past the corner of the midnight curtains. Darkness enveloped the beast and his eyes fought to capture the scene before him.

The curtain created a small inner room within the greater chamber. Set near the far wall of the enclosure was a large chunk of rock, seemingly hewn from solid granite. Standing at least three yards tall, the slab dwarfed the form of Izgra who stood arms raised and positioned in front of it. The edges of the giant obelisk were irregular and crudely cut. A polished black surface lay entombed within the rough-hewn edges of the slab. The black rock formed a void within the stone. The substance absorbed all light around it.

Izgra swayed unsteadily in front of the stone, arms raised in supplication. He chanted feverishly. Sulgor was unable to hear or understand any of the chant until the warlock threw back his cowl, exposing a hairless gaunt skull covered in tightly drawn, diseased and decaying flesh.

"Amird, my Lord and Master!" cried Izgra. "I have need!"

The smooth black surface of the obelisk changed. It no longer appeared rigid, but more an insubstantial sheath, shifting and changing before Izgra. Blackness flowed within blackness and bled across its surface.

"I HAVE NEED!" shrilled Izgra.

Abruptly, red flecks of flame appeared within the surface of the obelisk. They swirled and sputtered across the blackness, coalescing toward the center into an image. Smoke rose and slowly filled the curtained enclosure. At once the image in the center of the obelisk both heightened in clarity as more of the burning red flecks completed the image, and grew hazy as smoke obscured the vision of the Malveel Lord.

Sulgor curled a lip into a snarl of pleasure as the beast realized what he witnessed. There before him, on the surface of the black obelisk lay the likeness of his true master, Amird, Lord of Chaos. It took all of the Malveel's self control not to throw himself toward the base of the slab and declare his everlasting loyalty.

A deep voice filled the chamber. It boomed from the blackness and echoed against the walls of the room. A cavernous, pitiless howl, filled with rage and venom.

"Why do you call me?" demanded the voice as it faded into the hiss and crackle of a smoldering fire.

Izgra kept his head bowed and arms raised.

"Lord Amird. I have need," begged the warlock.

"You were warned, Izgra Admir," snapped the towering image of Amird. "I expend too much energy maintaining this form! The fiery winds of Chaos tear at my soul in this realm and force my disembodiment."

"I implore your forgiveness, my lord," pleaded Izgra. "But I seek knowledge."

"You were given all knowledge held for your task," snarled Amird. "You tarry! Finish your duties or others will finish in your stead!"

"I seek knowledge only you can provide, my lord," squealed Izgra. "I seek knowledge from within the mists of Chaos."

Amird's fiery eyes narrowed and glared at the warlock. He considered the request for a moment then replied.

"What do you seek?" questioned Amird.

"Answers, my lord," sniveled Izgra. "One of your servants was defeated and his soul was taken to the burning mists."

Amird's lips curled in a cruel smile.

"Methra the Beguiler. I brushed his presence here within the flames. He was one of my first," said Amird with an air of satisfaction.

Sulgor's lips quivered in ecstatic pride at the recognition Amird bestowed upon his kind.

"Yes, my lord," stated Izgra. "He was taken from your service. He was weak."

The sputtering image of Amird roared into flame.

"Did you summon me to curry favor and undermine the Malveel?" roared Amird as flame and smoke erupted from the shifting surface of the black obelisk. "Your task is all you require to be judged Izgra!"

The warlock took a step backward and lowered his head in deference.

"No! No! My lord!" whined the Half Dead. "On the contrary! Methra was close. He was sent to the edges of the Nagur to intercept Elven messengers. He was successful in his mission yet delayed return. I must know why. I must see what he has seen and know what he encountered. Only then will I begin to understand if he stumbled upon the new Seraph."

"Do you know what it is you ask? Methra has been torn asunder. He is scattered throughout the flaming mists. To call him back is to gather him in from the edge of madness and force his spirit together if only for a few brief moments," rumbled Amird. "I try to build my strength, not waste it!"

"It is crucial, my lord."

The image of Amird smoldered and sputtered. Finally, his red eyes brightened in intensity and rolled into his head. Sulgor heard more chanting and the fiery red flecks holding Amird's image dissipated. They were replaced by new red flecks struggling to coalesce near the center of the obelisk. An image formed then drifted apart, only to reform seconds later.

After several attempts to gain substance, the fiery image of Methra hovered in the center of the obelisk. The Malveel's image threw its head back and gnashed its fangs, slashing the empty air as if it were beset by stinging hornets. A deep howl of anguish filled the chamber as the beast thrashed in pain.

"Methra!" commanded Izgra.

The beast growled and attempted to focus on the warlock standing before him. Methra's body jerked in spasms, but his wide, madness filled eyes searched for Izgra.

"The burning never ceases!" growled the image of the Malveel.

The red flecks shifted and slid across the blackness of the stone obelisk. At times the image of Methra dissolved, only to reform moments later. Sulgor's black tongue ran along the knife-edge of his fangs in anxiety over the fate of all of Amird's servants. Victory over Avra in this world meant never having to face Methra's fate.

"Pain!" shrilled Methra. "Suffering!"

"Silence!" shouted Izgra. "Heed my words, snake! You failed your master and you suffer the consequences for such failure. Obey my commands and perhaps your suffering will be relieved."

Methra thrashed and spun within the obelisk, slashing at the burning mists of Chaos.

"What is it you ask?" howled the creature through his madness.

Izgra's lip curled in satisfaction, displaying rotting gums and broken, blackened teeth.

"You sensed the new Seraph in the Nagur Wood?" questioned Izgra.

"Yes!" cried out Methra.

"You were drawn to his location?"

"I was drawn toward the Nagur path," snapped the beast. "Toward power!"

"Whose power?"

"I found a boy," wailed Methra. "I killed it!"

"The new Seraph?" asked Izgra intently.

"The boy. I ... it was I. I killed him," raved the Malveel.

"What of the new Seraph?" commanded an irritated Izgra.

"He arrived within the day," slavered the beast writhing in agony.

"You sensed his approach?" asked Izgra.

"I sensed nothing!" snarled Methra halting his spasms and glaring at the warlock. "Power surrounded me. The power of creation shown like the surface of the sun and obscured my senses. Power in the wood. Down the path. At my feet. Power filled the Nagur. I could not distinguish between any of it. Great power! The power of Avra the Creator pushes forth to flood the world and drown you!"

Instantly, Methra shrieked in pain and flailed uncontrollably within the obelisk. His wails and howls filled the chamber with a deafening noise.

"I AM POWER!" boomed the voice of Amird from deep inside the obelisk.

Izgra stood patiently watching the creature's anguish. After a few moments, the shrieks died away and Methra slumped forward heaving. Izgra slowly continued.

"What of the new Seraph?" demanded Izgra.

Methra appeared not to hear the question. The Malveel's image churned within the obelisk, heaving and glaring at Izgra. Finally, a crazed smile crept across his face. Sulgor couldn't imagine anything eliciting pleasure in the horrific place Methra's spirit was cast into. Through lowered eyes the beast glowered at Izgra and with supreme pleasure he addressed the warlock.

"He comes for you," hissed Methra in a whisper. "The boy comes for you."

Izgra saw Methra's madness for what it was. No spirit could maintain a grip on itself when plunged into the realm of insanity Amird and Chaos created.

"The new Seraph comes for me?" questioned Izgra.

"The Old One assisted the boy within the woods. The boy was not defeated but raised up. I am the executioner's sword, but you are the hand that held the blade. Even now he moves closer to you. The Old One is with him and he is with the Old One. They are the same. The Father awaits them and the three King's are One. The end draws nigh," snarled Methra.

Izgra stared at the raving Malveel and considered his words. Surely this creature's madness affected much of what he said, but there could be no denying he encountered the new Seraph in the Nagur.

"Your rant has given me much to think on, Methra. Return to the mists," said Izgra with a wave of his hand.

The image of the beast shimmered. Izgra turned from the obelisk.

"What of my torment?" questioned Methra frantically.

Sulgor quickly ducked from the curtain and retreated to the main chamber's opening.

"Your torment is eternal," hissed Izgra.

The image of Methra the Beguiler flickered and disappeared.

CHAPTER 27: TAPESTRY

Aemmon stood on the Nagur path staring into the forest. Panic enveloped Kael. His brother was unaware. Kael wanted to shout to Aemmon. Warn him. Methra! Methra lurked in the woods! Aemmon turned and hobbled back toward the camp using a fallen limb to support his injured leg. Methra crept from the opposite side of the path. Kael's heart ached. His thoughts raged. Why can't I save you?

Aemmon turned as if in response. He stared directly into Kael's eyes. His expression was forlorn. He knew. Without seeing the rushing Malveel he knew it was coming for him, and he accepted it. Aemmon smiled weakly a moment before the Malveel's jaws widened and the creature leapt.

Light flashed. The figure of Aemmon transformed into a brilliant silhouette of blinding radiance. The light was so intense that Kael could see nothing else. The path was gone. Methra was gone. The trees were gone. Only the shimmering white magnificence remained. It hovered for a moment, strong and reassuring, flared once more and was gone.

In Aemmon's place stood Hilro, spirit of the Nagur Wood. The giant, old man calmly stared at Kael with the same winsome smile Aemmon had, but Hilro emanated the same reassurance Kael saw in the light. Kael knew things would be alright. Instantly, Hilro spun on the leaping Malveel and snatched it by the neck in mid flight.

CRACK!

Kael awoke with a start. He was curled on the small window seat in the Rindoran palace. The river's steady flow pushed past the fishing boats that worked below. The sun had shifted across the sky since his discussion with Ader. It must be afternoon. The boy's racing heart slowed. He stood and shook his head. His legs and shoulders were stiff from sleeping on the cramped seat. He walked about in order to get the blood flowing in his legs. After several tight rounds through the room, Kael stopped and frowned.

"This is silly," he mumbled to himself.

Kael walked over to the door and opened it a few inches. He peered down the hallway. No guards were posted outside his door or at the end of the corridor. He swung the door wide and stepped out. Heavy tapestries hung on either side of the hallway. A pair of tridents, nearly as tall as Kael, was affixed to the wall above the stairway. He strolled close and admired their workmanship. They were most certainly steel, and the craftsman embossed the image of an otter in the area where the three tines met.

Kael turned and studied the tapestries. One held the image of Rindor. Birds wheeled above the sun-dappled citadel as the river rushed past. Fish leapt from the river's water and otter basked on the muddy shoreline. The other tapestry displayed the image of an ancient battle. Men in armor and chain mail stood on barges and drifted toward ancient Rindor. The barges also held catapults clamped to their decks. Rindorans in small skiffs with crews of three or four moved amongst the barges. The Rindorans wore no armor. Their tridents and nets of meshed steel were their only protection.

The scene was utter chaos. Armored invaders spilled from floundering barges spinning in the strong currents of the Ituan. Images of struggling armored men sprang up all over the tapestry. Rindorans easily leapt from skiff to barge and back again. Their nets flashed out and incapacitated their rivals. The heavily armored assailants were unable to use their weaponry standing on such unsteady surfaces. The length of the Rindoran tridents kept the attackers at bay. The Rindorans were also able to use the tridents as boat poles, steering the barges away when they posed a threat and drawing them closer when their defenses were down. Kael marveled at the Rindoran mastery of the weapon.

A small image in the corner showed a Rindoran trident catching a heavy blade between its tines and locking it there. The Rindoran simultaneously whipped his net across the ridged armor of the assailant. With a tug of the net, the armored soldier lost his footing and teetered over the swirling water of the tapestry for an eternity.

Smoldering barges spun past the citadel to smash into the rocky shoreline. Steel covered arms and helms flailed in the water around the barges. Bodies littered the shoreline. Catapults launched ineffective salvos, unable to achieve a steady shot. Rindoran catapults returned accurate volleys from the parapets of the citadel.

Kael smiled as he looked at the other corner of the tapestry. The artist summed up the Rindoran concept of the battle. A tiny image portrayed a pack of hungry, gaunt wolves standing on the muddy shoreline. A group of river otters spun and played in the murky water just out of reach from the hungry pack.

Kael left the tapestry and moved to the stairs. Cautiously he stole down the stairwell. Corad and Lucyn had never granted them leave of the castle, but Kael was anxious. He yearned to see more of Rindor and couldn't do it from inside. Kael scampered down the stairwell passing several uninhabited levels along the way. A flurry of activity greeted him on the bottom floor. Pages, soldiers and maids hustled back and forth along the lower level.

News of the Army's imminent departure threw this part of the castle into a hive of activity. Kael passed an open doorway and was nearly bowled over by the rush of three exiting pages. Inside the room, a hulking, gray bearded man in an oilskin overcoat sat at a large desk covered in parchment. The man barked orders to pages and soldiers alike while he scribbled frantically on the parchment.

"You there," barked the man to a page as he held out an envelope. "Lord Yaw's estates in the north! As fast as you can!"

The page snatched the envelope from his hand and bowed deeply.

"No time for that now," snapped the man without ever looking up. "Off you go!"

The page spun and sprinted from the room. Once again Kael was nearly knocked to the floor as the page brushed past and headed down the hallway. Kael recovered and looked back into the room. A tall, thin woman was rapidly folding the parchment the graybeard had written on. She turned a burning red candle over the fold and dripped wax upon it. Before the wax cooled, she slammed a large forged seal down upon it.

"Remember, one and all!" bellowed the woman above the melee. "If the addressee obtains an envelope with a broken seal, they are ordered to detain you. So take care!"

The entire hive of activity paused momentarily and bowed to the woman. The graybeard flicked his hand toward another page.

"Lord Manfir's estates in the northeast! His people will know what to do!"

The page snatched the envelope and turned toward the door. Kael was ready. He quickly leapt aside. The page barreled through. Kael saw enough. He turned to follow the page toward the exit and nearly ran into a figure standing just inches behind him.

"Pardon," spluttered Kael and he backed away.

A young man stood staring into the room. The man was completely covered in a heavy, woolen robe. Hanging in the middle of the man's chest was a silver amulet. The amulet was fashioned into a swirling pool of water. A pair of dusty sandals sat upon his feet and he carried a long walking staff. Kael had never spoken to a Delvin Scribe before, though he saw a few travel through Kelky.

"I didn't see you there," apologized Kael.

The scribe lightly bowed and Kael returned the gesture. Kael stepped to the side and the scribe entered the doorway to monitor the activity in the room. Kael moved down the hallway. After a dozen steps he heard the graybeard shout.

"Where are those mapmakers? I want at least ten copies of each of these maps by week's end. I won't allow my people to go wandering aimlessly in a foreign land!"

Kael followed the hallway until it terminated at a large oaken door. Several pages and soldiers passed him in either direction. He exited and found himself standing on a small twisting street in the heart of Rindor. Castle personnel flitted about the massive building and citizens strolled past. Kael looked for the sun to get his bearings. He didn't want to lose his way. He might feel a bit silly asking directions to get back to the castle.

The Southland boy wandered the streets of Rindor taking in all his eyes could see. His first impression was one of confusion. The streets made no rhyme or reason. Twisting this way and that.

Also, the architecture was ridiculous. Structures were heaped upon structures. It was quite evident that the Rindorans ran out of room upon their island years ago and simply decided to build up.

Often, Kael walked under causeways built between structures. More often than not, these causeways were transformed from a means to travel between buildings into actual living spaces. Anyplace that could hold a small dwelling or apartment served as such. Laundry lines drifted like cobwebs throughout the entire city. Streets were crowded with men, women and children.

As Kael moved further and further from the castle, periodically he passed through gateways. The boy realized that these were the old walls of the city. As Rindor grew, new walls were built to protect outlying homes and shops. Eventually, the land between the new walls and the old filled in with more dwellings and buildings. He walked and imagined how the city evolved over time. He determined that from above the city must look like a huge, freshly cut tree stump, each ring of new growth capped by an ancient wall circling through the city's interior.

Kael stopped for a moment and breathed deeply. His nose informed him that he moved closer to the outer wall. The air from the river smelled heavy and dank. He paused and took in the hustle of the Rindoran folk around him.

The sight of two boys walking down the street to his left struck him as significant. The boys strolled a hundred paces away and something about them tweaked Kael's interest. He slid close to the wall of the nearest building and shadowed their progress. Kael slipped forward blending in with dozens of other Rindorans going about their business.

The boys arrived at the next crossroads and turned left. Kael raced ahead and peered around the corner of a building. He was close and took a good look at them. He was certain they were the same duo he saw playing in the marketplace. He was just as certain they were the lads he saw frolicking in the streets of Quay. The boys moved a good distance from the corner and Kael stepped into the street to follow. All at once he was knocked sideways.

"Oh, I'm terribly sorry," said a sweet voice beside him.

Kael turned to see a girl bending to retrieve a basket of flowers. Flowers littered the street beneath him. He began to apologize, but hesitated as she smiled and gazed at him with her stunning blue-green eyes.

"I, uh, no, it was my fault. I was not looking where I was going," said Kael.

He quickly bent down and gathered the flowers from the road.

"Oh, please don't bother," said the girl in her high pitched, lilting voice. "I can do that."

Kael fumbled with the flowers.

"No trouble at all. My mistake, so I should make it right," he replied.

"Well, that's a healthy attitude," replied the smiling girl.

Kael rose and laid the damaged flowers in her basket. The girl bowed and smiled. He was captivated. At first, he surmised she could be no older than thirteen, but the more he gazed at her the more uncertain he became. The girl was diminutive in stature. Her hands and arms were delicate. They reminded Kael of some of the beautiful porcelain statues he saw in the halls of the Rindoran castle. However, if her size hinted at youth, her demeanor and bearing told him otherwise. She spoke confidently and grinned at him as if he were an awkward puppy to be admired and played with.

Her clothing did not give away her age either. Simple Rindoran garb with no accouterments. Yet simple as her attire was, her beauty shone through. Ageless eyes penetrated his soul. There was both confidence and knowledge behind those eyes.

Kael suddenly remembered the boys.

"Once again, I humbly apologize for my clumsiness," said Kael. "Good day to you miss."

"Such manners too," said the woman. "You will make a fine catch one day."

Kael smiled and turned from the woman. He raced down the street trying to find the boys. At the nearest crossroads he made a guess and headed deeper into the city. He sidestepped carts and peddlers. There! He glimpsed the boys strolling toward an inn. A sign above the doorway read "The Rusty Nail". Kael held back and watched them disappear inside its doors. He waited until he felt he could enter inconspicuously then stepped into the inn.

A smoky common room held the usual array of shadowy figures. Several patrons at the bar hardly flinched as Kael stepped from the doorway and let it slam behind him. He halted a moment and let his eyes adjust to the darkness as he surveyed the room. The boys were nowhere to be seen. The door behind him swung open and a heavily cloaked figure pushed his way past the young man and took a seat near the bar. The figure waved a barmaid over and muttered something. She turned and headed toward a large, tapped keg. Kael felt uncomfortable and the feeling stirred him to action. The Southlander approached the bartender and quickly produced some silver coins from his pocket.

"Excuse me, good sir, perhaps you might help me?" said Kael sheepishly.

The barman hungrily eyed the coin as Kael flipped it in an open palm.

"What can I do ya' for, young master?" asked the barman.

"A pair of boys were just at my father's booth in the marketplace," began Kael, "and they overpaid for a service we rendered. My father, being an honest man, said he overheard them say they took lodging here. He sent me to return the extra coin."

The barman smiled and wiped his dirty hands on a towel that hung from a loop on his belt.

"Well now, your father is right. Always treat customers fairly to retain their business in the future," began the barman. "A couple of boys are staying here. However, I'm not quite sure if they're in at the moment. I've not seen 'em for most of the day. Perhaps you could leave the coin with me and I'll make sure it gets to its rightful owners."

The barman outstretched a hand and smiled deeply at Kael. The boy inched his hand toward the fidgeting barman, then snatched it back at the last moment.

"I'm afraid I can't do that, sir. You see, my father wanted me to talk with the lads about unscrupulous behavior in the city, and how they could get taken advantage of if they weren't dealing with someone as honest as him. I wouldn't feel right unless I said my piece. You understand, don't you?"

The barman frowned and rolled his eyes. His hand balled into a fist and dropped to the bar.

"Well, if ya' must. If they're in, and mind ya, I mighta been in the back and missed 'em, but if they're in, they'll be in the far room on the third floor," muttered the barman.

"Thank you kindly, sir. I'll attend to my business quickly."

Kael slid past the tables in the bar and made his way to the main stairwell. He wasn't sure what he was doing or why he was doing it. What did he hope to accomplish? What if he stumbled upon the boys? What would he say? They would probably play the part of clueless children and he would discover no more answers. However, he was sure of one thing. This was a sight better than sitting in a stuffy room, high in the Rindoran castle, staring at the river roll by.

Kael cautiously climbed the stairs. At the second level he surveyed the layout of the building. Two doors on each side of the hallway, and one facing down the hall from the end. On the third level, Kael stepped into the hallway. He silently tiptoed the length of the corridor on the old wooden floor and halted before the door.

Kael tilted his head close to the door and listened intently. The soft, muffled hum of conversation could be heard in the room. Obviously the boys were there. Kael recognized the sound of laughter from inside the room. It was hard to make out words. He closed his eyes and strained to hear. The sound remained fuzzy at first, then his mind just reached out to it.

"... Chimbre you possess plenty of money. Why you can't pay for it, I'll never know?" said a high-pitched voice.

"Why pay when I get it for free? Besides it keeps the skills sharp. If I don't snatch something now and again, I'll fall out of practice and make a mistake when it could cost us our lives. It was only an apple, Sprig," said a second slightly deeper voice.

"Only an apple! But it was the apple he was looking at when you took it. He didn't even see your hand. The apple was there, then it was gone," laughed the voice of Sprig. "I nearly died when he waved his hand over the spot it had been."

"You missed the best part," laughed Chimbre. "I slipped a copper coin in his other hand as I walked away. He felt its weight as we rounded the corner."

"Now that's more like it," chortled the first voice. "Nice job. Should we go and find ....."

"What are you doing?" whispered a voice several inches from Kael's ear.

Kael's eyes popped open and the rest of his body froze. His heart raced. He shot a glance to his right and saw the heavily cloaked and hooded figure that pushed by him at the inn's doorway. Kael swallowed hard and wondered how he should react. Before he could chance a decision, the figure's hand rose and pulled the hood back to reveal the smiling face of Eidyn.

"I'm following you. Lord Teeg isn't the only member of our party capable of disguise," whispered the Elven Prince. "Who are you listening too?"

Kael felt his entire body drop an inch toward the floor. He let out a deep breath, just now realizing he held it in. He rolled his eyes at the Elven prince in mock anger then smiled.

"Do you remember the two boys we passed on the outskirts of Quay?" whispered Kael.

Eidyn looked to the ceiling and searched his memory. He nodded his assent.

"Do you remember the boys that bowed to the captain in the marketplace?"

Once again Eidyn nodded. However, this time a look of recognition crossed his face. Kael smiled.

"If I'm right," began Kael. "Those boys are one and the same. We were followed. I don't know who they are, or what they're doing, but I'm determined to find out."

Eidyn's face grew stern. He motioned to the doorway then tapped his ear. Kael took his meaning and once again reached out for the sounds from in the room.

".... and I told her we would grab a bite and return to the room," said the voice of Chimbre the thief.

"I could use some shut eye as well. It's been a long week," squeaked Sprig.

"Interesting city don't you think?" said Chimbre.

"Quite," returned Sprig. "Such a mass of humanity. So easy to blend in. Sakes, even I get turned around by the hustle and bustle of this...."

Kael heard the creak of a door or window shutter in the room.

"Why hello," laughed Sprig. "Why didn't you use the door? It is a bit easier than the window."

"Where were you?" said Chimbre, a nervous edge creeping into his tone. "We considered going to..."

He halted abruptly. Kael heard the sound of rushing movement in the room. The shutter creaked once more and Kael heard a light thud. That was all he needed. Kael fumbled in his cloak for his dagger. Its absence shocked him. He didn't care. He reached for the door's latch. Eidyn's eyes went wide as he saw what Kael was about to do. The Elven prince drew his own dagger and moved behind the Southlander.

Kael threw the latch up and rushed in. Eidyn followed in his footsteps and leapt to Kael's side. The room was empty and the window shutter slowly creaked back against the wall. Eidyn pointed to the windowsill. Ten fingertips were visible along the sill for a moment then disappeared. Once again Kael heard a light thud. The Elf and Southland boy collided with one another as they tried to circumnavigate the tiny room's bed and reach the window. When they untangled, they popped their heads out the window above the alleyway.

Kael caught a glimpse of three running figures in the light at the end of the alleyway then they were gone. Eidyn threw a foot onto the sill and prepared to leap. Kael grabbed the prince's arm.

"I'm not questioning your abilities, Eidyn," said Kael shaking his head. "But you won't find those three in this maze of a city."

Eidyn frowned and lowered himself from the ledge.

"There's still something to be gained here," said Kael. "Return to your spot downstairs and I'll follow shortly."

Eidyn nodded his assent and flipped the cowl back over his head. The Elven prince stepped from the room and headed down the stairs. Kael waited a few moments then followed.

The common room was unchanged. All who were there earlier remained in their places. Kael approached the barman smiling.

"Innkeeper. Are you sure those boys lodge here?" asked Kael. "No one answered at the door. When I opened it, I found the room barren and uninhabited."

"What? Impossible!" said the barman. "They just ran through here not more 'n fifteen minutes ago. Did you knock on the right door? I said the door at the end..."

"I thought you said you didn't see them all day?" questioned Kael sternly. "What's going on? Are you toying with me?"

The barman fidgeted and bit his upper lip.

"My father encounters quite a few travelers at our shop," persisted Kael. "They often inquire after good accommodations. I was going to reference 'The Rusty Nail' due to your helpfulness earlier, but I question that decision. Perhaps I should spread word in the marketplace that you tried to cheat some guests out of coin that was rightfully theirs."

"No! No!" protested the barman. "My apologies. I host so many guests that I sometimes mix them up! By all means prompt your father to send anyone he can in my direction. I run an honest establishment. While you were upstairs I recalled seeing the boys pass. But, if you say they're not in, perhaps I saw them departing and not arriving."

The barman rubbed his sweaty palms on the towel hanging from his belt.

"Well, that may be," said Kael softening. "But I must be about my business today and become reluctant to leave this coin with you. I see no evidence that these lads are staying here."

Kael stared at the man as if working out a problem in his head. He smiled.

"I know of a solution," began Kael. "Do these boys owe you for their lodging?"

"It was paid through this evening," returned the barman. "But they ran up a small bill from food."

"I'll make you a deal. Give me any information you possess on the boys. Say, for example, the names they registered under. I'll canvass the other inns in the area, and if I find them I will return them here to settle their account before I give them their coin. If I don't find them, I'll use what I owe them to pay you. Either way you'll be paid and I'll feel I fulfilled my father's request."

The barman briefly smiled at the prospect then frowned.

"I'm afraid I can't provide you with their names," said the barman.

"Why not? My bargain is fair," said Kael.

"They didn't pay for their rooms. Another paid in advance and told me to expect their arrival sometime in the evening," replied the barman.

"Do you have that persons name?" asked Kael.

"Ah, yes," said the barman. "He's an old tinker by the name of Jasper."

A gray hooded patron at a table not far from Kael choked on his ale and spit half of it across the common room.

CHAPTER 28: KNOWLEDGE IS POWER

In the street in front of "The Rusty Nail", Eidyn raced to catch up to Kael.

"Hold a moment, Kael!" called Eidyn. "Will you hold?"

Kael stopped and turned on the Elven prince.

"Just when you think he's being honest with you," spluttered Kael. "More lies! More deception!"

Eidyn held up both hands.

"Now wait a moment, Kael," exclaimed the prince. "How has he lied to you?"

"You heard the man. Jasper, or whatever he wants to call himself, paid for the boys' room. They shadowed us all along."

"So, your point?" asked Eidyn.

"My point? My point is ...." shouted Kael. "Oh I don't know! It's wrong!"

"What's wrong? The fact that you aren't informed of everything?"

Kael clenched his teeth and seethed. His hands hung at his sides, balled into tight fists.

"Fine! Yes! You're right!" exploded Kael. "Why is everything a puzzle? Why do I feel like I don't know a thing? Why do Ader, Teeg, Manfir and even old Hamly feel like they need to teach me things? They give me scraps and pieces but keep whole volumes hidden in the dark!"

Eidyn smiled and crossed his arms in front of him. He looked at Kael with mock pity. Kael frowned at the Elven prince.

"Ader isn't lying to you, Kael," began Eidyn. "He merely keeps something from you, and from me, if that's worth anything. Also, we're unsure what he keeps from us. Who are these boys? What are they doing? Before we make accusations, we should find answers."

Kael's posture softened as he weighed Eidyn's words. The fact that they were in the same position did seem to help. He felt helpless. Something was going on, and he needed to know what.

"Actually, we hold Ader at a bit of a disadvantage," smiled Eidyn.

Kael furrowed his brow and looked at the Elf.

"How so?"

"His three companions are sure to report that you discovered them, but will assure Ader the secrecy of their connection is intact. But we know otherwise. The first thing Lord Teeg taught me," said Eidyn, mimicking Teeg to perfection. "Knowledge is power. Guard it with your life and spend it frugally, for there is only so much to go around."

Kael smiled and slapped Eidyn on the back.

"I'll do just that my friend. I'll do just that!"

As Kael walked back to the castle with Eidyn, he wondered what he might say to Ader about the missing dagger. He grew accustomed to its weight. Its presence provided peace of mind. He wasn't sure he would ever use it properly, but at least he might make an attacker think twice before advancing on him.

Eidyn walked along, lost in contemplation. Kael felt ashamed. He was so caught up in his own emotion, he didn't take the time to think about Eidyn. The young prince obviously struggled with this information as well. Was Manfir aware of the boys? If so, why didn't Ader share their presence with Eidyn? What about Teeg? Did the Master of Spies know, yet keep his own prince in the dark? Kael recognized the delicateness of the situation.

They fought their way through the teaming city. It was getting late, and the marketplaces and shops were closing. Workmen and servants headed home for the day. Each street held double the number of people as the street before it. Kael tried to squeeze past a slow moving ox cart. He jammed his hands into his vest pockets to make his frame smaller. In the right pocket, he felt a small scrap of parchment. He stepped past the ox cart and unrolled the tightly wound scrap. He read as Eidyn slipped past the cart and noticed the confused expression on Kael's face.

"What is it?" asked Eidyn.

"I've found another teacher," said Kael as he finished reading the paper and handed it to Eidyn.

Eidyn read the parchment aloud.

"A bit of advice. When you are trailing someone, be doubly aware of those who might be trailing you."

Eidyn turned and gave a questioning look to Kael. The Southlander just shrugged his shoulders. Kael wondered whose hand placed the note in his pocket. However, he was sure of one thing, that very hand now held the Needle of Ader.

In the morning, the king and queen called the travelers before them. Kael entered the meeting chamber and sumptuous smells greeted him. A large circular table stood in the chamber filled with trays of succulent food from the area. Corad and Lucyn rose as the group entered.

"Our meeting yesterday was somewhat forced," said Corad. "The situation required a ... harsh approach. Now that we come to terms, Lucyn and I desire to host you in a more suitable manner. Please, step forward and be seated."

The group bowed and moved toward the table.

"Ader, please sit here by me," said Corad as he pulled a chair out for the Guide. "I damaged our relationship these many years. I regret my actions and hope to make amends."

Ader nodded in Corad's direction and accepted the chair. Lucyn smiled at Manfir as he tried to take a place opposite her.

"For just a moment you may let your guard down, Manfir, son of Macin. You battle no Ulrog at this moment. Imagine that you are thirteen years old again and we are entertaining guests. You ate at this table so often it should be easy," began the queen. "Come. Sit beside me and be a stranger no longer."

Manfir hesitated for a moment. His stern expression finally relaxed and he smiled.

"I do not deserve such a place of honor. I'm not the best of nephews," replied Manfir.

"I do not give it as a place of honor, but as a place of love. Love overlooks transgression and accepts unconditionally," said Lucyn and she extended her arms.

Manfir stepped forward and embraced her. After a moment all stood at their places silently waiting for Lucyn to sit. Flair glanced nervously at Eidyn for clues on appropriate behavior. Lucyn looked across the table at the imposing figure of Granu. His granite jaw was set. His face was impassive.

"Before we sit," began the queen lightheartedly. "I must say well met Granu, son of Grannak."

Kael noticed surprise enter the giant's eyes and he lightly bowed.

"Your story is one of personal hardship and sacrifice," continued Lucyn. "Avra calls upon all of us to forgo the easy path and follow him up the steep road to the true riches of happiness. It is a challenging journey, and for some it is much more difficult than for others."

The queen lifted a goblet and raised it on high.

"May your endeavors to change this world be blessed by the hand of Avra," said the queen. "And may both enemy and friend alike learn from your example of sacrifice and personal fortitude. In my house you will be called friend."

"Here! Here!" added Corad as he raised his glass.

The remainder of the group raised their goblets and drank. Manfir looked as if the motion was painful, but he followed suit. Granu bowed much more deeply to the lady across the table.

"I entered your household under duress," stated Granu raising his own goblet. "However, the eloquence of such a speech disarms me. I accept your friendship and pledge mine in return."

The entire group drank once more. Lucyn sat and the men joined her. The meal carried on in idle chatter. Lucyn was anxious to know all of Manfir's whereabouts over the years. Corad entered a hushed conversation with Ader over spiritual matters. Kael realized he was famished, and tried not to embarrass himself by overfilling his plate.

The food was delicious. Egg soufflé, smoked ham and poached river cat were laid out on trays before them. Kael tried a filet of poached fish from another tray. The flavor was rich and earthy. At first, he was unsure whether he liked it, but as it settled on his tongue he found it to be excellent. Manfir looked up from his conversation with the queen.

"And how is the Urgron, Lord Kael?" asked Manfir smiling.

Kael stuffed another large piece of the filet in his mouth. His eyes went wide as he struggled to chew the piece and answer. Lucyn laughed and held up a hand.

"No need to answer, Kael Brelgson," laughed Lucyn. "The fact that half the filet is in your mouth speaks more resolutely than you are able at this moment."

Kael turned a bright shade of red and slowed his chewing.

"And what of you, Master Flair," asked Corad. "I see you are a man of expensive tastes."

Flair smiled and raised another soft pastry to his lips.

"The jelly in this pastry is fantastic. It is like nothing I have ever eaten," said Flair as he took a sizable bite out of the pastry.

The center was filled with a black, oily substance that dribbled down the youth's chin. Slightly embarrassed, Flair grabbed a napkin and wiped his chin as he munched on the pastry.

"Expensive indeed," exclaimed Teeg as the boy popped the last morsel in his mouth. "I have never seen a person eat eight Urgron roe cakes at one sitting."

Flair's chewing stopped abruptly.

"Eight cakes you say?" added Manfir. "And every last one of them filled with fish eggs. Extraordinary! Far too rich a meal for my constitution."

Flair's mouth was stretched wide in mid chew. His eyes widened and he quickly glanced around, lifting a napkin toward his face.

"Ah! Ah! Ah!" said Teeg wagging a finger at the boy. "Decorum at all times, my good man. You are a guest in this house!"

Flair's eyes bulged. Corad and Lucyn looked around the table puzzled, as the rest of the group snickered. Flair chewed slowly, then swallowed hard with a painful expression on his face. He slowly picked up his full goblet and raised it above the table.

"To our gracious hosts," whispered the boy and his voice cracked.

"Here! Here!" shouted the rest of the men at the table and they broke into a roar of laughter.

Flair drained the entire goblet.

After the meal, the company retired to their rooms and made ready to depart. Ader, Manfir and Teeg held a private audience with Corad and Lucyn. Assurances were made as to the speed at which the Rindoran Spear could be formed and sent north, but many crucial roles in the city needed to be temporarily manned. People must be trained. Supplies were required. Horses commandeered.

Before long, Kael found himself leading his chestnut through the crowded city streets. The group arrived at a gate similar to the one on the south side of the river. A few soldiers stood near the gate, but in the daytime it stood wide open and people came and went freely. A long, timbered bridge identical to the bridge on the south side of the island stretched from the mouth of the gate. Kael followed Eidyn and led his horse out onto the bridge. As before, it neither swayed nor buckled.

"I don't understand how the river affords Rindor such protection," said Kael, "if any army could merely march across these bridges to their door."

"Excellent observation, young man," smiled Teeg. "Exactly the type of observation the Rindoran generals hope an opposing commander might make."

"If it's too good to be true, Kael," said Manfir. "Quite often it's not true."

"What do you mean?" asked Flair. "I agree with Kael. You could roll several battering rams up to this tiny gate."

Manfir halted and motioned the boys to the side of the bridge. He pointed to the giant sturdy pilings that supported the structure.

"They look as strong as the granite foundations of the castle," stated Manfir.

Kael and Flair nodded in agreement.

"Now take a closer look. What do you see?" asked Manfir.

Kael looked hard at the crisscrossing maze of timber supports and pilings. It confused him, but he confidently believed he could glean the meaning of the design. Support after support buttressed one another to add to the strength of the bridge.

"What are those gears and cables for?" asked Flair.

Of course it was Flair who figured it out, thought Kael. The lad possessed such a logical mind.

"If that gear turns, the timber it supports will ..." he paused as he pondered it, "... slide out and each timber above will lose its support. This whole section of the bridge will collapse!"

Flair quickly grabbed the railing of the bridge and looked back toward the safety of the island.

"Easy lad," laughed Ader. "This bridge has stood as it is for decades. The discovery of its secret by Master Flair of Kelky will not send it crashing to the river's bottom."

The group moved across the bridge once more. Ader slid in next to Kael and put a hand inside his cloak.

"Speaking of discoveries," said the Seraph. "Please try harder to keep this safe. I'm quite fond of this bit of handiwork, and it just might save your life one day."

Ader slid Kael's dagger from beneath his cloak and handed it over to the boy. Before Kael could comment, the Guide prodded Tarader to the front of the procession. Kael clenched his teeth and glanced at Eidyn. The exchange was not lost on the Elven prince. Eidyn frowned and shrugged his shoulders.

As they stepped from the bridge onto solid ground, Kael noticed a smile play across Manfir's face. Manfir caught the boy looking.

"It's nice to be home, Kael. I never consider myself in Zodra until I cross north over the Ituan River," said Manfir.

The group mounted and began a light trot along the Northern Trade Route. The landscape contained marked differences between the South and the North. The South was dry sparsely vegetated grassland of gullies and washes. The North was a land of sharp plateaus overlooking leagues of gorse bushes and tree groves. In the South the road followed some of the flatter wash runs. Travelers circumvented the small hills by traveling around them. There was no such opportunity in the North. Sometimes the group traveled along a relatively flat stretch. Other times, the road halted at a tall ridgeline that ran for several leagues in either direction. Usually, a path wide enough for one rider was cut into the side of the plateau. The group traveled up these paths in a single file line.

The frequent elevation changes along the road made for a slow tedious journey. Kael broke up the monotony by taking in the scenery around him. However, the scenery failed to relieve the boredom. The narrow footing on the ridgeline paths made those stretches the most tedious. Kael was sure of his chestnut's agility, but the path never appeared substantial enough.

Periodically, Ader called for a halt. The air was dry and water for the horses was scarce. Tarader never seemed to need any type of sustenance, and Ader frequently wandered ahead of the group searching the horizon while the others watered their mounts.

"He has much to think about," commented Manfir to Kael.

During one of these stops, Kael was the first to water his mount at a small brook that ran near the road. Ader once again moved ahead. This time however, Tarader munched on the soft, new growth of blackberry bush. The horse lightly whinnied and swished flies with its tail. Kael moved away from the brook to let the others refresh their horses. The Guide sat with his back to Kael and the group. Ader looked unusually worn and tired. He was hunched forward on the stallion's back, barely moving.

Kael left his chestnut tethered to a nearby bush and quietly approached the Seraph. As he closed within a couple of yards, Kael realized Ader was not still at all. In fact, his hands were drawn in tightly to his chest and worked feverishly. Understanding came to Kael. He mistook similar movements by the Guide in the past. Ader did not fidget in the saddle in Quay or Rindor. Ader communicated. He used his hands to convey a bounty of information, just as the Guide communicated with Teeg at the court in Luxlor. Kael looked in the direction Ader's directed his hands. A thick grove of gorse bush grew at Tarader's feet and spread out into the surrounding country. The movement of Kael's head alerted the Guide. The hand motions stopped. Ader cleared his throat and glanced at the boy.

"Are you finished watering your mare, Kael?" asked Ader.

"Yes, I tethered her. Are you feeling all right?" replied Kael.

"Just fine. A bit tired. Happens to even me now and again," smiled Ader. "This terrain is rough on horse and rider alike. It is in our best interests to halt early this evening. I should consult Manfir and determine if there is a suitable place within striking distance."

The Seraph turned his stallion back toward the group and trotted away. Kael was left staring at the grove of gorse bush in front of him. A cool breeze stirred the tops of the bushes like a wave upon the water.

"Thank you for returning my blade," whispered Kael to the bushes, and he turned and walked away.

CHAPTER 29: THE FOX AND THE HAMMER

In the late afternoon, the troop made camp at the base of a large bluff just off the road. Once again Eidyn offered to stand guard for the group and once again Ader informed him that it was unnecessary. Kael recognized the tension in the Elven prince's face as Eidyn pursed his lips and walked off to help Flair gather firewood. All save one in the group seemed exhausted. Granu was unusually pleasant. His stern demeanor was melting away and he hummed as he went about his business.

"I like this country," Granu said offhandedly to Teeg.

The comment elicited a withering glare from Manfir, but no more was said. In the morning the group rose early and was quickly underway. Plateau to drop-off. Drop-off to plateau. The tedious journey dragged on. Finally, the group crested a large plateau and Kael felt a sense of relief. A rolling expanse stretched out before them. Grassland populated with small groves of trees pushed toward the horizon. Kael searched their path ahead and saw neither plateau nor drop-off. At last they could simply meander over rolling hills.

Manfir led them for over an hour. Suddenly, Eidyn pointed to the left of the road. Wisps of dust rose above the horizon.

"Manfir! Riders bear down on us from the West. They are still a few leagues off," shouted Eidyn.

A small, shadowy figure dashed across the top of a hill several hundred yards away. It ran in a crouch, darting from grove to grove.

"Who is that?" exclaimed Kael.

"It seems the riders drive a fox before them," said Eidyn.

Ader and Teeg edged closer to the side of the road. They remained motionless, following the progress of the diminutive figure. Eidyn and Kael rode toward the back of the procession. The Elven prince turned to Kael with a look of concern and confusion.

"Should we arm ourselves, Lord Ader?" asked Eidyn.

The Seraph did not reply. Ader's eyes followed the figure. Kael turned to Eidyn and shrugged his shoulders. Eidyn frowned and slipped his bow from his back. His hand slid down to the quiver slung on the side of his mount. Blindly he drew an arrow from the quiver and lifted it to the bow. The figure closed to within a hundred yards and the dust cloud billowed on the horizon.

Eidyn notched his arrow and his eyes bore down on the figure. Slowly he drew the bowstring backwards.

"It looks like a child, but it runs like the win ..... AYE!" shouted Eidyn.

Kael spun to look at his friend and was stunned. Another small figure sat on the stallion just behind the Elven prince. The figure was covered head to toe in a gossamer cloak. The cloak's colors shimmered and changed with each movement. A delicate hand reached around the prince and locked on the drawn bowstring. The other hand pressed a short, curved dagger against Eidyn's exposed throat. A small drop of blood slid down the edge of the blade. The runner closed to within fifty yards of the group.

"Eidyn!" boomed Teeg. "Stay your arrow! Tis an ally!"

The Elven prince was glaring over his shoulder at the figure holding him captive. Slowly he released the tension on the bow and let the point of the arrow dip toward the ground. The figure seated behind him removed its grip on the bowstring, grabbed the hood of its cloak and drew it down. Kael stared into the blue-green eyes of the beautiful young woman he met on the streets of Rindor. Eidyn's eyes went wide. She smiled, rammed the blade into a small sheath at her side and jumped into a standing position on the stallion's rump. In an instant the young woman laughed and did a flip off the horse's back. She executed a perfect landing a foot from a grove of gorse bush, darted into cover and disappeared from sight.

In that same moment, the "fox" leapt onto the back of Tarader from a full sprint. This figure wore a similar cloak to the young woman. Even though it stood on the back of the stallion, its head barely cleared that of the Guide. The "fox" drew its hood back and leaned in close to the Ader's ear. Kael was astonished to see the smaller of the two boys he tracked in Rindor. After a moment the Seraph nodded and the boy flipped from Tarader's back in the same way as the young woman. He darted into the bushes and was gone.

"A dozen riders approach, most of them Keltaran," stated Ader. "They will be upon us shortly."

"Who was that woman?" Eidyn asked Teeg.

The Master of Spies bit his lip and muttered an explanation. Manfir cut him off.

"There's no time for that now, Eidyn. We are set upon by the mountain dogs!" shouted Manfir as he glared toward Granu.

The giant was unfazed. A contemplative expression crossed his face.

"A Keltaran Hammer unit so far from the Anvil and deep in Zodrian land," stated the giant. "This is unusual."

The giant moved behind Flair's mare and threw his hood over his head. Manfir scoffed and wheeled his warhorse to face the growing dust cloud.

"Keep your ranks tight," barked Manfir. "And Flair, take care to watch your back."

The pounding of hooves filled the air. Kael stared out to see riders and their mounts filling the hilltop. Dust swirled and rose around the figures as their massive horses whinnied and stamped. Kael never saw anything like these horses. They were huge, easily as tall as Tarader, yet not nearly as sleek. Their backs were broad, built for power not speed. The horses' coats were long and shaggy. Clumps of hair hung over enormous shoulders. They were outfitted in steel, from a studded plate on their brow down to their shoes.

The Keltaran paused then began a slow trot toward the road. Kael noted several hooded and cloaked riders near the back of the formation. A leader separated from the crowd. His warhorse trotted a few yards ahead of the group. Eidyn slid the arrow back onto his bowstring.

"I'll wager they slipped through the Chimgan Pass," stated Manfir.

Granu's grunt from behind Flair was all the acknowledgment the group needed. Manfir, Ader and Teeg rimmed the edge of the road flanked by Kael and Eidyn to their left. Flair sat in the rear and Granu stood next to the boy's mare.

The Keltaran leader came within Eidyn's range and drew a large battle-ax from behind his back. Kael felt his heart begin to pound rapidly. The Keltaran lifted the ax high in the air, then grabbed the head and pointed the handle toward the road.

"He seeks parlay," stated Teeg.

"What does that mean?" Kael whispered to Eidyn.

"He wishes to talk," replied Eidyn in hushed tones. "He agrees to no violence and wishes to approach."

"Does he think we're crazy?" said Kael. "Look at those men!"

"He neither thinks you are crazy nor quite formidable," came a rumble from behind Flair. "He wishes to talk rather than fight. In his mind, a Keltaran Hammer unit against our ragged group is no match. If his first option were force, he would have used it. Accept his parlay and see what he says."

Manfir hesitated but after a nod from Ader the Zodrian prince drew his sword and extended the handle toward the Keltaran.

"Manfir accepts the parlay," Eidyn whispered to Kael.

The giants moved forward and halted twenty yards from the road. Many of the riders matched their horses, huge men with shaggy red and brown manes trailing over muscled shoulders. They wore helms of tight fitted steel with studded nose guards. Leather and steel were bound over forearms and legs. Their front line was armed with either battle-ax or cruelly barbed pike.

Tarader threw back his head and whinnied loudly. The Keltaran mounts startled and shifted under their riders. The mountain men struggled to gain control. In the confusion, Granu softly called to Ader.

"They wear the uniform of the imperial guard, my brother Fenrel's troops."

The Keltaran mounts regained their composure and the rank reformed. Kael noticed the ghostly image of a ram's skull emblazoned on each man's chest. Their leader removed his helm and rested it upon his saddle.

"Quite an odd company traveling the Northern Trade Route," he stated.

"No more unusual than a Keltaran Hammer this far from home in Zodrian territory," returned Manfir.

The leader smiled dismissively. The head of his giant ax rested in his lap, and the handle still pointed past his horse's head toward the road. His elbows rested on the flat of the ax blade as he lazed in his saddle.

"Ah, yes," smiled the leader. "We are a bit out of the way. We're on an errand for his majesty."

"Grannak has sent you this far into Zodrian territory?" questioned Ader. "Does he invite Zodrian retribution? What trifle tempts him to start another upheaval?"

"Ah ... 'twas not Grannak's order. I'm on direct orders from Fenrel," smirked the Keltaran.

"The last time I checked," began Teeg. "Grannak ruled in the mountain city."

"Oh he does, he does," exclaimed the leader through pouting lips. "But he grows so tired and old. Circumstances compelled Fenrel to relieve the king of certain responsibilities. Besides, I don't intend to alert Zodrian authorities of my presence. I come to retrieve something. Once I take what I want, I will go in peace. No one will be the wiser and we all gain from this meeting."

"What trinket does this motley crew possess, that interests the royal House of Hrafnu?" asked Ader holding a hand out toward his group. "And what do you possibly posses that we might want in exchange?"

A smug expression crossed the Keltaran's face.

"Did you not know, old man? You possess the House of Hrafnu itself, you fool. Fenrel wants it back!"

The leader shot a finger toward the cowled Granu.

"There stands Granu son of Grannak, heir to the throne of Keltar. All that is and will be Keltaran stands in his grasp. Fenrel wants it!"

Manfir glanced over his shoulder at the figure of Granu then spun back to the Keltaran war party.

"You talk in riddles, Keltaran. That is but the slow-witted nephew of the old man here," nodded Manfir toward Ader. "However, you still didn't answer the second question. What do you offer us?"

"A Southland farmer with the brains to barter," laughed the leader to his troops. "I offer you that which is most precious to you. I offer you your lives! You may ride from here unmolested. Go. Travel north and join the Guard. You will fall to a Keltaran ax or an Ulrog cleaver on some other day. Just ride away and say nothing of this event. The House of Macin will never be the wiser."

Manfir frowned and looked back at Granu. The giant stood immobile. Manfir furrowed his brow.

"You make a few mistakes in your logic, mountain dog," began the prince as his eyes narrowed. "First, your offer of our lives is invalid. They are not yours to give, only yours to take if you dare. Since you asked for parlay first, I think you don't dare. Second, the House of Macin already knows of your trespass on their lands and determined an appropriate response. You will take nothing from Zodrian lands without the Royal House's approval, and they do not give it."

"Under whose authority?" barked the leader as he sat upright.

Manfir slid the chain holding the ring from inside his cloak.

"Manfir, son of Macin," snapped the prince.

A murmur spread through the ranks of the Keltaran. The leader looked perplexed and hesitated.

"Kill two birds with one stone, Sherta!" called a familiar voice from the back ranks of the Keltaran.

The leader glared back over his shoulder.

"Silence! I'm in charge here!" bellowed Sherta.

The Keltaran leader swung back to face the road and encountered Granu as the giant stepped past his companions and threw back his hood. He stood leaning heavily on his staff surveying the mounted troop before him.

"Sherta? How do I know that name?" Granu questioned himself as he stroked his badly scarred head and inched forward. "Sherta?"

Finally, the giant snapped his fingers in recognition and stared hard into Sherta's eyes.

"Are you the same worthless Sherta who called for the retreat at Kel Moor and allowed the Ulrog to overrun the outpost?" began Granu. "You couldn't possibly be that Sherta! I hope that Sherta rests in chains somewhere for abandoning his post."

Sherta grimaced and ground his teeth.

"That situation was untenable," grumbled the Keltaran leader. "We were surrounded and our..."

Granu ignored Sherta's protest and focused on another member of the Keltaran group.

"Catra," called Granu. "Well met."

Sherta reddened in anger. A Keltaran soldier nodded and smiled to Granu.

"Well met, Prince Granu. Your barber was a little harsh with your last cut," returned Catra smiling. "I assumed it might have grown back by now?"

Granu gave a weak smile and rubbed his huge hand over the scars on his bald head.

"'Twas a punishment meant to shame me, but I grow accustomed to it. The scars will fade," murmured Granu. He frowned toward Catra. "You wear the skull of my brother's unit?"

"Fenrel disbanded the brotherhood. All of the faithful were assigned to military units. Are you fully recovered from your last encounter with your brother?" Catra nodded toward Granu's lame leg.

"It comes and goes," replied Granu rubbing his knee.

The display of weakness emboldened Sherta.

"Silence Catra! You are under my command now," shouted Sherta maneuvering to face Granu. "Under the authority of Prince Fenrel, I order you to..."

"I hold no quarrel with you, Sherta," barked Granu once again cutting off the Keltaran leader. "I'm no threat to my brother. Leave me in peace."

Sherta hesitated and looked uncertain of his next move. His eyes darted between his troops and Granu.

"Leave him, Sherta," called Catra. "He's a wanderer, an outcast. Grannak forbade anyone to harm him. He begs an existence off our enemies by using his name. He owns nothing more to give them and that will soon grow stale. Do not start another war over a lame beggar."

Sherta's eyes shifted between his troop and Granu.

"You requested parlay and it was granted," stated Granu. "Your request for my custody is denied. Honor your parlay and retreat for a measure of time. If you still wish to take me, only then may you use force."

Kael shot a glance at Eidyn.

"They are honor bound to retreat until the sun travels its width three times across the sky." whispered Eidyn.

Sherta glared at Granu and muttered to himself. He fidgeted with the heavy blade of the ax and glanced back to his troop. The Keltaran warriors murmured amongst themselves. Kael noticed one of the cloaked figures from the back of the formation moving up just behind Catra. Sherta mumbled loudly.

"We will... ah... must ... We need to consult on the matter."

"There's no need to consult," stated Catra. "Grannak banished Prince Granu and gave him an oath of protection from all Keltaran. To bring him home is illegal and to kill him is treason. When we rode from Keltar, Grannak was still king. It's time to end this farce and ride on."

Kael saw a flash of steel from the cloaked figure behind Catra. A powerful, tattooed forearm shot forward and slammed a blade into the giant's exposed ribcage. Catra's eyes went wide with surprise. The assailant's other hand looped a cord over Catra's head and yanked it tight around the giant's throat. At the same instant, the killer's motion caused his hood to fall away. Kael stared into the red glowing eyes of Tepi.

Illustrations of fire breathing Malveel covered the trader's arms. Strange symbols tattooed his face. He muttered incantations as he neatly dropped Catra's body to the ground. Suddenly, his voice boomed in fury.

"You are the Maul of Fenrel, his chosen warriors! Ignore this traitor who would force you to serve the Zodrians!" bellowed Tepi pointing to Catra's body. "Do your master's bidding and you will receive glory in the halls of Keltar! Take Granu the lame and make him a sacrifice to Amird!"

Events were happening so rapidly, Kael felt overwhelmed. He watched green fire crackle about the hands of Ader. The Seraph grew as he stared down from atop his stallion.

"You seal the fate of your soul today, warlock," shouted Ader raising his hands.

The sight of Ader caused the Keltaran to hesitate. Kael was unsure if the giants would charge or run. Tepi's eyes widened in shock as green Seraph fire encased Ader, revealing the old man's identity. However, the evil warlock quickly recovered.

"Save your breath, lapdog," snarled Tepi. "It is known to all, you cannot hurt another human. Your weakness allows you only to protect yourself."

The entire assembly froze for a moment like the tapestry Kael viewed in Rindor then erupted in action. Sherta flipped the blade of his battle-ax. In one smooth motion he snatched the handle out of the air and directed the blade toward Granu. The Keltaran leader's shaggy warhorse bolted forward. Granu leapt aside, dodging the heavy blade and thrusting his staff at Sherta. The momentum of Sherta's mount carried him directly into the tip of the staff. Granu stood firm, legs braced against ground. The staff's tip hammered Sherta across the bridge of the nose and the Keltaran leader's head snapped back with a sickening crunch. Sherta's entire body rose a few inches off the saddle of his warhorse then flopped lifelessly to the ground.

The roadside flared into a swirling confusion of noise, weapons and horses. Kael quickly drew the Needle of Ader and was stunned to see it glowing with the same green flame that surrounded the Seraph. Keltaran charged toward the road with weapons drawn. Kael heard a strum to his left as Eidyn loosed an arrow into their midst. Tepi wheeled his mount and shouted to the back ranks of the Keltaran formation.

"Concentrate on the old man, fools!" blared the warlock.

The remaining two hooded figures threw back their cowls. For the first time in his life Kael's eyes fell upon the sight of every Zodrian child's nightmares. Two hulking Ulrog, nearly as large as the Keltaran, raised rusty cleavers and charged through the Keltaran formation toward Ader. Kael's frightened childhood visions didn't compare to the waking horror that rushed the old man. Sloping, hairless heads covered in bits of rock and filth sat upon huge rounded shoulders. The Ulrog were built with no necks to speak of. Their heads simply connected directly to their powerful shoulders. Cords of knotted muscle and chunks of rock covered long, mud colored arms. Kael was amazed at the reach of the beasts as they raised their cleavers on high.

Red flame shot past him and slammed into Ader. The boy flinched and covered his eyes. Tepi sat near the back of the formation, eyes aglow. Flame covered the bald man's hands and he raised them above his head.

"He's weak from his encounter with Lord Methra. Finish him!" cried Tepi.

The Seraph threw up a wall to protect himself from Tepi's assault and was distracted. The Ulrog were almost upon him. Manfir slammed his warhorse into their path. His sword slashed down at the nearest Ulrog. The beast threw an arm up and met the blade. Kael sat stunned. Manfir's sword glanced off the rock-encrusted arm in a shower of sparks.

The Keltaran giants moved in. Granu stood at the forefront of Kael's group spinning his staff and blocking ax chops. Eidyn worked feverishly with his bow, slowing the enemy with a quick rain of arrows. Several found their mark. Two Keltaran dropped to the ground clutching arrow shafts. However, the enemy was too close and heavily armored for the arrows to halt their charge. Kael sat helplessly while the enemy remained focused on Ader, Granu and Manfir.

The Zodrian prince drew a second blade and struggled to protect himself from the cleaver wielding Ulrog. Tepi allowed the battle to move away and blasted fire at Ader. The Seraph worked hard to shield himself and Manfir from the fiery assault. Many of the Keltaran focused on Granu, but several finally realized the damage Eidyn's bow accomplished. Three swung free and stormed toward the Elven prince.

Instantly, Teeg blocked their path. The lead Keltaran snarled and hefted his heavy ax in his left hand. Teeg sat motionless as the Keltaran charged and cocked the ax head back. The old Elf leapt to a standing position on the back of his horse as the Keltaran approached within five yards. Teeg smiled. The Keltaran swung the ax at the old Elf. An instant before contact, Teeg leapt into the air throwing his feet up over his head. The Keltaran's ax whistled through emptiness. The Elf twisted and spun, tucking his arms in close to his body. The giant's arms and shoulders lurched forward and he desperately tried to slow the movement of his heavy ax. A glint of steel flashed from the Elf's cloak and hammered into the back of the giant.

Teeg affected a perfect landing on the broad back of his mount. Kael recoiled in fright as the Keltaran rumbled toward him. The giant dropped his ax to the roadside and both of his hands struggled and fumbled with something on the back of his neck. His eyes were filled with dismay. His huge, shaggy horse galloped past Kael. The giant's hands were wrapped around the hilt of Teeg's dagger. It protruded from beneath the rim of his steel helm. The doomed Keltaran slumped forward, dead in the saddle.

"Kael! Move!" shouted Eidyn

Kael wheeled to face Eidyn. A second Keltaran chose the Elf prince as his quarry. Eidyn bumped Kael from his way and loosed an arrow at his attacker, but it glanced off the Keltaran's armor. Eidyn fumbled with a second arrow while the Keltaran charged from his left. The giant's ax came down hard toward the Elven prince. Eidyn quickly slid from the mare's back to her side, nearly falling to the ground. The ax glanced off the back of the beast tearing its flesh. Eidyn squeezed his legs around the stallion's midsection and avoided being unseated. The Elf loosed another arrow from this prone position as the Keltaran passed. The bolt shot upright and glanced off the breastplate of the giant. Its steel tip ricocheted off the armor and traveled upward, catching the Keltaran under the chin and driving into his head. He too traveled a few more yards before falling to the ground dead.

    The third rider was focused on Kael. Eidyn was unable to right himself in order to notch another arrow and Teeg was just dropping onto his mount's back. Kael panicked. He yanked hard on his mare's reins and turned her from the fight. Frantically he hammered her flanks with his boots. The mare lurched forward and sprinted across the road. The Keltaran howled and gave chase. Wild-eyed, Kael stared over his shoulder at his pursuer. The Keltaran leveled a long, barbed pike at Kael and gained ground. The boy's vision shot forward searching for an avenue of escape.

    Movement in the bush caught his eye. A red flash whistled past his head. Kael rode hard for a few moments more then dared a glance over his shoulder. Shockingly, the Keltaran halted. He sat clutching his throat as his mount slowed to a walk. Kael stopped and circled. The boy saw red feathers protruding from between the Keltaran's fingers. After a moment, the giant's face turned a deep crimson, followed by a sickening purple. He finally succumbed to the poison that tipped the dart in his throat and he too fell to the ground dead.

    The Ulrog surrounding Manfir chanted and pressed their attack. They hacked and slashed at the Zodrian prince, keeping him on the defensive. Tepi pressed his assault upon Ader and Manfir. Several Keltaran lay scattered around Granu either dead or severely wounded.

    The stones and rocks embedded in the Ulrogs' skin flared red. The beasts' cleavers burst into flames and they attacked with renewed strength.

    "Ulrog priests!" shouted Manfir.

    Worry crossed Ader's sweating face. The Seraph encountered tremendous difficulty with Tepi. The warlock's robe fell away. Tattoos marked his arms and symbols scarred his skin. Tepi raised his right arm and Kael saw Amird's name deeply carved upon it.

"That is correct Seraph. You contend with three of us. Fear the power of my Lord Amird!" squealed the warlock and flame shot from his hands.

Ader narrowed his eyes and produced a wall of green fire to deflect the onslaught. The Ulrog slammed their fiery blades down upon Manfir. The stone men drove the prince low against the back of his mount. As the Ulrog raised their blades once more, Manfir slid from the back of the Black and rolled to the ground. He darted under his horse's belly. The Ulrog were momentarily confused.

The Zodrian prince dashed forward between the horses of his opponents. The Ulrog tried to hack at him with their weapons, but their long arms made it difficult to fight in close quarters. Manfir rammed one of his blades into the knee of an Ulrog. The monster howled in pain as thick black blood oozed from the wound. The beast's mount wheeled in fear, knocking into his companion's horse. The second Ulrog lost control.

Manfir struck. He leapt into the air and plunged the second of his blades into the exposed back of the Ulrog. The creature howled and gnashed its crumbled, stone teeth. The blade lodged deeply in the Ulrog's rocky hide.

The fire faded from the stone men's blades as they struggled with their wounds. The pair turned upon the unarmed Manfir. The Zodrian prince lie trapped between the Ulrog and the melee that surrounded Granu.

Flair rushed past the green, sputtering fire of Ader. The Ulrog were unaware of his approach from their rear. The Southland boy's horsemanship rewarded him. Flair drew a hatchet from the pack slung by the side of his horse. In his other hand he held the sword given to him by his grandfather. He directed his chestnut with his knees. The horse dodged past the conflagration created by Tepi and Ader. The horse spun to its left then charged directly between the Ulrog attackers. Flair stretched to meet their height. The young man's right hand whipped forward launching the hatchet. It spun through the air and caught one Ulrog at the base of its head. The sharply honed blade sparked against the Ulrog's rock encrusted skin, but penetrated and wedged there tightly. Flair's right hand quickly met his left on the hilt of his Grandfather's sword. The boy howled and he rammed the blade into the second Ulrog as the chestnut sprinted past. The sword caught hard and was ripped from his grip. The mortally wounded Ulrog lost control of their mounts. Flair shot between them and leaned over extending an arm to Manfir. The Zodrian prince locked forearms with the boy and swung onto the chestnut as it passed. The crazed mounts of the Ulrog slammed into one another once again and spilled their riders to the ground.

The momentum of Flair's mount carried it into the fray around Granu. Flair's chestnut hammered into the back of one of Granu's remaining opponents as the Keltaran prince expertly unarmed the second. Manfir leapt from the back of Flair's horse and retrieved a Keltaran battle-ax from one of the dead. A giant lie face down sprawling on the ground. The prince screamed as he raised the ax and sent it crashing toward the Keltaran. Granu's staff slammed into the ax and deflected it harmlessly into the earth.

"Hold, Manfir!" boomed the giant.

Manfir glared at Granu with a look of shock, followed by fury.

"You will not butcher my brethren. They're beaten!" shouted Granu.

The two remaining Keltaran lay at the feet of Granu and Manfir.

"You ask me not to butcher butchers," cried Manfir in exhaustion.

"I tell you not to." stated Granu.

"Look!" cried Flair pointing west.

Tepi the warlock fled. His mount galloped to the hill upon which he and the Keltaran appeared.

"Amird, the Lord of Chaos, will claim your souls!" cackled the trader.

Eidyn sprinted forward and notched an arrow. The warlock was already out of range.

"Eidyn, save your arrow," wheezed an exhausted Ader. "Behold."

Tepi laughed insanely as he reached the hill and realized no one pursued. His mount galloped up the hill past a large clump of gorse bush. Two small figures darted from the cover of the bushes. They sprinted to within a few yards behind the trader. The frontrunner was the larger of the two. He spun and braced himself. The second was the "fox".

The "fox" leapt forward and planted a foot in his partner's locked hands. He flipped through the air, landing on the back of Tepi's huge, shaggy warhorse. A frenzy of activity ensued. Tepi waved his hands in horror and confusion. The attack reminded Kael of a swarm of bees around a dog that disturbed their hive. The warlock was bewildered by this creature that set upon him.

The fox's hands darted and thrust about the head of the warlock. Tepi's horse slowed and halted at the top of the hill. In an instant the tiny figure flipped from the back of the shaggy horse, met his counterpart, and they dashed back into the thick cover of the gorse bush. Tepi sat howling on the top of the hill, clutching his throat and chest. The sound lasted a few moments then the warlock shuddered and dropped to the ground.

Granu stood calmly facing Manfir. The exhausted Zodrian's chest heaved. He stood hunched over by the weight of the Keltaran battle-ax.

"Avra calls for mercy, Manfir," said Granu softly. "Do not become that which you abhor."

The battle rage in Manfir's eyes faded.

"Whatever ills these men commit, they don't deserve to be butchered like cattle," said Granu. "Stay your bloodlust, Zodrian prince."

The ax slid from Manfir's hands and fell to the ground. Teeg and Eidyn moved amongst the fallen checking for signs of life. Special care was taken with the Ulrog. All were dead except the two spared by Granu. Ader slid from his horse and inspected the Ulrog as well.

"Is anyone suffering from a wound?" called out the Guide. "Kael, come over here. Are you all right?"

The Southland boy tapped his heels into his chestnut's flanks and trotted back to the group.

"I'm fine," said Kael. "What of the others?"

Ader turned and inspected the group. His eyes widened at the sight of Eidyn covered in blood. He raised his hands and approached the Elven prince.

"Save your powers, my lord," said Eidyn pointing to the body of his fallen horse. "Tis not Elven blood that stains this soil."

Ader nodded and smiled, throwing an arm around the prince's shoulder.

"Good," sighed the Guide. "We cannot afford to lose you."

"What of you, Granu?" asked Teeg pointing to a large welt on the giant's skull.

Granu raised a hand to his bald head and gingerly massaged the protruding lump.

"Sometimes it is to your advantage to lean into the path of a swung ax. The handle may catch you squarely, but it will do far less damage than the ax's head," stated Granu.

A low chuckle passed through the exhausted company. Ader snapped the group back into action.

"We must be away from here. Keltaran troops roam the Zodrian hills freely. The Guard is too busy protecting the borders to stop small groups such as this," began Ader. "Eidyn, gather in one of the Keltaran mounts, and retrieve another for Prince Granu. The fewer nights we spend in the open country the better."

"My people must receive proper rights," said Granu solemnly.

"Granu, we have no time for..." started Ader.

"No matter their crimes, these men were children of Avra. They must return to the soil and we must ask for their acceptance into Avra's world," stated Granu.

Ader threw up his hands.

"Bury them. But be quick about it. Manfir, help him while I discuss matters with our guests," stated Ader pointing to the pair of Keltaran.

Manfir started to protest, but Ader would not allow it.

"Will you all begin to bridle against me? I cannot accomplish what I need to if you all refuse the simplest tasks. You made a pledge to me, Manfir. Please do as you are told."

Ader strode to the Keltaran that knelt before Granu.

"Do you know me?" boomed Ader.

"Yes... yes, Lord Ader," stammered one and his counterpart nodded.

"Then know this. I will ask you a few questions. I possess the wonderful ability to read a man's intentions. If I feel you are lying to me I will hand you over to the Zodrian. He will not handle you quite so delicately as your brother, Prince Granu. I've been at this for centuries, and the lives of two sinful Keltaran will not matter to me in the least. You'll do what I say and tell me what I want to know. Understand?" demanded Ader.

"Yes, my lord," replied the Keltaran in unison.

"Stand and walk," commanded Ader.

They rose and fell in next to Ader. He led them down the road and out of sight, the entire time snapping questions at them. Kael was unable to hear what the Seraph was asking.

Granu lifted a battle-ax from the ground and pried up the soft earth around the Keltaran dead. Manfir grimaced and followed suit. Shortly, the men excavated several shallow ditches about the battle site. Eidyn moved amongst the dead, salvaging arrows. Teeg rifled through the Keltaran's belongings for any information he might find useful. Flair walked to his horse and retrieved the small collapsable shovel he used to dig fire pits. He stepped in beside Manfir and shoveled dirt from the graves.

Kael intended to help dig, but as he passed the fallen Ulrog, he stopped, transfixed. Hideous was the only way to describe them. Small tufts of matted hair grew sporadically from a tough, grayish hide. The rocks Kael believed encrusted on their skin were actually embedded within it. The skin grew around and over hunks of black shale and lumps of granite. Their huge, powerful arms were tipped with razor sharp, flinty claws. Their large oval shaped eyes were completely black. It was as if their eyes were a window into the oily black blood that Kael saw spill from the creature's wounds.

Irregular shaped teeth were crowded into the mouth surrounding a swollen, purple tongue.

"A seemingly impenetrable, unstoppable creature of death."

Kael started and tried to catch his breath. Teeg stood next to him looking down. The Elf leaned over and worked Flair's hatchet free from the skull of an Ulrog.

"However, hit them hard enough and they die like the rest of us." stated the Elf.

"Yes, I guess they do," mumbled Kael.

He stared at the nightmare at his feet for a moment longer.

"Priests as well," said Teeg pointing to the Ulrog's arms.

"How do you know that?" asked Kael.

"It has to do with how they are .... born, for lack of a better word," said Teeg.

Kael never thought about that. Do Ulrog come from families? Do they have a mother and a father?

"Are they born?" asked Kael.

"Not exactly," stated Teeg. "They are created."

Kael frowned. Teeg knew the young man wanted a better explanation.

"Ulrog are a bastardization of Amird's doing," began Teeg. "The Seraph joined forces with ancient Chaos and spawned beings of his own. He never hid his dislike for the weaknesses and failings of humans. He was trying to form a race that stood up to his beliefs of success.

"Think about it, Kael. What is an Ulrog? Incredibly strong. Unbelievable stamina. A hide as tough as iron. They can eat anything. They rarely need water. They follow their leaders unquestioningly. Their loyalty is to their master and his servants. They care only for Amird's desires and hold none of their own. Most of all, they are expendable. Lose one hundred and more will be produced."

"How?" asked Kael.

"Torn from the rock and earth of their homeland. Molded in pits of fire. Given life by the Malveel. Their spirit force is weak. Their life force comes from Amird and his ally, Chaos. They live but a fraction of a human life, but as Amird's power grows, so do their numbers," said Teeg.

"The Malveel create them?" questioned Kael.

"They channel a small bit of Amird's will into the Ulrog. Remember Kael, this is a creature that requires little and hardly thinks at all. It doesn't take much of the force of Amird to animate an Ulrog. Besides, the Fallen One draws his power from the vast energy of Chaos. If he continues to rally, he may be able to overrun our world with Ulrog," stated Teeg. "These two were not molded haphazardly. Look at the rocks embedded in their arms."

Kael studied the Ulrog. He noticed patterns in the rock. Bits and pieces were aligned to form similar symbols to those carved in the arms of Tepi. The symbols were unfamiliar to Kael, but definite in their appearance. Additionally, the name of Amird appeared all over the two creatures in the form of scars. The lettering was crude and irregular, but the name was unmistakable. Teeg pointed to the stony emblems.

"These are the Chaotic Symbols, Kael," said Teeg. "They call upon the powers of Chaos to give their wearer power. The scars invoke the name of Amird for strength. These were no ordinary Ulrog. Tepi summoned priests with special powers to help him battle Ader."

Kael heard a yip and a snarl in the distance. The group halted their work and looked to the hill where Tepi's body lay. A pack of wild dogs snapped at one another and tore into the remains of the warlock. Flair groaned and grabbed a large rock. The boy stepped toward the hill hefting the rock.

"Leave them, Flair," said Manfir. "Tis what the warlock deserves."

The boy hesitated for a moment then released the rock and returned to his work. The dogs yelped and growled. Manfir turned back to the grave he was digging and his eyes met those of Granu. The giant leaned on his ax and arched a thoughtful eyebrow toward the scene on the hill.

"Trouble dogs the wicked." quoted Granu from scripture.

The duo looked at one another for a moment, then a wry smile passed between them and they returned to their work. After a few moments Ader walked back to the roadside followed by the Keltaran soldiers. Granu and Manfir were piling rocks on the tops of the graves. Eidyn led several of the Keltaran horses down the road into the midst of the travelers. Teeg retrieved and cleaned Manfir's blades. The Zodrian prince thanked him and returned them to the sheaths on his back. The Elf lord hefted Flair's hatchet in his hand.

"Light enough to throw a fair distance, yet heavy enough to cleave the head of an Ulrog," commented Teeg. "A fine weapon."

"I never used it as a weapon before," stammered Flair.

"An extremely successful first outing for you, I should say," commented Teeg. "Don't you think, Prince Manfir?"

Manfir turned from a pack he cinched to his horse and bowed.

"I owe you my life, Corporal Flair," said the prince.

"Corporal?" said a wide-eyed Flair.

"Of course," said Manfir approaching the boy. "During training at the Hold, a student or two are chosen from among the recruits to help lead them. The best of the class is chosen and given authority. Someone who stands out. You will be that man in the next class."

"But I still need to pass the test. I'm not sure I'll be accepted to the Guard," stated Flair.

Teeg and Eidyn suppressed a chuckle and Manfir frowned at the boy.

"You really possess no idea what you just accomplished do you?" asked Manfir.

Flair shook his head and looked questioningly at the group around him.

"Perhaps we should allow him to wallow in ignorance," laughed Teeg. "The boy will unwittingly destroy the entire Ulrog army before the concept of fear ever crosses his mind."

"Please don't make sport of me," pleaded Flair. "I was plenty afraid."

"Then what possessed you to charge between two Ulrog priests like that?" exclaimed Eidyn.

"Someone needed to do something, and I was the only one left," shrugged the boy.

Manfir laughed heartily and threw an arm around Flair.

"Thank Avra for that!" exclaimed the prince.

"We must be on our way," announced Ader. "Is the site to your satisfaction, Prince Granu?"

"I wish to say a few words over these men. Catra was a friend and the others are brothers who fell under the spell of the Great Deceiver. You may journey on if you choose. I will make up the ground and be with you shortly," stated Granu.

Eidyn led two giant horses over to Ader. The pair was tethered together by a long rope.

"We can transport the prisoners on these," stated the Elf.

Granu stepped over and untied the lead between the horses.

"There will be no prisoners," stated the giant.

"What?" exclaimed Manfir. "Of course there will be prisoners. These men tried to murder us today! They violated the honor of parlay."

Ader stroked the gray stubble on his chin and stared at Granu. The giant remained steadfast. His eyes searched those of the Seraph.

"What do you recommend?" asked Ader calmly.

"If they are transported to Zodra they will be executed for entering Zodrian land and betraying parlay," stated Granu.

"As they should be," snapped Manfir.

"This does no one any good," said Granu.

"Except the Zodrians they may kill in the future," grumbled Manfir.

Granu ignored him and turned to address the Keltaran.

"You will carry one of two messages to the city of Keltar for me," commanded Granu. "If you love your king and brethren, you will go to the city with news of my brother's treachery. Fenrel is in league with the Ulrog and trades the future of the Keltaran people for conquest and revenge against the Zodrians. A deal struck with the Deceiver and his horde gains us naught but our own doom.

"If you choose Fenrel over the king and his rightful heir, you may carry a different message of doom. Fenrel's doom. Tell my brother I come for him. I'm uncertain of the time and I'm uncertain of the day. However, one thing I am certain of, Fenrel and I will meet and I will exact his penance for the treachery he commits."

Granu stepped over to Eidyn and grabbed the reins of the Keltarans' horses. He led the mounts to the soldiers and handed the reins to them.

"Either choice you make serves my purposes," said Granu. "You are weapon-less strangers in a strange land. A long dangerous ride lies ahead of you. Now go, and may Avra guide your path."

The pair nervously glanced at one another, then back to Granu. Their faces were full of fear. Both of the soldiers grabbed the reins and readied themselves to mount. As the first threw himself into the saddle, the second stopped and turned to Granu. The soldier looked down to the ram's skull tunic that covered his armored chest. He quickly tore it from his body and dropped to one knee before Granu.

"My lord, I ask your forgiveness and that of my Creator," sobbed the soldier.

"I can only offer mine," said Granu, "and that is freely given. Go now and serve your people."

The Keltaran leapt to his feet and swung onto the back of his mount. The pair drove their heels into the flanks of their horses and rumbled over the hill to the west. The dust cloud created by their departure settled and Manfir turned to face Granu.

"I... I think you make a mistake," said the Zodrian through clenched teeth.

Granu smiled.

"Vengeance and death are not the only tools of a leader, Zodrian prince. Compassion and mercy are a powerful ally. In your world, two more graves are filled and two more children of Avra are gone. No use to anyone," said Granu. "In mine, I may add two more friends among my people. Two who strayed may take the path to righteousness. Two may be willing to turn their lives over to Avra."

"May," stated Manfir.

"What if they don't? Then they will deliver my other message. A message almost as useful. They will set doubt and fear in my brother's mind. Allies as strong as an armed man. The uncertainty Fenrel harbors will cause him to falter."

Manfir's expression softened and he pondered Granu's words.

"You cannot win this war merely with daring and guile in battle," stated Granu. "We are at war for the hearts and souls of our people. They must believe and be led by those who believe. When we capture their hearts, then we will raise an invincible army."

The group stood in silence for a moment and let the giant's words wash over them. Kael tried to understand the incredible resolve Granu possessed. He wondered if he could ever commit himself entirely to a cause like this man.

The group mounted. Eidyn led one of the Keltaran mounts to Granu.

"I'm more comfortable on my feet," stated the giant. "Besides, how could I disappear when the mood struck. The horse is more of a burden than a help."

The travelers set off down the road at a slow trot. Granu pulled a small book from his robes and stood over the graves of the Keltaran soldiers. Kael crested a low hill up the road and heard Granu softly chanting. The boy turned to see the giant, head bowed, outstretch one hand over the graves and hold it there as he sang. Kael frowned. Granu was certainly challenging the boy's notions concerning the giant and his people. Kael spun his mount north and knew that no matter how hard Prince Manfir pushed the group, Granu Stormbreaker would join them eventually.

CHAPTER 30: THE GATES OF ZODRA

Several more days in the saddle passed. On the third of these days, Kael woke and prepared for the day's ride in the usual manner. Ader stepped into the center of the encampment as saddlebags and bedrolls were tied onto the backs of the horses.

"Manfir," called the Seraph. "It's time for you to lose the trappings of Rin the tinker. There is no hiding who we are now. The enemy knows, so let those we hope to call friends know as well. We'll tarry here a short time longer for you to make the appropriate changes."

Manfir pursed his lips and contemplated Ader's words. He ran a grimy hand across his bristly chin then pulled his tattered cape in front of him for inspection.

"We will not make the same mistake in Zodra as we did in Rindor," continued Ader. "We will not skulk into the kingdom in the dead of night. Today, the prince heir of Zodra returns from his long hiatus. Those who are present will see a man proud to have served, even if they know not how."

Manfir smiled and unstrapped a large pack from the back of his midnight stallion. The pack slammed to the ground with a loud clang. The Zodrian prince snatched the pack from the ground and spun toward a shallow brook running near the encampment.

"I'll be but a moment," announced Manfir over his shoulder.

He disappeared from sight behind a thicket of gorse bush. The men remained silent for a time then Ader turned to the remainder of the group.

"It's been a long journey, and you all performed admirably," stated Ader. "However, we are now in Manfir's land. If you know anything of Zodra, you should know this. She is a kingdom of contradictions. She is home to more people faithful to my Lord Avra than any other place in all the lands, yet she was thrust into prominence by the Master of Deceit. Her numbers grow tremendously as more and more seek her protection, yet she fears outsiders and treats them ill. Her streets are renown for safety and freedom from violence, yet her people have been at war with much of the known world for millennia. In short, you can never trust logic in Zodra. The moment you relax is the moment you falter."

The Guide paused and let his words take hold.

"Therefore, I ask you all," said Ader glancing toward Teeg. "To stand back and follow the lead of Manfir and myself. The prince heir left under secretive circumstance. His reputation suffers. The enemy exploits this occurrence and the rumors grow. It is Manfir's time to claim his place. No other can do it for him."

Teeg bowed toward the Guide.

"It shall be as you ask, my lord," said the old Elf somberly.

"Granu," continued Ader. "Your disappearances are at an end. You arrive in Zodra as an emissary of the Elven kingdom and with all the protections such an office affords you. I don't wish to parade you down the main street to the palace, but we shall not send you over the wall in the cover of darkness. Remain in your robe and cowl, but stay with the group as we approach the capital."

"As you command, Lord Ader," rumbled the giant. "I lay my life in the hands of Avra."

"Actually, your life will lie in my hands," came a voice from behind the gorse thicket. "A prospect you may find troubling."

Manfir stepped through the thicket and into the center of the encampment. His unkempt hair was combed and fashioned into a braid on the back of his head. His grimy, scruffy face was cleansed and shaved clean. A maroon cloak was clasped with an ornate silver hook around his neck. The cloak draped over his shoulders and bordered a polished, silver breastplate. Copper was fashioned on the center of the breastplate into the image of a diving bird of prey.

"When you embrace a faith in the Creator, you find nothing troubling," replied Granu.

Manfir smiled and nodded to the giant. The Zodrian prince walked through the encampment to his stallion and threw the saddle pack onto the horse's rump. He quickly secured it with straps and lifted himself onto the animal's back. The others in the party did the same. Once they settled, Manfir kicked his horse's flanks and the group started forward.

Half a day passed and finally, Kael beheld signs of civilization. Homesteads and ranches appeared sporadically as the group crawled north. Periodic plateaus and ridges still broke up the countryside, but they were less pronounced. After climbing one of these low ridgelines, Kael looked to the north and saw the capital.

Zodra was nothing like Rindor. The river city rose up to the clouds from the swirling mists of the Ituan River. Zodra, on the other hand, lay squat and wide across the arid, dusty floor of a huge plateau, encircled by a massive wall. Rindor's structures increased in height toward the center of the city, culminating in the royal palace. Zodra followed no such plan. Buildings of all shapes and sizes stood buttressed to one another.

The troop headed toward the southern wall of the city and passed weary workers exiting to their homes in the country. The Zodrians stared at the strange group and many broke into excited conversations. More than a few muttered Manfir's name.

Manfir led the group to within one hundred yards of the massive city wall. The structure stood at least twenty yards high, and was tipped by a row of three-foot iron pikes. It arched above the spot where the road entered the city. Two heavy iron doors stood wide open.

Soldiers patrolled the top of the wall that lay thick enough to allow a cart to rumble across. More guards took stations atop the arch and stared at the approaching riders. They called to the gates below and another group of soldiers turned and moved in front of the gate.

Manfir cupped a gloved hand to his mouth and called to the causeway above.

"Sergeant of the guard! We seek entry to the capital!" shouted Manfir.

The soldiers near the gate tensed and slid their hands over the hilts of their sheathed weapons. The travelers streaming from the city slowed and stared at the encounter. Manfir reined in his stallion and the entire group halted. A broad shouldered soldier on the causeway above turned and eyed the group beneath him. He stepped to the low, granite step that ran the length of the upper wall and removed his helm. Kael noted the weathered features of an old soldier.

"The day grows long and an armored company requests entry into the capital," stated the Sergeant. "Not altogether unusual, except that their leader wears the royal crest of the city and the cloak of a superior officer of the Guard. Why don't you simply order the sentries to stand down and enter of your own volition?"

Ader slid in next to Manfir.

"Our group requests parlay with the house of Macin, King of Zodra," called the Seraph.

"Parlay!" exclaimed the sergeant. "Forgive me if I don't make myself clear. I served his highness for almost forty years and I'm sure I'm not mistaken that I recognize his son Manfir."

A murmur ran through the citizens spread across the gate's opening. Several travelers and soldiers alike dashed from the gate into the city's interior.

"What need does the prince have of parlay with his own house?" persisted the sergeant.

Ader rolled his eyes and sighed.

"Sergeant Deling, will you humor me and grant our group parlay?" asked Ader.

The sergeant's face broke into a broad smile and he nodded to Ader.

"Well, of course I will, Lord Ader. I'm merely questioning the point of it," he mumbled.

"Thank you, Sergeant Deling. How fare you?" asked Manfir.

"No complaints," smiled Deling. "Twenty years watching the north gate and welcoming back our men from battle. They said I was getting too old, inattentive. So they sent me down here to the south to keep an eye on wagons of grain and pickpockets. If you ask me, some of them don't want my eye on what they're doing up north."

The sergeant pointed to several guards on the road.

"You and you! Clear the entryway to the city! Move those people back and let the prince heir and his companions enter!"

barked Deling as he turned back to Manfir. "I'll meet you 'neath the gate your highness. Welcome home!"

The sergeant spun and stepped from the edge of the wall. He disappeared from view and a few moments later he stood in the arching tunnel formed by the causeway. Recesses in the tunnel walls provided places for more guards. Zodrians attempted to exit the city, but slowed as they encountered the burgeoning crowd around the gate. Deling stepped into the road.

"Clear a path there! Clear a path!" barked the sergeant.

Manfir tapped his heels into the flanks of his stallion and the group trotted forward. The people backed away and a wide path opened through their midst. As Manfir passed Deling, the sergeant saluted. Deling cleared his throat and glanced at his troops. The guards who stood scattered throughout the tunnel stared in confusion at the event unfolding before them. The prince regent, unheard from in seventeen years, rode up in full regalia. One of the guards recognized Deling's hint and snapped to attention. He joined Deling's salute, and the others quickly followed suit. Manfir smiled at the sergeant and returned the salute.

"Thank you, sergeant," smiled Manfir. "I'll be heading to the Hold before presenting myself to his highness. Perhaps a runner should be sent to inform my father of my return."

"It's already been done, sire," nodded Deling.

"Always one step ahead," laughed Manfir.

The old sergeant leaned in and lowered his voice.

"I waited on you for several days now," whispered Deling with a wink. "When good old Brelg passed through a couple of days ago, then Cefiz the day after, I knew I would be seeing you shortly."

Manfir nodded and moved forward.

"Good fortune to you, sergeant," called the prince over his shoulder.

"And to you, my prince," replied Deling.

The group slowly made their way through the city. Word quickly spread concerning the return of the prince regent. Zodrians crowded the streets along the path to the Hold. Kael fidgeted. The crowd acted uncertain and edgy. Manfir certainly wasn't receiving a hero's welcome. Many of the citizenry pointed and stared at the passing troop. Whispers and knowing looks passed between some of the Zodrians. Granu remained cloaked and hooded, but his presence drew many of the looks and whispers. More than a few catcalls were thrown in the troop's direction. Kael drew in next to Teeg.

"I'm feeling a bit uncomfortable," Kael stated in a low voice. "These people aren't ecstatic over Manfir's return."

Teeg frowned and nodded to the boy.

"I forced myself to ignore events in the capital recently, too much going on elsewhere. When last I left, feelings weren't this sour," replied Teeg. "I believe the enemy is busy spreading lies and innuendo about our loyal prince. Manfir returns now and only he may repair the damage done to his reputation."

The troop rounded a bend in the road and a group of horsemen raced in their direction. Manfir reined in and his body tensed. Zodrians straggling in the street jumped from the path of the cavalry. Others were knocked aside as the heavily armed soldiers roared to a stop ten yards from Manfir's coal black steed. The Zodrian horsemen blocked the roadway. Several citizens in the crowd cheered as a pair of riders separated from the group. The larger of the two soldiers addressed Manfir.

"I am Colonel Udas ..." stated the leader and he paused.

Manfir remained silent and expressionless. The eyes of the smaller man at Udas's side darted in panic and distress.

"The hero of Rimdar Pass!" announced Udas's aide.

Another small cheer broke from the crowd. The colonel sat ramrod straight. One gloved hand rose and lightly waved in acknowledgement to the crowd. The other lay stiff and immobile, folded over the horn of his saddle. Upon his chest he wore a gleaming gold breastplate. His red robe was immaculate.

"A member of the General Staff in charge of supplies," whispered Teeg to Kael. "His breastplate is engraved with the emblem of the supply staff."

Kael lightly nodded and noticed the other horsemen bore the same insignia on their vestments.

"What is it you wish, colonel?" asked Manfir.

"It has come to my attention that Sergeant Deling allowed a heavily armed group to enter from the South gate without first appropriately checking their credentials," snapped Udas. "The old fool has spent too many years in the noon day sun. I'm afraid he neglects his duties."

Manfir pursed his lips and leaned forward in the saddle. He glared at Udas.

"I ask again, what is it you wish, colonel?" growled Manfir.

Udas sucked in a quick breath and arched an eyebrow at Manfir.

"Put 'im in his place, Udas!" shouted a Zodrian from a group of men in the crowd.

"Show 'em what a real fightin' man looks like, Udas!" called another.

Kael looked to Ader and found the Guide calmly sitting on the back of his stallion. Ader's hands lay in his lap, subtly shifting. Kael's eyes searched the crowd and immediately he found what he was looking for. A beautiful young woman with dark hair and blue green eyes stood on the stoop of a storefront staring at the Seraph. Ader's hands worked a moment longer then stopped. The young woman nodded, then threw her green cowl over her head and turned. She hesitated a moment then spun back to the group and stared past Kael to the other side of the road. Eidyn sat on his Keltaran warhorse, eyes fixed upon the woman. She smiled and lightly bowed to the Elven prince. Eidyn's face remained expressionless, but he returned her bow with a nod of his head. She quickly turned and disappeared into the crowd.

Udas gained courage from the crowd's comments.

"You and your companions will be checked like any other unauthorized, armed party which enters the city," blurted Udas. "Your weapons will be confiscated and you will be interviewed to determine your business here in Zodra! The majority of your group is not Zodrian and its suspicious constituency requires immediate attention. Those of you I determine to be enemies of the state, will be detained!"

Manfir tapped the flanks of his stallion and moved alongside Udas. The colonel shrank back as Manfir glared at him.

"You'll do nothing of the kind, hero of Rimdar Pass. I speak for all the men in this group," growled Manfir. "And the last time I checked, I held a general's commission in the Guard. The next time you fail to salute a superior officer before addressing him, you will find yourself confined to the Hold. Do you understand me?"

Udas's eyes shifted nervously between Manfir, the crowd and his troops.

"I uh ... I.." stammered Udas.

"DO YOU UNDERSTAND ME COLONEL? YES OR NO?" demanded Manfir rising in his saddle.

Udas's eyes widened and he nearly slid from the back of his mount. He fumbled awkwardly with his right hand in an attempt to extract it from the reins of his stallion then stiffly raised it in salute. His unit followed his lead as Manfir glared at them. The prince spun his mount and cantered toward the area of the crowd that shouted support to Udas. The men standing there shrank back against the wall of the nearest building. Manfir leapt from his stallion and walked amongst them. Fire raged in his eyes.

"How I served this kingdom and my Lord Avra over the last seventeen seasons is no one's business but my own and the ruler of this great land. Any man willing to question that service and take exception to my duty may do so now!" bellowed the prince.

Manfir drew one of the dual sabers strapped to his back and held the hilt out to the crowd. The group shrank further away. Manfir's hard eyes bore into them.

"No one?" questioned the prince as he shoved the hilt toward the face of the man who shouted the first comment.

The Zodrian averted his eyes to the cobblestone street and shook his head in dissent.

"No, my lord," muttered the man.

Manfir flipped the sword over and deftly slid it back into its scabbard. The prince spun and marched to the middle of the street. He swept his hand across the growing crowd.

"Zodrians! Now is the time for faith!" shouted Manfir to the crowd. "Now is the time for unity. The forces of evil bear down upon us! They hope to overwhelm and destroy us! We live in fear of an enemy poised to sweep down upon us unleashing murder and Chaos. The Ulrog strain upon their master's leash, desiring nothing more than to overrun beautiful Zodra!

"However, the arena for this destruction is not solely the battlefield! They also fight for our hearts and minds. These too are battlefields to our enemies. They hope to twist and corrupt all that is good in our society. They hope to turn us against our allies, our neighbors and our brothers. When the final battle begins, do not spend your last hours questioning whether your neighbor is doing enough. Ask yourself whether YOU are doing enough. Make sure that your own house is in order before you wonder about your brother's house!"

Manfir walked confidently to his stallion and threw himself in the saddle. The crowd's eyes remained fixed on the Zodrian prince. The street was quiet and still.

"As for me," stated the prince. "My house remained faithful to the wishes of Avra these last seventeen seasons, and I am ready to sacrifice all for the good of Zodra. I call upon those of you who can say the same to ride with me in defense of the kingdom!"

Manfir reined the stallion to face Udas.

"Now out of my way, colonel. I wish to go home!" called the prince.

The black stallion charged in Udas's direction as the colonel and his aide scrambled to get free of its path. Ader and the remainder of Kael's group followed closely and a cheer went up from some gathered in the street.

Udas's face boiled with rage and embarrassment as he glared at the retreating figure of Manfir. He dropped his right hand onto the horn of his saddle with a hollow clunk. Hatred filled his eyes and the supply commander's left hand mechanically rose and rubbed the elbow of his stiff and immobile right arm. His subordinate pulled beside him.

"Prince Manfir was absent from these lands for quite some time," chattered the aide as he nervously glanced to the area Udas caressed. "Perhaps he is unaware of the pain and sacrifice that both you and the great General Ellow endured at the hands of those Keltaran monsters, my lord."

Udas's attention was broken from the departing troop and he turned to the young officer. A sneer spread across his face.

"The sacrifice and pain I endured for the good of my nation is nothing compared to that which Manfir son of Macin will face before he ever sets foot outside his beloved kingdom again," snarled Udas. "Spread word to our men. The time comes to show this kingdom where its power lies!"

NOW ENDS BOOK I OF THE SERAPHINIUM

GLOSSARY OF CHARACTERS AND LOCATIONS

Ader: One of the second generation of Seraphim created by Avra to fill the gap after Awoi and Amird left the world. Ader represents the voice of Avra, commanding those on this world who will follow.

Aemmon Brelgson: The second son of Brelg, an innkeeper in the small town of Kelky.

Alel: One of the second generation of Seraphim created by Avra to fill the gap after Awoi and Amird left the world of Vel. Alel represents the Ear of Avra, hearing all the prayers and praise of his people.

Amird: One of the first two Seraphim created by Avra to help and support the human race. Amird represents the intellect and creativity of the Creator.

The Anvil: The military of the Keltaran Empire. All men past a certain age are members of the Anvil.

Astel: Once thriving kingdom on the plateaus to the East of the Mirozert Mountains. Astel has been conquered by the warlock Izgra and his Ulrog stone men. The palace and ruins surrounding it have been renamed Kel Izgra.

Avra: The Lord God and Creator of the Nearing World.

Awoi: One of the first two Seraphim created by Avra to help and support the human race. Awoi represents the heart and compassion of the Creator.

The Black: Manfir's battle mount. Also referred to as the Prize by the Eru.

Brelg: Owns a small inn, "The King's Service", in the town of Kelky. Raising two sons on.

Cefiz: The cook at "The King's Service" in Kelky.

Chani: Commander of the Grey Elf army.

Chimbre: Mysterious figure Kael spies upon.

Corad Kingfisher: King of the island kingdom of Rindor.

Delvi: A small enclave on the shores of the Lake of Calm Waters (Lake Eru) in the heart of the Eru plains. It houses the archives of the Delvin Scribes.

Delvin Scribes: A group of men dedicated to observing and recording all that takes place in the world of Vel. The Order of Delvi is led by a prelate who directs all their efforts. The Order also has been known to prognosticate future events within their writings. The Book of Delvi is a collection of written works compiled by the Delvin Scribes.

Diom: Grey Elf soldier in charge of the bridge over the Efer River set in the heart of the Nagur Wood.

Eidyn Valpreux: Grey Elf heir to the throne of Luxlor. Accomplished soldier and officer in the Grey Elf Army.

Eirtwin Admir: Queen of the Grey Elves of Luxlor. Wife of King Leinor Valpreux. Mother of Eidyn Valpreux.

Ellow: Former commander of the Zodrian supply corps. Ellow was ostensibly killed by a group of Keltaran soldiers who ambushed him and his aide, Colonel Udas, at Rimdar Pass.

Eru: Nomadic tribesmen of the Eastern plains. They protect long stretches of the North country from invasion by the Ulrog Horde. They are master horsemen and have extensive herds of the animals.

Fenrel Stormbreaker: Captain of the Kings Guard in Keltar. Heir to the throne now that his brother has been exiled.

Flair: A young man and hand at his grandfather Hamly's ranch.

Grannak Stormbreaker: King of the Keltaran people.

Granu Stormbreaker: Exiled prince of the mountain kingdom of Keltar. Son of Grannak Stormbreaker. Brother of Fenrel Stormbreaker. Chief Abbott of the Monastery of Awoi.

Gretcha: An ancient princess of the Zodrian kingdom. She was born unusually large and grew to a giant stature. Her father first kept her locked up then banished her from the kingdom.

The Guard: The military of the Zodrian Empire. Recruits are selected and volunteers are typically rejected. It is quite an honor to be selected for the Guard.

Hamly: An old man used by Brelg to perform odd jobs around the inn.

Hilro: A mysterious figure that patrols the Nagur Wood.

Hindle: Blacksmith's apprentice in the town of Quay.

Hrafnu: The son of Gretcha and the Seraph Awoi. He is the father of the giant Keltaran race.

Ituan River: A great river that gets its start in the Zorim Mountains to the West of Zodra. The river flows west to east across the lower third of Zodra and washes into the vast waterways of the Toxkri Swamp.

Izgra the Half-Dead: Warlock and worshipper of the Deceiver. Izgra is a usurper on the throne of Astel. The warlock has taken the reins of control over the minions of Amird upon the Nearing World.

Jasper: An old tinker and tradesman who travels amongst the villages in the south of the kingdom of Zodra providing goods and sewrvices to the people.

Kael Brelgson: The eldest son of Brelg, an innkeeper in the small town of Kelky.

Kelky: A small village in the southernmost part of the kingdom of Zodra. Kelky's location has made it a forgotten outpost of the great kingdom.

Keltar: City and surrounding lands set within the steep peaks of the Zorim Mountains. Keltar is inhabited by a race of people known for their extraordinary size and heartiness. At war with Ulrog invaders from the north and in a centuries long blood fued with the Zodrian kingdom.

Leinor Valpreux: King of the Grey Elves of the Kingdm of Luxlor. Husband to Eirtwin Admir, Queen of the Grey Elves. Father of Eidyn Valpreux.

Lilywynn: Mysterious girl Kael encounters on his journey north.

Lintos: A captain in the Rindoran army.

Lucyn Kingfisher: Queen of Rindor.

Luxlor: Kingdom of Grey Elves set in the heart of the southern Nagur Forest. Luxlor is a secluded and isolated kingdom.

Macin of Zodra: Current king of Zodra.

Malveel: Amird the Deceiver began his rebellion against the Creator by fashioning beasts to enforce his will upon the Nearing World. The thirteen Malveel rule all the minions of Amird.

Manfir of Zodra: The prince heir to the throne of the mightiest nation in the world.

Mestor and Wist: Former rulers of the kingdom of Astel. Overthrown by Izgra the Half-Dead and his army of Ulrog Hackles.

Methra the Worm: The 5th of the thirteen Malveel. Methra was once a powerful Malveel lord known as the Beguiler. However, failures and indecision have marginalized his power. Now, he does the bidding of Sulgor in hopes that it will ingratiate him with the Malveel king.

Netur: Eldest son of Hrafnu and Uttren of Keltar.

Nyven (Jilk & Trawney): Cattlemen from the Zodrian town of Trimble.

Olith Stormbreaker: Brother of King Grannak. Commander of the Keltaran army, the Anvil.

Order of Awoi: A religious order of monks dedicated to the ways of the Seraph Awoi. The monks of the order are known for their peace and compassion but are equally adept at defending themselves and considered fierce fighters.

Paerrow Admir: Nobleman in the court of King Leinor in Luxlor. Paerrow often represents the voice of the Grey Elf people in the confines of the king's court.

Quirg Firebreather: The 9th of the Malveel. Quirg is of the lesser order of the beasts and as all Malveel he is to be feared but he does not command a high rank in their order. He is known to be impetuous and rash.

Rin: The son of Jasper the tinker. Rin is a silent and expressionless man.

Scythtar Mountains: A range of treacherous peaks that runs west to east across the northern reaches of the Nearing World.

Seraphim: Beings created and set upon the world to care for and direct humans. Often referred to as Guides by the people.

The first two Seraphim were Awoi and his brother Amird. The second pair was Ader and his brother Alel.

The Spear: Name given the Rindoran army.

Sprig "The Fox": Mysterious figure Kael spies upon.

Sulgor the Magnificent: The first of the thirteen Malveel beasts created by the Deceiver to be his emissaries on the Nearing World. Sulgor is the King of the Malveel and rules them as they in turn rule the multitude of Ulrog stone men. Sulgor has had his power wrested from him by Izgra the Half-Dead.

Tarader: The mightiest of horses. Ader's mount.

Tay: Rindoran noblewoman married to Macin of Zodra. Manfir's mother. She has passed away.

Teeg Cin Fair: Old nobleman of the court of King Leinor in Luxlor. Friend of Brelg of Kelky.

Toxkri Swamp: A gigantic maze of bogs, quicksand and jungle. The Toxkri lies on the southern border of the Eru plains. Its geographical distinction lies in its central location. A part of the swamp touches the Derol forest, the Eru plains, the Borz desert, the Nagur Wood and the Southlands of Zodra.

Ulrog: Men fashioned of stone and mud and given chaotic life by the Malveel. The Ulrog army is referred to as The Horde and units of 13 stone men are packs. An individual Ulrog is often call a Hackle. They populate the Scythtar Mountains. (Knife Mountains).

Udas (The Hero of Rimdar Pass): A Zodrian colonel in command of the supply lines of the Zodrian army (The Guard).

Uttren: Zodrian refugee who becomes the wife of Hrafnu.

The Nearing World: The world created by Avra.

Wynard: Zodrian commander of the cavalry corps.

Yanwin: Kael and Aemmon's mother who passed away many seasons ago.

Zodra: The most powerful kingdom in the Nearing World. Zodra has stood for centuries as the main protector of the world against the forces of evil. Both the capital city and the kingdom go by this name.

Zorim Mountains: Mountain range that runs north to south forming the western border of the kingdom of Zodra. Home to the Keltaran Kingdom.

GLOSSARY BY LAND OR RACE

ZODRIANS

Zodra: The most powerful kingdom in the Nearing World. Zodra has stood for centuries as the main protector of the world against the forces of evil. Both the capital city and the kingdom go by this name.

Aemmon Brelgson: The second son of Brelg, an innkeeper in the small town of Kelky.

Brelg: Owns a small inn, "The King's Service", in the town of Kelky. Raising two sons.

Cefiz: The cook at "The King's Service" in Kelky.

Flair: A young man and hand at his grandfather Hamly's ranch.

General Ellow: Former commander of the Zodrian supply corps. Ellow was ostensibly killed by a group of Keltaran soldiers who ambushed him and his aide, Colonel Udas, at Rimdar Pass.

The Guard: The military of the Zodrian Empire. Recruits are selected and volunteers are typically rejected. It is quite an honor to be selected for the Guard.

Hamly: An old man used by Brelg to perform odd jobs around the inn.

Hindle: Blacksmith's apprentice in the town

Jasper: An old tinker and tradesman who travels amongst the villages in the south of the kingdom of Zodra providing goods and services to the people.

Kael Brelgson: The eldest son of Brelg, an innkeeper in the small town of Kelky.

Kelky: A small village in the southernmost part of the kingdom of Zodra. Kelky's location has made it a forgotten outpost of the great kingdom.

Macin of Zodra: Current king of Zodra.

Manfir of Zodra: The prince heir to the throne of the mightiest nation in the world.

Nyven (Jilk & Trawney): Cattlemen from the Zodrian town of Trimble.

Rin: The son of Jasper the tinker. Rin is a silent and expressionless man.

Tay: Rindoran noblewoman married to Macin of Zodra. Manfir's mother. She has passed away.

Udas (The Hero of Rimdar Pass): A Zodrian colonel in command of the supply lines of the Zodrian army (The Guard).

Wynard: A general in the Guard. Zodrian commander of the cavalry corps.

Yanwin: Kael and Aemmon's mother who passed away many seasons ago.

ELVES AND GREY ELVES

Luxlor: Kingdom of Grey Elves set in the heart of the Southern Nagur Forest. Luxlor is a secluded and isolated kingdom.

Chani: Commander of the Grey Elf army.

Diom: Grey Elf soldier in charge of the bridge over the Efer River set in the heart of the Nagur Wood.

Eidyn Valpreux: Grey Elf heir to the throne of Luxlor. Accomplished soldier and officer in the Grey Elf Army.

Eirtwin Admir: Queen of the Grey Elves of Luxlor. Wife of King Leinor Valpreux. Mother of Eidyn Valpreux.

Leinor Valpreux: King of the Grey Elves of the Kingdm of Luxlor. Husband to Eirtwin Admir, Queen of the Grey Elves. Father of Eidyn Valpreux.

Paerrow Admir: Nobleman in the court of King Leinor in Luxlor. Paerrow often represents the voice of the Grey Elf people in the confines of the king's court.

Teeg Cin Fair: Old nobleman of the court of King Leinor in Luxlor. Friend of Brelg of Kelky.

KELTARAN GIANTS

Keltar: City and surrounding lands set within the steep peaks of the Zorim Mountains. Keltar is inhabited by a race of people known for their extraordinary size and heartiness. At war with Ulrog invaders from the north and in a centuries long blood fued with the Zodrian Kingdom.

The Anvil: The military of the Keltaran Empire. All men past a certain age are members of the Anvil.

Fenrel Stormbreaker: Captain of the Kings Guard in Keltar. Heir to the throne now that his brother lives in exile.

Grannak Stormbreaker: King of the Keltaran people.

Granu Stormbreaker: Exiled prince of the mountain kingdom of Keltar. Son of Grannak Stormbreaker. Brother of Fenrel Stormbreaker. Chief Abbott of the Monastery of Awoi.

Gretcha: An ancient princess of the Zodrian kingdom. She was born unusually large and grew to a giant stature. Her father first kept her locked up, then banished her from the kingdom.

Hrafnu: The son of Gretcha and the Seraph Awoi. He is the father of the giant Keltaran race.

Netur: Eldest son of Hrafnu and Uttren of Keltar.

Olith Stormbreaker: Brother of King Grannak. Commander of the Keltaran army, the Anvil.

Order of Awoi: A religious order of monks dedicated to the ways of the Seraph Awoi. The monks of the order are known for their peace and compassion but are equally adept at defending themselves and considered fierce fighters.

Uttren: Zodrian refugee who becomes the wife of Hrafnu. First queen of Keltar.

Zorim Mountains: Mountain range that runs north to south forming the western border of the kingdom of Zodra. Home to the Keltaran kingdom.

THE SERAPHIM

Ader: One of the second generation of Seraphim created by Avra to fill the gap after Awoi and Amird left the world of Vel. Ader represents the voice of Avra, commanding those on this world that will follow.

Alel: One of the second generation of Seraphim created by Avra to fill the gap after Awoi and Amird departed the Nearing World. Alel represents the Ear of Avra, hearing all the prayers and praise of his people.

Amird: One of the first two Seraphim created by Avra to help and support the human race. Amird represents the intellect and creativity of the Creator.

Awoi: One of the first two Seraphim created by Avra to help and support the human race. Awoi represents the heart and compassion of the Creator.

THE MALVEEL

Malveel: Amird the Deceiver began his rebellion against the Creator by fashioning beasts to enforce his will upon the Nearing World. The thirteen Malveel rule the minions of Amird.

Methra the Worm: The 5th of the thirteen Malveel. Methra was once a powerful Malveel lord, but failures and indecision marginalized that power. Now, he does the bidding of Sulgor in hopes that it will ingratiate him with the Malveel king.

Quirg Firebreather: The 9th of the Malveel. Quirg is of the lesser order of the beasts. Like all Malveel he is to be feared but he does not command a high rank in their order. He is known to be impetuous and rash.

Sulgor the Magnificent: The first of the thirteen Malveel beasts created by the Deceiver to be his emissaries on the Nearing World. Sulgor is the King of the Malveel and rules them as they in turn rule the multitude of Ulrog stone men. Sulgor defers in power to Izgra the Half-Dead.

GLOSSARY OF MAPS

The Southlands

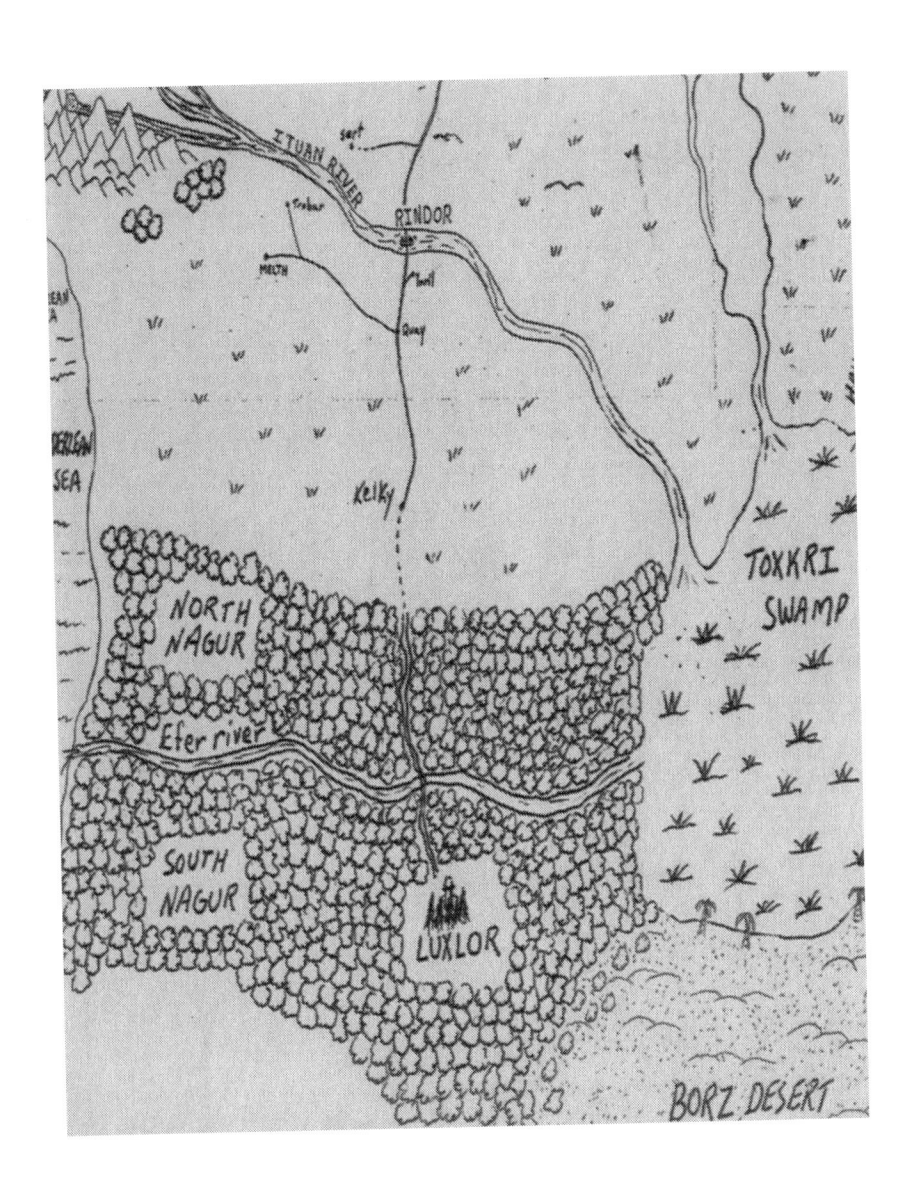

Nearing World

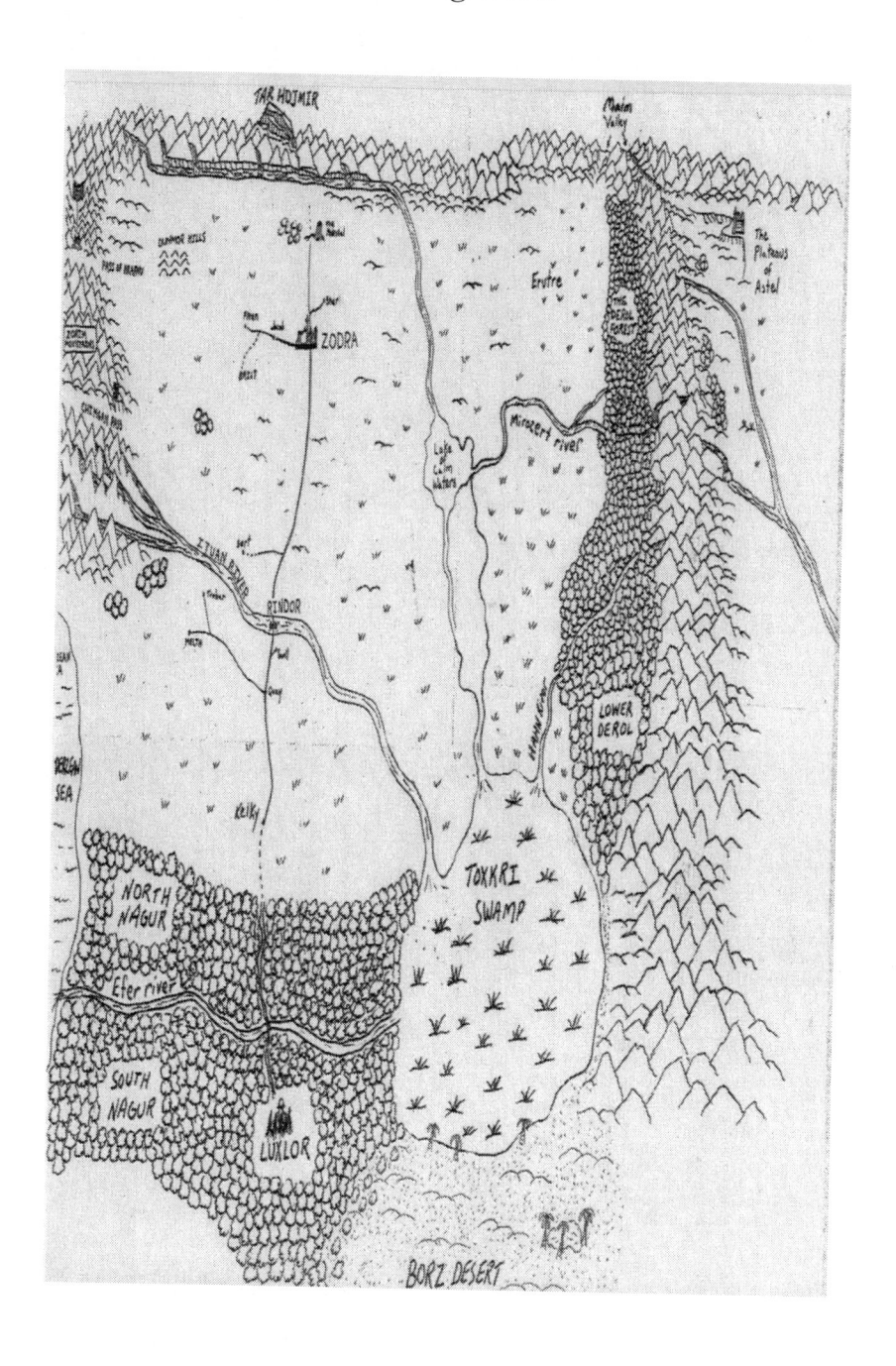

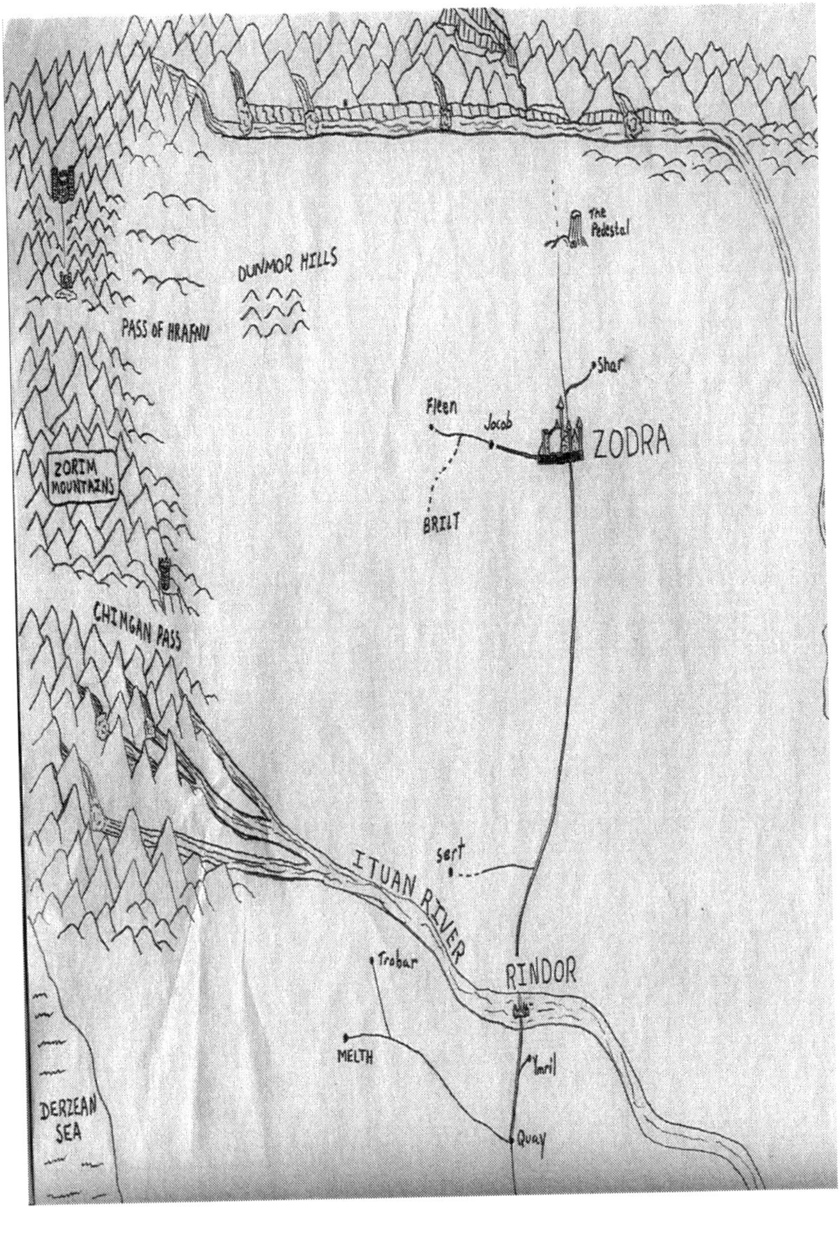

The Pedestal
DUNMOR HILLS
PASS OF HRAFNU
Shar
Fleen
Jocob
ZODRA
BRILT
ZORIM MOUNTAINS
CHINGAN PASS
Sert
ITUAN RIVER
Trobar
RINDOR
MELTH
Imril
DERZEAN SEA
Quay

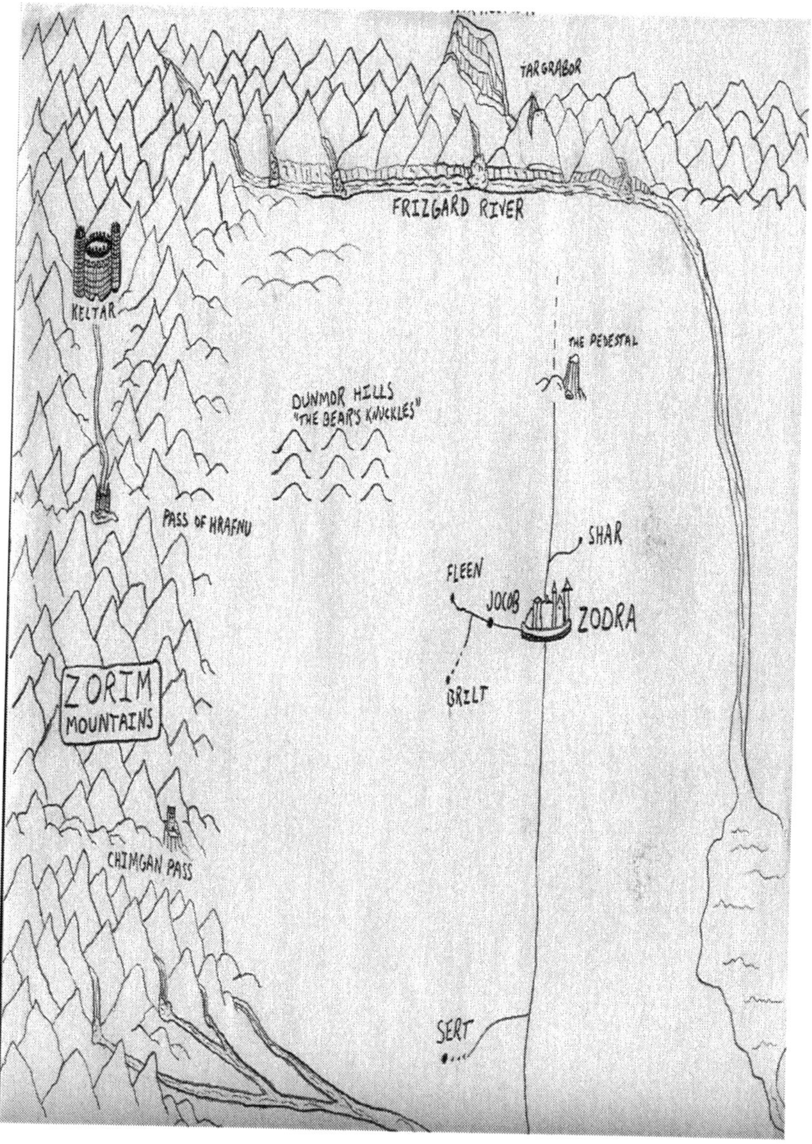
TARGRABOR
FRIZGARD RIVER
KELTAR
THE PEDESTAL
DUNMOR HILLS
"THE BEAR'S KNUCKLES"
PASS OF HRAFNU
SHAR
FLEEN
JOCOB
ZODRA
BRILT
ZORIM
MOUNTAINS
CHIMGAN PASS
SERT

Made in the USA
San Bernardino, CA
29 April 2019